She is a survivor!

Nhamo was alone on this island. Now and forever. She would slowly grow old, without family or children, until she was too feeble to climb the tree. Her eyes would grow too dim to find water and her fingers too weak to dig for yams. She would starve like the baboon on the little island, unless a predator found her first.

"No! I will build a boat and sail away!" Nhamo cried stoutly. "I am Nhamo Jongwe, whose totem is the lion and whose people are descended from kings. I am a woman, not a little girl. I have Mother and Crocodile Guts for company, and—and—the njuzu."

And she moved everything to the sleeping platform and began working on her ladder.

"[Readers] will place Nhamo alongside Zia (*Island of the Blue Dolphins*) and Julie (*Julie of the Wolves*)."
                    —*School Library Journal*, starred review

OTHER PUFFIN BOOKS YOU MAY ENJOY

A GIRL
NAMED
DISASTER

Nancy Farmer

PUFFIN BOOKS

PUFFIN BOOKS
Published by the Penguin Group
Penguin Putnam Inc., 375 Hudson Street, New York, New York 10014, U.S.A.
Penguin Books Ltd, 27 Wrights Lane, London W8 5TZ, England
Penguin Books Australia Ltd, Ringwood, Victoria, Australia
Penguin Books Canada Ltd, 10 Alcorn Avenue, Toronto, Ontario, Canada M4V 3B2
Penguin Books (N.Z.) Ltd, 182-190 Wairau Road, Auckland 10, New Zealand

Penguin Books Ltd, Registered Offices: Harmondsworth, Middlesex, England

First published in the United States of America by Orchard Books, 1996
Reprinted by arrangement with Orchard Books, New York
Published in Puffin Books. 1998

30 29 28 27 26 25 24 23 22 21

LIBRARY OF CONGRESS CATALOGING-IN-PUBLICATION DATA
Farmer, Nancy.
A girl named disaster / Nancy Farmer.
   p. cm.
Summary: While fleeing from Mozambique to Zimbabwe to escape an unwanted
marriage, Nhamo, an eleven-year-old Shona girl, struggles to escape drowning and
starvation and in so doing comes close to the luminous world of the African spirits.
ISBN 0-14-038635-1 (paperback)
1. Shona (African people)—Juvenile fiction. [1. Shona (African people)—Fiction.
2. Survival—Fiction. 3. Supernatural—Fiction. 4. Mozambique—Fiction.]
I. Title.
[PZ7.F23814Gi 1998] [Fic]—dc20 97-28173 CIP AC

Printed in the United States of America

TO HAROLD
Light of my life
and spirit guide

CAST OF CHARACTERS

THE VILLAGE

NHAMO: The girl named "disaster."
AUNT CHIPO: Nhamo's aunt and Uncle Kufa's wife.
AUNT SHUVAI: Nhamo's aunt.
MASVITA: Aunt Chipo's eldest daughter.
RUVA: Aunt Chipo's second daughter.
UNCLE KUFA: Aunt Chipo's husband.
GRANDMOTHER (AMBUYA): Nhamo's grandmother;
    mother of Chipo, Shuvai, and Runako.
RUNAKO: Nhamo's mother, who was killed by a leopard.
TAKAWIRA: Grandmother's brother. A very old man.
VATETE: Uncle Kufa's sister, who lives in a village five
    miles away.
CROCODILE GUTS: A fisherman.
ANNA: Crocodile Guts's wife.
TAZVIONA: Village girl, born with a twisted foot.

THE TRADING POST

THE PORTUGUESE TRADER (JOAO): Owns the trading post.
ROSA: The trader's Shona wife.
THE MUVUKI: The witch finder.
GORÉ MTOKO: Murdered by Nhamo's father.
ZORORO MTOKO: Goré Mtoko's brother.

THE JOURNEY

THE *NJUZU*: Water spirits.
LONG TEATS: A witch.
RUMPY: A baboon with a twisted foot and half a tail.
FAT CHEEKS: The baboon chief.
DONKEYBERRY: An old female baboon.
TAG: Donkeyberry's baby.
OPPAH: Woman in a village near the Zimbabwe border.

EFIFI

DR. HENDRIK VAN HEERDEN: Afrikaner scientist.
DR. EVERJOICE MASUKU: Matabele scientist.
SISTER GLADYS: The nurse at Efifi Hospital.
BABA JOSEPH: *Vapostori* Christian in charge of
    experimental animals.

MTOROSHANGA

PROUD JONGWE: Nhamo's father, who has deserted her.
INDUSTRY JONGWE: Nhamo's uncle.
EDINA JONGWE: Industry's wife.
MURENGA JONGWE: Nhamo's grandfather; also called
    Jongwe Senior.
CLEVER: Son of Industry by his junior wife.
THE *NGANGA*: Nhamo's great-grandfather, head of the
    Jongwe clan.
GARIKAYI: The *nganga*'s assistant.

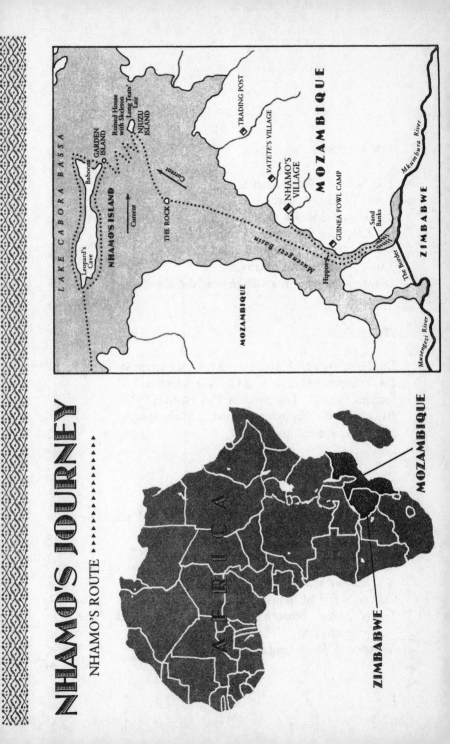

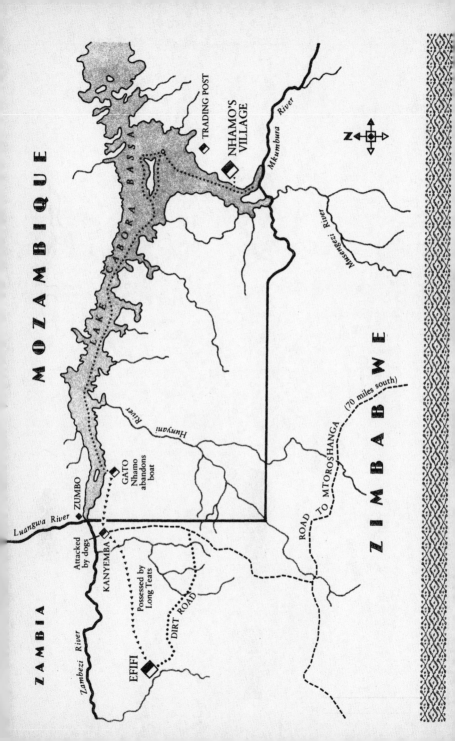

1

Crouched on a branch of a *mukuyu* tree, a girl tore open a speckled fruit. She grimaced as ants scurried over her fingers. So many! And the inside was full of worms, too.

Even Nhamo, hungry as she was, couldn't eat it. She dropped it to the ground and searched for another cluster of figs.

"Nhamo! Nhamo!" came a voice not far away. The girl rested her head against the trunk of the tree. If she was quiet, no one would find her. The thick, green leaves formed a bowl around her.

"Nhamo! You lazy girl! It's your turn to pound the mealies," called the voice. Footsteps trudged along the path below.

It's always my turn, thought Nhamo. She watched Aunt Chipo disappear behind some bushes. She much preferred to sit in the shade and gather figs. Almost without thinking, she observed the dusty path below: Aunt Chipo's footprints were short and wide, with the little toe tucked under. Nhamo could recognize the footprints of everyone in the village.

Nhamo didn't know why she had learned this. It was simply a way to calm her spirit. Her body worked all day planting, weeding, baby-sitting, washing—oh, so many chores!—but her spirit had nothing to do. It became restless, and so she gave it work, too.

It learned how the Matabele ants carried their

young at the center of a line while the soldiers ran along the outside. It learned that when Uncle Kufa pursed his lips as he was eating, he was angry at Aunt Chipo. It learned that the wind smelled one way when it blew from the stream and another when it came from the forest.

Nhamo's spirit had to be kept very busy to keep her from losing her temper.

The other girls in the village never felt restless. Nhamo was like a pot of boiling water. "I want . . . I want . . . ," she whispered to herself, but she didn't know what she wanted and so she had no idea how to find it.

"Nhamo!" bellowed Aunt Chipo from directly under the *mukuyu* tree. "Selfish, disobedient child! I know you're up there. I can see fresh fig skins on the ground!"

Then she had to come down. Aunt Chipo switched her across the legs with a stick before dragging her back to the village.

Nhamo went to the *hozi,* the communal storehouse, to fetch mealies. The *hozi* was up on poles, and in the shade beneath was Masvita, Aunt Chipo's oldest daughter. She was making a pot from wet clay. Nhamo squatted beside her.

"That's beautiful," she commented.

Masvita grinned. "The last one fell apart when it was baked. I've been working on this one all day."

"It's so nice! I'm sure it will be all right." Nhamo stuck her finger into the reserve clay and tasted it. "Mmm! Termite nest!"

"It's good, isn't it?" Masvita licked some of the clay off her fingers.

"Nhamo!" shouted Aunt Chipo from her doorway.

Nhamo climbed into the *hozi* and selected a basket of mealie grains. She hauled it back to the kitchen hut and poured the grains into a mortar made from a tree trunk. *Stamp, stamp, stamp!* She pounded the mealies with a long pole until the tough outer husks came loose. It was extremely hard work. The sweat ran down into her eyes. She had to stop and retie her dress-cloth from time to time.

She rested her skinny arms whenever she dared and

watched Masvita in the cool shade of the *hozi*. Her cousin wasn't exactly idle, but she was never given the really difficult tasks. If a heavy pot of boiling porridge had to be lifted from the fire, Nhamo was told to do it.

Once, when she was smaller, she had dropped a pot. The scalding porridge spilled over her feet. She screamed. The other villagers ran to help her. They blew on her skin, but in spite of their care Nhamo's feet had blistered and scarred. "Such a shame!" cried Grandmother. Aunt Chipo only remarked, "Yes, but think if it had happened to Masvita!"

Stamp, stamp, stamp! Nhamo watched her cousin in the shade of the *hozi*. She was beautiful, no question about it. Nhamo had seen her own face reflected in a pool. She thought she didn't look too bad. Masvita was sweet-tempered, though, and Nhamo had to admit her own manners left a lot to be desired.

But who wouldn't be sweet-tempered if she could sit in the shade all day?

When the husks were loosened, Nhamo poured the grain into a winnowing basket. She tossed it repeatedly until the breeze blew the chaff away. She put the crushed maize into a clay pot with water to soak overnight. She would dry and grind it into flour tomorrow.

Then Aunt Chipo sent her to fetch water from the stream. Nhamo filled the cooking pots and watered the pumpkin mounds. She weeded the fields carefully with her hoe—*chop, chop, chop*. Next, she collected fresh cow dung for her grandmother's floor.

Grandmother sat in the shade outside her hut and puffed on a clay pipe. It wasn't a nice habit for a woman, but no one dreamed of telling her so. *Ambuya* was old, so old! She was close to the spirit world, and everyone respected her for it. "Welcome, Little Pumpkin," she called as Nhamo arrived.

Nhamo swept the floor with a bundle of grass and rubbed the dung in with her hands. "If only we lived when Mwari's voice was still heard," sighed Grandmother. "In those days, when people clapped their hands and asked God for food, pots of porridge and honeycombs came out of the earth."

Nhamo smiled as she polished. She had heard the story dozens of times, but it didn't matter. She liked being close to *Ambuya*.

"At first, the ancient kings were good," Grandmother said, her eyes dreamy, "but gradually they became cruel. Mwari withdrew into his country to show his displeasure. He didn't want to abandon his people entirely, so he still spoke to the spirit medium Tumbale, and Tumbale told everyone what God wanted.

"The worst king of all was called Mambo. He flew into a rage when people praised Mwari. 'Who is this creature no one can see? How can he have more power than me?' And Mambo hated Tumbale because he was good.

"One day all the people were gathered in a field. They were celebrating a victory against their enemies. Mambo sat on a carved chair and accepted plates of food from his wives, who approached him on their knees. Suddenly, the grass in the field began to whisper, 'If not for Tumbale, there would be no victory.'

" 'What's that?' roared Mambo. 'How dare the grass talk back to me! Set it on fire!' The soldiers soon had it ablaze, and it burned to ashes.

"Then the trees all around began to murmur, 'If not for Tumbale, there would be no victory.'

" 'Chop those trees down!' screamed Mambo. His soldiers reduced the forest to a heap of kindling.

"The rocks began to say the same thing, so Mambo had fires kindled on them and split them into pieces. Still the voice was heard whispering, 'If not for Tumbale, there would be no victory.' Now it came from the king's youngest wife.

" 'You traitor!' shouted Mambo, but all the people gathered around and said, 'Great chief, please do not blame her. She is only a child.'

"The king said, 'Let there be an end to it. Kill her!' The soldiers killed the girl, skinned her, and used her skin to cover a drum. They burned the body. Then Mambo had the drum beaten, but the sound disturbed the hearts of the people so much that they crouched on the ground and covered their ears. A voice came out of the wind, saying, 'You have shamed me with your evil ways. Now feel my anger. I will send armies against you. I will reduce your houses to sand and your fields to ashes.'

"And Mwari's voice withdrew from the people forever. Since that time people have had to work hard, and their lives have been full of strife and danger."

Grandmother's voice died away. Soon Nhamo heard a gentle snore from outside and she knew *Ambuya* had fallen asleep in her chair. She leaned against the wall of the hut and thought about the story. Imagine having your skin used to make a drum! Would your spirit know what had happened?

Nhamo knew that the spirit stayed close to one's body, but Mambo's poor wife had been burned. Except for the skin. Did that mean the girl lived in the drum?

"Aren't you finished yet?" exclaimed Aunt Chipo from the door. Nhamo sighed. She washed her hands and prepared to grind the maize from yesterday. Nhamo used a flat, hollowed-out stone for a base and a smaller stone for a crusher. *Crunch, crunch, crunch* she went, grinding the maize into flour. All this time, Masvita had been sitting under the *hozi*. She had two half-completed pots sitting on wooden plates to dry.

"Come and drink *maheu*," called Aunt Chipo to her daughter. Nhamo thought longingly of the cool, sour taste of the fermented mealie-water.

"What beautiful pots! We'll have to decorate them," said Aunt Shuvai, Chipo's younger sister. Masvita got up gracefully and clapped to thank them. They went inside to escape the heat.

Soon it was time for Nhamo to gather firewood.

2

Most girls were afraid to gather firewood by themselves. The village was surrounded by a forest where almost anything might hide. Nhamo was afraid, too, but she had a compelling reason to venture out alone. She didn't expect to meet elephants—although they migrated to the river at certain times of the year. She wasn't likely to run into a buffalo—although someone had done so a few months earlier. Her most persistent worry was leopards. She feared leopards with a terror so complete that she couldn't breathe when she thought of them.

Her mother had been killed by one when Nhamo was only three. The child was sleeping by the door of the hut, but the animal walked past her and attacked Mother instead. Grandmother rocked back and forth, wailing with grief, when she recounted the story. "In daylight, Little Pumpkin! With the sun streaming in the door, that disgusting beast killed my poor, poor daughter! It wasn't *her* fault. It was that hyena-hearted husband of hers—may he fall into a nest of flesh-eating ants!"

The hyena-hearted husband was Nhamo's father.

Nhamo couldn't remember the tragedy, yet somewhere inside her was a memory of flowing, spotted skin and terrible claws.

Now she followed a broad path from the village to the stream. She saw women beating clothes on rocks; their round-bellied babies were deposited on a mat in the shade of a tree. A small girl watched to be sure they didn't crawl away.

Nhamo followed the stream to an area of yellow sand where she could see the bottom clearly in both directions. No crocodile could creep up on her here. She waded across. The water came up to her shoulders. She always experienced a moment of panic in the middle because she couldn't swim, but she planted her feet firmly in the coarse sand and struggled on. When she got to the other side, she scrambled up a rock and picked off a leech that had managed to fasten onto her ankle.

She hid behind a bush to wring out her dress-cloth. The wetness against her skin was very pleasant, but she couldn't waste time enjoying it. Aunt Chipo would be waiting for her firewood. Even more important, Nhamo had to return before dusk.

Dusk was when the leopards came out to hunt.

She followed an old, overgrown trail for a long time until she came out into a meadow. It wasn't a natural clearing. A few poles remained of the village that had once been there, and a few pumpkin mounds with vegetables gone wild. Nhamo wasn't sure who had lived here. It might have been her own people, but they no longer visited the site. Masvita said the place was haunted.

With a nervous look at the shadows under the trees, Nhamo crossed the clearing and quickly gathered firewood from a deadfall in a dry streambed. That was the good thing about this place: The wood was easy to find. It took her far less time than Aunt Chipo suspected. She tied the wood into a bundle with vines and deposited it by the trail.

She climbed a hill at the edge of the deserted village. It was really only a large, round boulder, but it allowed her to see in all directions from the top. On one side was the stream and wavering smoke from her village; everywhere else was a sea of low, gray-green trees. In the distance she saw the river where the stream ended: a flat brightness at the edge of the forest.

At the very top of the hill a perfectly round and deep hole had been worn into the rock. Rain filled it in the rainy season; even now it was half-full of water. Nhamo leaned over and studied her face. She didn't think she was ugly.

Now came the moment she was waiting for. She dragged aside a slab of stone from a smaller, dry hole in the rock. Inside were the treasures Nhamo had managed to collect. She removed pots, wooden spoons, a drinking gourd, an old cloth Aunt Chipo once used to cover her hair, and a knife Uncle Kufa had hurled into a bush when the tip broke off. (He was even angrier when he couldn't find it again later.) She left a few things inside the hole: a precious box of matches, some glass beads that had come off Aunt Shuvai's bracelet, some of the copper wire Uncle Kufa used to decorate his snuffboxes.

Reverently, Nhamo smoothed out the cloth and put the utensils on it. Last of all, she reached into a pot and removed—a roll of paper.

She weighted the edges down with stones. It was a picture torn out of a magazine.

Books were unheard of in Nhamo's village, but very occasionally a magazine found its way from the distant cities of Zimbabwe. Only two men in the village could read. They retold the stories for everyone's entertainment. The women studied the pictures of clothes and houses, gardens and cars with great interest. They tried to copy the hairstyles in the photographs. Eventually, the magazines fell apart and were used to light fires.

This picture had been on the cover, so it was of sturdier paper. The minute Nhamo had seen it, her heart beat so fast it hurt. The picture showed a beautiful woman with braided hair decorated with beads. She wore a flowered dress and a white, white apron. She was cutting a slice of white, white bread, and next to her was a block of yellow margarine.

Nhamo didn't know what margarine was, but Grandmother told her it was even better than peanut butter.

The room behind the woman was full of wonderful things,

but what interested Nhamo most was the little girl. She was wearing a blue dress, and her hair was gathered into two fat puffs over her ears. The woman smiled at her in the kindest way, and Nhamo *knew* the white bread and yellow margarine were meant for the little girl.

She thought the woman looked like Mother.

She couldn't remember Mother, and of course no one had a picture of her, but the way her spirit leaped when she saw that picture told her this was how Mother had looked.

Nhamo hadn't waited for the magazine to get old. Right away, when Aunt Chipo wasn't looking, she'd torn off the cover and hidden it. Aunt Chipo was terribly cross. She accused her sister of doing it, but it never crossed her mind that Nhamo was responsible. What would Nhamo want with a new hairstyle, anyway?

Nhamo pretended to pour tea into the pots. She cut bread and covered it with margarine. "I climbed the *mukuyu* tree and got so many figs, *Mai*," she said. "But they were full of worms. I had to throw half of them away. Then I saw a yellow bird—the kind that builds a basket over the water— and it ate the worms. Do you think they grow inside?"

Nhamo paused to let Mother answer.

"I didn't think so either. I saw a swarm of bees fly overhead—oh, so many! But fortunately they didn't land."

Sometimes Nhamo tried to imagine her father at the tea party, but she knew almost nothing about him. He had run away before she was even born. Grandmother said he was working in a chrome mine in Zimbabwe. How she had learned this was unknown, but visitors did wander through the village from time to time. Father was at a place called Mtoroshanga and someday, *Ambuya* said, he would return to claim his daughter.

The thought was frightening. A stranger could merely show up and take her away from everything she'd ever known. No one would stop him. But probably—or so Aunt Chipo said—he had found himself another wife and forgotten all about his daughter by now.

Nhamo suddenly realized the light was going. *Maiwee!*

She had been so absorbed, she had forgotten the time. Scrambling, she packed everything and dragged the lid over the hole.

She slid down the hill and tied the firewood to her back. Oho! In this light, the trail was almost invisible! The air was a strange, silvery color, and the gray-green trees melted into the sky. It was the moment when the day animals passed the night animals on their way to hunt. Nhamo listened for the stream. The air was so still she couldn't smell it.

Sh, sh—there it was in the distance. She made more noise than usual, smashing through the bushes in her haste. All at once, she was by the stream. The surface of the water gleamed with silver light, and it was impossible to see underneath. Crocodiles liked this time of day. They floated just beneath the water, where their flat, yellow eyes could watch anything that approached.

"Oh," whispered Nhamo. She lifted the bundle of firewood to her head and slowly approached the stream. *Sh, sh* went the water as it rushed along the banks. By the trail, in the bushes, was a spotted shadow. It was sitting on its haunches, barely visible in the speckled light.

Nhamo froze. Behind her was no safety. If she returned to the deserted village, the creature would only follow her. She could throw the firewood at it and hope to frighten it. Or she could wait. The villagers would come to look for her.

Or would they? Nhamo wasn't sure.

The darkness increased. Then, quite suddenly, the strange, silvery quality of the air faded. A half-moon lit the path, and Nhamo saw that the leopard was merely a tangle of leaves by the water. It had been a trick of the light. She could even see faintly into the water. The sand lay in a pale sheet without any crocodiles floating over it.

Shaking with relief, she edged past the spot and entered the water. It felt warm now in the cool air of evening. She held the firewood up high to protect it, and presently she came up the other side and hurried toward the cook-fires beyond the trees.

3

Where have you been?" said Aunt Chipo crossly as Nhamo dumped the firewood onto the ground.

"She probably fell asleep under a tree," Aunt Shuvai said.

Masvita was cutting up onions and tomatoes for relish. She looked up and smiled at Nhamo. "It was very hot, *Mai.* I dozed off myself several times."

"The lazy thing was probably stuffing herself with wild fruit." Aunt Chipo scowled at the worms in the figs she was preparing.

Nhamo didn't say anything. She broke up the wood and began to feed the fire. Not far away, other women knelt by other outdoor hearths, preparing the evening meal. The men, tired from fishing, farming, and hunting, had gathered in the *dare,* the men's meeting place. Now and then, laughter reached her on the cool evening breeze.

Soon the air was full of the comforting smell of food. Nhamo's mouth watered, but she didn't dare help herself to anything. First, the men must be fed, then Grandmother and the small children. Aunt Shuvai nursed her baby while busily shoveling porridge into the mouths of her two smallest sons. The older boys were at the *dare* with their father. Nhamo fed Aunt Chipo's three smallest children, Masvita carried pots of beer to the *dare,* and Ruva, Masvita's little sister, carried back empty plates. Ruva had just graduated from being hand-fed herself. She was finding it difficult to wait for dinner.

Grandmother sat contentedly smoking her pipe as Aunt Chipo, Aunt Shuvai, Masvita, Ruva, and Nhamo settled around the fire with bowls of their own.

No one spoke. Eating was much too serious. They ate mealie porridge, called *sadza*, with tomato, onion, and chili sauce; boiled pumpkin leaves; and okra with peanut butter. Everyone had a piece of boiled fish with some of the water for gravy. It was a good, full meal. The only thing wrong with it was the lack of salt. Salt had to be traded for from the seacoast far away, and they used it sparingly.

"Ah, that was good," sighed Aunt Shuvai, mopping up the last of her relish with a chunk of stiff porridge.

"Nhamo, fetch the men's bowls," Aunt Chipo said lazily. "You can wash them outside."

Nhamo hurried off to perform this last chore. She bowed respectfully as she entered the *dare*. Uncle Kufa was telling one of his favorite stories about a willful girl who insisted on running off with a strange man her parents didn't like. "She went up the mountain with him," said Uncle Kufa.

"Go on," said the other men and boys, joining in with a polite response. They knew the tale, but they looked forward to the ending.

"Her husband walked too fast. He left her behind. 'Wait!' called the girl."

"Go on," said the men and boys.

"He turned back and his head began to grow. He opened his mouth wide."

"Ah! So wide," said the men and boys.

"He took the girl's head in his mouth and began to swallow. *Gulp, gulp, gulp.* Her head went in. Her body went in. Her legs went in until she was all gone!"

"All gone!" everyone responded.

Nhamo slowly gathered the dishes. The fire in the *dare* crackled as a breeze came up from the stream.

"He had turned into a big snake," Uncle Kufa said with satisfaction. "He swallowed the willful girl right down to her toes. And *that* is what happens to children who don't obey their parents."

"A true thing!" cried another man, relishing the fate of the bad girl.

"Imagine what it was like inside that snake," Uncle Kufa said.

Nhamo shivered. She could easily imagine it.

"It happened on the flat-topped mountain a day south of here, and the girl lived in the ruined village across the stream."

That village? thought Nhamo. Where she had poured tea for Mother? Perhaps the girl's spirit still wandered, looking for her people. What happened to your spirit if it was swallowed by an animal? *What had happened to Mother?*

A rap on the side of her head made her gasp and almost drop the dishes. She saw Uncle Kufa's cane by her knees.

"Speaking of willful girls," said Uncle Kufa. The other men laughed. "Get back to your chores. You aren't allowed here."

Nhamo, burning with embarrassment, gathered up the dishes and fled. She dumped them outside the kitchen hut and fetched a pot of water. She rinsed the cooking pots but used ash and sand to get the wooden plates clean. Then she lined them up on a rack inside.

What happened to your spirit if it was eaten by an animal?

The thought had never occurred to Nhamo before. She assumed Mother's spirit hovered near her grave, as the other ancestors did, but what if her body had been carried off by a leopard?

She found her female relatives and the children settled around Grandmother. *Ambuya* was telling one of her stories. Ruva sat with her thumb in her mouth. Masvita mechanically jiggled the baby as she listened. Aunt Chipo braided her oldest daughter's hair into a new pattern she had seen in a magazine. Masvita's skin shone with butterfat applied earlier.

They sat comfortably together, like kernels on a mealie cob. There was no space where Nhamo might fit herself in, and so she waited patiently in the doorway as Grandmother finished her tale. The others added bits of gossip from the events of the day.

Nhamo wanted badly to ask about Mother's spirit, but didn't know how to introduce the subject. Suddenly, she had an idea. "*Ambuya,* a very strange thing happened at the stream this evening," she began.

"See how the hollow gourd rattles with stones inside it," said Aunt Chipo.

"Oh, let her speak," Aunt Shuvai intervened. "She's been quiet up till now."

"*Ambuya,* I was coming back from gathering wood. I was very late."

"You're telling me," muttered Aunt Chipo.

"The light was bad," Nhamo went on. "I was almost to the stream where the sand is yellow, when I saw a leopard—"

"*What?*" everyone cried.

She had their attention now, all right. "It was big, with terrible claws. It was watching the path. Oh, oh, I thought. How will I ever get home? I almost dropped the wood, but I said to myself, 'I'll throw it at the leopard. I'll ram it into its teeth.'" Nhamo was so pleased with the unusual attention she had attracted, she began to embroider the tale.

"It growled low down in its throat—*rrrrrr!* Its tail lashed the grass. I thought, That leopard could swallow my bundle of sticks and still have room for me."

Masvita's eyes opened wide and she stopped jiggling the baby.

"*Maiwee!* What could I do? 'Oh, Mother, help me,' I cried. All at once, the moon shone brightly. It shone onto the leopard—and turned it into a bush! It was only a donkeyberry bush! I kicked it hard as I went by and came straight home." Now Nhamo planned to ask about Mother, but she became aware that the room was unnaturally quiet.

Grandmother, Aunt Chipo, Aunt Shuvai, Masvita, Ruva, and even the little children were all staring at her.

"I—I don't think it was a good idea to kick the bush," said Aunt Shuvai.

"*A spirit leopard,*" Aunt Chipo said in horror.

"The light was bad. Probably it was a bush all along," Nhamo amended.

"No, you said it growled," said Grandmother. "This is very serious. I must talk to the *nganga* about it."

Nhamo's heart sank. The *nganga* lived in the next village and didn't do anything without being paid.

"Perhaps it was just passing through," argued Aunt Shuvai.

"But it was waiting for *Nhamo.*" Aunt Chipo pulled Masvita closer.

"Mother sent it away. Her spirit *is* nearby, isn't it?" Nhamo asked.

"Well, of course, Little Pumpkin." Grandmother smiled sadly.

"I mean—I mean—" Nhamo didn't know how to put it. "Mother was eaten by a leopard, so—her body—"

"Oh, listen to her!" exploded Aunt Chipo. "Go to bed, Nhamo, before you make *Ambuya* cry!"

But Grandmother was already weeping silently. She beckoned for Nhamo to sit beside her. Nhamo tucked herself in between Aunt Shuvai and *Ambuya*. She felt tremors of grief run through the old woman's body.

"I should have explained before," Grandmother said after a few moments. "Little Pumpkin, we found your mother's bones in the forest. She was a small woman, and the leopard was able to drag her away. When someone is carried off in this way, we sacrifice a cow and lay it in the grave. This replaces the body so the spirit can return home."

Nhamo was awestruck. Cattle were extremely valuable and they were almost never killed. How much *Ambuya* must have loved Mother to do that! Tears began to roll down her face, too.

"So you see, your mother *was* able to protect you from the spirit leopard."

Nhamo wanted to say she had made up the part about the growl, but it was too late. *Ambuya* hugged her tightly. Nhamo was almost never shown affection and she liked the feeling. She didn't want *Ambuya* to stop. She often wondered why her aunts didn't like her, but it probably had something to do with Father.

No one ever talked about Father. Nhamo didn't even know why he had run away, although she was well aware of the results. Mother had died because he hadn't been there to protect her. Normally, a child was sent off to its father's family if the mother died. A child's totem, and therefore its true kinship, came from the male parent. Nhamo had not been sent away.

Sometimes she felt bad about this: Her *real* family would have welcomed her. At other times, such as tonight, she was content to bask in *Ambuya*'s affection. After all, Father's family might be as vicious as a pack of starving hyenas. She had no way of telling.

"Time for bed," said Aunt Shuvai.

Nhamo, Masvita, and Ruva rounded up the little girls and took them to the girls' sleeping hut. The little boys were fetched by their older brothers.

Nhamo lay awake and tried to sort out her thoughts. Could she have been mistaken about the shadow by the stream? She was certain it was a trick of the light, but everyone else took the appearance of a spirit leopard seriously.

It was almost, she thought as she rolled a sleeping toddler back onto her own mat, as if they were expecting it to appear. And as if they were expecting it to come looking for *her*.

4.

Very early next morning, Masvita left the girls' hut. This was most unusual. Nhamo quickly tied her dress-cloth and went to investigate. She looked in all directions, but her cousin had already vanished. Takawira, Grandmother's brother, was coughing and groaning in his hut. Soon he would call for someone to take him into the bushes.

Nhamo bent to study the ground. Masvita's footprints went across the compound to Grandmother's hut. That was a surprise! Grandmother was the only person in the village who regularly gave Masvita any chores. Her cousin usually avoided her.

"Help me!" came Takawira's querulous voice. One of the boys appeared instantly from the boys' hut. To hesitate when the old man needed to relieve himself was to invite disaster.

Nhamo hurried off to begin her chores. Soon she had water boiling actively in a three-legged pot. She measured tea leaves in her hand and threw them in. Tea was a luxury. Only Grandmother and Takawira drank it regularly. They liked it as sweet as possible, so Nhamo measured six spoonfuls of sugar into the pot.

Uncle Kufa and the other men traveled to a trading post to barter for tea, sugar, salt, cloth, and matches. Nhamo had never seen the place. The trading post was located where many trails from various villages converged, and once a month (she had been told) a tractor slowly made its way to the store from a tar road. It pulled a wagon piled high with goods and people who wanted to visit the villages. Uncle Kufa said a child could walk faster than the tractor, but of course *it* never got tired. The travelers had a good time swapping stories as they rode.

After the goods were delivered, the tractor slowly ground its way back with a load of people returning to the outside world. That was why sugar, like salt, was so rare and why, much as she wanted to, Nhamo didn't dare take a spoonful for herself. Aunt Chipo watched the supply too closely. Nhamo contented herself with licking a few grains from her fingers. By this time Takawira was perched on the bench outside his hut.

She poured him tea.

"I want milk," complained the old man, but unfortunately none of the cows was producing at the moment. He wrapped his old gnarled fingers around the enamelware cup.

Masvita emerged from *Ambuya*'s hut with Grandmother close behind. They wore broad smiles, and Masvita hurried off to the stream. Grandmother came to the fire to drink her tea. She didn't offer any explanation, so of course Nhamo couldn't ask her anything.

She pounced on her cousin when she found her packing a basket in the girls' hut. "All right, what's happening?" Nhamo said.

Masvita grinned. "I'm going to stay with *Vatete*." *Vatete* was Uncle Kufa's sister in the next village, five miles away.

"Whatever for?"

"I'm a *mhandara* now," Masvita said proudly.

So that was it: Masvita's first blood had shown, and she was going to stay with her father's sister to be instructed in the secrets of womanhood. No wonder she was smiling!

Nhamo felt her *mutimwi* hidden under her dress-cloth. Everyone, boys and girls, wore a secret cord to protect his or her fertility. Masvita's *mutimwi* would be broken with great ceremony because now she had proven her readiness to bear children.

It was hard to dislike Masvita—she was so good-natured—but Nhamo felt a little serpent tongue of envy wriggle inside because her cousin had crossed the river into womanhood first.

"How long will you be gone?" she asked.

"Until the full moon. That way we can have a party all night," Masvita replied.

Flicker, flicker went the little serpent tongue. Of course there would be a party with dancing and good food.

"Nhamo! Hurry up and give the little ones their breakfast," said Grandmother as she entered the hut.

Feeding the toddlers was Masvita's job. Ordinarily, Nhamo would have enjoyed the chore, but her pleasure was spoiled by her cousin's triumph. She spooned the porridge with such bad grace the little ones complained and cried for Masvita. She told them to be quiet if they didn't want a smack, and they watched her with round, accusing eyes.

Even the babies liked her cousin better! It wasn't fair!

At midmorning, Grandmother placed the broken *mutimwi* and a stamping pole from one of the mortars across the doorway of Uncle Kufa and Aunt Chipo's hut. Gravely, the parents stepped over these, to show that they accompanied their daughter on her journey to womanhood. The old *mutimwi* was burned, and Masvita, who was hidden in Grandmother's hut, was presented with a new one. She wasn't allowed to see her parents until after her visit to *Vatete* was over.

As soon as Masvita left, Nhamo stalked off to the deserted village. Let Aunt Chipo beat her! She didn't care. She bent over the rock pool and studied her body. She didn't look like a *mhandara* yet. Her chest was as flat as the top of a drum.

"At least I won't have to get married soon," she told Mother when she had laid out the utensils and picture. "Masvita will probably go to someone with two wives already. They'll beat her when he isn't looking."

She listened to Mother's reply.

"Oh, I don't really want Masvita to suffer. Or not much," Nhamo added honestly. "But sometimes I wish Masvita would do something *bad*. It would feel so good to have a reason to dislike her!" She cut slices of sponge cake and served them with ice cream. She had never seen ice, let alone ice cream.

Then she laid out a plate of fried chicken. She and Mother were going to celebrate today. They finished up with lemonade sweet enough to make their jaws ache.

"When I become a *mhandara*," she announced, "I'll get a new dress-cloth and a necklace of blue beads. I'll have pink plastic shoes like that pair Aunt Shuvai got from the trading post. When I come back from *Vatete*'s house, I'll have a party, too."

A sudden thought struck her. Masvita's *vatete* was, of course, Uncle Kufa's sister. Who was hers?

Father must have a sister. Where was she? Not in any village Nhamo knew about.

A child belonged to its father's family. No matter that Nhamo had spent her entire life with Mother's relatives. When the time came for her to marry, Father would arrange the bride-price.

"Grandmother will send a message to him," Nhamo assured Mother. "*Ambuya* says he is at Mtoroshanga. She must know how to call him."

By now Nhamo's stomach was grumbling. It was all very well to eat pretend cake and chicken, but her real stomach felt like the two sides were stuck together. She repacked her treasures, slid down the rock, and built a fire in the dry streambed. Nhamo dug around the deserted gardens until she had found several sweet potatoes to roast.

Then, driven more by thirst than by any desire to return home, she gathered a bundle of wood—to mollify Aunt Chipo—and trudged back to the stream.

She entered the village nervously. She had been gone for hours. The water pots had been neglected, the pumpkins unwatered, the mealies unstamped. Aunt Chipo would be furious! Nhamo dropped the firewood outside the cooking hut and braced herself.

But Grandmother came out instead. Aunt Chipo was

squatting inside, her mouth set in a sour line. She didn't say anything. *Ambuya* beckoned for Nhamo to follow her. In amazement, Nhamo saw Ruva and the other girls hauling water from the stream.

"It won't hurt them to bend their backs for once," Grandmother remarked. "I need my granddaughter's company today."

"Masvita is your granddaughter, too," Nhamo couldn't resist saying.

"Yes, but she's off getting her skin oiled and her mouth sweetened with honey. Anyhow, Little Pumpkin, sometimes I find Miss Masvita just a little *dull*."

Nhamo was astounded by this. It was the first time anyone had hinted Masvita might be anything less than perfect.

Grandmother took Nhamo into her hut and gave her—wonder of wonders!—lemonade with sugar. Exactly what she had pretend-given Mother.

"Your mother grew slowly," said *Ambuya,* startling Nhamo out of her reverie. "I worried a great deal at the time, but people are like plants. Some shoot up like weeds, and some are slow like fruit trees. In the end, the fruit trees are worth more."

That sounded all right to Nhamo: Masvita was a weed.

"Runako, your mother, was worth waiting for. Did you know she could read?"

Nhamo shook her head. Things were getting more surprising by the minute.

"Your grandfather and I used to live at Nyanga in Zimbabwe. It's cold there. Ice forms on the water in winter."

Nhamo tried to imagine it.

"Grandfather cut trees for a white farmer. Oh, such strange trees! They were tall, with leaves like needles. Every one was exactly alike, and they grew in rows like vegetables. Every week, the farmer's wife gave us a sack of mealie meal, sugar, cooking oil, and meat. She also gave me cloth once a year and, when your mother and Chipo were old enough, school uniforms. Shuvai was still a baby."

"What's a *un-i-form*?" said Nhamo, stumbling over the unfamiliar word.

"A dress. All the girls at school wore exactly the same thing. It looked very smart to see them lined up with their faces scrubbed and their hair combed." Grandmother sighed. She didn't speak for a while, and Nhamo knew she was remembering. *Ambuya* wept when she thought of Mother, so Nhamo had always been afraid to ask questions. She was excited to learn that Mother had gone to school. Perhaps she ate ice cream, too.

"Runako was so clever! The headmaster said she could go to university someday. Chipo, on the other hand, forgot everything as quickly as possible. How different things might have been. . . ."

Grandmother trailed off again. Nhamo sipped her lemonade slowly, to make it last. Outside, crows cawed and someone shouted at them. They must be trying to raid the garden.

"One day Grandfather was killed by a car as he was walking along a road. The farmer gave me his pay for that month—ten dollars—and turned us out of the house. His wife gave me two old dresses and a photograph of herself— I tore the picture up the minute I was out of sight! We had no house, no money, no work. This village was the only place we could survive. Runako cried when I took her books back to the school."

Ambuya fell silent. Quite soon, she began to snore. Nhamo gently helped her lie down and stretched out on the mat herself to think.

Masvita returned the day of the full moon. Her head was shaved and she wore a new dress-cloth. It was yellow with dark-blue fish and a red border. Aunt Chipo killed a chicken in honor of *Vatete,* who had returned with her, and several other relatives arrived from the other village with baskets of food.

Technically, the party was merely a family gathering on

a full-moon night, but everyone knew it was really to celebrate Masvita's new status. She would be a fine woman, everyone said. She was modest and obedient. She never put herself forward, but kept her position respectfully equal with other people, and she did not say irritatingly clever things. The praises became more extravagant as the beer flowed.

Nhamo padded from group to group with snacks. Old Takawira sang in a reedy voice as his son played an mbira, a hand piano. Someone else was beating a drum. Nhamo's feet danced along to the music. Uncle Kufa sent her to fetch more bananas from the grove at the edge of the village.

She could see the party from the shadows of the banana trees. If she made a circle with her hands, the whole village fit inside. Here and there were small, lively fires. People danced and chattered, and she smelled popcorn and beer. It suddenly seemed that she held everyone in her hands, like a picture in a magazine. She could almost roll them up and hide them in a pot.

Cough-cough.

From the dark forest behind her came a noise.

Cough-cough.

Nhamo didn't have to think. She burst out of the banana trees and ran faster than she dreamed possible. She fled back to the campfires and fell on her knees in front of her astonished relatives.

"Nhamo," cried several people, springing to their feet.

"Did you hurt yourself?"

"What's the matter?"

Nhamo lay on the ground, moaning with terror. "Leopard," she finally managed to gasp.

Everyone grabbed branches from the fire and ran off to protect the animal pens. For a while, all was confusion. Men shouted; women dragged babies into huts. Then, gradually, the commotion died down.

"All that exercise has given me a powerful thirst," said a man, tossing his burning branch into the fire.

"Me, too," agreed his friend, settling next to a pot of beer.

"I didn't see any leopard tracks," Uncle Kufa said in a dangerous voice.

"It—was in the forest behind the banana trees." Nhamo was huddled against Grandmother's knees.

"If you ask me, she made it up," said Aunt Chipo. "She's always trying to grab attention."

"Look how she's trembling. She isn't making that up." *Ambuya* patted Nhamo's shoulder.

"It's so dark in the banana grove. I've often been frightened there," Masvita added kindly. Uncle Kufa scowled, but he didn't say anything more.

Quite soon, everyone was singing and dancing again. Grandmother kept Nhamo by her side and refused to let her run any more errands. After a while, the conversation reverted to *roora,* the bride-prices that had been paid for various relatives. This was a very popular topic of conversation. Fathers counted on the wealth they would get for their daughters. How else could they be rewarded for raising otherwise useless girls? How else could they afford to buy wives for their sons and insure that they would eventually become ancestors?

Sometimes it took many years to pay the *roora;* sometimes—there were several sly looks—it took no time at all. Nhamo understood that a woman's value was determined by the size of her bride-price.

Vatete told them all about someone who had earned a whole herd of cattle for her family. Years and years the son-in-law slaved to pay for his wife.

"Ah," everyone sighed with envy.

On the other hand, *Vatete* said, even a barren goat was too much for some women, not mentioning names of course.

"We won't have that problem with Masvita," said Aunt Shuvai.

No indeed, everyone agreed.

"Or with Ruva," added *Vatete.* "She's so plump and pretty."

Ruva ducked her head with embarrassment.

What about me? Nhamo wanted to ask. I'm older than Ruva. What about me?

She waited for Grandmother to introduce the subject, but *Ambuya* merely signaled for Aunt Shuvai to massage her feet. Not long afterward she sent Nhamo and the other girls to bed.

5

"Wake up," said Masvita, shaking Nhamo. Nhamo sat up and rubbed her face to clear it of sleep. It was still dark, although the crowing of a rooster told her dawn was not far away.

"What's the matter? Did the leopard come back?"

"No. *Vatete* is sick. They're sending for the *nganga*."

Nhamo got up at once. Nhamo's village had no *nganga,* and sick people had to travel five miles to be treated. *Vatete* must be extremely ill to ask the doctor to come from her village.

"She was tired by the walk yesterday," Masvita said as they hurried through the dark. "We had to rest every mile or so. I thought she was better last night, but she began to vomit after the party."

By now they were at Aunt Chipo's hut. *Vatete* was curled up on a mat inside, and Aunt Shuvai was wiping her face with a wet cloth. Nhamo saw at once that *Vatete* was extremely ill.

"Thank goodness! Nhamo, cut some thatching grass. We need it for bedding." Aunt Shuvai dipped the cloth in water and bathed the sick woman's arms and chest. "She's very hot. I don't think this is food poisoning."

Nhamo took a sickle and hurried off. The first streaks of light were turning the clouds pink. She could see well enough, but she moved cautiously after leaving the village. No one else had seen any trace of the leopard, but Nhamo had no doubts about its existence.

Presently, she came to a stand of dry grass and sliced off as much as she could carry. When she returned, Aunt Shuvai and Masvita packed a layer under the sick woman. Aunt Chipo attempted to give her water, but *Vatete* only moaned and pushed her away. The sick woman was curled up in a ball as though her stomach hurt. Her face was gray and her eyes were squeezed shut.

"Don't just stand there, Nhamo," Aunt Chipo snapped. "Fix breakfast and feed the babies. Don't think you're going to sneak off to the bushes today, my girl!"

Nhamo spun around and left. She felt stung that Aunt Chipo thought she would run away during an emergency. It hadn't escaped her notice either that *she* had been the one awakened to cut grass.

At least it shows they believed me about the leopard, thought Nhamo with a bleak smile. She blew last night's coals into a flame and hauled a large pot to the fireplace.

All day she ran from one chore to another. Inside Aunt Chipo's hut, Masvita fanned *Vatete,* and Nhamo's aunts watched with expressions of great worry. Uncle Kufa sent another messenger to urge the *nganga* to hurry.

But at midday Aunt Chipo and Masvita suddenly broke into wild cries. Aunt Shuvai rushed out of the hut, pulling her hair. "She's dead! She's dead!" she wailed. She fell on her knees. Nhamo caught her emotion and began to wail, too. Other women rushed to add their cries.

Poor, poor Vatete, Nhamo thought as she rocked back and forth with her arms tightly wrapped around her chest. *Only last night she was joking about roora. She was so happy!*

People hurried off to carry the message to the other village. A woman poured ashes into a mortar and pounded them as she called the names of *Vatete*'s relatives who lived too far away to attend the funeral. "Cousin Kuda," she cried, "Great-aunt Misodzi. Uncle Tendai. Please do not be frightened. Your relative has died here. We know you would come if you could." The ashes blew away on the wind, carrying the message.

But when evening came, grim news arrived. People were dying in the other village. Even the *nganga* lay in his hut, unable to rise. None of the relatives would be able to come.

"What is this illness?" Nhamo whispered to Masvita.

"*Ambuya* says it's cholera," Masvita whispered back.

Nhamo's eyes opened very wide.

"She says we must boil our water. We must wash our hands carefully and go far from the village when we have to—"

Nhamo nodded. They would have to provide old Takawira with a pot.

"But Father"—Masvita meant Uncle Kufa—"says it's witchcraft."

Nhamo sucked in her breath. That meant a witch-finding ceremony. She had never seen one, but she had heard about them. The most horrible thing was that a person could be a witch *and not even know*. He or she—it was usually she—could ride hyenas at night and spread sickness, *and in the morning she wouldn't remember anything about it*.

"There's not much we can do until after the funeral. *Vatete*'s sisters are supposed to prepare the body, but for all we know they're dead, too." Masvita began to cry again, and Nhamo waited patiently for her to be finished. She didn't feel like crying. She knew this showed lack of proper feeling, but she had barely known *Vatete*.

Aunt Chipo washed the dead woman's body. She broke *Vatete*'s *mutimwi* and laid it aside to give to whichever female relatives might survive. This cut *Vatete*'s last tie with life. No longer would she tend her garden or prepare food for her family. She would not sit by the fire, nor would she clap respectfully when her husband returned from hunting. Now she belonged to the spirits and would dwell in the land of her ancestors forever.

Aunt Chipo dressed the dead woman again and wrapped her in a cloth to await the funeral.

A brooding sense of disaster hung over the village that

night. The men ate silently in the *dare*. The women sat drawn and worried inside their huts. This death was not natural. Trouble would surely come of it.

Uncle Kufa and one of his brothers set out at first light to dig the grave. They had already selected a termite hill about half a mile away. They dug a shaft downward and then sideways in the tough clay. When they returned, they broke a hole in the side of Aunt Chipo's hut—for the dead must not leave by the same door as the living—and carried *Vatete*'s body out on a litter.

The mourners followed in single file to keep witches from following them. Witches knew that many footprints meant a funeral, and they stole bodies for their own evil purposes.

Uncle Kufa laid out a mat in the grave. He placed a pot of ground millet, a packet of snuff, cooking utensils, and a calabash of beer at the top. Then *Vatete* was laid down on her right side with her hand under her head as though she were sleeping. Her face was uncovered. Uncle Kufa and those few blood relatives who could be present each threw a handful of sand over her. "Farewell," they murmured. "Keep us a place in your new home, for we will surely meet again."

Afterward, the grave was securely filled. Stones were piled on top and the sand around it was smoothed. It would be checked the following day for evidence of witchcraft.

"I'm exhausted, but I can't sleep," said Masvita as she lay on her mat in the girls' hut.

"Me neither," said Nhamo.

"I keep remembering last week. *Vatete* took me to the trading post. Did I tell you?"

"No."

"I saw so many people. The tractor had just come in. I had a choice of a hundred different patterns for my new dress-cloth. The owner of the trading post was Portuguese, very pale, with a big gold cross around his neck. He shouted at *Vatete* when she squeezed the bread on his shelves. I wonder if she's lonely."

"Who?" said Nhamo.

"*Vatete*. She's out there somewhere."

"Don't!"

"I can't stop thinking about it. She has to wander until the welcome-home ceremony." Masvita began to cry again.

Where was *Vatete*'s spirit? thought Nhamo. Was it walking along the roads calling for her children? Had Mother called for her? No, that was too terrible to think about. "Let me tell you a story," she said aloud to keep the fear away.

"Do you know how?" said Masvita.

"I've listened to *Ambuya* often enough. She says a good story makes almost anything feel better."

Masvita sighed and turned on her side. Nhamo could hear her mat rustle. The hut was filled with girls, big and small, and all the breathing noises made Nhamo feel safer.

"Once upon a time there was a man and his wife who had fine cattle and rich farmland, but no children," she began. "The woman went to the *nganga,* and he made her a little baby out of millet flour. 'Take this home and greet it as though it were your child. Tell it your praise names and totems. Then you will become pregnant. But you must be careful not to harm it in any way.'

"The woman obeyed, but one day the millet-flour baby slipped out of her hand. 'Oh, oh,' she cried. 'My child has broken in two.' Still, there was nothing to do but fit the two halves together again.

"After nine months, the woman gave birth to twins, a boy and a girl. Now the parents' joy turned to grief, for the law said that twins were evil and must be killed. The mother and father hid the children in the middle of the forest for six years. For six years, everyone in the kingdom had bad luck. The rivers dried up; the rains refused to fall; the cattle and people died of disease. Finally, the king ordered everyone to appear before him. His witch finder would smell everyone's hands and discover who was responsible.

"The parents knew they could hide the children no longer. The father took them to a deep pit behind a waterfall and threw them inside. With a heavy heart, he returned to his wife.

"But the boy and girl were swept away by the water to an underground country. This land had a blue sky like ours. It had fields and rivers and villages. It was very beautiful, but the people and animals there were all damaged in some way. They had broken wings or legs or hearts. In spite of this, they appeared cheerful and they welcomed the twins.

" 'Where are we?' asked the boy and girl.

" 'This is the country of all those who were thrown away by the world above,' the people and animals replied.

"The twins lived there for a long time. One day, when they were playing by a hill, a crack opened up in the rock. They saw their father weeping on the other side.

" 'Father! Father!' they cried. They climbed through the crack and went home with him. Their mother had become old with grief, but she cried with happiness when she saw her children again.

"The parents gave the twins anything they wanted. They never scolded them or made them work. In spite of this, the children didn't feel happy. 'We don't belong in this world anymore,' they decided. So one night, they left the house and went back to the waterfall.

" 'Farewell, Father and Mother,' they called as they held hands. 'We are sorry, but we belong with the creatures who have been broken and thrown away.' They jumped into the pit and were swept off to the underground country. And their parents never saw them again."

Masvita's regular breathing told Nhamo she had fallen asleep. She had never attempted such a long story before, and was pleased with the results. Too bad her audience had deserted her!

Grandmother thought that killing twins was wrong, but Aunt Chipo and Aunt Shuvai were of the opinion that one, at least, should be allowed to die. It was necessary, to protect the village from evil. Nhamo hoped she would never be faced with the problem. Wrapped in the comforting presence of the other girls, she drifted to sleep beside Masvita.

In the morning Uncle Kufa returned from *Vatete*'s grave and said the sand had been marked by the prints of a leopard.

6

Witchcraft," whispered Masvita in the girls' hut. The others watched her with frightened eyes. The only light came from a burning wick in a tiny bowl of cooking oil. The smell made Nhamo's nose twitch.

"Are they sure?" said Tazviona, a large girl who had been born with a twisted foot. Nhamo knew that witches caused deformity, but no one had ever discovered who was to blame for Tazviona's misfortune. Perhaps it was Anna, who was married to Crocodile Guts, the boatman. Anna had a nasty disposition, and everyone knew that her great-grandmother had been a witch.

"They were talking about it at the *dare,*" Masvita said in a low voice. "I listened outside after I brought the food. Father says witches send animals to dig up bodies."

"They didn't get *Vatete*?" cried Ruva.

"No, no. Of course not. Father surrounded the grave with branches of *mutarara,* wild gardenia, to confuse them."

Nhamo thought about her young cousin. Ruva was known to sleepwalk, which could be the first sign of witchcraft. Aunt Chipo was certainly worried by the habit, and slapped her daughter whenever it happened. But it was hard to think of the little girl as a horrible witch. Anyhow, *Ambuya* said she would grow out of it and

that they should worry more about Ruva falling over a cliff.
"—especially because it was a leopard," finished Masvita.

"What? I didn't catch that," Nhamo said.

"We've had a lot of visits from leopards recently: first the spirit animal by the stream, and then the one in the banana grove."

"I didn't really see a spirit leopard! It was a trick of the light."

"It *growled* at you," Masvita gently reminded her. Nhamo felt trapped. If she protested now, everyone would think she was trying to hide something.

"Will Father send for the *nganga*?" Ruva asked.

"The *nganga* isn't good enough," Masvita explained. "The elders are going to wait until *Vatete*'s relatives can visit us. Then they'll call in a specialist."

"The *muvuki*!" gasped Tazviona.

It made sense, Nhamo thought. The *muvuki* lived near the trading post, where he could be consulted by people from many villages. He could *smell* witches by their evil thoughts, and it was useless to lie to him.

"I—I heard that he got his powers in a bad way," stammered Tazviona. The other girls eagerly bent forward. "He studied with a famous doctor in Maputo. The doctor told him to kill a close relative so he could force the spirit to serve him."

"Ah," sighed the girls.

"Which relative did he kill?" Nhamo asked.

"His oldest son!"

Everyone was speechless with horror. That made the *muvuki* very close to being a witch himself.

"I think the *nganga* is perfectly able to solve our problems," Nhamo declared. "*Ambuya* says witch-hunting is a way to get rid of people nobody likes. She says it's illegal in Zimbabwe."

Everyone looked at her in surprise. It was all right for Grandmother to say outrageous things, but not for a girl like Nhamo to repeat them.

"You're only saying that because the leopard appeared to *you*," said Tazviona.

"I am not! Ask *Ambuya,* if you don't believe me."

"Don't shout. The elders will hear," said Masvita.

"Of course you don't want to admit it," Tazviona said.

"I suppose you think *I* twisted your foot! I wasn't even born when it happened."

"Your mother was there!"

Nhamo threw herself at Tazviona, and the bigger girl punched her right in the stomach. It only made Nhamo angrier. She grabbed Tazviona's ears and wrenched for all she was worth. "Take back what you said about Mother!" she screamed.

"She was a bad woman! Everyone knows!" Tazviona shrieked back. The other girls fell on the pair, trying to pull them apart. Ruva tipped the light over onto a sleeping mat. It flared up instantly.

Masvita kicked open the door at once and dragged the mat out before it could set the whole hut on fire. Everyone struggled outside. The mat crackled as it burned. Red gleams shone on everyone's faces.

"You girls are a disgrace!" shouted Aunt Chipo as she ran toward them. She was followed by people from the nearby huts. "We're all worried sick, and you have to throw temper tantrums! Bad, bad children!" She dealt out blows in all directions.

"Who was fighting?" said Uncle Kufa in a terrible voice. The girls were silent, but it was clear who had been involved. Nhamo and Tazviona were breathing heavily. Tazviona was clutching her ears; Nhamo had deep scratches on her arms. Tazviona's mother led her off to be punished privately, and Aunt Chipo took Nhamo off to an empty storage hut.

Aunt Chipo pinned Nhamo's head between her knees and lashed her with a leather strap until her arm was tired. "You can sleep here. You won't find anyone but the mice to fight with!" She slammed the door shut and secured the bolt outside.

At first Nhamo barely noticed the welts Aunt Chipo had inflicted. Her spirit was too angry. But gradually, as the excitement of the fight wore off, she began to hurt. She huddled next to the wall with her knees drawn up almost to her chest. "I'm glad Tazviona's foot is twisted," she said to the dark hut, but almost at once Mother's voice whispered inside her head, *You don't really think that. You're angry because she insulted me.*

"I *should* be angry," Nhamo said. "You weren't bad."

Of course not. I'm proud of you for sticking up for me.

It was so dark Nhamo couldn't see anything, even with her eyes wide open. If she concentrated, she could imagine Mother sitting across the room from her. Mother wore a bright blue dress and pink plastic sandals. A flowered scarf covered her hair.

Nhamo stretched out, wincing as the marks of the lash met the floor. Most girls would have been terrified to be left alone, but Nhamo rather liked it. She had never let Aunt Chipo realize this, however.

I wonder if they really will call the *muvuki,* she thought sleepily. Uncle Kufa might think twice after he considered how much a specialist cost. He would have to bring him from the trading post and entertain him until the judgment was given. Uncle Kufa was so stingy, he would rather eat boiled weevils than admit porridge had gone bad.

Could the *muvuki* really have killed his own son to get power? A man like that wouldn't think twice about killing anyone else. What happened to the people he smelled out?

Nhamo understood that most witches were tolerated, as you might tolerate a bad dog in the neighborhood. But if someone had done something really evil—like spread cholera, for instance—wouldn't that person be punished? Nhamo had heard a story of a witch who had her eyes poked out with a sharpened stick.

"They don't do that anymore, do they?" she asked Mother, but Mother's spirit had stolen away, and the hut was silent.

Takawira was the next to fall ill. He was dead in less than a day. "He was very old," everyone whispered. "He had reached the end of his natural life."

But when Crocodile Guts got sick, everyone was shocked. Crocodile Guts owned the only boat in the village. No one else cared to go out on the river, where hippos could chop your boat in half or crocodiles could pull you overboard. No one else knew how to swim. The boatman plied his homemade nets not far from shore and brought in fat bream and tiger fish.

Everyone liked bream; the tiger fish weren't as popular. They spoiled rapidly in the heat. Crocodile Guts sometimes tried to sell them after their eyes had gone milky, but people weren't often fooled. If he couldn't unload his catch, Crocodile Guts would merely laugh—he was a large man with a booming, hearty voice—and eat the fish himself. That was how he got his name. Crocodiles could eat meat that had rotted in the water for several days without getting sick. The boatman seemed to have the same ability, and people made detours around his cook-fire.

If he could get sick, everyone whispered, no one was safe.

The villagers watched in horror as, day by day, the big man shrank with illness. His eyes turned milky as a sun-ripened tiger fish, and then he died. His wife, Anna, howled with grief. No one had suspected how attached she had been to her husband. She was such a sour, complaining woman that everyone expected her to dance with glee. But Anna wept bitterly for Crocodile Guts and then she, too, fell ill and died.

In spite of Grandmother's precautions, cholera had already found its way to the heart of the village. Suddenly, it was everywhere. Some people were only lightly affected; some were stricken with all the savage force of the illness. A few didn't get sick at all. Aunt Shuvai lingered for a week before she died. Then Masvita wasted away until she was barely recognizable. Aunt Chipo, far from well herself, implored her daughter to live with heartbreaking cries until Grandmother ordered her to sleep in another hut.

Ambuya was one of the lucky ones. So were Nhamo and Uncle Kufa. They boiled water and mixed it with the precious sugar and salt to feed the weakest people. Grandmother explained that this would keep everyone's strength up until he was ready to eat again. It seemed to work. Nhamo patiently dribbled the liquid into Masvita's mouth. Slowly, the gray pallor faded and the killing fever cooled from her cousin's skin. Her body was skeletal and her hair, which had begun to regrow after the coming-of-age ceremony, fell out.

Nhamo was so exhausted she could hardly move, what with running from one patient to the next. In some huts, bodies lay unburied because no one had the strength to bury them. Ruva wasn't ill, but she was half-mad with fear and grief. She curled up next to Masvita and refused to eat. Very early on, Nhamo dragged her off to stay with a family at the other end of the village. She visited frequently to cuddle her little cousin, rocking her back and forth while the tears silently ran down her own face.

Nhamo plodded from one chore to the next like a small donkey pulling a cart too heavy for it. Sometimes she sat down in the road like a donkey, too, and stared into space until she regained the energy to go on.

"Masvita is looking so much better," she whispered to Ruva. "Your mother isn't sick at all anymore. Would you like me to tell you a story?" Nhamo really didn't have time for this, but she needed the escape almost as much as Ruva did. Besides, stories kept the little girl from asking for Aunt Chipo, who proved useless even after she recovered. The woman spent her days demanding to be waited on and weeping over Masvita. She had forgotten all about Ruva.

"Once upon a time," Nhamo said, "there was a hunter with two dogs. The dogs were called Bite Hard and Grip Fast."

"What color were they?" asked Ruva. Nhamo had a bowl of porridge in her lap, and as soon as the little girl opened her mouth, she popped a spoonful of it inside.

"Brown, with a white tip on their tails and four white paws," Nhamo said quickly. "The hunter went out one day and saw a dassie* hunched on a rock. Just as he was about to shoot it with an arrow, a honeyguide bird flew over his

*dassie: An animal that resembles a large guinea pig. Also called a hyrax or rock rabbit.

head and cried, 'Leave it, O hunter. Better things are ahead.' The hunter called his dogs away and walked on." Nhamo popped another spoonful of porridge into Ruva's mouth.

"After a while, the man came upon a rabbit. He lifted his bow, but the honeyguide flew over his head and cried, 'Leave it, O hunter. Better things are ahead.' He obeyed the bird, and soon he encountered a kudu. 'What a fine, fat antelope!' he said. 'This is certainly a better prize.'

"But the honeyguide still sang, 'Leave it, O hunter. Better things are ahead.'

"Grumbling to himself, the man went on until he found a buffalo. It had just fallen over a cliff and was already dead. 'Wonderful!' cried the hunter. 'I didn't even have to waste an arrow.' He sat down to carve up the buffalo and roast the meat. But the honeyguide flew over his head and sang, 'Leave it, O hunter. Better things are ahead.'

"By now, the man was getting angry. Pesky bird, he thought. I have never seen a finer prize than this. There *can't* be anything better ahead. But he was afraid to disobey the honeyguide because it was a magical creature. I know what, he thought. I'll hide from it in a cave. When it flies away, I'll go back and get the buffalo.

"He went into a cave. It got bigger and bigger as he walked farther into the mountain. At the back was an entire village, with fine houses and pens of cattle and goats. The village was ruled by an old, old woman who had only one long, sharp tooth, and the only inhabitants were women. All the men had been eaten by the old woman. They were her favorite food.

" 'Welcome, welcome,' said the old woman, eyeing the hunter up and down. 'Please stay at my house this evening.' She gave him a bowl of food and showed him a soft bed. But during the night, she sharpened her long tooth—*whisk, whisk, whisk*—and prepared to eat him. The dogs Bite Hard and Grip Fast stood in front of their master and growled to protect him. So the old woman ate a goat instead.

"The next morning, she said, 'There's a dead tree in the forest. Could you help me gather firewood from it?'

" 'Certainly,' replied the young man.

" 'But you mustn't take those dogs with you. They are too frisky and might knock me over.' The man shut the dogs away in a goat pen. He and the old woman walked far into the forest until they came to a tall, dead tree. 'Start at the top,' ordered the old woman.

"The man climbed until he was at the very top. He began to break off branches and throw them down. Meanwhile, the old woman sharpened her long tooth on a stone—*whisk, whisk, whisk*—and prepared to chop down the tree. He'll fall and break his neck, she thought. Then I can have him for lunch.

"The honeyguide saw her sharpening her tooth. It flew away to the cave. 'Quick! Quick! Turn the dogs loose,' it called to the women. The women turned the dogs loose. Away flew Bite Hard and Grip Fast. They caught up with the old woman, knocked her down, and broke all her bones.

"The hunter went back to the cave. All the women greeted him. They showed him pens of cattle, sheep, goats, pigs, and chickens. They showed him storehouses of grain and springs of fresh water. 'Please be our husband,' they said. 'The old witch ate all of ours.'

"So the young man became a great chief, and he always remembered to leave honey out for the honeyguide."

By now the porridge bowl was empty. Ruva lay relaxed in the arms of the chief wife of the house, who had also been listening to the tale. "You're a fine storyteller," the woman complimented Nhamo. Nhamo smiled and stood up. Her body felt so heavy, she thought she couldn't move, but she had to keep going. Masvita had to be fed, and there were dozens of other chores waiting.

Nhamo returned to find Aunt Chipo hunched over her oldest daughter's bed. *Ambuya* sat in the corner, grinding peanuts in a small mortar. "Let her sleep," Grandmother snapped. "You make her twice as sick with all your wailing."

"She was such a beautiful girl!" Aunt Chipo moaned.

"She's alive, isn't she? The hair will grow back."

"She looks like an old cooking pot," blubbered Aunt Chipo.

"You're such a fool. I must have dropped you on your head when you were a baby."

"That's right! Attack me. You always liked Runako and Shuvai better!" Aunt Chipo snapped right back at Grandmother.

Nhamo shrank against the wall in dismay. Never had she heard her elders arguing like this.

"Runako was worth ten of you. She could have gone to university."

"Oh, sure! Who came home with a fat belly and a no-good husband? Clever Runako! Too bad she and Shuvai are dead. I'm all you've got left!"

Grandmother began to weep stormily at this. "I can't stand it! My good daughters are gone, and the last one wants to feed my heart to the vultures!"

"You don't deserve anyone as nice as me," shouted Aunt Chipo. She broke into noisy sobs herself. "Day and night I wait on you—'Bring me tea, bring me sugar, rub my feet!' No one else would put up with such selfishness!" Aunt Chipo had forgotten that Nhamo did all these chores.

Over their cries, Masvita whimpered, "Please don't fight. I can't bear it."

Nhamo immediately scrambled to her cousin's side and began stroking her as she would a terrified infant. "It's all right," she whispered. "Everyone is too tired. They aren't really fighting." She lay down next to Masvita and held her in her arms. She couldn't think of anything else to do.

She was dazed by all the illness around her, and by her elders shouting at each other. Masvita was so thin. She might die at any moment. Suddenly, Nhamo began to shake all over. She gasped for breath and clung to Masvita as though she were trying to keep her from being dragged off by lions.

Uncle Kufa entered to find Grandmother rocking back and forth on her knees. Aunt Chipo howled like a dog. Masvita produced thin, wailing cries as she lay on her mat, and Nhamo trembled as though she had malaria. He backed out of the hut and ran into the forest.

By the time Uncle Kufa returned several hours later, the madness had lifted and everyone was on speaking terms again. It was as though the cholera had wrung everything out of the villagers' bodies and found nothing left to attack except their spirits. When the strange fit was over, the disease was truly defeated. Every hour saw its strength ebb away.

The men dug a mass grave in the forest, and the bodies were buried with as many of the proper ceremonies as possible. *Ambuya* and Aunt Chipo behaved with affection toward each other once more. Masvita took over the care of Aunt Shuvai's children, a task she enjoyed in spite of her extreme weakness. Everything appeared to be healing. But Nhamo felt that something was not right.

She had difficulty putting it into words. The conversation at the *dare* was too quiet; the women no longer clustered in groups at the stream. Rather, there was a space between one person and the next. It was as though a necklace had come apart and each bead rolled separately across the floor. The village had broken somewhere deep inside, and she had no idea how to mend it.

7

Is that basket too heavy?" Masvita asked as Nhamo carefully took a few steps.

"I don't think so. I'll tell you if I need help," Nhamo said. In fact, the basket was larger than anything she had ever attempted, but Nhamo was afraid to ask her cousin to take some of the load. Masvita was so thin! She had been over the cholera for weeks, but she was still skeletal. It wasn't from lack of food. Every time she turned around, someone tried to feed her. Aunt Chipo killed one of her precious hens and forced her daughter to eat all of it. *Ambuya* toasted pumpkin seeds and sprinkled them with salt.

But Uncle Kufa had made the greatest sacrifice. Accompanied by Nhamo, he went into the forest and found a wild beehive. The bees had taken up residence in an old termite nest. First Uncle Kufa checked the opening. A blackish opening would show that the hive was new, and they would have to find another one. But the opening was the color of earth. That meant the bees had had time to store honey.

Uncle Kufa sealed the hole and dug another entrance close by with a hoe. He made a smoky fire of grass and leaves to make the bees drowsy. In spite of this, when he thrust his hands into the new opening, some of the insects were alert enough to sting.

Nhamo bit the inside of her cheek as she watched. She didn't dare get close. The tears ran down Uncle Kufa's face as he grimly scooped out honey-combs. He placed them in a pot of water to keep the bees from finding them again.

It was Nhamo's job to carry the pot. Her uncle's hands were so swollen, he couldn't pick up his hoe, so Nhamo carried that as well. They hurried away before the bees woke up.

Aunt Chipo squeezed the honey out of the combs and boiled it with millet meal to make delicious cakes. Every time Masvita showed the slightest willingness, a cake was thrust into her mouth. Still she didn't gain weight and, most upsetting of all, her menstruation didn't occur at the expected time.

"She's very young," *Ambuya* told Aunt Chipo. "Girls are often irregular at that age."

"She's sterile," moaned Aunt Chipo. "I'll never have grandchildren."

Ambuya pursed her lips in annoyance.

This was why Nhamo was unwilling to share her load with Masvita, even though she suspected the heavy basket would make her neck ache. Nothing worse could happen to a woman than sterility. She felt terribly sorry for her cousin.

She hoped they would find a cure for Masvita on this journey, although it was filled with potential danger for everyone. Someone—probably a witch—was responsible for the deaths and Masvita's condition. They were about to find out who that person was.

Masvita tied Aunt Shuvai's baby to her back and lifted a much smaller basket to her own head. The baby had been weaned far too early and was unhappy with a diet of watery porridge and weak, sweetened beer. He cried continuously, adding to Nhamo's gloom.

Would she ever see the village again? Nhamo had been quite wrong about Uncle Kufa's willingness to pay the *muvuki*. Masvita's condition worried him too much. She had been wrong about the specialist coming to the village as well. Common *ngangas* could be coaxed into making house calls, but not the *muvuki*. He was far too important. People had to travel to *him,* and they might have to wait a long time to attract his attention.

Uncle Kufa, Aunt Chipo, *Ambuya,* Masvita, and Nhamo waited for the others to show up. At least half the families had lost someone. The rest of the villagers would remain behind to care for the children, although Aunt Shuvai's baby was being taken along in hopes that they could buy milk at the trading post.

Eventually, a crowd of twenty gathered, and they started off down the trail. Nhamo's neck began to hurt after a few minutes, but she gritted her teeth and endured it. They rested frequently because *Ambuya* and Masvita were unable to keep up the pace.

By early afternoon they arrived at the next village, where *Vatete* had lived. "What kept you so long?" complained *Vatete*'s husband. He would be joining them on their trip to the *muvuki.*

"Masvita," Uncle Kufa replied in a low voice. *Vatete*'s husband glanced at the wasted girl as she tottered to a log and sat down.

"That's her? I didn't recognize her," he whispered to Uncle Kufa.

Nhamo took the baby from her cousin and dribbled porridge into his mouth with her hand. His skin was loose and he seemed to have already given up the battle to live.

"I suppose I should see *Vatete*'s children," Masvita said in a dull voice.

"We can do that on the way back," said Nhamo. She didn't want her cousin to start crying. "Tell me about the trading post. It sounds so exciting."

So Masvita described the tractor and the bolts of cloth again. She said that the Portuguese trader had a yellow-and-blue parrot in a cage. It could talk, but only in Portuguese, and it bit anyone who stuck his fingers through the bars.

They spent the night at *Vatete*'s village, and early the next day they moved on. Nhamo noticed that quite a few people had *zango*s, or charms against witchcraft. Everyone, of course, already wore the bark cords of mourning, the men around their heads and the women around their necks. The men's faces, too, were covered with stubble because they would not be allowed to shave until the period of mourning was over. What Nhamo saw now was the sudden appearance of small red-and-blue packages containing magic roots or feathers. Aunt Chipo and Uncle Kufa each had one tied around an arm, and even Aunt Shuvai's baby wore one around his waist.

They must have visited the *nganga* last night, Nhamo thought. But who are they protecting themselves against? A thrill of terror ran through her. No one had given *her* a charm. The sunlight grew dark before her eyes. She stumbled along with the heavy basket on her head, but she couldn't feel the ache in her neck anymore. She couldn't feel anything. *She* was the one they were worried about! She was the one they thought rode hyenas in the middle of the night.

Nhamo was so distracted, she banged into a tree. The bark cut her forehead, but she didn't react. She stood still, dazed by her thoughts.

"Please let me take some of that," came Masvita's gentle voice. "Mother is carrying the baby now. I can help out."

Nhamo didn't protest as her cousin took some of the heavy packets of mealie meal from the basket and transferred them to the sling on her back.

"If they keep loading you like that, you're going to grow up crooked. Here, let me tie a *zango* on your arm. I have more than I need."

Hypnotized, Nhamo watched Masvita fasten a blue charm around her arm. She wiped the cut on her head with some leaves and smiled in a glassy way at her cousin.

"I think the heat's bothering you," said Masvita, worried.

"No, no. I'm fine." Nhamo forced herself to continue walking. It took a while for the shock to wear off, but presently she found an explanation for what had happened. Uncle Kufa had given the *zango*s to Masvita, expecting her to share them with the younger girls. It made perfect sense to protect everyone from sorcery. They were visiting the *muvuki*, who had killed his own son to gain power. Uncle Kufa wanted to be sure they didn't go home with more witchcraft than they arrived with.

Late in the afternoon, they came to the trading post. In spite of the somber reason for the journey, everyone cheered up. The trading post was so lively! Dozens of little camps surrounded it. Dozens of campfires threaded blue smoke through the *musasa* trees. Large women in bright head scarves sat behind heaps of vegetables outside the Portuguese store. Their faces shone with butterfat.

Men wove baskets out of reeds. Fishermen laid out bags of dried fish. Food sellers roasted mealies and peanuts—the smell almost drove Nhamo mad. She turned this way and that, eager to see everything.

A farmer played a one-stringed harp like a hunter's bow and sang to himself as he waited for someone to buy his chickens. The chickens lay in a mournful row with their legs tied together. A man sat on the steps of the trading post and tootled a lively tune on a *pakila*, or panpipes. He was joined by another man with a Portuguese guitar. Nhamo had never seen a guitar, and the music took her breath away. She stood perfectly still, hardly believing the beauty of the sound, until Aunt Chipo yelled at her to move on.

They made camp along a stream. Nhamo found stones for a cook-fire. She swept the ground to prepare sleeping areas, hauled water from the stream, and began the long process of preparing food. It made no difference that she was tired. The work still had to be done.

But when all was finished, she was too excited to rest. She ran back to the trading post. The guitarist was gone, but something equally interesting had appeared. The Portuguese trader had brought out his radio. It was loud, so loud! No mere human could have made so much noise. Nhamo discovered that if she leaned against it, her ribs quivered. She seemed to be made all of music. It was wonderful!

She stayed there until someone grabbed her by the arm and dragged her away. Nhamo stumbled off—the music still made her ears ring—and squatted in the shadows nearby.

"Go home, *picanin*!" shouted the Portuguese trader in bad Shona. "You no old enough for here!"

Gradually, she understood what the man was trying to tell her. Kerosene lamps—another amazing thing—hissed as they hung from hooks over the porch. Beneath sat a mob of men and women with buckets of beer. Each person had his or her own bucket, and it was clear the group had settled down for a night of serious drinking.

A vague sense of danger hung over the gathering, although Nhamo wasn't sure why. Regretfully, she returned to her camp.

"The *muvuki* can't see us for weeks! He wouldn't even talk to me!" Uncle Kufa was shouting as she arrived. "How are we supposed to wait—with all of you eating like starving hyenas? I suppose he plans to push up the price, the dirty child murderer!"

"Please don't shout. You don't know who's listening," begged Aunt Chipo.

Uncle Kufa stopped abruptly and looked around at the dark trees. "You're right. I wouldn't put it past him to have spies," he muttered.

"What kind of spies?" asked Nhamo as she stretched out next to Masvita later.

Masvita thought for a moment. "Owls?" she guessed.

Nhamo digested this idea as she stared up at the stars. She didn't like sleeping outside, even with a crowd of people. "I thought only witches kept owls."

"Don't ask so many questions. Go to sleep," said Masvita.

Nhamo thought about the *muvuki*. Grandmother said that perfectly good *nganga*s were sometimes tempted to use their power for evil. Once they did, she said, you didn't go near them, any more than you would approach a dog that had gone rabid.

In the distance, she heard the radio and the loud voices of the drinkers. The music let her know she was in a truly exotic and exciting place. "I'm glad we have to wait," she whispered to herself.

Every day Nhamo saw interesting things. A group of Frelimo soldiers gave a speech outside the trading post. They told everyone the people of Mozambique must work together to build a new nation now that the Portuguese colonialists had been defeated. Nhamo had no idea what a *nation* was, but she listened politely. Some of the soldiers were women. They dressed in the same clothes as the men, and they swaggered around like the men, with guns slung over their shoulders.

"I wonder what kind of *roora* they'd bring," remarked Uncle Kufa to *Vatete*'s husband.

"None at all," he replied. "Frelimo says paying for women is bad."

Everyone was shocked. Not pay for women? How were fathers to get back their investment in raising daughters?

"They're no better than animals," declared Aunt Chipo. "Marriages that haven't been paid for can be broken like old pots."

One night, for entertainment, the Frelimo soldiers set off flares and fired tracer bullets into the sky. The bullets flew like sparks, and the flares went right up into the stars. The explosions made Nhamo and Masvita clutch each other in alarm.

"Stupid soldiers," muttered *Ambuya*. She was irritable most of the time now. Whether it was caused by the long walk or by grief, Nhamo didn't know, but the old woman seemed to age more every day. She no longer bustled around. Instead, she sat against a tree and stared at the stream.

Often Masvita sat with her, too exhausted to work. Then Nhamo wished the *muvuki* would see them quickly, although she was afraid of what he might say.

"Come with me to the trading post, *Ambuya*," she said one day. "It's so very interesting."

"It's new to you, Little Pumpkin. Nothing surprises me anymore." *Ambuya* pulled a blanket around her shoulders.

"You can listen to the radio."

"Shake-shake music," grumbled *Ambuya*, referring to the shake-shake, or beer, the trader sold. "I should rack my bones to see a pack of drunk fools."

"The guitarist sits there in the afternoon," Nhamo coaxed.

"A guitar?" Grandmother's eyes showed a flicker of interest.

"It sounds like water pouring over a rock. You have no idea how beautiful it is!"

"I know what guitars sound like," Grandmother said crossly. "I've heard them hundreds of times." But she allowed Nhamo to draw her to her feet. Nhamo supported the old woman as they walked toward the trading post. When they arrived, the guitarist was already playing, and someone had thoughtfully provided him with a bucket of beer. Several people moved to allow *Ambuya* to make her way to the porch. The Portuguese trader found her a stool.

"He good," the trader confided to *Ambuya* in his bad Shona. "I pay his way to Maputo for play in nightclub. We make money like bandits."

Ambuya nodded graciously. Her nose twitched, and Nhamo knew she could smell the alcohol on his breath.

The trader clapped when the guitarist finished, then shouted something in Portuguese. The other people complimented the musician and made requests.

The sun slanted through the *musasa* trees as it lowered toward the horizon. It turned everything gold. For the first time in several days, Grandmother smiled. It made Nhamo's spirit happy to see the old woman nod her head in time to the music. If only the golden afternoon could go on forever, with *Ambuya* and her at the center of this friendly crowd. But eventually the musician grew tired and the sunlight faded. The trader's assistant brought out the hissing lamps and hung them over the porch.

"He go for Maputo soon," said the trader as the musician slung the guitar over his back. "Make money like bandits."

Still, the enchantment lingered as the blue twilight flooded the land. No one was willing to ask for the radio just yet. "You have many death in your village, hey?" said the trader suddenly. Nhamo could have killed him.

Grandmother's face became sad again. "Many people died," she agreed.

"Cholera a bad bugger. Frelimo send soldiers with *muti*,* but too late. *Muti* no work good, anyway." He shook his head. "You lose someone special, *ambuya*?"

Nhamo wanted to drop a lantern on his head.

"Yes," Grandmother replied.

"Me, too. My little Maria. My wife cry. I cry, too." The trader took a picture from his shirt pocket. He signaled to the assistant to lift down one of the lamps. Nhamo saw a girl about Ruva's age, wearing a beautiful dress covered with ruffles. The girl had on shiny black shoes and she carried a small purse. Pinned over her hair was a lace handkerchief. Maria was almost as dark as herself, so Nhamo guessed that the trader's wife wasn't Portuguese.

"I don't have a picture of Shuvai," *Ambuya* said with the tears rolling down her face.

"No matter. Her picture here, no?" The trader slapped himself on the chest. "Inside have best photo."

Grandmother was too overcome to answer. Nhamo was desperate to get her back to camp.

"Can we have the radio?" someone called hopefully.

"Shut up," roared the trader. "Me and *Va-ambuya* talk seriously. You rascals can get drunk without music." Nhamo heard murmured grumbles, but no one spoke out loud. The

muti: Medicine.

assistant began bringing out buckets of beer. "Bring something for this old lady, hey? Nice stuff. Not the swill these buggers drink."

Nhamo's spirits rose. It was unheard of for *Ambuya* to drink with strangers. Now she would surely ask to go home. But to Nhamo's horror, Grandmother accepted the dark bottle the assistant brought. He provided his boss with a bucket of "shake-shake." Apparently the trader had no qualms about drinking swill himself.

Nhamo brooded in the shadows as *Ambuya* and the trader discussed dead relatives. It seemed an insane thing to do, but gradually she noticed that Grandmother appeared more lighthearted. Perhaps, in remembering, her spirit let go of the unhappiness.

Soon, on her *third* bottle of the dark beer, *Ambuya* was recounting how Ruva squealed when a fish she had been given by Crocodile Guts wriggled in her hands. The trader responded with a tale of how his wife heated a can of peas on hot coals without opening it first. "Boom! Peas on the walls. Peas on the ceiling. 'Ah! Ah!' my wife cried. 'It's a hand grenade!'" Grandmother shook with laughter.

"Come here, Nhamo," she called. "Tell him about the time you put a grass snake in the boys' hut."

Nhamo burned with embarrassment. She still remembered the beating Aunt Chipo had given her.

"They left puddles on the mats, I can tell you," Grandmother recalled.

"Nhamo mean 'disaster,' no? She's a nice kid. No look like a disaster to me."

"She's my wonderful Little Pumpkin," Grandmother said warmly. "She's my Runako's only child, but her birth caused trouble, I can tell you!"

"How so?" The trader called for his assistant to bring them bowls of *sadza* and relish from his kitchen. Nhamo brightened up at once. Her stomach was growling with hunger.

"Runako was so clever! After we left Zimbabwe, her headmaster sent a letter to our village. 'I have spoken to the nuns at the Catholic school,' he wrote. 'They have agreed to give Runako a—a *scholarship*.' " *Ambuya*'s tongue stumbled over the English word. "That's a kind of *bonsella,* a gift. Imagine! They would pay for her food, books, everything. I was so excited. I sent her off at once. She was only fifteen."

The assistant arrived with three large bowls of food. As much as Nhamo was riveted on the story of her birth, her stomach demanded that she pay attention to dinner. The *sadza* was white and beautifully cooked. The relish was like nothing she had ever seen. It was a rich tomato stew flavored with strange spices—and full of chicken! Nhamo, who hardly ever got meat, had to control herself to eat politely. Grandmother was equally delighted by the meal and for a few moments applied herself to steady eating.

"Now can we have the radio?" someone asked.

"Silence, you *tsotsis*!*" shouted the trader. "Why do I let you drunks sit on my porch? You better off with the goats."

"If only I had kept Runako at home," said Grandmother as she cleaned the last crumbs of *sadza* from her bowl. "She met a boy at that school. He was called Proud Jongwe." *Ambuya* spat out the words. "Proud! I should like to know what he was proud of. *Useless* would have been a better name."

"But nice-looking," guessed the trader.

"Oh, yes." Grandmother sighed. "Poor Runako. She seemed so intelligent, but they say girls turn stupid for a few years after they become women."

"That's true," said one of the drinkers. "It's a well-known fact."

"You be quiet!" the trader shouted.

"They got married in a Catholic church. Wicked, disobedient children!"

"Not bad to marry in the church," the trader said, slightly offended.

"It's all right for you. You're Portuguese. Among us, the son-in-law has to get the family's permission—and arrange

*tsotsi: A hoodlum.

the *roora*. One day I saw Runako walking along the trail to our village. 'What happened?' I cried. 'Did the nuns send you away?' Then I saw her stomach." *Ambuya* paused to finish the beer. She waved a fourth bottle away, for which Nhamo was thankful.

"He was right behind her, the scheming hyena! Not a coin in his pockets, not a cow to his name."

"Sometime poor man work for pay *roora*. That okay," the Portuguese man said.

"*If* the man works! I never saw Proud Jongwe do anything. Oh, he was full of plans! He would find gold; he would build a square house like they have in Zimbabwe—our huts weren't good enough. But the only talent he had was to empty beer pots!" *Ambuya* glared at the shake-shake customers, and they nervously looked away.

"One night . . ." *Ambuya* paused dramatically until everyone had turned back to watch her. Nhamo held her breath. No one had ever told her about Father. If she approached when someone was speaking of him, people immediately changed the subject—and here was Grandmother revealing the secret to a whole crowd of strangers!

"One night Proud went to a beer-drink in the next village." *Ambuya* straightened up and put her hands on her hips. The lanterns painted her face with a harsh yellow light. The shake-shake drinkers bent close to listen. "He got into a fight with a man called Goré Mtoko," she said in a hushed voice. "They were both *tsotsis*, both useless. Goré knocked Proud into a bed of hot coals, and Proud was so enraged he—he grabbed a rock—*and he smashed in Goré's skull!*"

"Hhhuuu," murmured all the beer drinkers.

Nhamo felt like screaming, but her throat had closed up so tightly she could hardly breathe. So that was the secret! Her father was a murderer! Her stomach twisted with nausea. No wonder Aunt Chipo and Uncle Kufa didn't like her!

"Proud ran away like the mangy dog he was. He never even said good-bye to Runako. Later I heard he returned to the Catholic school and borrowed money from the nuns—

told them it was for his wife. He went to Mtoroshanga to work in a chrome mine."

So much for thinking her father would return to arrange a marriage for her! Nhamo clenched her teeth to keep from crying out loud. Her mother had had no *roora* paid for her. She was one of those women *Vatete* meant who wasn't even worth a mangy goat. Everyone in the village had known about it except her. Nhamo wanted to tear out her hair with shame. She crouched next to Grandmother's stool, hugging her stomach.

"*Va-Ambuya,* we were so worried about you," came Uncle Kufa's voice. Nhamo squinted at the market area in front of the trading post. She could just make out his figure in the shadows, and that of Aunt Chipo beside him.

"We thought you had fallen into the stream," Aunt Chipo called.

"As if I would do such a foolish thing," Grandmother said. She rose unsteadily, and Nhamo rushed to support her. "Thank you, my friend," she told the Portuguese trader, clapping her hands respectfully.

"You always welcome, *Va-ambuya.* You got sense in that old head. Not like these buggers." The trader scowled at the beer drinkers.

"*Now* can we have the radio?" someone called plaintively.

Grandmother leaned heavily on Nhamo as they made their way back to camp. "You—you've been drinking," murmured Aunt Chipo.

"What of it?" *Ambuya* said belligerently.

When they were well away from the trading post, Uncle Kufa said quietly, "I thought we agreed never to talk about Runako's husband."

"Am I to fill my mouth with clay? Am I to be lectured by one who was wetting his loincloth when I was out buying cattle for my family?"

"Mother . . . ," faltered Aunt Chipo.

"Yes! I am your mother, and you would do well to remember it!"

No one said anything for a while as they felt their way

along the dark trail. Nhamo was too disturbed to pay much attention, but gradually she began to sense that something was very wrong. It wasn't common for women to drink, of course, but it wasn't unheard of. Grandmother had always been independent. She smoked a pipe. She sometimes sat in the men's *dare*. She maintained far more control of her wealth and affairs than any woman Nhamo knew. That was Grandmother, and no one expected her to behave any differently. Uncle Kufa and Aunt Chipo were too quiet, however. Nhamo sensed a current of disapproval; for once it wasn't directed at her.

"There's nothing wrong with visiting people," *Ambuya* said suddenly.

"You don't know who was in that crowd," Uncle Kufa replied in a tight voice that told Nhamo he was struggling not to get angry.

Grandmother thought for a moment. "The whole business was laid to rest years ago."

"Maybe it was, and maybe it wasn't."

More silence. More unspoken disapproval.

Nhamo couldn't make sense out of the argument, but she knew better than to ask questions. When they at last arrived in camp, Nhamo helped Grandmother to bed. Then she presented herself at the makeshift cooking area to clean dishes. Her mind was whirling with what had happened. She barely heard the other girls' voices, and as soon as possible she stretched out on a sleeping mat. She pretended not to notice when Masvita lay down beside her.

Father was a murderer. He ran away before he could be punished, and that meant Goré Mtoko's family hadn't got revenge on him. A crime like that cried out for punishment. Nhamo remembered *Ambuya* telling a story about a man who murdered his wife in Zimbabwe. He was sent to a whiteman's prison. That was all very well, Grandmother said, but everyone knew the wife's spirit wouldn't be satisfied. When the murderer was finally set free, he began to act very strangely. He dressed in women's clothes and spoke in a high-pitched voice. He shouted at his sisters and said, "Why did your brother kill me?" Then everyone knew he was possessed by the spirit of the dead wife. He wandered around, Grandmother said, until he was run over by a bus. "*She* made him walk in front of that bus," *Ambuya* said with satisfaction.

Perhaps Goré's spirit pursued Father even now. And yet Grandmother had said the whole business had been settled years ago. Did she pay compensation to the Mtoko family? That would have been unfair—after all, she was no blood relative of Father's—but perhaps they blamed Mother. *Ambuya* would have done anything for Mother.

Nhamo's throat ached from holding back tears. A daughter belonged to her father's family. Most people would have sent her away after Mother died, but not *Ambuya*. Grandmother had insisted on keeping her, had treated her kindly and called her Little Pumpkin. When she remembered this, Nhamo's control broke down. Tears poured out of her eyes and she clenched her teeth to prevent herself from making a sound. Her whole body trembled, but she managed to keep from disturbing Masvita at her side. Lucky, lucky Masvita! *Her* name meant "thank you." Her birth had been welcomed and, in spite of recent troubles, everyone would rally around to make her future as pleasant as possible.

9

I t's happened!" cried Masvita, pushing through the reeds of the stream. Nhamo was perched on a rock, watching the effect of a fish trap she had made.

"What's happened?" she said.

"The *muvuki*." Masvita had been running so hard, she had to sit down to catch her breath. "He says we can see him tomorrow. Ah! That's a clever device."

Nhamo bent down, whisked a smallish fish from the cone-shaped trap, and popped it into a basket. Her heart was beating very fast, but she didn't want to show her cousin how frightened she was. "Thanks. I learned to make it at the trading post. There's a man there who can weave almost anything. Are . . . we all going?"

"Oh, yes! We have to be present in case, in case . . ." Masvita's voice trailed off.

In case one of us is discovered to be a witch, Nhamo thought.

"It'll be wonderful to get it over with. I want to go home. I thought I'd like travel, but really all I want to do is stay in one place and never, never have any surprises." Masvita opened Nhamo's basket and counted the fish inside.

"I don't like surprises either," murmured Nhamo, thinking of Father.

When they returned to the camp, everyone was busy packing. They would return home soon if everything went well. Uncle Kufa went to the trading post to buy powdered milk for Aunt Shuvai's baby. The infant was recovering rapidly—his face had already rounded out, and he seemed to have accepted Masvita as his new mother. This, in turn, had an excellent effect on Masvita.

She already looks like a mother, thought Nhamo. She could be five years older than I—but then, she grew rapidly like a weed. Grandmother's comment had once made Nhamo smile, but now it only aroused a dull ache in her heart. It doesn't matter if I turn into a fruit tree in five years, she thought. Who would want to marry the daughter of a murderer then—or ever?

Early next morning everyone dressed with particular care. Masvita combed Nhamo's hair and rubbed her skin with butterfat. Her cousin's hands were cold, and Nhamo knew that she was frightened, too. They set off just as the sun rose in a dull red ball beyond the *musasa* trees. The trail was damp under Nhamo's bare feet, and the forest was full of glossy starlings with dark blue-green feathers and orange eyes.

The settlement was built in a long line close to the stream. The trader's house, Nhamo had learned, lay at one extreme, with the *muvuki*'s house nearby. The Frelimo camp was at the other. The store was at the center. The villagers followed the stream past clusters of huts and granaries perched on stilts. Uncle Kufa was at their head, and the men carried presents for the doctor.

One mile, two miles passed. They came at last to the *muvuki*'s garden. He had a square house with a red tile roof, and his garden was full of heavily laden banana and papaya trees. A boy passed them on the way, herding a flock of sleek nanny goats. Each one was fitted with a cloth bag over her udder to keep the milk from being stolen. Nhamo thought that was ludicrous, but she was far too worried to laugh.

"*Takutuka chiremba*," the adults shouted in unison before they entered the garden: "We have scolded you, doctor." Nhamo didn't know the meaning behind this strange saying, but Grandmother said it was the correct way to enter a *muvuki*'s yard. The doctor was dressed in a gray suit like a picture in a magazine, and he was eating breakfast at a table on the porch. Nhamo saw with fascination that he used a knife and fork instead of his fingers. Suddenly, he looked up and gazed straight at her. She felt as though her bones had turned to water.

"*Vahukwu*. Welcome," he called. He put down his utensils, and a servant removed his plate.

"I see you, *Va*-Nyamasatsi," he said, giving *Ambuya*'s real name. "And you, *Va*-Kufa." Nhamo felt goose bumps on her arms as he singled out every person in the group. How could he do this? He had never seen them before.

He then slowly and impressively listed all the people who had died. When each name was uttered, everyone cried, "*Womba!* Amazing!" He pointed at a grove of trees at the far end of the garden and abruptly entered the house.

"What happens now?" whispered Nhamo.

"That is his *vukiro*, his sacred grove," Grandmother whispered back. "We must wait there until he is properly dressed."

Everyone sat in a semicircle. Presently, the *muvuki* emerged, still wearing his suit but with two ceremonial cloths crossed over his chest and tied behind his back. He wore a leopard-skin cap and a necklace of small bones and glass beads. He carried a clay pot.

Is that the pot where he keeps his son's spirit? thought Nhamo with a stab of pure terror. But the *muvuki* unrolled a reed mat on the ground and removed four *hakata*, or divining sticks, from the pot. Nhamo shivered with relief.

Following the doctor came a younger man who knelt beside him and waited. "I request my *gogodzero*, the opening fee," said the *muvuki*. Uncle Kufa quickly took three trussed-up chickens from the other villagers and laid them before the doctor.

"I will keep them for you, *baba*," said the younger man. He removed the chickens to the shade of a tree nearby. So that's one of the *muvuki*'s sons, thought Nhamo. I wonder what he thought when his brother was sacrificed.

Now the doctor took up two of the *hakata* sticks in one hand and two in the other. "These people have come to me, a son of an *nganga*, and want to be told who killed their relatives. Was it a *mudzimu,* a family spirit?" he asked. His hands opened, and the sticks fell to the mat. He quickly scooped them up, but Nhamo saw that two were faceup and two were down. She knew each stick had a patterned and a smooth side. Three of the designs were abstract. The fourth was the outline of a crocodile. She didn't know what the symbols meant.

"Is this diagnosis true?" asked the doctor, and he let the *hakata* fall again. This time three were up and one down. "*Zaru,*" he said. "The sticks disagree. These deaths were not caused by a family spirit."

He proceeded to ask whether the trouble was caused by a *shave,* a wandering spirit. He threw the *hakata* twice to see if they agreed. Again the answer was no. "Was an *ngozi** responsible?" the doctor said. The sticks fell with three down and the fourth up, showing the crocodile. "*Ngwena.* Bad luck. Is this a true diagnosis?" Again the *hakata* fell three down with the crocodile up. "They agree! An *ngozi* has done this."

"Hhhuuu," everyone sighed. Now no one would be pointed out as a witch.

"A man has been murdered," the *muvuki* went on. "His spirit wanders. He has become an *ngozi* without a resting place, without heirs. He seeks revenge. *He* is the one who slew your relatives—and that one's father is responsible!" He pointed straight at Nhamo. She flinched back so abruptly, she fell against Masvita.

"His spirit is crying out, 'Why did you kill me? Why is my family calling for vengeance?'"

"We paid compensation," *Ambuya* objected.

"Hush, hush," everyone murmured. Masvita helped Nhamo sit up. They clung to each other.

"Who is this who questions the *hakata*?" demanded the *muvuki.* "Is she a spirit medium? I do not recognize her."

"Ten years ago I paid compensation. I wasn't even a relative of the man who committed the murder, but I paid. Goré

**ngozi:* An angry spirit bent on revenge.

Mtoko's father demanded ten cattle, one for each of the fingers on his son's hands. Such a price for a *tsotsi* whose only skill was to prop open a door!"

"Please don't say any more," whimpered Aunt Chipo. *Ambuya* impatiently waved her daughter away.

"And did you pay ten cattle?" inquired the *muvuki* in a quiet voice.

Grandmother became uneasy. "Well, how could I? I didn't have that kind of wealth. Besides, nothing would have happened if Goré hadn't knocked Proud into the coals. They were both at fault, really."

"And what *did* you pay?" The *muvuki*'s voice was smooth as the passage of a snake through reeds.

"Two cows," admitted *Ambuya*.

"Two cows for a man's life? Two cows for depriving someone of becoming an ancestor? Is it any wonder his spirit has returned *in the form of a leopard*?"

Everyone gasped.

"Oh, yes." The *muvuki* smiled. "You think to hide it from me, but I know. *I have seen it, Va-Nyamasatsi.* Your daughter Runako was killed by a leopard, is it not so?"

"Yes," whispered Grandmother.

"It walked into the village. It did not kill a goat or a chicken. It walked past a small child and took her mother, is it not so?"

Grandmother was unable to speak.

"Then, when this girl approached the age of womanhood, the leopard came again. It appeared to her by the water—to her alone—and it spoke to her in the banana grove by night. Its footprints were seen in the dust of graves. You all know that the totem of Goré Mtoko's family is the leopard. The solution to this problem is very clear."

"Aaugh!" screamed Aunt Chipo, falling to the ground. "Eh! Eh! Why did you kill me? What had I done to you? Aaugh!" She tossed from side to side, her eyes rolled back in her head. Everyone jumped up at once. Masvita dragged Nhamo away from Aunt Chipo's writhing body.

Nhamo almost fainted from shock. Goré's spirit had possessed her aunt! He was right there, demanding vengeance!

"I had no cloth to cover my body, no goat for the people who dug my grave! I had no food for the people who mourned me! These things I demand now!" screamed Aunt Chipo. Uncle Kufa knelt beside her and tried to wipe her face with a cloth, but she threw him back with surprising strength.

"I have no son to offer sacrifices for me! I demand vengeance! I demand the daughter of my murderer! Eeeee!" Aunt Chipo gave a heart-stopping shriek and fainted. Her body became perfectly limp as the spirit of Goré left her. Several women hurried to rub her arms and legs. Uncle Kufa asked the *muvuki* for a calabash of water. The doctor sent his son to the house.

Masvita was crying and trembling, but Nhamo barely noticed. She felt turned to stone. Only Grandmother maintained her self-control. She faced the *muvuki* squarely. "I agree that two cows was too small a payment, but after all, the murderer's family should have handled the situation. They're in Zimbabwe. I sent them a message telling them about the problem, but they never answered."

The doctor's son arrived with water, and Uncle Kufa splashed it over Aunt Chipo's body to cool her down. She moaned and opened her eyes.

"*One* member of the murderer's family is not in Zimbabwe," the *muvuki* said.

"I will send cloth and food to Goré's family, and a cow to take the place of this girl. That, surely, will please the Mtokos."

"We aren't speaking of what will please the Mtokos," the *muvuki* said in his smooth voice. "It's the *ngozi* who has to be satisfied. Life must be given for life."

Nhamo was jolted from her state of shock. Was the *muvuki* talking of sacrificing her? Surely not!

"The girl must be given to the brother of Goré Mtoko as a junior wife. As you know, she will really be the bride of the *ngozi*, and her first son will bear his name."

"No! *Ngozis* can no longer demand human beings as

payment! That custom is illegal—and it's stupid—and cruel! I will not agree!"

"Please, *Va-Ambuya*. Don't make things worse," pleaded Uncle Kufa.

"They could hardly be any worse. Let me tell you, *Muvuki*. The brother of Goré Mtoko is a beast. He's riddled with disease, and so are his miserable wives. As if I would give the child of my Runako to that animal! I would sooner die—and *then* you would see an avenging spirit. Not one of you would get a good night's sleep! Let go of me!"

Several of the women present tried to hold on to Grandmother. They murmured anxious words as though they were calming an angry infant. "She isn't well, *Muvuki*. Please forgive her," one of them said.

"There's nothing wrong with me!" Grandmother shouted. "We live in modern times, and girls don't have to be given away as slaves. What kind of doctor are you, anyway? Someone who killed his own son to gain power? Ha! Only witches do that!"

"Mother!" shrieked Aunt Chipo.

"She's sick," Uncle Kufa cried. "She doesn't know what she's saying."

Nhamo was dizzy with fear. The worst, the very worst thing you could call anyone was a witch. *Especially* when it might be true. The *muvuki*'s face was expressionless, but his clenched fists showed the rage that bubbled inside him. Even Grandmother seemed appalled by what she had just said.

"If there's a witch present, she arrived this morning," the *muvuki* snarled. "And if someone tries to cast a spell on *me*, the force of my ancestral spirits will cast it right back." He thrust his walking stick, carved in the shape of a serpent, at *Ambuya*.

Nhamo screamed. She thought the heavy cane was going to smash Grandmother's face, but it stopped a finger's breadth away. The effect was as though the blow had actually landed, however. *Ambuya*'s head snapped back and she bared her teeth in a terrible parody of a smile. Then she collapsed into the arms of the women around her.

"Grandmother," wailed Masvita.

"Get back. Let her breathe," Uncle Kufa ordered.

The women laid Grandmother on the ground, and Aunt Chipo began rubbing her hands and feet. The *muvuki*'s son grabbed the calabash and ran for more water.

To Nhamo, the rest of the world seemed to disappear: All she could see was Grandmother's face with one side crumpled and one eye open and unblinking. Nhamo closed the eye gently. She massaged *Ambuya*'s face and felt the teeth clenched beneath the wrinkled skin.

"Can you help her, honored doctor?" said Uncle Kufa.

"Why should I aid someone who called me a witch?" said the *muvuki*.

"She is the oldest person in our village. She suffers from a misguided fondness for her granddaughter, but otherwise her life has been blameless. I will pay you, of course."

The *muvuki* considered. "It is a good thing to care for one's elders. I see you are a considerate and honorable son-in-law. Very well, I will make a poultice to draw out the illness, but you will have to find someone else to carry on the treatment after you return home. This kind of sickness takes a long time to heal."

"How long?"

"Weeks. Perhaps months."

The *muvuki* returned to his house to prepare the medicine, and Uncle Kufa removed more gifts from the packs carried by the villagers. He took out two brand-new hoes, a knife with the hilt wrapped in copper wire, a length of dress-cloth, and a small amount of real money. Grandmother's breathing was ragged, almost like snoring.

"Go on to the Portuguese trader's house, Nhamo," said Uncle Kufa. "Ask him to send us something to help move *Ambuya*."

Nhamo hurried farther along the trail. The trader didn't open his store until noon, so he was still sitting on his porch enjoying the cool morning breeze. He sent his assistant off at once with a stretcher. "Bring her here," he told the man. "No leave alone with witch doctor. Maybe he cut her into steaks for dinner." Nhamo looked so alarmed, he added, "I make joke, little Disaster. Your *ambuya* too tough for him anyhow."

After a while the villagers arrived with Grandmother. The side of her face and body was plastered with a brown-gray mud. Everyone's forehead was marked with chalk to show that the *muvuki* had been satisfied with his payment and that everyone had been satisfied with his diagnosis. The trader told them to put Grandmother on a bed on the covered porch.

"She's not used to sleeping off the ground. She might fall," whispered Nhamo.

"You watch her, then," the trader ordered. "Me, I no sleep on the ground. Centipedes crawl up my nose and make nest." In spite of her misery, the idea was so silly Nhamo gave him a watery smile. "That better, little Disaster. You stay by your *ambuya* and hit the centipedes with a stick when they show up."

Uncle Kufa was amazed that the trader wanted no payment for keeping Grandmother, but he was quick to take him up on the offer. He assigned several women to take turns watching her.

All day they sat, keeping Grandmother's body warm and flexing her hands and feet. By afternoon, the old woman was able to move one side of her body, but the other side remained paralyzed. She was unable to speak. There was no question of moving her until she recovered more of her strength or— Nhamo swallowed back the tears—died. At night, the women returned to the camp by the stream. Only Nhamo remained, patiently changing the cloths beneath *Ambuya*'s hips and dribbling water into her mouth. Finally, in the middle of the night, she was too exhausted to go on. She stretched out on a mat by the bed and, worn out by fear and misery, sank into a dreamless sleep.

10

The next day, Uncle Kufa sent Masvita, Aunt Chipo, and Aunt Shuvai's baby to stay in *Vatete*'s village. *Vatete*'s husband and one other man went along to protect them. The rest of the villagers remained to carry Grandmother home when she was able to travel. Nhamo hugged her cousin. They both cried, and the baby, who was tied to Masvita's back, picked up their mood and began to howl.

"He looks strong," said Nhamo, wiping tears from her face. "Good lungs, anyway."

"He's beautiful," Masvita said. "If I—if I never have babies, I'll at least have had him." Then she cried some more until Aunt Chipo called her away. Nhamo watched them disappear down the trail with mixed feelings. On one hand, she hated to see them go. On the other, no one else would expect her to discuss that terrible, terrible meeting with the *muvuki*. Uncle Kufa would make only brief visits to see how *Ambuya* was doing.

The other women didn't speak to her at all, and Nhamo had plenty of time to think about her situation. Her father was a murderer. The *ngozi* had demanded that she marry a diseased man with several wives. Goré's brother wouldn't pay *roora* for her, so she wouldn't have any status in her new household. The other wives would beat her. Perhaps her husband would beat her, too, to get revenge for his brother's death. She

wouldn't see Masvita anymore, or Ruva or Grandmother—
if Grandmother even lived.

The future was so bleak, Nhamo refused to think about
it. She pretended that she lived on the trader's porch instead.
It was what she did in the deserted village back home. She
knew, of course, that Mother didn't really drink tea with her
on top of the hill there. She knew she sat with a scrap of
paper held down by pebbles—but the pictures in her mind
were so real, she thought they must somehow exist. They
might live in the underground country where the thrown-
away animals and people went. And someday, if she could
find the way, she might join them.

Nhamo applied herself to caring for *Ambuya*. When an
unpleasant thought occurred, she shook her head to clear it
out. Nothing existed for her but the trader's house, the porch
with Grandmother's bed, and an endless present.

Three or four times a day she made up a poultice. The
muvuki had provided powdered bark from a tree that had
been struck by lightning. This was the correct treatment, he
said, for someone who suffered from *chikandiwa,* or a stroke.
Nhamo boiled the powder with water, soaked it in a cloth,
and applied it to Grandmother's paralyzed side. Between
times, she rubbed *Ambuya*'s arms and legs, and told her
stories. She couldn't tell whether the old woman understood
her.

The other women helped during the day, but they talked
to one another and ignored Nhamo.

During the afternoon, when the trader was at work, his
wife sat on the porch. She was a plump, cheerful woman
called Rosa. "I used to have a Shona name, but Joao changed
it when we got married," she explained. Joao was the trader.

"Is that their custom? To change a wife's name?"

"If she joins the church," said Rosa. "I became a Catholic
to marry Joao. You're an excellent storyteller."

"Thank you. *Ambuya* taught me." Nhamo was pleased
to have company and even more delighted with the snacks
Rosa produced. Never had she encountered such food! Some
of it came out of cans—delicious, oily fish, and peas already

shelled and cooked. Rosa had paper packages of cookies and glass bottles full of honey. What a wonderful thing it was to be married to a storekeeper! Nhamo would have joined the church, too, to have such riches.

Other things about Catholics made her uneasy, though. Across from Rosa and Joao's bed was a huge cross with a man nailed to it. His head was crowned with thorns. Rosa said he was called Jesus. She said bad people had murdered him, but he came back to life after three days.

"Did he get revenge on his enemies then?" inquired Nhamo.

"Oh, no! He *forgave* them. That's the Christian way."

Nhamo didn't want to be rude, but she thought it was creepy to have a dead man on the wall of your bedroom. Also, if compensation hadn't been paid, Jesus would have turned into an *ngozi* and made his enemies suffer anyway. Nhamo shook her head violently to keep from thinking about *ngozis*.

Slowly, Grandmother improved. She could move both sides of her body, although she was too weak to stand and she still couldn't talk. Her eyes had expression in them now. They followed Nhamo and sometimes they welled over with tears.

"Does it hurt, *Ambuya*?" whispered Nhamo as she wiped the tears away. Grandmother couldn't answer; the tears continued to flow.

One afternoon, Uncle Kufa decided the old woman was well enough to travel. "The basket maker has made a traveling chair for you, *Va-Ambuya*," he said. "It hangs on long poles, which we can carry on our shoulders. You should be very comfortable." He instructed Nhamo to have everything ready to leave the next morning.

Nhamo felt stunned as her uncle strode off. All at once, the thoughts she had pushed away came back in a rush. She wasn't going to live on this porch forever. No one would speak to her kindly anymore or worry about her welfare. She would go to a strange house where the women would hate her and her husband would beat her. Even her own people couldn't wait to get rid of her.

Nhamo sank to the ground and burst into wild sobs. Rosa came running from the house. "What is it? Are you hurt?" She knelt and took the girl into her arms. Nhamo wept until she was exhausted. Rosa led her into the house and made her lie down on the big bed across from Jesus.

"Drink this, little Disaster," she whispered, holding a glass of dark red liquid to Nhamo's mouth. Nhamo almost choked on the sweet, fiery substance, but Rosa refused to go until she finished. "Stay here. Sleep," Rosa murmured, stroking Nhamo's forehead.

Nhamo woke with a start later. The first thing she saw was the dead man on the wall. He was a murder victim, so he had certainly turned into an *ngozi*. Was he still wandering around, looking for his enemies? Nhamo rolled off the bed and crouched on the floor where Jesus couldn't watch her. She heard voices outside, speaking Portuguese.

Her chest ached from her crying earlier. A heavy feeling of despair weighed down her arms and legs, but she realized that *Ambuya* needed care.

"Little Disaster!" cried the trader as she came out to the porch. He and Rosa were sitting next to Grandmother.

Nhamo was surprised. It was daytime, and the trader was supposed to work until midnight.

"I come home special for you," Joao explained. "Rosa send message: You cry, cry. Make yourself sick. She explain better what we got in mind. Speak better Shona."

"We know all about the *muvuki*. He's an evil man!" began Rosa.

"Bad bugger ten times over," Joao added.

"He tells people to wait, so his spies can find out their secrets. Then he pretends the spirits told him everything. It's all lies."

Nhamo was worried. It was dangerous to criticize the doctor. He might find out and harm Joao and Rosa.

"He always has someone at the trading post because, sooner or later, everyone goes there," Rosa went on.

"I big fool, getting this old lady to talk. The witch doctor hear about you, Nhamo. He smack his lips, you bet. Get out the salt and pepper." The trader nodded at *Ambuya*, and she watched him intently.

"We've met your grandmother before, when she came to trade livestock and gold," said Rosa. "She's a remarkable woman, intelligent and independent. Look at the way she sent your mother off to school. We know she wouldn't want you to be an *ngozi* bride."

Nhamo hung her head. It was kind of the trader and his wife to be sympathetic, but they had no idea how desperate the villagers were. They were fighting for their lives. The happiness of one girl wouldn't concern them.

"We think—although we aren't sure—that your mother became a Catholic before she was married. That makes you a Catholic child, Nhamo. You *can't* be given away in a pagan ritual."

Nhamo looked up, startled.

"Our little Maria die of cholera," said Joao. "Rosa sad all the time. No have any baby. She want for you to be hers." Rosa took Nhamo's hands, and her eyes glistened with tears. Nhamo was astounded. Live here? With these kind people? Was it possible?

"Your *ambuya* would like that," said Rosa. Nhamo looked down at Grandmother. The old woman brought her withered hands together as though she were trying to clap, the way one did to say thank you.

"Oh, Grandmother," murmured Nhamo. She felt dazed. Could she really stay here—and talk to Rosa all day—and listen to the guitar—and eat fish from a can? She would work in the garden and kitchen—she would work day and night to make them like her! But she wouldn't see Grandmother or Masvita anymore. And what about Mother! Would she still be able to have tea with her?

"You wouldn't be able to see your family anyhow, if you got married," Rosa said, understanding Nhamo's sudden look of dismay. "You'd be nothing but a slave. Do you think your husband would let you run off on visits? Husband! How could anyone think of marrying you off? You don't look over *eleven*."

"I'm the same age as Masvita," said Nhamo.

"Going by her, you might be as old as twelve. That's still a shocking age to get married."

"Uncle Kufa will never agree," Nhamo said. She didn't dare let herself hope for too much.

"I deal with him," declared the trader. "I fill him up with presents. He fat as hippo by time he go home."

But the trader had underestimated the depth of Uncle Kufa's fear. "No!" Uncle Kufa shouted that night. "No! The *ngozi* killed my relatives. It made my daughter sterile. It will kill us all if it doesn't get satisfaction." Uncle Kufa's brother, waiting in the shadows near the porch, grunted in agreement.

"I talk to Goré Mtoko's brother, make big offer. He happy, Goré happy. Go back to boneyard where he belongs."

"You don't understand! What the *ngozi* wants is a *son*. No one can give it to him except Nhamo." Uncle Kufa talked as though Nhamo and Rosa didn't exist, although they were standing right in front of him.

"She too small for wife," Joao said. "You leave her here one year. Then she marry."

"No one expects her to behave like a grown woman yet, but she has to move into her husband's house," said Uncle Kufa. "The *ngozi* has to understand that we're serious. And I see right through your schemes, Portuguese. If I leave the girl here, you'll hide her next time I visit." His brother moved from the shadows to sit on the edge of the porch. Nhamo's hopes evaporated.

"Make *Ambuya* happy," Joao pleaded. "She old, old. Have much love for granddaughter." Grandmother lay on the bed, watching the argument. Her eyes flickered from one man to the other.

"*Ambuya* is my greatest concern. She won't recover until the *ngozi* is satisfied."

"*I* think Nhamo's father was Catholic," said Rosa suddenly.

Uncle Kufa looked straight past the woman and addressed the empty air. "The girl grew up in a traditional village. She belongs to us, not the *Catholics*." He said the word as though it were a curse.

"She belongs to her father," Rosa emphasized. Nhamo was impressed. It was a good argument: Perhaps her uncle didn't have the right to dispose of her after all.

"He caused the problem," Uncle Kufa said, still speaking to the air. "It is right and fitting that his daughter pay for his evil deeds."

"A true thing," commented Uncle Kufa's brother from his perch.

"The problem was cholera," Rosa cried. "Hundreds of people died. Do you think your *ngozi* was responsible for them all?"

"I have no idea. Perhaps someone should ask the *muvuki*."

"That monster who keeps his son's heart in a pot? Anyone who consults him is an idiot!"

"Rosa . . . ," said Joao, putting his hand on her arm.

"You ought to be ashamed of yourselves, throwing this child away to save your miserable skins!"

"I see your wife has forgotten the traditional humility of our foremothers. Or perhaps it is the teachings of the *Catholics*." Uncle Kufa might have been discussing the weather with the trader, but Nhamo could tell by the stiff way he stood that he was in a cold fury.

His apparent indifference drove Rosa into a rage. She thrust herself forward and screamed in his face, "Don't pretend I'm not here! I'll make you listen if I have to ram the words down your throat!" Nhamo covered her ears. Joao grabbed his wife and pulled her away.

"Stop it, Rosa! You make things worse!"

Uncle Kufa signaled to his brother that they were to leave. "Be ready at first light," he told Nhamo. He left the porch without a backward glance.

Rosa struggled in Joao's arms. "You can't let them take her."

"*Minha vida,*" whispered the trader. "My love. I no can stop them."

"Go to the Frelimo soldiers, those women with men's clothes and guns."

"No want guns here, my darling."

"Frelimo is against the old ways. They'll stop this craziness."

"Is too dangerous!"

"If you won't go, I will!"

"Okay, okay." The trader sighed. "But *minha vida,* the soldiers no like visitors after dark. Maybe they use me for target, bang-bang. You cry if I come back full of holes?"

"You can't get out of it that easily. I know they all like you," said Rosa, smiling through her tears.

"Oh, yes! All the time threaten to pour beer into stream."

Nhamo knew Frelimo was opposed to alcohol, but they had reached a truce with the Portuguese trader. Him they could control. They knew where he operated and could round up the shake-shake drinkers if they became too rowdy. Any other beer seller might hide in the forest and cause more trouble. Joao took a lantern and set off down the trail.

Nhamo and Rosa bathed Grandmother and fed her chicken broth and thin porridge. They arranged her again on the bed.

"How far is the army camp?" asked Nhamo.

"About an hour's walk, on the other side of the trading post."

"Isn't that dangerous?"

"Joao won't go alone. He'll pick up his assistant."

The conversation lapsed. Nhamo's nerves were strung as tightly as a bowstring. She didn't know what to hope for. She wanted to stay with Rosa—but she didn't want her family hurt. What would happen when Frelimo showed up with their guns? And if she didn't marry Goré Mtoko's brother, wouldn't the *ngozi* kill the rest of her family?

Nhamo sat on the floor next to Grandmother's bed and held the old woman's cold hand. "What should I do, *Ambuya?*" she pleaded. "If you want me to stay with Rosa and Joao, please move your fingers." But Grandmother did nothing, either because she hadn't understood or because she, too, couldn't make up her mind.

In the distance, Nhamo heard voices and saw lights moving among the trees. They were coming from the direction of the trading post. "Rosa!" she cried.

"That can't be the soldiers yet," Rosa said. Very quickly a crowd poured into the trader's garden, trampling the plants and forming a semicircle in front of the house. Nhamo was startled to glimpse Joao's pale face. The crowd consisted of Uncle Kufa and the villagers, the *muvuki,* and his son and servants. They carried blazing torches.

"Ah!" cried Rosa as Joao and his assistant were thrown to the ground. Their hands were tied behind their backs.

"By what authority do you challenge me?" roared the *muvuki.* He drew a small gun from his belt and pointed it at the trader. Rosa screamed. "You can't tell me what to do!" the *muvuki* went on. "You are not my father, and I am not your child. You will not be permitted to interfere."

"I only go for check store," Joao protested.

"You liar! You were on your way to the Frelimo camp. I heard you talking to your assistant," Uncle Kufa shouted.

"If the Catholics want war, then war it shall be," the *muvuki* screamed. "We'll see who wins, your dead man on a stick or the living spirits of Africa!" He fired the gun into the air. Nhamo gasped with terror.

"I go for take brandy to soldiers," said Joao, suddenly inspired. The *muvuki* stopped and considered his captive. The two men stared at each other for a long moment. Something about their expressions seemed odd to Nhamo. In spite of his threatening words, the *muvuki* didn't look particularly angry, nor did the trader appear frightened.

"Frelimo is against alcohol," the doctor pointed out.

"Big boys on top no like," Joao said craftily. "Little guys on bottom drink, drink. Chase women, too."

"That's so," agreed one of the villagers. "You can tell Frelimo women are trashy. They wear pants like men."

"Is this true? You were taking brandy to the soldiers and not asking them to rescue the girl?" the doctor said.

"Delivering drinks in the middle of the night? Don't be ridiculous," said Uncle Kufa.

"If I go in daytime, the big boys shoot me."

"It makes sense." The *muvuki* put the gun away. Suddenly, Nhamo understood that an agreement had been reached between the doctor and the trader. They had to live together in this community. They might dislike each other, but they were both businessmen, with the same customers. As long as the *muvuki* maintained his supremacy, he was quite willing to let a Catholic trader operate in the same area. Joao, for his part, had to protect Rosa. Uncle Kufa was an outsider.

"Aren't you going to punish him?" said Uncle Kufa.

The *muvuki* ignored him. He called for his son to bring him a seat. The young man went into the trader's house as though he owned it and returned, lugging Joao's easy chair. After the doctor had settled himself down, he told his servants to untie Joao and the assistant. Rosa ran to her husband, crying.

Uncle Kufa didn't understand the delicate trading that had gone on under his nose. He looked both angry and bewildered, something Nhamo would have enjoyed if her own situation hadn't been so desperate.

She knew the battle was over. She was doomed. She watched passively as Grandmother was bundled into a carrying chair. Rosa wept in Joao's arms, and he looked past her into the dark forest. Nhamo turned away, resolutely following *Ambuya*'s chair as it swayed along the trail. Perhaps the trader and his wife saw her leave, perhaps not. It didn't matter. The sooner she was gone, the safer they would be.

11

Nhamo stared at the open door of the hut. The light outside was blinding; inside, it was cool and dark. She heard Grandmother's steady breathing from the mat behind her.

Tomorrow was the first day of the handing-over ceremony. Beer had been brewed and the *nganga* from *Vatete*'s village had arrived. During the ceremony, he would be possessed by Goré's spirit and would list the things it required to leave Nhamo's family in peace. All the conditions had already been decided. The ceremony was only a formality.

The following day, Nhamo and her relatives would travel to Goré's village for the second part of the marriage. She would wear a red cloth over her head until she sat beside the ceremonial pot shelf in her new home.

For the first time in her life she wasn't burdened with chores from dawn to dusk. It was as though the village had already said good-bye to her. Masvita, Tazviona, and the others gathered wood and weeded the gardens. They spoke politely to Nhamo when she ventured from Grandmother's hut, but there was already a wall between them and her. The only encouraging event was the reappearance of Masvita's menstruation. It seemed the *ngozi* had forgotten some of his anger.

What would her new life be like? She knew

that Goré's brother, Zororo, had three wives already. They were all older than Aunt Chipo and so they would be jealous of her. She had seen Zororo. His hair was peppered with gray, and the whites of his eyes had turned a dull yellow. When Uncle Kufa's hunting dog growled at him, Zororo gave the beast such a kick in the ribs that it ran yelping into the forest. Goré's brother clearly didn't tolerate opposition.

And what would she do about Mother? Only once, in the weeks since her return, had Nhamo gone to the ruined village. It was too disheartening! "Could I take you with me, *Mai*?" she asked. It might be better to leave the picture where it was. She could always imagine Mother waiting for her there.

"Little Pumpkin," came a faint voice behind her.

Nhamo was so startled she almost screamed. She spun around and saw Grandmother watching her from the mat.

"D-did you speak, *Va-Ambuya*?" she quavered.

"Come here." The old woman's voice was low, but perfectly clear. "I don't want anyone else to listen."

Nhamo crouched next to the mat, trembling.

"I've been able to talk for several days. And to listen for much longer. I had to think about what to do."

"D-do?" murmured Nhamo.

"I'm very, very weak," Grandmother went on. "I doubt whether I can argue with Kufa about your marriage."

"You know about it?"

"I remember everything, including the night we were taken from the trader's house. I've had a long time to think about what Rosa said. Little Pumpkin, you might be a Catholic."

"How can I tell?" Nhamo automatically dipped a cloth in a pot of water. She had been cooling *Ambuya*'s skin so often during the hot days, she hardly noticed what she was doing.

"I don't know. But I do know the Catholics would protect you if they thought you belonged to them."

Nhamo felt like crying. Why had Grandmother waited so long to give her this information? Any help *Ambuya* sent for now would come too late. She gently wiped the old woman's face and arms with the wet cloth.

Grandmother was silent a few moments. Perhaps she had exhausted herself.

"*Ambuya,* would you like some food? Or should I call Aunt Chipo?"

"No!" Grandmother said with surprising strength. "The last thing I need is a fit of hysterics in this hut. My beloved child, what I have to say is for you alone."

At the words *beloved child* Nhamo began to cry silently and hopelessly. Never in her life had anyone called her that.

"You must run away to the Catholics today."

Nhamo sat up straight. Had she heard correctly? "You mean walk to the trading post by myself?"

"No. Kufa and that misbegotten brother of Goré would find you in no time. Besides, Joao and Rosa can't protect you. They are only two against hundreds. You must go to Zimbabwe."

"Zim-bab-we?" gasped Nhamo.

"I've been lying here thinking, thinking, thinking. How is it to be done? And at last the solution came to me. The stream flows down to the river—the Musengezi River. I followed it when I came from Zimbabwe. You can use it to go back."

"I—don't know." Nhamo was aghast. The edge of the river was thickly forested. Not only was it difficult to walk through, but all the animals went there to drink. She would be someone's dinner before the first day was out!

"You could take a trail, but you'd probably get lost. Besides, one girl alone wouldn't last long."

Exactly my idea, thought Nhamo.

"So you'll have to take a boat. Crocodile Guts's boat was pulled up on a sandbank when he died. I doubt whether anyone has disturbed it."

"It's still there," Nhamo said.

"Good! You're an observant girl. I'm sure you noticed how Crocodile Guts maneuvered his boat."

Nhamo had, in fact, often watched the fisherman. Boating was one of the many things she had studied without having any clear reason to do so. He had a pole with a flat paddle that he used first on one side, then the other, to move himself along.

"When it gets dark, you pull the boat into the water and let yourself float downstream. After a while you'll come to the Musengezi. Then you must use the paddle to force yourself *against* the flow. You have to go upstream, not down. When you need to rest, go toward shore and tie up to a tree. Crocodile Guts always kept a coil of rope in his boat. Be sure it's still there. It's perfect! You'll be safe from animals all the way."

Nhamo was stunned by the idea. It was so unbelievably daring! Could she really float—or row—all the way to freedom? "How will I know when I've gone far enough?"

"When you come to electric lights," said *Ambuya*. "You've never seen them, but they're bright—bright as a hundred fires! You must be very careful crossing the border, though. Don't get out of the boat. The ground is full of land mines." Grandmother explained about land mines, and Nhamo felt queasy.

All at once, they heard Aunt Chipo's voice outside. *Ambuya* lay flat and closed her eyes. The woman brought in food and *maheu*. There was a special dish of treats for Nhamo. "Since it's your last day," Aunt Chipo explained. She lifted Grandmother's hand, which was perfectly limp, and laid it back down with a sigh.

When they were alone again, Nhamo shared her treats with *Ambuya*. "I had to lie to her," the old woman explained. "If Kufa knew I could give you advice, he might guess where you went after you escaped. I'm hoping he'll think you went back to the trading post." The two of them ate and talked more as if they were two girls rather than a revered elder and a child. It was like the afternoon they had listened to the guitar at the trading post.

But finally, Grandmother told her to close the door for privacy. "Move that chest at the end of my bed," she ordered. When Nhamo had done so, Grandmother told her to dig a hole in the floor. A few inches down was a small pot. It was full of gold nuggets.

"I collected those from the stream. I used to trade them with Joao, but I'll never do that again."

"Don't say that," begged Nhamo.

"I'm only telling the truth. When I go to my ancestors, Chipo will hunt around until she finds it. She can dig up a pot of earthworms for all I care! I want you to have it."

Nhamo poured the nuggets into her hand. They were colder and heavier than she'd expected.

"Put them into a cloth bag and tie them around your neck," instructed *Ambuya.* "Don't try to sell them without advice—ask the nuns for help."

"At Nyanga?" said Nhamo, remembering the place her mother had gone to school.

"You won't be able to walk that far, but there are nuns all over Zimbabwe. Just find the nearest ones and tell them you're Catholic. They can send a letter to your father."

Her father! Nhamo had forgotten about him. Suddenly, Grandmother's daring plan took on reality. Nhamo had a family in Zimbabwe. She had a name: Nhamo Jongwe, member of the Jongwe clan, which might include friendly aunts and uncles and even grandparents.

"He's as trustworthy as a rat in a grain bin, but he's all you've got," said *Ambuya,* spoiling Nhamo's enthusiasm. Still, Grandmother didn't really know Father that well. He might have a very nice family.

"Go for a walk now, Little Pumpkin. Take food from the storehouse. Get matches, a calabash, and whatever else you can manage without getting caught."

"That's stealing," protested Nhamo.

"That's *survival.* I, your elder, command you to do it. Now go. I'm exhausted with talking and need to sleep." Grandmother closed her eyes and this time really dozed off. Nhamo tore a square of the red cloth she was to use for the wedding ceremony and tied the gold pieces inside.

My *roora,* she thought with a bitter smile. Then she set about following *Ambuya's* directions.

All went with amazing smoothness. Crocodile Guts's boat was still jammed into the reeds, and the mooring rope was still attached. Nhamo removed a sack of already ground and dried mealie meal from the storehouse. She visited Aunt Chipo's hut and took a box of matches and a bag of beans. Here and there she went, removing odds and ends. It was wicked to steal—she knew that—but worse to disobey an elder. And so she entered into the adventure with a clear conscience. No one bothered her or even stopped to talk. She was a ghost in her own village, already seen as the bride of the *ngozi*.

Only Masvita gave her an uncomfortable moment. "I'll miss you," her cousin said tearfully as Nhamo bent over Aunt Shuvai's baby. "I want you to know . . . if it doesn't work out . . . if he's cruel . . . come back. I couldn't bear to see you suffer. I'll argue with Father until he lets you stay. You'll have to return anyway to have your first child."

Nhamo knew that Masvita would never find the courage to argue with Uncle Kufa, but she appreciated the thought. She felt slightly guilty because she had just stolen a pot of the millet-and-honey cakes Aunt Chipo kept to fatten her daughter up.

Nhamo stored everything in the boat. In the late afternoon, she went to the ruined village and fetched Mother. "You'll never guess what I'm going to do," she whispered to the clay pot. "I know it seems wrong, but Grandmother commanded me to do it."

As the shadows grew and the time for departure approached, however, Nhamo began to have second thoughts. It had been a wonderful plan when the sun was high. *Ambuya* had seemed full of confidence and even—if such a thing were possible with an elder—mischief.

Now the spaces between the trees filled up with blue-gray shadows as Nhamo halted by Crocodile Guts's boat. *Quelea* birds flew to safety in the reeds. The moment, when day had not quite become night, held the forest enthralled. A kudu stood, one foot poised, near the water; a monkey gazed at Nhamo from his perch in a *mobola* plum tree. Nhamo hesitated, holding the clay pot with Mother's picture inside.

Then the light shifted; the kudu snorted and backed away to find another path. The monkey fled. "Oh, Mother, I'm so frightened," murmured Nhamo. She placed the pot in one end of the boat and packed grass around it for protection.

12

As usual you've arrived too late to help," grumbled Aunt Chipo as Nhamo entered Grandmother's hut. "Don't think you'll get away with such laziness with your new husband. He's a man who knows what's what." She leaned against the wall with a bowl of *sadza* and relish. Masvita was carefully spooning food into *Ambuya*'s mouth.

"She looks better, don't you think?" said Masvita. "I almost think she understands what we say."

"Poor Mother! If it wasn't for Nhamo, she wouldn't have angered the *muvuki*. Well, what are you looking at, girl? *I'm* not going to wait on you."

Nhamo helped herself to the pot of relish and platter of *sadza* next to Grandmother's pot shelf.

"You be ready bright and early—no running off to the forest," Aunt Chipo said.

"Please come to the girls' hut tonight," begged Masvita. "I'll ask Tazviona to watch Grandmother."

Nhamo almost choked on her *sadza*. "I'll see you again, lots of times. I don't know when I'll see *Ambuya*."

"Then I'll stay with you," her cousin said warmly.

"Oh, no! You won't get any sleep," snapped Aunt Chipo. "You have to do this one's chores, now that she's running off to a new home." She made it sound as though Nhamo were marrying Goré's brother out of spite.

Masvita made a few gentle protests and dropped the argument. "Don't worry. I'll come and see you as often as possible after you're married," she whispered. Nhamo doubted this very much. Her cousin had a kind spirit, but she was no match for her mother.

And it didn't matter. Masvita wasn't going to visit her in her *real* new home.

Nhamo hurried to perform the final chores of the day after Aunt Chipo and Masvita had left. She helped *Ambuya* sit up to relieve herself. She tidied the hut and made sure a water jar was close to the bed. She discovered that Grandmother could hold a cup and drink without any help at all.

"You fooled everyone," she said with admiration.

"In a day or two I'll magically recover." The old woman smiled serenely.

Nhamo glanced out the dark door. "Grandmother . . . if I run away, won't the *ngozi* punish everyone?"

Ambuya paused before she answered. "I've been thinking about that a long time. Many people died of cholera, not just our family. I believe Rosa was right: Goré Mtoko couldn't be responsible for a whole epidemic."

"But the *muvuki*—"

"Was wrong. I know that's a surprise," said Grandmother when Nhamo's eyes widened. "You see, spirit mediums are ordinary men and women when they're not being possessed. A few of them fake messages when they can't manage a real one."

Nhamo was deeply shocked.

"I've lived a long time, Little Pumpkin. I honor and revere *nganga*s; I believe they can tell us what our ancestors want, but a few—a very few—are dishonest. Now and then one is downright wicked."

"Like the *muvuki*."

"What kind of decent person would kill his own son? Really big problems, like drought or swarms of locusts or epidemics, are dealt with by the *mhondoro,* the spirit of the land. The *muvuki*'s spirit is only a flyspeck compared to it."

Grandmother's words were disturbing. Nhamo had never heard anyone question the authority of an *nganga*—except the trader and his wife. They were Catholic, so their opinion didn't count.

An idea suddenly occurred to Nhamo. "Aunt Chipo! She was possessed by Goré's spirit."

"Oh, yes. Chipo," Grandmother said bitterly. "Listen, Little Pumpkin. What I'm about to say will be upsetting, but you need to understand. Your aunt has hated you from the moment you were born. She hated your mother, too. Runako was the one everyone said was pretty. She was the one who did well in school, and the very worst thing Runako did was have a beautiful child one month before Masvita was born. It took all the attention away from Chipo."

Beautiful. They thought I was beautiful, Nhamo said to herself.

"She's always wanted to get rid of you, and her chance came when we visited the *muvuki.*"

"You mean she was *lying?*"

"It's been known to happen."

Nhamo's world turned upside down. First *Ambuya* had accused the doctor of making things up, and now she said Aunt Chipo had pretended to be possessed. What could anyone believe when things like that happened?

"You can't wait any longer," Grandmother said softly.

"Now? I don't want to go!"

"You have to. If I could come along . . ." *Ambuya* sighed. "Well, I can't, and that's that. I know all about Zororo. Believe me, you wouldn't last a year before he either beat you to death or one of his wives poisoned you. Your only hope of survival is to go. I gave Runako her chance long ago. Now I'm giving you yours. I only wish you were older."

"I'm frightened," sobbed Nhamo, clinging to Grandmother.

"I know." *Ambuya* smoothed her hair, and Nhamo felt a tear drop onto her head. "The journey will be the hardest thing you'll ever do, but it will be worth it. Just think of finding your father. I don't expect the trip will take more than two days—we're very close to the border. Remember to push yourself *against* the current when you reach the Musengezi. Close to the border the river divides in two, but it doesn't matter which branch you take. They both go to Zimbabwe."

"What lies in the other direction?" Nhamo asked.

"Lake Cabora Bassa. The Musengezi used to flow into the Zambezi River until the Portuguese dammed it up. Now the Zambezi's become a huge lake. You can't even see across it." Nhamo nodded. She had heard many tales about Lake Cabora Bassa. *Ambuya* gently removed her granddaughter's arms from her neck and pushed her toward the door.

"You might get sick in the night," Nhamo protested.

"I'll be fine. Remember, Little Pumpkin, your mother's spirit is watching over you. She'll warn you of any danger."

"I'll never see you again!"

"Sh. Sh. Someone might hear us. If I go to my ancestors before we meet again, my spirit will come to you in a dream. I promise it."

Nhamo felt sick with grief as she crept out. She removed the small oil lamp that lit the interior of the hut and put the wooden door in place to keep out predators. She heard Grandmother sigh as the old woman lay back down.

All around stood the dark huts of the village. A quarter moon lay low in the west, not giving enough light to tempt anyone to stay up late. Nhamo took the lamp along to light the way. Far off, in the distance, a lion roared. *He* was not the dangerous one, the girl knew, but his mate who padded noiselessly through the trees.

Every trickle of noise made Nhamo freeze and her body break out in sweat. Every rustle of leaves made her want to flee back to *Ambuya*'s arms. But it was a false safety. Besides, she had been ordered to go by her elder. "Please protect me, *Mai*," she prayed as she tiptoed along.

Eventually, she pushed aside the reeds and saw Crocodile Guts's boat floating right where she had left it. She climbed in. Oho! It swayed like a tree branch. Nhamo had never been in a boat, and she didn't like the sensation. She lay on her stomach with her arms over the stern, untying the rope. A puddle of water in the bottom soaked her dress-cloth.

Once free, she took the oar, as she had seen Crocodile Guts do many times, and pushed herself away from shore. The boat moved! At first it edged by inches, but it drifted more swiftly as it reached the middle of the stream. Nhamo held tightly to the sides. The quarter moon was almost down.

She could see the sky over the trees. Now and then she glimpsed a round boulder or a patch of sand. Of her village there was not a trace.

In spite of her fear, Nhamo felt a little thrill of excitement. She was really doing it! She was sailing away from Zororo and his jealous wives. In two days she would arrive in Zimbabwe and ask the first people she met to find her some nuns. And then—oh, then!—they would send a letter to her father at Mtoroshanga.

Thinking happily of the aunts and uncles she was soon to have, Nhamo watched the dark shore slide by as she floated on toward the Musengezi River.

13

Nhamo woke with a start. At first she was completely confused. The floor rocked and her dress-cloth was soaked. I'm on the boat, she realized after a moment. She sat up cautiously. A faint light marked the eastern horizon, and the shoreline seemed very far away.

Fighting back a surge of panic, she scanned the water for clues as to where she might be. The current was moving much more swiftly than it had in the middle of the night. That was what had awakened her. "This must be the Musengezi," she said aloud. Nhamo took the oar and began to paddle against the flow, first on one side, then the other, as she had seen Crocodile Guts do. But she didn't make much headway. The river was very strong.

The light increased, and pink wisps of cloud appeared in the sky. Nhamo felt chilled by her wet dress-cloth. Surely there was more water in the boat than she remembered? Meanwhile, it took all her strength to make any progress. Her arms ached; she clenched her teeth to keep them from chattering. Soon the villagers would discover her absence and search parties would go out. She would have to be either far away or hidden before anyone decided to visit the river.

The red ball of the sun appeared to her left over the gray-green smudge of the shore. Red ripples dimpled the water, and the odor of cooking fires stirred on the sluggish morning breeze.

Nhamo's chest began to hurt. She badly needed rest, and so she turned toward land.

It would have been safer to go to the farther bank—the villagers wouldn't be able to find her—but she could barely see it. A heat haze lay over the water and hid all but the tallest rocks. Sometimes even they disappeared. Nhamo doggedly plied the oar. The trees drew closer with painful slowness. Her dress-cloth untied and fell into the murky water sloshing around her feet, but she couldn't take the time to retrieve it. If she paused, the current rocked the boat in a frightening way.

Finally, with a last burst of energy, she drove the craft toward a stand of reeds and stood up to catch an arm of willow protruding from the water. The boat spun around. Nhamo fell back. "No, no, no, no," she whimpered as the prow swung toward shore and crunched into a mass of acacias. Wicked-looking thorns passed within inches of her face. She stared up wildly at the branches crackling around the boat. Dust, ants, and twigs showered over her, but the trees also caught the craft and kept it from being swept away. After a few moments she felt secure enough to creep forward and tie the rope to an acacia. Then she lay still with her cheek pillowed on the soggy lump of her dress-cloth. Her body trembled with fatigue.

So much for her first attempt to sail to Zimbabwe!

Nhamo rested for a long time. The water smelled of rotten fish—an odor she had always associated with Crocodile Guts. Now it seemed to sink into her skin as thoroughly as it had permeated the fisherman. People always said you could smell Crocodile Guts before you saw him. Perhaps she, too, would advertise her presence in this way. Nhamo smiled bitterly. Would Zororo be as anxious to marry her if she smelled like a sun-ripened tiger fish?

As the heat of the day rose, Nhamo's stomach began to churn. Her fingers wrinkled from being immersed in water and, perversely, her mouth dried up with thirst. Still, she was unwilling to move. In the distance she heard voices. They grew and then faded as the searchers combed the forest. It didn't seem likely that anyone would venture into the acacia thicket and, fortunately, the village had possessed only a single boat.

Grandmother said that once many people had owned boats. At that time the Musengezi was a tame river. When the Portuguese dammed up the Zambezi, it pushed water back up the mouth of the Musengezi, widened it, and made it a dangerous place to sail. During the civil war, Portuguese soldiers came through the village and destroyed all the boats to keep them from being used by Frelimo. Only Crocodile Guts managed to hide his, and only he continued to fish until Frelimo took over the country.

Now, as Nhamo lay in speckled shadow and watched the ants wander over acacia thorns, she considered the implications of this story. Frelimo had defeated the Portuguese several years ago. Why hadn't anyone rebuilt the boats? Could it be that only Crocodile Guts had the *strength* to maneuver against the new, strong current? Of course, the water must always have been swift, but the shore was once much more reachable. Lesser men could have managed it.

It had looked so easy when she watched the fisherman set off on his travels. It must have looked easy to *Ambuya,* too. For the first time a thread of doubt entered Nhamo's mind. How did Grandmother know it took only two days to reach Zimbabwe? Perhaps it only took Crocodile Guts that long.

"Ah!" gasped Nhamo as she suddenly noticed that water had crept halfway up her body. The boat was sinking! The sacks of food were dangerously close to getting soaked, and Mother's pot was actually floating at the far end! She twisted herself into a kneeling position, getting several bad scratches from the acacias in the process, and pulled the clay pot back. She cradled it between her knees and began bailing with her drinking calabash for all she was worth.

Oh, but she was being foolish! She had often seen Crocodile Guts do the same thing. In the morning, before he set out, he had always spent time getting rid of the night's accumulation of water. When she recalled this, Nhamo felt better.

Bailing out water was a normal activity on a boat. Crocodile Guts had sailed around safely for years, leaks and all.

Nhamo stopped to dip up clean drinking water and to nibble some of Masvita's honey-and-millet cakes. The food made her feel immensely better.

Later, when the boat was as dry as she could manage, she took Mother out of the pot and propped her against the sack of mealie meal. "We're going to Zimbabwe, *Mai*," Nhamo said. "I'll try to find the nuns at your school—I'm sure you'd like that. I'll visit the place you lived and talk to your friends. Did you ever meet Father's relatives? I hope they like me."

Nhamo listened for Mother's reply.

"Of course I'll go on to Mtoroshanga. I imagine Father has a home there—*Ambuya* said he liked square houses." Did chrome miners make a lot of money? Nhamo asked Mother. It would be wonderful if his place was as fine as Joao's.

Mother told her not to expect too much.

"I have gold to help pay my way." Nhamo jiggled the sack of nuggets tied around her neck. She put Mother away before an accident could happen, rinsed her dress-cloth over the side, and spread it out to dry. Then she stretched out naked in the speckled light and waited for late afternoon. She wanted to give everyone time to get tired of searching before she ventured into the current again.

Sometime later she perched her bottom over the side and relieved herself. The heat in the acacia thicket was overpowering. Even the ants seemed dazed by it. They sat on the thorns and waved their antennae slowly. A small, green snake slid along a branch, causing Nhamo's heart to speed up, and disappeared into a crack in the bark. A *Nephila* spider spun a golden web, lazily swinging from twig to twig. It finished the beautiful pattern and settled itself at the center with blue-furred legs outspread.

By now Nhamo had to admit she was stalling for time. She was afraid to venture out onto the dangerous river again. The sun slanted lower and lower in the west. *Quelea* birds swooped in flocks over the water as they searched for a place to spend the night.

"I can either go home and marry Zororo," said Nhamo to Mother in the jar, "or I can try to reach Zimbabwe. The only thing I *can't* do is stay here. I wish I knew how far Zimbabwe was."

She tied her dress-cloth as best she could while lying down in the boat, untied the rope, and pushed herself away with the oar. Ah! The minute she was free, the water had her in its grip again. She paddled vigorously. She seemed to have learned something about boats because it was easier to control her direction. Rowing was still tiring.

Nhamo kept close to shore. The sun went down, casting red gleams across the water. A hippo complained loudly from somewhere near the middle of the river. Nhamo shivered. What was its opinion of boats? Did it think she was merely a log floating upstream? Hippos were quite intelligent—and curious, unfortunately. They sometimes watched the women wash clothes. They considered anything that happened to the water to be their business.

Fortunately, this hippo floated off in the opposite direction. Its head formed a black bulge in the reddening river.

Twilight came and swiftly departed. The moon was slightly larger tonight, but still gave little light. Nhamo kept checking the dark shore on her left. She didn't want to drift too far from land. On and on she went until her arms ached and her breath came in short gasps. It was impossible to tell how far she had traveled. The shore was lightness. No cook-fires shone beyond the trees, and there was no trace of the electric lights Grandmother had described.

Nhamo had to make for land again. This time she glided into a little bay where the current was sluggish, and tied up to what she thought was a willow. She filled her calabash and ate more of the honey-and-millet cakes. "I'll have to go ashore to build a fire, if this journey takes much longer," she whispered to herself. It seemed proper to whisper in the dark.

As Nhamo bailed out the boat, a strange sensation came over her. It was extremely unpleasant. For a minute she thought she was going to be sick, but then she realized that this illness came from her spirit, not her body. For the first time in her life she was completely alone.

She had been by herself in the deserted village—and when Aunt Chipo locked her into a hut for being bad—and when she went off to cook private meals. This was different. No one was waiting for her to come home, not even a bad-tempered aunt. For all the villagers knew, she was dead. Masvita would cry because her spirit might be wandering along the dark roads.

At the thought of spirits, Nhamo lay down in the boat and covered herself with as much of the dress-cloth as possible. She felt around until her fingers touched Mother's jar. I'm not alone. Mother is with me, she thought. But the pictures that seemed so real by day were unconvincing after dark. She heard disturbing sounds in the water. Was that a crocodile swimming by? She didn't know what they did at night. A troop of bush babies chattered as they made their way along the shore. A ground hornbill grumbled deep in its throat— *hhuhh-hhuhh, hhuhh-hhuhh.*

Worse than the feeling of danger was the sheer loneliness. Nhamo had never, ever, spent a night alone. She generally slept in the middle of a troop of girls. Their breathing surrounded her, their bodies warmed the air, their movements formed a barrier between her and the dark. Suddenly, without even expecting it was going to happen, Nhamo began to cry. She did it silently, to keep the creatures on the shore from hearing. Tears rolled from the corners of her eyes and soaked into her hair.

Eventually, she went to sleep with her arms around the sack of mealie meal and her nose buried in its dusty cloth.

She set off before dawn. "I wasted too much time yesterday," she said. In her mind was the possibility that if she tried really hard, she might reach Zimbabwe by dark. She didn't want to spend another night alone. She was terribly stiff from rowing and sleeping in the damp, but as she paddled, the soreness went away. The sun dried her dress-cloth and raised her spirits.

The honey-and-millet cakes were almost gone. Good as they were, at any rate, Nhamo craved variety. In the middle of the day she tied up to an immense strangler fig and clambered over it to reach land. There she set about making a fire. She boiled mealie meal and sprinkled it with dried fish. She had even taken a precious packet of salt for flavoring. This was living! With her stomach comfortably stretched, she dozed awhile and set out again.

In midafternoon, a hippo rose out of the water right beside her and opened his huge mouth. He roared—she could see right down his pink gullet—and snapped his teeth at her. Nhamo threw herself flat in the boat. *Aunh-aunh-aunh* went the hippo. A splash told her he had submerged. A second later the boat rocked. He was bumping it!

Nhamo grabbed the oar and began rowing for shore. Other hippos surfaced around her. They kept pace, their piggy eyes just above the water. The male yawned again, terrifyingly. Nhamo had never seen a hippo's mouth so close-up. It looked like a slab of raw meat studded with teeth. *Aunh-aunh-aunh* went the beast, rearing his head toward the sky. He looked as though he wouldn't mind chopping her boat in two!

She saw babies on the outskirts of the group. She knew that few things were more dangerous than hippos with young.

Nhamo paddled. She used muscles she hadn't known she possessed. She prayed to every spirit she could think of, even her great-grandfather whom she had never seen. The water became shallow—the boat scraped on stone—and she despaired of escaping. But the hippos didn't care for the shallows. They fell back to the deeper water and floated there in a long line.

Nhamo jumped out and splashed up to her waist in water. Without her weight, the boat floated free. It began spinning away downstream. She caught it with the tips of her fingers and fought desperately until she was able to plant her feet firmly on the riverbed and pull the craft within reach of a tree.

She sat on shore the rest of the day. The hippos floated near and far. They returned frequently to observe her. It was too unfair! She had been making such good progress. She could almost imagine the electric lights of Zimbabwe, but when darkness fell there was not a shred of light in the forest. She was utterly alone.

The hippos talked among themselves. Finally, silence fell as the huge animals left the water and went foraging for grass. Nhamo climbed back into the boat and resigned herself to another miserable night.

She didn't sleep well. When the hippos were silent, she imagined them creeping around the tree where she had tied up. Toward dawn, when they returned to the water, their grunts echoed distressingly close by. The red sunlight on the water showed their glistening heads in the deeper channel. They kept sinking and surfacing, but Nhamo thought she could see twenty adults and six babies.

Her bones ached, and her skin itched from the constant damp. Around midday she finished the last of the honey-and-millet cakes. Now she would have to go on shore to cook, but she couldn't bring herself to face the danger. It was easier to lie in the boat and tell herself stories: the many, many stories she had soaked up from Grandmother and from hiding in the darkness near the men's *dare*.

"One day Mwari was thinking about the things he had made," Nhamo told Mother in the jar. "He looked at the sun, the moon, and the stars. He looked at the sky and the clouds. 'I think I'll make something even more beautiful,' he said, so he created Mother Earth.

"He made her in the shape of a winnowing basket and gave her water from the clouds and fire from the sun. He covered her with trees and bushes and grass. 'I give you the power to make these things grow,' he told Mother Earth.

"Mwari spoke so often of his beautiful Earth, the sun and moon became jealous. The sun grew hot and tried to burn her; the moon chased away the clouds to dry her up. But the trees and grass continued to grow. The heat only made them put out more flowers.

"The sun and moon complained so much, Mwari decided he would have to make something to eat the plants. Then Mother Earth would not be quite so beautiful. He took clay and made the animals. He worked quickly because he had a lot of animals to create. He worked so fast he forgot to give horns to some or tails to others. Some animals had big ears, others no ears at all. As the day passed and the sun began to go down, Mwari became tired. He took a big lump of clay, poked holes in it for eyes, and stuck a few bristles on its rump. 'There! I'm too tired to create anything else,' Mwari said.

"The last animal was only half made. It was very ugly and bad-tempered. It was the hippopotamus.

"Even Mwari doesn't like you," Nhamo called out over the river. "He makes you hide in the water so he doesn't have to look at you."

The hippopotamuses continued to doze with their noses above the surface.

"The next day, the water complained," Nhamo went on. "'The land is full of creatures. What about me?' Mwari took more clay and made the fishes, only he didn't have much left, so he couldn't give them legs. He told Mother Earth to bring everything to life."

Nhamo looked over the edge of the boat. A big catfish foraged along the bottom. She could roast it over *mopane* coals with a little salt for flavoring. Ah! She could almost taste it now! Her mouth watered. Slowly, stealthily, she slid her hand into the river and wiggled a finger very slowly. The fish drew closer; its fins stroked the sluggish current. It hesitated, watching the finger.

Nhamo lunged with both hands, but the catfish was even faster. It shot out of the shallows and disappeared under a raft of water lettuce. She sat back down with her hands clasped across her grumbling stomach.

"Well, anyway," she continued, "Mwari decided to make a master for all the animals. He took clay from deep in Mother

Earth's womb and formed a man. He had barely finished when Mother Earth said, 'My creator, this is a fine creature, but it looks like you, not me. Why don't you make another one?'

"Mwari took more clay and formed a woman. He took a little of the rivers and mountains, the grass and flowers, and added them to the clay to give Earth's beauty to the woman. He took a pinch of fire for her heart and a handful of water for her womb, so she could grow new life.

"When he was finished, he let his shadow fall over the pair. The animals had received only one spirit from Mother Earth, but the people had one from her and one from Mwari.

"Oh, why won't they go!" Nhamo cried out suddenly. "I'll die out here. My spirit will be trapped forever with those ugly animals watching me. I wish I'd never left home!"

She curled up into a ball. The water in the bottom of the boat soaked into her dress-cloth. It clung to her like a second, evil-smelling skin. She was alone, alone, alone and she was going to die.

Nhamo lay in a fit of grief with her eyes squeezed shut. But presently a breeze stirred the forest. The leaves tossed with a rushing sound and the scent of wild gardenias hidden somewhere in the trees blew from the shore. It was as if a hand stroked her hair—lightly, swiftly passing, but most certainly there. Nhamo opened her eyes.

Sometimes, when she was in the deserted village at dusk, the wind awoke as day shifted into night. It had a different quality from other breezes, just as the silvery air was different from the harsh light of noon. It seemed to have a voice, as of people talking far away, but she could never quite make out the words. She heard that voice now.

Nhamo . . . Nhamo . . . , it whispered. Or perhaps it only said *Aauuu,* the usual sound of the wind. Yet, if she strained her ears, she could almost hear it: *Nhamo. . . .*

"Mother?" said Nhamo.

The wind blew away, riffling the water.

She sat up. The hippos were still floating in the central channel. The sun slanted through the trees, low and golden, sending showers of light around their drifting hulks. Something let go deep in Nhamo's spirit. She lay down again in the boat and fell into a sleep as profound as any she had had surrounded by the breathing of her cousins in the safety of the girls' hut.

14

She slept soundly until dawn and awoke with a feeling of hope. "I'm being silly," she declared. "Hippos never stay long in one area. They run out of food." She scanned the water carefully for crocodiles and then eased herself over the side for a bath. It felt wonderful! She was no longer quite as afraid of the river.

I wonder if I could learn to swim, she thought. Hippos do it. Even people swim where there aren't crocodiles. Nhamo shivered at the thought of crocodiles. This corner of the Musengezi, however, flowed over a wide, flat expanse of stone with the remains of trees jutting out here and there. It had recently been dry land, she realized. When the Zambezi was dammed, the water had pushed up into the river and drowned part of the shoreline.

Nhamo hung on to a low-hanging branch and experimentally lifted her feet from the bottom. Oho! The branch moved! She put her feet back down quickly.

How *did* you keep your nose up when your body wanted to go down? Nhamo found a place where the water barely came to her knees. Here she practiced, holding on to a jutting rock and letting her body float out straight. Once she tried to let go, but panic made her claw her way back. Still, she was pleased with her progress. Eventually, her grumbling stomach told her it was time to think about breakfast.

She collected supplies and climbed onto shore. Nhamo set about making a cook-fire in a clearing next to a jumble of boulders. Not far away was a grove of *muzhanje,* or loquat, trees. It was too early for them to have fruit, so Nhamo paid them little attention until she noticed a stealthy noise in the dry, brittle leaves that littered the ground. She came instantly alert.

Crick-crack went the leaves. Nhamo's heart raced. The trees lay between her and the boat. She squinted at the loquats. Their massed branches created deep shadows, among which streaks of harsh sunlight confused the image of what lay beneath. Flames caught the dry twigs of the cook-fire and smoke spiraled up, but Nhamo's attention was riveted on the trees. The fire flared briefly and died. *Crick-crack* went the leaves.

She didn't know whether she was looking for something very large or very small. Hippos were enormous, but they could glide like spirits when they wished. On the other hand, a lizard could make as much noise as an elephant.

Crick-crick-crack-crack! Nhamo was up the rocks between one breath and the next. So what if she was fleeing a lizard? No one was around to make fun of her. She scrambled higher until she was at the top of a huge boulder that leaned out over the clearing. She peered over cautiously.

Crack-crack-crick went the leaves, and out of the dappled shade came a fat guinea fowl—and another and another. It was a whole flock! They patiently hunted for seeds in the clearing.

Silently, Nhamo edged back from the cliff. She found the biggest rock she could lift.

Slowly, the guinea fowl approached the cook-fire, which was now only a drift of ashes. They found the sack of mealie meal. It was tied up, but they clearly sensed it was something they might enjoy. They clustered on top and pecked at the fabric. One of the birds wandered close to the bottom of the cliff. Nhamo slowly lifted the rock over the edge. Her arms began to tremble from the weight.

Closer, closer—ah! She lost her grip. The rock fell straight down. The guinea fowl panicked—and fluttered in the wrong direction. The rock caught it squarely on the back. The other birds blundered into the air, their heavy bodies crashing through branches as they fled.

Nhamo slid down. The guinea fowl was squashed flat as one of Masvita's honey cakes. She cleaned it as well as she could with Uncle Kufa's broken knife and soon had it boiling over a crackling fire. As it cooked, Nhamo made up a song. It was like the boasts the boys chanted when they wanted to show off. Girls weren't supposed to use them, but Nhamo was so elated, she didn't care. It went:

> *"I am she who lifts mountains*
> *When she goes to hunt,*
> *Who wears a mamba* for a headband*
> *And a lion for a belt.*
> *Beware!*
> *I swallow elephants whole*
> *And pick my teeth with rhinoceros horns.*
> *I drink up rivers to get at the hippos.*
> *Let them hear my words!*
> *Nhamo is coming*
> *And her hunger is great."*

She sang it over and over. After a while, she hauled everything back to the boat and ate as much of the guinea fowl as she could manage. She had to pick numerous fragments of bone from the stew. She ate and dozed and ate again. The only way she could store the meat was inside her round belly.

The hippos floated far and near, unmoved by Nhamo's threats. They paid no attention to the boat or to her when, late in the day, she attempted another swimming lesson. All in all, it was a most successful day.

Still, when darkness fell, so did her spirit. "*Why* do I need people?" she wondered as she huddled in the damp boat.

---

*black mamba: The largest and most feared of African snakes. It is quick to bite if disturbed. Its poison can cause death within minutes.

"I'm full of food and comfortable—well, fairly comfortable. I'm safe—well, fairly safe. Soon I'll go on to Zimbabwe. But right now I wish I could see Aunt Chipo. I don't care if she beats me. I even want to see Zororo, and he's a pig! I don't understand it."

As for *Ambuya* and Masvita, Nhamo didn't dare think of them. Her longing was so great, she might throw herself into the river. She fell asleep with her arms around the mealie bag. "If I eat all the grain, I'll have to fill the bag with grass," she told Mother. "I seem to need *something* to hold on to."

Nhamo stayed at what she named the guinea-fowl camp for several more days. She didn't try to flatten another bird— that had been sheer luck, and besides, it wasn't exactly pleasant finding shreds of bone and intestines in her soup. Instead, she made a trap. She laid a trail of beans leading to a very deep, circular hole in the ground. Then she hid nearby in a clump of elephant grass.

After a while a guinea fowl discovered the new source of food. It foraged along with one beady eye fixed on the next morsel. Soon it came to the hole and stuck its head inside. At once, Nhamo sprang out and wrung its neck. The trap was simplicity itself. If guinea fowl had been slightly more intelligent, it wouldn't have worked, but fortunately they were as dull-witted as earthworms.

Nhamo ate one of the heavy birds every single day. Even in the village she hadn't done as well. The birds around her home had been thinned by hunting, and the survivors were wary. For variety she found straggly *mhuvuyu*, blackjack weeds, and cooked their leaves as a kind of spinach.

One day she fashioned a fish trap, following the pattern she had learned at the trading post. She peeled off the bark of a *musasa* tree, then chewed and rolled it until it formed a kind of twine. She used this to bind strips of reed into a cone. She wedged the cone into a side channel of the Musengezi, with the narrow end pointing toward a fenced-in pool. The little fish swam into the wide end and slipped through to the pool. Then they couldn't get back. The sharp points Nhamo had thoughtfully carved at the narrow end discouraged them. They swam round and round until she scooped them into her basket.

Nhamo gutted the little fish and smoke-dried them over her cook-fire. She wasn't sure how to store guinea fowl, but she had often preserved fish. "Now I not only smell like Crocodile Guts, I *act* like him," she told Mother. "Soon I'll sit on my haunches and scratch." The boatman had been alive with lice, which had disgusted the other villagers but seemed not to worry Crocodile Guts at all.

Nhamo practiced swimming several times a day. Part of her intense fear of water was due to crocodiles, but she saw no sign of any in the shallows, nor did she find tracks or the slidy print of their bodies in the mud. "Maybe they don't like hippos,"she concluded. "Or, more likely, hippos don't like *them*." She remembered seeing a crocodile once in a mud hole near the village. It had been bitten in two, with its head at one end of the pond and its tail at the other. A hippo wallowed in between. No, the animals weren't friends.

The absence of crocodiles made her swimming lessons slightly less frightening. Nhamo willingly let go now—if she was within reach of the rock. She could float and maneuver her feet to the bottom. She could even turn over onto her back, but she hadn't figured out how to propel herself forward.

One morning, she sat up from the bed of grass in the boat and found the river deserted. She felt a sudden, odd stab of loneliness. Not that she liked the hippos—far from it—but they had become a familiar part of her world. Nhamo waited all day to be certain. They didn't come back. After darkness fell, she couldn't hear them snorting and complaining to one another. The night felt strangely empty. When Nhamo went to sleep with her arms around the mealie bag, she missed their constant muttering almost as much as the breathing of her cousins in the girls' hut.

She untied the rope before dawn. "Today we're going to Zimbabwe, Mother," she said as she pushed away from the shallows. The current caught her, but Nhamo plied the oar expertly. She not only had learned a lot about boats, but she was less afraid of water. And her muscles were fueled with roasted guinea fowl. She sang:

> "I am she who tosses trees
> Instead of spears.
> The ostrich is my pillow
> And the elephant my footstool!
> I am Nhamo
> Who makes the river my highway
> And sends crocodiles scurrying into the reeds!"

All day she paddled, with stops to rest and eat. She went on through the sunset on a blood-colored river. The moon was three-quarters full and cast a silvery sheen when the red faded. The forest was an indistinct shadow, now near, now far, as she struggled against the current. She kept turning at right angles and having to fight her way back. Eventually, she gave up and made for shore. Or where she imagined the shore to be.

That was when she discovered the sandbanks. The boat scraped alarmingly, broke free, and scraped again farther on. It took every ounce of strength to fight her way past. She didn't dare get out to lighten the load. Nhamo began to pant with exhaustion and fear. It sounded as though the sandbanks were ripping out the hull. For a few moments the boat eased into deeper water, and she breathed more easily, but then it crunched into another obstacle. Something slapped Nhamo in the face: It was a sharp-leafed reed.

She reached out in the dark and felt plants all around her. Water rushed by on either side. This must be an island, she thought. She fastened the rope to a bundle of reeds and sat back to rest her aching arms. Suddenly, the many hours of fighting the river caught up with her. Her body shook as though she had a fever, and she leaned over the side to vomit what little she had in her stomach. She rested her cheek on the smooth wood until her head stopped swimming. Far ahead, she saw a bright star on the horizon.

It's awfully low to be a star, she thought, and awfully *big*. Then it came to her: She was looking at an electric light.

As she studied that part of the horizon, she detected other lights winking as they were hidden or eclipsed by trees. It was Zimbabwe. "Oh, Mother! Oh, Mother! I wish we could go there tonight!" Nhamo cried from sheer disappointment.

When she tried to lift the oar, it slipped out of her hands and clattered to the bottom of the boat. She began to tremble again. All she could do was sit dumbly and watch the lights winking beyond the far trees. Eventually, she curled up with Mother's jar at her side, but now and then she lifted her head to check that Zimbabwe was still there. And once, when the wind was blowing the right way, she thought she heard music.

15

Nhamo was walking in a strange place. It was very beautiful, with trees full of fruit. Cattle grazed in thick grass that rippled about their legs, and goats with fat udders wandered with clanking iron bells tied about their necks. On either side she saw hillocks covered with pumpkin vines, while beyond stood row upon row of ripe mealies.

She, herself, felt unusually light. Her feet barely brushed the ground, and when she jumped, her body moved through the air in a slow, dreamy fashion.

Is this Zimbabwe? No wonder Mother was sorry to leave, she thought. Nhamo followed a path that wound through the hillocks. The earth was soft beneath her feet. Presently, she came to a cluster of huts in a clearing: fine huts that looked as though they had been built yesterday. The thatching was evenly trimmed, the walls freshly plastered, the ground smooth without the print of a foot.

Two girls sat on a bench outside. Nhamo's spirit leaped. People! And what wonderful ones! They were even lovelier than Masvita before her illness. Their skin shone with oil. Their hair was woven into an intricate pattern, more like the scales of fish than like any style Nhamo had seen. They smiled at her with even, perfectly white teeth.

"*Masikati!* Good day!" said Nhamo.

"*Masikati!*" responded the two beautiful girls.

"Have you spent the day well?"

"We have done so if you have done so," they answered politely. Around their necks and looped over their arms were many, many strands of black beads. These rippled like drops of water when the girls moved.

"Your village is very fine," Nhamo said, uncertain how to strike up a conversation.

"Come and eat with us," they called. Nhamo needed no second invitation. She quickly settled herself on the ground. The girls produced plates of *sadza,* white as gardenias, and pots of steaming relish. Nhamo clapped in thanks before accepting a bowl.

She dredged a morsel of *sadza* with relish, lifted it to her mouth—and sprang to her feet, knocking everything to the ground. Crocodile Guts suddenly stood in the doorway of the dark hut!

"*Maiwee!* A ghost!" she cried. The girls twined around her; their long arms held her prisoner. "Please don't hurt me," Nhamo moaned.

"As if I would hurt you, little Disaster," Crocodile Guts said cheerfully. He sat down on the bench and helped himself to the food. He smacked his lips and scratched his neck with long, dirty fingernails. Even in death, his hair swarmed with lice—or ghost lice.

The fisherman belched satisfyingly. "I see you have my boat, little Disaster. Well built, isn't it? You have to remember to bail it out every morning, though. I never did get all the cracks filled."

Nhamo felt tongue-tied. What was the polite way to address a ghost?

"I carved it out of *mukwa* wood," Crocodile Guts continued. "That's the best. The termites won't touch it. But after many years, even a good boat gets cracks. I used to plug them with sap from the *mutowa,* the rubber tree. Most of the time it was easier to bail the thing out."

"*Baba . . . ,*" Nhamo began uncertainly.

"Yes, little Disaster?"

"Forgive me, *baba,* but aren't you . . . dead?"

The fisherman roared with laughter. "Of course! Why else would I be in this fine place with two beautiful *njuzu* girls to wait on me?"

Njuzu! Water spirits! Nhamo felt the long arms of the girls twining around her—or were they arms? She was afraid to look.

"Most people wander on land between the time they die and the *kugadzira* ceremony, when their family welcomes them home," the fisherman explained. "I was so fond of water, I came here instead."

"I—we—are *underwater*?"

Crocodile Guts pointed up.

For a moment Nhamo didn't know what she was seeing. The sky rippled as though the wind had become suddenly visible. Above hovered a small, dark shape.

"The boat!" moaned Nhamo, struggling against the girls. They slithered around her with a whispering, rustling sound. Their faces were still those of beautiful humans, but their bodies had turned into long, black snakes! Nhamo screamed. The *njuzu* shrugged themselves off and rippled over to Crocodile Guts.

"You mustn't be afraid of *njuzu,* child. They taught me everything there is to know about water."

But Nhamo screamed again and again, and stretched her arms toward the distant boat.

"I'm drowning!" cried Nhamo. She flailed wildly, and the sky rocked back and forth. Mother's jar rolled on its side. In spite of her panic, Nhamo automatically grabbed it before it could fall into the water—

—in the bottom of the boat. She was still in the boat! She wasn't drowning. It had only been a dream. Nhamo was flooded with relief. She had been soaked by the water that seeped in overnight, and that must have been what gave her the nightmare. "It was so real, *Mai,*" she told Mother. "Those girls . . . and Crocodile Guts. . . ."

The sun was nearly overhead. "*Maiwee!* I've slept a long time!" she said, shielding her eyes from the glare.

She lay on the soggy grass bed and went over all she had heard about *njuzu*. They lived in bodies of water and kept these from drying out. They were far wiser than humans. For this reason, they often instructed *nganga*s in their craft. Occasionally, they pulled unwilling people into their pools. Sometimes they took the shapes of humans, and sometimes of snakes or fish or, if they were bent on evil, crocodiles. They could melt from one form to the other.

If the *njuzu* offered you food, you must refuse it or be doomed to stay forever in their watery realm. Nhamo shivered. She had come *that* close to eating the *sadza* and relish.

She sat up and looked around. A mist lay over the horizon. Only a few yards away, the river faded into a haze. She dipped her calabash over the side and noticed that the water didn't look quite the same. The stream by the village had been clear. The Musengezi was dyed the color of tea, although it tasted perfectly clean. This water was blue-green. Or perhaps it was only the hazy light.

Nhamo remembered tying up to the reeds the night before. She crawled to the stern and pulled on the rope. It came up easily. The loop at the end had a single broken reed still attached.

Nhamo stared at the rope and then at the water. She was drifting! The motion had been so gentle, she hadn't noticed it. I must have crossed the sandbanks into a side channel, she thought. She began to paddle against the current, but the movement was so slight she couldn't keep track of the direction. For all she knew, she was traveling away from, not toward, Zimbabwe. "It's better to wait until I can see the shore," she decided.

Nhamo drank water and munched a few of the fish she had dried at the guinea-fowl camp. The clear area around the boat gradually widened out, and still she couldn't see the edge of the river. She listened for birds, but there was only the light slap of water against the hull. The air was empty of the smell of plants or flowers. Nhamo became uneasy.

Presently, a breeze stirred. The haze dispersed, and Nhamo realized she was in a far worse situation than she could ever have imagined. *The shoreline had completely vanished.* This was no side channel. This wasn't even the Musengezi. The boat had been scooped up and dropped into a boundless ocean. It had to be the country of the *njuzu.* "I didn't eat the food. I didn't!" she told the water spirits. But perhaps by merely accepting a bowl from them, she had fallen into their power.

As the breeze freshened, small ripples became wavelets; the wavelets grew into swells. Nhamo yelled when the boat began to sway. "Oh, *njuzu,* I didn't mean to insult you by screaming," she cried. "I've always been afraid of snakes. Please forgive my rudeness!" She begged and wept, but the boat continued to pitch, with Nhamo clinging to the sides.

When the craft leaned over, she could see right into the water. It was deep, so deep! The *njuzu* girls were coiled up in the depths, watching her with bright, human eyes. Mother's pot rolled; the mealie bag shifted. Nhamo desperately opened the bag with one hand as she clung to the boat with the other. She retrieved the pot and stuffed it inside.

"I think your pool is beautiful, Spirits of the Water. I am so lucky to be allowed to see it. Please don't drown me!" she cried. "I'm sorry I didn't ask permission to use your boat, *Va*-Crocodile Guts. I didn't know how."

You mustn't be afraid of njuzu, *child. They taught me everything there is to know about water.*

"You're already dead," Nhamo wailed. "You don't have anything to be afraid of!" But her mind began to work very fast. What would Crocodile Guts do in this situation? He must have encountered it. People said he went everywhere, even Lake Cabora Bassa. She grabbed the oar. Every time the boat tipped, she tried to push it back. This didn't work very well. Eventually, she discovered she was in less danger of capsizing if the prow faced into the waves.

Now she could slide up and down the swells without tossing the contents of the boat around. It was hard work, and the waves made her queasy. If she tried to rest, the craft swung sideways with a terrifying seesaw motion. On and on Nhamo forged, not knowing where or for how long, only that she had to keep going or die. Her head swam with fatigue; the sunlight glittering off the water made her eyes ache. She noticed a patch of whiteness ahead.

A dip in the waves revealed the top of a rock. Ah! She veered away before it could rip out the bottom of the boat. Suddenly, white foam frothed all around her as other rocks made their presence known. Nhamo was bewildered by so much danger. Directly in front of her was even more whiteness, a ring of it, and in the center a low shelf of land almost hidden in the glare of sunlight. It was an island!

Nhamo discovered she wasn't quite out of energy. She made for the island, and when her oar struck bottom, she jumped out and dragged the craft onto shore. The boat wasn't light. Nhamo had no idea she was strong enough to lift it, but terror gave her supernatural strength. She pulled the boat away from the foaming water and collapsed on the warm stone. Then she must have fainted, because the next thing she noticed was the sun, lying very low in the west. All around her was the *slap-slap-slap* of waves.

"Thank you, *Va*-Crocodile Guts," she whispered. "Thank you, *Va-njuzu*." She didn't know whether they had anything to do with her rescue, but it was safer to be polite. She watched the shadow of the boat lengthen and the sunlight creep away from the rock. She sat up.

It was a very small island, hardly a man's height above the waves at its tallest point. As far as Nhamo could see, there was not another speck of land in any direction. And her new home had not a bush or a tree or a blade of grass.

16

Nhamo stretched out with the mealie bag for a pillow. Mother's pot was wedged into a crevice at her side. She slept heavily, without interruption. In one sense, it was the safest place she had been since she left the village. No leopards could creep up on her here. No hippos would be attracted to a grassless rock.

The wind died in the night and so, then, did the waves. A haze blotted out the stars, and when dawn came, the sky turned a milky pink. Nhamo opened her eyes briefly onto a glory of shining mist.

When she finally awoke, the sun was a furious, white ball in the east, the air already unpleasantly hot. Nhamo stood up and stretched. *Hezvo!** She had never imagined so much water was possible. Twenty long steps took her from one end of the island to the other; fifteen steps took her from side to side. She hunkered down to consider the situation.

She had tied up within sight of Zimbabwe. The river had been flowing rapidly all around her, and if the rope came loose there (or was untied by an *njuzu,* she thought uneasily), the boat would have been rapidly swept downstream. She had slept soundly. Perhaps she had sailed all the way back past the guinea-fowl camp and the stream that went by the village.

***Hezvo!* Good heavens!

What had Grandmother said? The Musengezi used to flow into the Zambezi River until the Portuguese dammed it up. Now the Zambezi had become a huge lake.

Lake Cabora Bassa.

You couldn't see across Cabora Bassa. Even Crocodile Guts had approached it with caution because of the great waves that sometimes arose. Nhamo felt slightly happier that this was a real lake and not the ghostly realm of the *njuzu*. Still, water spirits no doubt inhabited the place, as they did any body of water.

She couldn't stay here long, that was certain. The island was barren. Her fish trap was useless without a narrow channel, and no birds ventured this far from shore. The thought of leaving filled her with dismay. The lake was calm now, but who could say how long that would last? Meanwhile, her stomach felt as if its two sides were glued together. She ate more of the dried fish and drank as much water as she could manage. For a few moments her belly felt comfortably stretched, but the sensation quickly vanished. She was afraid to eat the uncooked mealie meal: *Ambuya* said raw flour swelled up inside and made your stomach burst.

Nhamo laid out the matches to dry. She unrolled Mother's picture and saw that it had survived the journey unharmed. "Well, *Mai*," she sighed. "We don't have many neighbors in our new home—unless you count the *njuzu*. I imagine there are a lot of *them* around here. I'll make you some tea, and we can talk."

Nhamo pretend-boiled the tea and poured it into pots. She didn't have the heart to cut bread and spread it with margarine. She placed the fish trap over Mother's head so she wouldn't get too hot.

"Grandmother told me a story once about a man who had many wives and sons, but no daughters." Nhamo sipped her tea as though it were really hot. "The man called his sons together when he was dying. 'I have no money to buy you wives, or daughters to exchange for them,' he said. 'All I have is a single black bull and the friendship of the *njuzu* who lives in the river.'

"You can listen, too," Nhamo told the snake-girls under the water. "This story is about your people.

"The old man said, 'My sons, I can give you only good advice. Before you do anything important, sprinkle mealie meal on the black bull's head. If he shakes it off, it means I agree with your plan. I will speak through the bull. As for getting enough money for *roora*, you must jump into the deepest pool in the river!

"The old man died. His sons thought he was making fun of them with his advice. They planted their crops and toiled in the fields. Not one of them made enough money to buy a wife.

"One day, when they were discussing the problem, the youngest boy, who was called Useless, said, 'Don't you remember? Father told us to jump into the river.'

"'You have the brain of a flea, Useless. If you jump into the river, you will drown,' said the oldest.

"Useless went to the black bull and sprinkled mealie meal on his head. 'O Bull of the Ancestor, I am going to jump into the river. Do you think that's a good idea?' The bull shook his head vigorously. 'That means yes!' cried the youngest son.

"'That means we will have one less mouth to feed around here,' replied the oldest.

"All the sons went to the river to watch Useless throw himself in. The boy sank like a stone. His brothers waited and waited. All day they waited, but Useless never returned. They went to the boy's mother and told her what had happened.

"His mother wept and cried. She put on the bark cord of mourning and refused to cut her hair anymore. The older brothers hired themselves out to other farmers. They worked for many years to earn enough to marry the farmers' daughters. 'Still, we are more clever than our youngest brother,' they said. 'His bones are rolling around in the mud somewhere.'

"One day Useless's mother went to the river to get water. She found a beautiful girl sitting on a rock. 'Cut your hair and put on your finest clothes,' the girl told the astonished woman. 'I will give you a horn full of oil.'

"The mother didn't understand, but she obeyed. Soon she saw a great herd of cattle, goats, and sheep approaching with many servants. Leading them was a handsome young man dressed in a lion skin and wearing a crown of reeds. On his right side hung a sword and on his left a bag. He carried an animal tail and a black horn full of oil. Behind him walked the beautiful girl who had been at the stream.

"'Mother! Mother! Don't you recognize me?' called the young man. 'I am your son, Useless!'

"'Oh, my son! What happened to you?'

"The man explained that he had turned into a tiny fish when he threw himself into the river. He went through a crack in the rocks and found himself in an underground country as big as the earth. It had fields and cattle and houses.

"'I lived there, *Mai,* with a giant snake as big as a river. Plants grew along his back, and my job was to weed them. He was the *njuzu* Father told us about. He told me I must eat only mud and never touch mealie meal. If I ate real food, I would be trapped forever in his country. Finally, he gave me a horn of oil to cure people and a bag of medicine. He gave me a crown of reeds and a sword to rule my brothers with. Last of all, he gave me an *njuzu* bride.'

"Useless had learned how to be an *nganga* from the water spirit. He became a great chief, and his mother, who had been mistreated by everyone, was treated like a queen from then on."

Nhamo lay on her stomach and watched the waves lap against the shore. The wind was rising. She had been wise not to venture out in the little boat. She gathered up the matches before they could blow away, and stored Mother's picture in the pot. When this was done, a heavy feeling of despair fell over her.

It had been all right when she was telling the story. Somehow, she was transported away. Mother had been there; even the *njuzu* girls had listened from their watery houses. Now she was all alone on a tiny island. The waves foamed around the shore and the rocks that lurked beneath the surface.

"If I threw myself in . . . ," she began. But with her luck, she wouldn't find any underground country. She would merely drown, and her spirit would wander without any hope of rejoining her relatives.

The spray left Nhamo feeling damp and irritated. She would like a bath. It was unfair to be surrounded by bathwater and unable to use it! She squatted next to the shore and doused herself, using the calabash. Then she took out her treasures from the boat and went over them.

She had one box of matches, five pots, the calabash, Aunt Chipo's old head scarf, the red cloth (minus a corner) she was supposed to wear for her marriage ceremony, Uncle Kufa's broken knife, the lamp she had used to light her way from Grandmother's hut, four wooden spoons, a few glass beads, a packet of salt, dried chilies, the bag of mealie meal, a small bag of dried beans mixed with ash to discourage weevils, and the sturdy rope Crocodile Guts had left in the boat.

And around her neck was the red cloth bag containing *Ambuya*'s gold nuggets.

"If I was in the village . . . ," Nhamo said dreamily. "Well, I wouldn't be in the village. I'd be at Zororo Mtoko's house. I'd be stamping mealies for his three wives. They would be sitting indoors with pots of *maheu*." Nhamo imagined the sour, rich taste of *maheu*. Her mouth watered. "They wouldn't give me any, oh no! They'd make me eat rotten porridge and wormy fruit."

Nhamo closed her eyes, seeing the three angry women inside the hut. Their skin was blotched with disease. Their heads were almost bald. "Their children are rude and stupid," Nhamo went on. She didn't know this, but it gave her spirit pleasure to imagine it. "They fight among themselves. Zororo can hardly bear to look at them. They're ugly, like him. He comes home drunk and swings his knobkerrie* in all directions. His wives think about putting poison in his food, but they don't dare."

Nhamo felt satisfied with the dismal scene she had imag-

*knobkerrie: A club.

ined. "And I am not there! I, Nhamo, am visiting the country of the *njuzu*. They will tell me their secrets and send me home with cattle and goats."

But when she opened her eyes, she was still alone in the middle of a vast lake. The lonely-sickness came over her again, and she pressed her fists to her temples to force it away.

You mustn't be afraid of njuzu, *child. They taught me everything there is to know about water.*

"What can I learn, *Va*-Crocodile Guts?" Nhamo cried.

For one thing, swimming.

Now where had that come from? Nhamo so badly wanted to hear a voice, she wasn't sure whether someone had actually spoken or whether she had imagined it. She considered the shoreline. The lake was shallow where she had pulled up the boat, and farther out were clusters of rocks. She waded in, keeping a sharp eye on the bottom. By slowly feeling her way around—and scrambling back onto shore when a large wave came through—Nhamo staked out a sizable area where the water reached no higher than her chest.

She perched on the island again and rewarded herself with a few tiny dried fish and a pinch of chili powder.

Njuzu took the shapes of snakes and fish and—ugh!—crocodiles, Nhamo thought. How did they move? She tried to wriggle like a snake. No, she wasn't long and thin enough. Crocodiles floated. She knew how to do that. But they moved along by swishing their tails from side to side. She didn't have a tail.

She tried to remember how other animals swam. Most creatures didn't venture to try if they could avoid it. The ones that did—hippos and elephants—were too dangerous to spy on. Very occasionally, Uncle Kufa threw a stick into the stream for one of his dogs to retrieve. The dog swam back with its legs going as though it was racing across a field. It looked relieved to get back on land—not that she could blame it. Even dogs understood about crocodiles. But wait! There was one animal who swam readily, even joyfully. The otter, or *binza*.

Nhamo had often observed *binza* hunting in the stream.

They skimmed along the bottom and turned over rocks to flush out frogs and fish. They caught these in their hands just like people, rose to the surface, and ate while treading water. Again and again they dove with restless energy until, sated, they bobbed around on top with their heads out of the water.

They were fascinating, but dangerous. An enraged otter would hurl itself at an enemy far larger than itself. One of Uncle Kufa's hunting dogs had been drowned by a mother protecting two cubs.

But they certainly knew how to swim.

Nhamo waded out on the shallow shelf of rock. She practiced floating like a crocodile. She kicked her legs like an otter. She trotted like a dog running across a field. Little by little she began to understand how a creature could maneuver in such a treacherous medium. She practiced until dark, by which time she was exhausted. For dinner she had two small fish and another pinch of chili powder. She drank two calabashes of water to stretch her stomach.

Days passed; Nhamo lost count. After the dried fish were gone, she suffered from gnawing hunger for a day before a new plan occurred to her. *Ambuya* had told her often enough of the dangers of eating uncooked flour and beans. She no longer had a choice in the matter. She soaked a handful of mealie meal in a pot. Hopefully, if it swelled enough *outside,* it wouldn't swell *inside* and burst her stomach.

The beans provided a more hopeful solution to the problem of food. Until now, Nhamo had only considered cooking them, but they could be soaked, too. And would begin to grow. The young plants were perfectly edible.

Why didn't I think of it earlier? she wondered.

She changed the water frequently, but the mealie meal spoiled anyway. When she touched it with her finger, ropes of slime pulled away from its surface. Even so, Nhamo attempted to eat a small portion. It made her vomit, and she threw the rotten meal away.

The beans sprouted. She devoured them as soon as she dared and set the rest to soak. The future was too terrible to contemplate, and so Nhamo didn't. It was like the time she had cared for Grandmother on the Portuguese trader's porch, an endless present. She spent the day telling stories to Mother and the *njuzu* girls. She talked to Crocodile Guts, too, in case he was visiting down below.

When the lonely-sickness came over her, she plunged anew into the blue-green waves. Danger kept her from despair. Farther and farther out she swam. She clung to submerged rocks and lifted her head above the water. She ventured out beyond the safe shallow area. She skimmed along under the surface like an otter. As long as she kept busy, she didn't think. But at night, in the middle of the night, she woke up without any defenses and cried hopelessly until dawn showed in the sky.

One day she didn't have the strength to return to shore. She turned over on her back to catch her breath. The lake roared in her ears, and sunlight jagged off the waves. When she eventually regained the island, she was so overcome with dizziness, she had to lie half out of the water for a long time until her strength returned.

Nhamo couldn't hide the facts from herself anymore. She had gone past hunger to real starvation, where the body no longer struggled against its fate. She would become progressively weaker until her arms and legs refused to move at all, and then she would die.

17

Nhamo slowly dragged the boat down to the water. She rested frequently, having no desire to reach her destination, but she couldn't postpone the journey any longer. "It seems you insist on me visiting you, *Va-njuzu*," she said bitterly as she wrestled the heavy boat over the rocks. It was early morning, when the water was generally calm. Nhamo floated the boat and walked it out of the shallows. On one side of the island was a field of dangerous rocks; on the other, as far as she could tell, was a deep, clear area.

Nhamo didn't allow herself to think. She clambered into the boat, waited for it to stop rocking, and started out. She didn't allow herself to look back at the island. A pinch of the precious salt and a few bean sprouts filled her with energy for a while, but it wore off.

For once, the waves remained small. Unfortunately, the still air brought a heat haze that covered the water and made it difficult to see very far. Midday came and passed. Nhamo rested and ate more beans. They rumbled inside her stomach. Long before sunset, Nhamo was too exhausted to row, so she brought the oar inside and stretched out with Aunt Chipo's scarf over her head.

"*Mother, how will my spirit return to the village if my body is at the bottom of the lake?*" she asked.

Mother smiled at her over the white tablecloth, where she was spreading bread with margarine. "I got home, didn't I? The paths of the body are long, but the paths of the spirit are short."

"Don't worry, little Disaster," said Crocodile Guts, who was lounging in a chair. "You've got my boat. It's made out of mukwa wood. Even the termites won't touch it." He scratched his head, and ghost lice crept over his fingers.

Two njuzu girls coiled up the table legs and bent gracefully over cups of tea that Mother had poured. They lapped at them with forked tongues.

Nhamo woke in the middle of the night. Mwari's country spread out above her. It was a region of which she knew little. Nighttime was too full of danger to encourage anyone to relax and study stars. Mwari, of course, was everywhere, but his special place was the sky.

The air was still, and the boat drifted gently. Nhamo thought about the dream. She knew that her spirit wandered with the ancestors when she was asleep. It made perfect sense that Mother would speak to her, but the presence of Crocodile Guts was puzzling. He wasn't a relative. Perhaps he was attracted by the boat.

As for the snake-girls, Nhamo would have preferred them to slither off to someone else's dream.

Dawn came. She continued to rest. It seemed too much trouble to sit up and row. Where could she go, anyhow? The sunlight crept up behind Nhamo's head and finally bathed her in uncomfortable heat. The air was motionless. She covered her eyes with Aunt Chipo's scarf. Slowly, the sun rose until it shone directly on her face. She could see beads of brilliant light through the weave of the scarf.

She attempted to paddle in the afternoon, but the oar threatened to slip out of her fingers. Nhamo gave herself up to the inevitable. Now and then she drank water and nibbled the rest of the beans and salt. At night she fell into confused dreams. How long had she been out here? How many times had the sun passed overhead? It was just peeping over the rim of the boat now, although she had no memory of a dawn.

And then it came to her that the boat had been drifting in the same direction all that time. It was moving toward the rising sun, which meant the current was flowing east. All she had to do was paddle west, and eventually she would reach Zimbabwe.

Nhamo sat up. Lights flashed before her eyes and her head swam. *Oh, yes! I'm going to row to Zimbabwe. I can barely move,* she thought. It took a while for the fit of dizziness to pass, and then her eyes couldn't focus. A dark smudge floated over the water.

Nhamo rubbed her eyes; the smudge didn't go away. In fact, it became clearer as the boat floated toward it. A strip of sky separated it from the lake, but it was most definitely a patch of land with trees. A thrill of terror shot through Nhamo. Whoever heard of land floating? It had to be connected to the spirit world.

As the boat approached, the strip of sky wavered and melted away. Suddenly, Nhamo realized she was looking at an island. She grasped the oar and was swept with another fit of dizziness. No matter! She began paddling anyhow, trying to make out the island through the haze of light blurring her vision. The shoreline rose up steeply. Here was another problem! This island didn't slope gradually into the water. She couldn't see anywhere to tie up.

On she went, bumping now and then against rocks. Even if she did manage to tie up, she didn't think she had the strength to climb any cliffs. Nhamo prayed to her ancestors and then, to be on the safe side, asked the *njuzu* for help, too. She hadn't forgotten the strip of sky. This land might very well belong to supernatural creatures.

As she was almost past the island, she spied a giant fig tree with long roots snaking down to the water. Nhamo made for it and secured the boat. She lay down to rest.

The roots twisted and interlocked above her. They made a natural ladder and even provided places to sit and catch her breath. It was perfect. *I can build a fire,* Nhamo thought. *I can eat. Thank you, Mother and Grandfather. Thank you,*

Great-grandparents. And of course you, too, *Va-njuzu*. And *Va*-Crocodile Guts. I couldn't have done it without your boat.

Nhamo thought about what she should do to express her gratitude. Beer was what one generally offered the ancestors, but she hadn't learned how to make it yet. She did know how to make *maheu*, though. She could use some of the cooked mealie meal and have it ready tomorrow.

What would the *njuzu* like? Here, Nhamo was completely stymied. They seemed to have plenty of food and drink in her dream. They had houses and livestock, too. Really, it was difficult to know what such powerful spirits lacked. Then she had it: They liked jewelry. The snake-girls had been covered with beads.

Nhamo hunted in her stores until she found the beads from Aunt Shuvai's bracelet. She looked at them sadly, remembering when she had gathered them up long ago after her aunt had thrown them away. They were one of her few remaining links to the village. But she must not be cowardly. The *njuzu* had brought her to this island, and it would be extremely ungrateful not to repay them.

Nhamo closed her eyes and flung the beads into the lake. She heard a light patter as they struck the water. "I hope you like them," she whispered. "They were very beautiful."

Nhamo made ready to climb the fig-tree roots to the top of the island. She packed a cooking pot, mealie meal, and matches into the fish trap. This she tied to her back. Then she filled the calabash with water and began her journey.

Step by step, with many rests, she worked her way to the top. The most difficult job was keeping the water in the calabash. She would have to work out a better method for transporting it. Nhamo fought against dizziness, but the promise of cooked food kept her going. She finally hauled herself over the top of the cliff and stopped.

And stared, open-mouthed.

The island was covered with greenery as far as she could see—not with ordinary forest plants, but with tomatoes, mealies, and bananas. Nhamo's eyes grew wider and wider as she took in the unbelievable scene.

"Oh! Oh! Thank you!" she cried. She fell to her knees by a banana tree and began cramming the ripe fruit into her mouth. Then she forced herself to eat more slowly. *Ambuya* said it was dangerous to eat too much after starving. Nhamo nibbled and waited and nibbled again. She ate some tomatoes next. They were little and egg-shaped, not like the tomatoes they grew in the village, but she had seen ones like them in the Portuguese trader's garden.

After a while Nhamo curled up in the shade of a tree and went to sleep. She knew this was foolish—after all, she hadn't explored the island—but she was so weak she couldn't help herself. And besides, she thought as she snuggled into the grass, this place must belong to supernatural beings who wouldn't allow wicked things to stay. Hadn't it floated over the water?

She awoke shortly before sunset, found a rocky area to build a fire on, and prepared dinner. She added tomatoes for flavor. Before it got dark, she boiled water and added it to the leftover mealie meal. "I am preparing *maheu* for you, O *vadzimu*. Please understand that I am very, very grateful for your help," she said.

Nhamo climbed down the fig roots and spent the night in the boat. The wind came up and tossed it around, but she barely noticed.

Most of the island's trees were fairly small; the fig was the main exception. They were scattered here and there among untidy stands of mealies, rioting pumpkin vines, and sweet potatoes. Nhamo found papayas, okra, chilies, onions, and peanuts as well. They were at all stages of development. The mealies grew in clumps as though they had sprouted from entire ears dropped from unharvested plants. In some places, though, she could see evidence of systematic farming. In the center of the island was a ruined house, behind which stood a lemon tree.

Nhamo walked around the structure. It was a square, Portuguese house, not as grand as Joao and Rosa's, but not small either. The windows were boarded up, and the remnants of iron grillwork hung from the frames. A door stood slightly open, showing a dark and forbidding interior. Nhamo wasn't tempted to go inside. She fetched the *maheu* pot and sat under the lemon tree to think.

Grandmother said this area had once been dry land, except for the Zambezi. The Portuguese dammed up the river and flooded the whole valley. Only the high hills poked out above the water now.

The villagers who had lived in the Zambezi Valley dug up the bones of their ancestors and carried them to new places beyond the edge of the lake. It would have been unthinkable to leave the bones behind. The ancestors were as much a part of the family as the children, and to abandon them would have been wicked beyond belief.

The mud huts of the villagers would perish after several rainy seasons, but a Portuguese house was made of stronger materials and would survive. As this one had.

The island was part of an abandoned village, much like the place where Nhamo used to have tea with Mother. There were no baboons or porcupines or wild pigs to ravage it, as there had been at the other place. As far as Nhamo knew, it contained no animals larger than mice, and the shore was too steep for hippos to invade. That was why food still abounded.

The place was part of the real world, then, and not a supernatural realm. Nhamo was relieved to find a logical explanation. It didn't mean her ancestors weren't responsible for *finding* it, though. She had no doubt that spirit hands had directed the boat when she was too weak to row.

The *maheu* smelled delicious, but she wasn't even slightly tempted to drink it. This food was for the ancestors. She knelt under the lemon tree and clapped her hands respectfully. "I have prepared this for you, O *vadzimu*. When I get to Zimbabwe, I'll go to an *nganga* and ask him to make a better offering with real beer and snuff. I hope you don't mind waiting. Please understand how very grateful I am for your help."

As Nhamo spoke these words, she slowly poured the *maheu* onto the earth. It soaked in quickly. When she was finished, she sat back and smiled at the beautiful green island. The lonely-sickness seemed far away at that moment. It was as though the place was filled with the presence of her ancestors. The paths of the body were long, but the paths of the spirit were short, and the *vadzimu* had gathered to witness her gift, and to protect their wandering child.

18

And yet she couldn't bring herself to spend the night on the island. Nhamo had been over every part of it now. She was sure there weren't any dangerous animals. It was unreasonable to return to the damp boat except to bail it out, but she felt safer there. The ruined house gave her a bad feeling. She knew that in the middle of the night, she would think about the door and what might push it the rest of the way open.

She wedged the boat between the fig-tree roots that snaked down into the water, to keep it from battering against the rocks. Even so, the waves tossed her around, sometimes violently.

Nhamo brought everything from the boat to her cooking area. She made a frame from branches and tied bundles of grass across it. This she leaned against two small trees to form a kind of shelter. With her belongings arranged at one end, she could curl up in the shade and feel almost as if she had a home.

She reserved the mealie meal for her eventual trip to Zimbabwe. Instead, she feasted on the riches the island provided. With careful management, she could live there for years, planting at the beginning of the rainy season and harvesting at its end. But of course she didn't want to stay for years. Father's family was in Zimbabwe. The thought of aunts and uncles and grandparents waiting for her there was cheering.

Nhamo dried chilies and roasted peanuts. Sweet potatoes and pumpkins would store for weeks or even months. She had ample food for a journey, and her supplies were limited only by the size of the boat. She made herself a grass ring for the top of her head. Now it was much easier to transport water from the lake. She had only to wedge a pot into the grass ring and climb the fig roots. Her hands were free to hold on. Years of practice kept her from spilling so much as a drop.

In the heat of the day, Nhamo sat under the lemon tree at the highest point of the island and made twine. She found young *mupfuti* trees, broke away the outer covering with a rock, and pulled the inner bark off in long strips. These she alternately chewed and rolled between the palm of her hand and her thigh. Her twine wasn't as strong as Crocodile Guts's thick rope, but it had more uses. She could make animal snares and lash together tools or thatching grass.

In the meantime, she thought about the people who had lived here. Once this had been the top of a hill where the owners of the ruined house could catch an afternoon breeze. At the front were traces of a wooden porch. Behind, near the lemon tree, Nhamo had discovered a variety of unfamiliar flowers. Rosa, too, had had a flower garden.

Nhamo closed her eyes and imagined the scene. The parents sat at a table with three—no, *six*—children. She felt kindly toward them, so she gave them enough offspring to be happy. They ate fish out of cans and used knives and forks. They had a nice, loud radio and a cage with a parrot.

And now they were gone.

Nhamo opened her eyes. The afternoon breeze whistled through the partly open door with a mournful, far-off sound. "They went back to Portugal," Nhamo said firmly. The civil war had gone on for ten years, with many deaths on both sides. When it was over, many of the Portuguese had returned home. She tried to imagine the inhabitants of the ruined house in their new country, but she knew too little about it.

Sometimes the afternoon breeze turned into a real wind. The trees shook and the waves dashed against the rocks.

Nhamo inched the boat out of the water. She had regained her strength, but the craft was still too heavy for her to lift. She wrestled it into the tangle of fig roots. It was safe there, but far too unstable to sleep in. At night she had to let it down again. One evening the weather was too wild to permit this.

"Now what," said Nhamo, perched in a curl of tree root. "*Hezvo!* That was a big wave!" The spray blew across her face; she rubbed her eyes. Twilight didn't last long, and already the lake had turned dark blue. The first stars were appearing in the fading light of the sunset.

Nhamo checked Crocodile Guts's rope again and the smaller rope she had made. The boat was tied as well as she could manage, but it wouldn't take her weight. "I'd better find a bed before it gets completely dark," she sighed. She climbed back to the place where she did her cooking. The fire was never allowed to completely die, and it took only a moment to blow the coals into flame. The wind threatened to scatter the fire. Nhamo rolled rocks around it for a windbreak and tucked her jars, a half box of matches, and supplies into a crevice between two boulders.

She hated being so exposed! She tied the grass shelter more firmly to the trees and crept as far inside as she could manage. It was still unpleasant. The wind seemed like a live thing determined to drag her out of her hiding place. She remembered that *njuzu* sometimes traveled as whirlwinds.

"Please don't carry me off," she prayed. Far off she could hear the waves splashing and, if she concentrated, the voices of the *njuzu* as they went about their business in the water. Nhamo lay wakeful and nervous for a long time. After a while, she dragged another log onto the fire and retreated to her shelter to sleep.

She was in the girls' hut. Tazviona had lit an oil lamp, and she could see everyone's faces by its feeble light. Masvita, Ruva, and the others sat in a circle, waiting expectantly. "Go on, Nhamo. Tell us a story," whispered Masvita.

"A *scary* one," said Tazviona.

Nhamo held up her hand for silence. "In the forest, in the deep, deep forest lived an old, old woman."

"Go on," whispered the girls.

"She wore no clothes. She didn't need to."

"Go on."

"Her breasts were so long, she could wrap them around herself, round and round like a blanket!"

"Hhhuuuhh," murmured the girls.

"Her name was Long Teats. When she got pregnant, she didn't give birth to babies, but to swarms of locusts!"

"Go on."

"They ate everything: the plants, the houses, the stored grain. They even fastened onto the cattle and drank their milk."

"Horrible! Horrible!" responded the girls.

Nhamo went on with the tale of Long Teats, who, when she wasn't giving birth to locusts, was finding children to devour. Ruva hid her face in Masvita's lap.

Afterward, Nhamo had to go outside. To her surprise, she didn't see the village at all. She was in a strange place where the trees tossed in a high wind. *Hhhuuuhhh* went the wind, moaning over the rocks. She tried to return to the girls' hut, but it had vanished. In its place was the black outline of a square house, a Portuguese house. Its door creaked on rusty hinges, *eeeee, eeeee.*

Inside the house something moved. Something put its hand on the rusty door and flung it open. It was Long Teats! She sprang outside, wielding a giant knife, a *panga*. "Whhhooo's going to be my next meal?" she cackled. "Whhhooo's going to sweeten my cooking pot?"

Nhamo screamed and ran down to the lake, where the boat lay smashed to bits and the *njuzu* girls swam among the pieces in the pounding waves.

"Yiiii!" screamed Nhamo. The wind had torn away the grass shelter, and she was exposed. She grabbed a burning branch from the fire and backed into the crevice where she had stored her belongings. The flames danced; the trees groaned.

"Oh, Mother, protect me!" Nhamo cried. "Oh, Grandfather, help!" She trembled like a calf confronted with a leopard.

Whhhooo's there? whistled the wind over the trees and rocks.

"I didn't know this was your island," whimpered Nhamo. "I'm sorry I ate your vegetables. Please don't eat me, *Va*-Long Teats."

She crouched down—and remembered the *zango,* the charm against witchcraft that Masvita had tied around her arm so long ago. She always removed it to bathe or swim, but carefully replaced it when her skin was dry. Now she felt it beneath her fingers. The *zango* bristled with tiny bones and feathers, a comforting shape that spoke of powerful charms.

"I am Nhamo, your child," she whispered to her ancestors. "I gave you *maheu* when you brought me here. Please tell Long Teats to leave me alone."

The wind gusted in a new direction, blowing from the jumbled saplings on the far side of the island. She smelled *mutarara,* the wild gardenia. What was it Grandmother had said about the *mutarara?* Its branches were very thick and complicated. It was used to keep away leopards and—and— she almost had it—to keep witches from plundering graves! That was it! Uncle Kufa had put gardenia branches on *Vatete*'s grave.

Ah! Her ancestors were sending the scent of *mutarara* to confuse Long Teats. The old witch would stumble into the sapling grove and fall over a cliff—Nhamo hoped.

Sometimes the wind blew away from the grove and sometimes toward it. And gradually, the wind's fury died down. The sky changed from black to a wash of deep blue. Nhamo was wedged so far into the rock crevice, her hips were bruised. She wriggled out when dawn was near and rubbed her body to get the stiffness out.

The sky brightened rapidly. Soon she was able to see the green of trees and brown of bark. Nhamo huddled next to the fire with her hand on the *zango.* Finally, when the sun cast blue shadows through the trees, she carefully made her way to the fig tree.

The boat was unharmed. It had tipped sideways, but since it was empty, nothing was lost. "So that part of the dream wasn't true," she said. "Maybe Long Teats wasn't real either." But Nhamo knew that dreams always had some significance. The ancestors were telling her something was wrong, or perhaps they merely wanted her to stop putting off her trip to Zimbabwe.

Nhamo climbed down and checked the ropes holding the boat. The waves were higher than she liked, but safe enough. Holding on to a fig root, she got into the water and refreshed herself with a quick swim.

19

I can't stay here anymore," she said as she feasted on bananas and roasted yams by the fire.

I agree, said Mother, who was sitting under a tree.

"I'm afraid, though. What if the wind comes up while I'm out on the water?"

You've got the best boat in the country, boasted Crocodile Guts from his perch on the rocks. *It's made out of* mukwa *wood. Even* njuzu *can't sink it.*

"The *njuzu* like you. They don't think much of me," pointed out Nhamo. Still, she had to admit that the snake-girls were friendlier than Long Teats.

After breakfast, Nhamo began selecting things to take with her. It would take careful planning. She didn't know how far she had to go, but she didn't dare load the boat too heavily. By afternoon the wind rose, and she realized it would be impossible to sleep in the lake. The thought of another night on the island was depressing, even if Long Teats was only a bad dream. "I'll put a barrier of *mutarara* branches around my bed," she decided.

Nhamo crossed the island, skirting the clearing where the Portuguese house stood. She didn't like to go that way, but it was by far the quickest path to the sapling grove. She glanced nervously at the house and almost fainted. The door was standing wide open!

Nhamo wanted to scream. If she spent the night within reach of that open door, she would be nothing but a pile of bones and gristle by morning. "Oh, what will I do?" she moaned.

Close the door, whispered Mother.

The suggestion made sense—except when Nhamo thought about actually doing it.

The afternoon sun shone directly into the dark opening, but she couldn't make out anything from that distance. "I'll stay on the boat no matter how bad the waves are. If anything tries to get me, I'll untie the rope," she said.

I would never sail in bad weather on purpose, little Disaster, warned Crocodile Guts.

Nhamo shifted from foot to foot, staring miserably at the door. Things weren't going to get any easier when the sun went down.

"Why don't I get the *mutarara* branches first?" she suggested.

Close the door now, the voices of the *njuzu* girls hissed.

Nhamo walked slowly to the Portuguese house with Uncle Kufa's knife held out in front of her. She didn't know if knives could hurt Long Teats, but it was worth a try.

Her eyes searched the dark interior. She noticed a pile of twigs and dirt. She leaned inside to grasp the edge of the door.

What she had taken for twigs were bones.

They lay in an orderly pattern, ribs here, legs there, showing through the remains of black pants and a black shirt. The skull sat where it should, and all was arranged on a metal frame. It was a Portuguese bed like the one Joao and Rosa had owned. Nhamo couldn't move. She stood with one hand reaching for the door and the other holding Uncle Kufa's knife.

The wind began to pick up again, causing the cloth shreds to flutter.

What struck Nhamo, when her shock began to ebb, was

the peacefulness of the scene. A small table in the shadows bore a plate and a glass, thickly covered with dust. The remains of a rug were blown against a wall. A wooden chest sat under a boarded-up window. It didn't look like a witch's lair. She had poured *maheu* to the ancestors only a few feet from here, and they had drawn near to watch. They surely wouldn't have been comfortable in the presence of wickedness.

Nhamo lowered the knife. She took a few deep, almost sobbing breaths. Nothing awful had happened so far, but you never knew. Dead bodies were not to be approached lightly.

She squatted in the doorway and tried to sort out her thoughts.

This was a Portuguese body. It was laid out carefully, not sprawled like a murder victim. She didn't know what Portuguese did with their dead, but they might seal them in houses, as her people occasionally did. Then the house, or hut, was left to decay. The wind had blown the door open, though, and the man—Nhamo guessed it was a man by the clothes—was upset.

She could understand that.

A witch might get interested in an unguarded body. The man's spirit was worried, and he had sent her the dream to tell her about his fears. Nhamo suddenly understood what she had to do. "Please excuse me, *Va*-Portuguese," she said, inching into the room. "I'm only trying to protect your grave." Other rooms lay beyond the one where she stood, but Nhamo didn't have the courage to explore them. She went to the chest under the window and looked inside.

She found more black clothes and a necklace of beads with a cross attached. Ugh! It was another portrait of Jesus-*ngozi*. She dropped it at once. She found books with no pictures, a tobacco pipe, bottles with beads inside. Nothing she could use.

Then she saw a glint of metal in the heap of rug fragments. It was even better than she had hoped for: It was a big, beautiful, strong *panga*, the perfect tool for cutting *mutarara* branches.

She hurried to the sapling grove before the sun got any lower. She sharpened the knife on a convenient stone and began hacking at the gardenias, scratching herself on the thorns. She worked as though possessed, and maybe she was possessed. Nhamo had never been taken over by a spirit, so she didn't know what it felt like.

She carried branches to the house and went back for more. She wanted enough to protect herself as well. She also found, and uprooted, a small *muzeze* sapling covered with bright yellow flowers.

She laid gardenias across the bones and, because she thought it might scare off Long Teats, draped Jesus-*ngozi* on top. She closed the door tightly, placing more branches in front of it. Last of all, she used the *muzeze* roots to sprinkle water all around the outer walls. Nhamo had seen *Ambuya* do this around Aunt Chipo's hut after *Vatete*'s body had been removed. It insured that wandering spirits stayed where they belonged.

Nhamo went back to her cooking area and made a barrier around the place where she intended to sleep. This, too, she sprinkled with water from the *muzeze* roots. By now the sun had set and the wind was again tossing the trees.

Nhamo built up the fire. She ate roasted yams and mealies. She lay down in the *mutarara* ring with a nice, warm feeling that everything had been done properly. "Isn't it lucky I watched Grandmother so closely?" she congratulated herself. "I could have spent every night on the island if I'd remembered about witch repellent sooner." And then she realized she hadn't returned the *panga* to the house.

It was lying under the lemon tree, where Long Teats could find it.

"Sometimes I think I was given the right name," Nhamo sighed. "Although *Stupid* would have done as well as *Disaster*."

Don't worry, Mother said kindly. *The* mutarara *will con-*

*fuse Long Teats so much, she'll walk right over a cliff, and
the wind will blow her away.*

"I hope so," murmured Nhamo. The bed was hard. If she
stretched her toes out, they met the gardenia thorns. In spite
of everything, she fell into a deep, dreamless sleep and woke
long after the sun had lifted from the edge of the lake.

The wind blew steadily for one more day. Nhamo waited
two days longer to be sure the weather had calmed down.
She gazed intently across the water to find signs of land.
When the wind blew, she thought she saw a shadow to the
east, but calm air brought a heat haze. Perhaps there was
another island, perhaps not. At any rate, it wasn't in the right
direction.

She had no more bad dreams, but the presence of the
grave had spoiled the island for her. The *panga* lay where
she had dropped it. It was more than two hands long, with
a curved blade. Even Uncle Kufa hadn't possessed anything
that fine, and it seemed a shame to leave it behind. It was,
however, the property of the Portuguese spirit.

The correct thing, of course, would be to open the grave-
house and throw it inside, but Nhamo didn't want to touch
the door. The exorcism ceremony had worked so far. Why
stir things up? She whetted the knife on a stone and polished
it with damp leaves. Ah! It was a beautiful thing! She laid it
next to the cook-fire.

All the supplies were ready to load early in the morning.
Nhamo fixed dinner and retired to her nest. "I'm leaving the
panga where you can get it," she informed the Portuguese
spirit. "Of course, it would make an awfully nice gift—if you
didn't mind—in return for protecting your grave from Long
Teats. Not that I expect payment. You've already let me stay
on your island. Don't think I'm not grateful. But if you don't
need the knife, I could certainly use it."

The wind was perfectly still this last night. She could hear
the water lapping in the distance. Long Teats had blown
away, no doubt searching for another grave, and the *njuzu*
were coiled up in their houses at the bottom of the lake.

Early next morning Nhamo sat up and looked around. A chill, blue-gray light filtered down from the sky. Trees were silhouetted beyond the rocks, and she could see the cleft where she had hidden from the witch. Stores of cooked and raw food lay in the makeshift baskets Nhamo had been able to produce. The island didn't provide good weaving material.

Shining dully, the *panga* lay on the other side of the clearing. The middle of the blade had vanished. Nhamo rubbed her eyes. No, the blade was unbroken. It was covered with something of the same color and texture as the ground.

As she watched, she noticed a mouse pilfering a basket of peanuts. It sat up with a nut between its paws, nibbling busily. Now and then it paused to check its surroundings. The light strengthened. Nhamo could see its whiskers and shiny black eyes.

Suddenly, like a bolt of lightning, the thing on the *panga* struck. It snapped up the mouse, which uttered a forlorn squeak before being hurried off to the crevice in the rocks.

It was a puff adder. Its yellow-and-brown-patterned body had faded easily into the rocks. Nhamo was startled, but also impressed. Puff adders came from the spirit world. Although dangerous, they were even-tempered and slow to anger, faithful to their chosen homes, and bringers of good harvests.

The message was perfectly clear. Nhamo had drawn the mouse with her store of peanuts. The spirit that possessed the snake had accepted the present and in return had given her the *panga*.

"Thank you," she cried, clapping her hands in gratitude. The knife could mean the difference between life and death.

Nhamo made a final breakfast and scattered some of her precious mealie meal as a sacrifice to whatever ancestors might be present. "You have some, too," she told the Portuguese spirit as she gave him an extra helping.

Then she quickly bailed out the boat, loaded it, and cast off, paddling away from the rising sun. Occasionally, she looked back—somewhat regretfully. The island had given her a much-needed rest. She could have lived there forever. She could have built her own hut to shelter from the rain and devised fishing lines to satisfy her need for meat. But the one thing the island could never provide was company. Spirits were thin fare, compared to people. They didn't breath comfortingly in the middle of the night, and they couldn't hold her in their arms—not even Mother.

The island slowly dwindled until it disappeared in a glimmer of light. Now she was truly alone on the water, without a trace of land and with no idea of how far away it might lie.

But at least, Nhamo reminded herself, she was paddling toward Zimbabwe.

20

All day Nhamo toiled, with pauses to rest and eat. When she stopped, the boat very gently drifted east. She wore a basket on her head when the sun bothered her. On and on she went, singing to pass the time, or talking to Mother, Crocodile Guts, and the *njuzu*. Eventually, she got so tired she couldn't do anything except doggedly move the paddle, first on one side, then the other.

She had hoped to find land before sundown, but she didn't. It was difficult to see when she was crammed down next to the water with all her stores. "I wish I could climb a rock," she grumbled. The light reflected off the lake and hurt her eyes. Sometimes the horizon disappeared in a confusing glimmer that seemed to be neither earth nor sky. Nhamo found this extremely disturbing. "I think it's the opening to the *njuzu* country," she told Mother. "I don't care what Crocodile Guts says; *I* intend to stay away from it." Fortunately, no matter how vigorously she paddled, the opening never got any closer.

When it was too dark to be sure of her direction, she brought the oar inside and wriggled down between the baskets of food. She ate peanuts, roasted yams, and tomatoes. The boat gently floated back the way she had come.

Before dawn, Nhamo began again. At midmorning, she found a line of trees protruding from the water. They must have grown on top of a hill before the river was dammed. She stayed there the rest of the day, resting and treating herself to baths. She could see a definite shadow now to the north.

It was far away, hardly a smudge on the horizon, but clearly something other than water. "That must be the north shore of the lake," Nhamo decided. "I ought to keep going west, though." She debated the problem for the rest of the day. "It can't make any difference whether I follow the north or south shore. I'll still be heading for Zimbabwe."

You'd be safer close to land, Mother agreed.

You forgot to bail out the boat again, complained Crocodile Guts. *Next time I'll lend it to someone else.*

Nhamo hurried to placate the irritated fisherman.

The smudge had disappeared in haze by morning, but she soon found it again. Nhamo pressed on, watching the smudge grow into a definite strip of land. By nightfall it was still too far to reach. "Stupid water!" she shouted at the lake. "Why can't you flow in *that* direction for a change?" Her legs ached with the need to walk on solid ground. Her body was hot and sticky, and she was beginning to feel hysterical.

Nhamo spent half of the next day recapturing the distance she had lost. When she *still* hadn't reached the land by nightfall—it stretched away from a headland and was covered with tall trees—Nhamo burst into noisy sobs. "Nobody wants me to reach Zimbabwe. Nobody cares what happens to me!" Between fits of weeping, she ate cold cooked yams, which were beginning to taste moldy, and peanuts. Some of the peanuts had worms. She chewed them up before she realized it.

"Horrible!" she screamed, spitting out the vile mix. "Oh, I wish I was dead!" She threw herself down, beating the hull of the boat with her fists and howling insults at the lake. Eventually, she fell asleep in the remains of a tomato basket, with the juice soaking into her dress-cloth. Sometime during the night, she awoke with a strange feeling of peace.

"I don't really think your lake is nasty," she assured the *njuzu*. She didn't want to anger them when they had been keeping the water calm.

The land was farther away at sunrise, but it looked reachable. Nhamo had something far more momentous to deal with, though. Her legs were streaked with blood. During the night she had become a woman.

"I'm a *mhandara*, just like Masvita," she told Mother. She smiled at the shining water and tantalizing strip of land. She was someone important now, a future ancestor. She had proven her willingness to bear children. She wouldn't have a party, but that didn't take away from the importance of what had just happened. When a girl became a *mhandara* in the village, they said she had crossed the river into womanhood.

"I'm the only girl who ever crossed a whole *lake*," Nhamo boasted. She tore the red marriage cloth into three wide strips and folded them around grass from her bedding to make pads. She held them in place with twine tied around her waist. Later she would hunt for wild cotton to use instead of grass. She began paddling with new spirit. On the way she made up a song:

> "I am Nhamo, a tree full of fruit,
> Not a weed.
> Pay attention, little girls!
> I am now a woman
> And allowed to scold you.
> My pots will be stronger, my baskets finer.
> The roofs of my houses will not fall in.
> I am Nhamo, a mighty woman
> For whom crossing a measly river was not enough!"

By midday she neared the land. It should have stretched east and west, but it extended north instead. The view south was blocked by a headland. This was somewhat puzzling. "I'm probably at the mouth of a river," Nhamo decided. She tied up to a convenient tree on a small island offshore.

Maiwee! It felt good to stretch her legs. She squatted by the water to douse herself with the calabash and to wash out her dress-cloth. Then she touched her toes and wriggled her shoulders to take the stiffness out of her body. She spent the afternoon lounging in the shade of a tree. Before dark, Nhamo hunted for a sleeping site. The lakeward edge of the island was steep enough to discourage hippos, but the landward side sloped gently into the water. As Nhamo climbed over a rock, she saw something rise from the ground and hurl itself into the lake. It was a crocodile!

She hastily retraced her steps. She had felt safe in the deep water. Now things were back to normal. She had been extremely lucky the crocodile hadn't been watching her bathe.

Feeling irritated, she resigned herself to another uncomfortable night on the boat. The yams were definitely moldy now, and she was sick of peanuts. But she had come to land safely. *And* become a woman.

"All in all, it hasn't been a bad day," Nhamo told Mother.

21

Nhamo rounded the headland and saw, to her relief, that the shore did extend west. She paddled vigorously, looking for signs of people in the early-morning light. She sniffed the air for cook-fires. A troop of baboons trotted along the bank to observe her, and the males uttered threatening cries. Springbok, duiker, and waterbuck hid in the shadows of *musasas*. *Shoko*, vervet monkeys, leaped from tree to tree.

But there were no people. Nhamo went ashore at midday. She built a fire and boiled mealie meal with the remains of the tomatoes. She wasn't discouraged. She had only to keep going, and eventually the huts, fields, and brilliant lights of Zimbabwe would appear. Nhamo filled one of the pots with live coals and perched it in a pool of water at the bottom of the boat. There was no use wasting matches until she knew how far she had to go.

After four days, she came to the end of the land. Nhamo was horrified. What had happened to the shore? Beyond lay nothing but featureless water. She directed the boat around a peninsula and began to paddle east. She searched the distance anxiously for the shadow that would surely connect the trees, the rocks, and the abundant animal life to the north shore. But it never appeared.

"At least the current's with me," she murmured as the boat slid along. She camped again and hunted for food rather than depend on her stores. As long as she kept busy, she didn't have to think about the significance of her new direction.

Finally, after threading her way through a cluster of rocks surrounded by foam, she came again to an endless stretch of water. With a pounding heart, she turned south. When she spotted a small island at the end of a headland, she couldn't avoid the truth any longer. There was the place she had taken a bath. There was the branch she had tied up to—the low-hanging tree was unmistakable—and yes, she even saw the same crocodile watching her with yellow, slitted eyes.

"It's another *island,*" wailed Nhamo. Lake Cabora Bassa was so huge, it could contain a place this large and still give no hint of where the shore might be. "I hate you!" she screamed at the big island. "What are you doing out here? Why aren't you in Zimbabwe where you belong?"

Snap! The boat jolted in a sickening way. Nhamo had been paddling rapidly, not paying attention. The boat had driven right onto a sharp-edged spur of rock just under the water. Nhamo wrestled it free, but water began to seep in at an alarming rate. One of Crocodile Guts's old cracks had opened up! She had no time to waste, so she drove the craft toward the low-hanging tree. The crocodile fled into the lake as she approached. Nhamo dragged the boat out of danger and sat down to catch her breath.

"I shouldn't have insulted the big island," she moaned. Aunt Chipo had often scolded her for speaking without thinking first. It was always dangerous to say bad things about an unknown place. Who knew what spirits were listening?

"Well, I've *really* got myself into a mess this time," she told Mother. "I've wrecked the boat, I'm nowhere near Zimbabwe, and my only neighbor is a big, hungry crocodile."

Nhamo soon discovered she had more than one neighbor, however. As she unpacked the boat, she saw a furtive movement in the bushes. She grabbed the *panga* and watched the shadows with her heart pounding.

After a few moments, the bushes moved again. A shrill

bark made Nhamo jump back with the knife raised over her head. This was followed by a soft churring as though someone were talking to himself. "Go away!" shouted Nhamo. The creature uttered four or five staccato cries and retreated.

It was a baboon.

Nhamo realized at once that she had a serious problem. Baboons could destroy her entire food store in a matter of minutes. Normally, she could have floated the supplies in the boat, but the crack made this impossible. "Why didn't I see them last time I was on the little island?" she wondered. They must have been watching her from the trees.

It was still morning, so she kindled a fire from the pot of coals and roasted yams while she thought. Baboons hated to cross water, she knew. They avoided it for the same reason people did: Crocodiles lurked under the surface.

Nhamo considered the line of rocks between her and the large island. It would be just barely possible to leap from stone to stone—if you were a baboon. A person couldn't do it. But why go to the trouble? The little island was too small to feed a troop.

Nhamo ate the yams with an uncomfortable feeling that she was being observed. She turned quickly. The bushes moved as though something had recoiled, and she hurled a rock at it.

She moodily watched the flames die down. A termite mound rose not far from where she was sitting. "I could fill the crack with clay," Nhamo suggested.

It's worth a try, said Mother.

"Of course, it would be better if I could *bake* the boat like a pot."

Don't you burn my mukwa *wood,* Crocodile Guts cried. He stood in front of the craft to protect it.

Nhamo chipped off a portion of the termite nest with Uncle Kufa's knife, while watching carefully for the mambas that inhabited such places. She crushed the clay between two rocks and made a thick paste with water to smear over the outside of the boat. She would have to wait for the seal to dry.

"Go away!" she screamed, hurling a stone at a baboon. He had almost reached the food stores. She rained missiles at him as he scampered clumsily into a tree. He clambered to the top branches and hooted at her with a grimace of fear.

"I don't like you either!" yelled Nhamo. She noticed that the baboon's tail ended in a lumpy scab: Something had recently chopped it in two. His left hind paw was twisted to one side like Tazviona's foot. It looked like a birth defect, not an injury, so it could have been caused by a witch.

Did baboons even have witches?

The longer Nhamo studied the miserable creature, the more certain she was that he was the only member of his troop on the island. He was too nervous to have companions. By now she should have heard the barks of the other animals.

He must have been chased by something extremely frightening to make him cross the water. She wondered what it was. Now he was trapped. Unless he worked up the courage to return, he would starve.

"It's not my problem," Nhamo said, turning her back. She applied another coating of termite mud, turned the boat over, and winced when she saw the damage caused by the spur of rock. Outside, the crack was tiny, but farther in it grew as wide as her little finger. She forced clay into the opening.

One baboon wasn't a serious problem, especially such a timid one. He wouldn't forage at night. The crocodile might be out after dark, but it wouldn't be interested in her food stores. "Although I'm sure it would be delighted with *me*," Nhamo said bitterly.

She built a large half-circle of fire in front of a rocky bluff. The crocodile wouldn't attempt to crawl over hot coals. The baboon would spend the night cowering in a tree. Feeling reasonably safe, Nhamo settled down inside the half-circle of fire with her head on the shrinking mealie bag. She stared up at the stars as she thought of a story to tell Mother, whose jar rested at the base of the cliff with the rest of Nhamo's belongings.

"Once upon a time there was a man with two wives. The senior wife, whose totem was the baboon, gave birth to many daughters. But the junior wife, whose totem was the zebra, gave birth to many sons. Because of this, everyone treated the junior wife with greater kindness and respect. The senior wife was so unhappy, she became thin as a rake.

"In our family," Nhamo remarked to Mother, "Grandmother had only daughters, and no one complained about it." At the thought of *Ambuya*, Nhamo felt such a wave of lonely-sickness sweep over her, she had to swallow hard several times to keep from crying out loud.

"One day," Nhamo said when she had recovered, "a hen belonging to the junior wife wandered into the senior wife's hut and broke three pots. 'Eh! See what your animal has done,' the older woman cried. 'An ordinary chicken wouldn't hunt out my things to break them. A witch must have trained it!'

"'What kind of family do you come from?' retorted the younger woman. 'Your father begged on the roads, and your mother's *roora* was a basket of stale millet! *My roora* was a herd of fine cows.'

"'Be quiet! You bring shame upon us all with your fighting,' the wives were scolded by the oldest woman in the village.

"The two wives went into their huts to sulk, but the next day the older woman sang a loud song as she ground mealies into flour:

> "*Why am I plagued with someone*
> *Whose mother is a witch,*
> *Who scoops up water with the tail of a hyena?*
> Ihe! Ihe! *Her ears are round as dinner plates,*
> *And her skin feels like the bark of a tree!*"

"The junior wife heard the words, as she was meant to do, and became very angry. The next day *she* ground mealie meal and made up a song:

"Ihe! Ihe! *The women in this area have no brains.*
Their lips hang open like cooking pots,
Their hair is grass left over from the dry season.
Their skin feels like burned logs,
And their nostrils yawn like old warthog burrows!"

"Every day one or the other of the wives would make up an insulting song. Everyone in the village was secretly amused by the battle, and only the husband was unaware of what was happening. Finally, the junior wife became so angry she crept into the senior wife's hut and dropped a chunk of baboon meat, the older wife's totem, into her cooking pot.

"That night at dinner the senior wife suddenly began to grow hair. She sprouted a tail, and her nose stretched out long. Barking like a baboon, she ran off into the forest. Everyone was horrified. They suspected what had happened, but no one had any proof.

"The daughters of the senior wife went into the fields to work the next day. They took the youngest girl, who was only a baby, with them. She cried loudly for food, and at once a female baboon burst out of the forest and snatched her up. She breast-fed the baby, laid it on the ground, and ran away.

"After that the daughters took the baby to the baboon-mother every day. Still, they were afraid the creature might run away with the child, so they told their father what had happened. He went to the *nganga* for help. The *nganga* put poison on bananas and left them where the baboon-mother could find them. She vomited up the chunk of baboon meat and turned back into a human at once.

"Now everyone learned about the nasty trick the junior wife had played. The husband sent her back to her parents, and gave all her jewelry to the senior wife."

Nhamo added wood to the ring of fire. In spite of the

precautions she had taken, she was too nervous to sleep. Her father's totem—and therefore hers—was *shumba,* the lion, or so Grandmother believed. "That's what he told me, anyhow," she said. "In my opinion, it should have been the hyena. Don't look like that, Little Pumpkin. I'm sure you aren't related to hyenas."

Nhamo's clan name was Gurundoro, which, Grandmother explained, meant "the people who wear the *ndoro.*" *Ndoro* were round disks worn by kings. Nhamo rather hoped this meant she came from a royal family, but Grandmother said the old kings had dozens of wives, so of course they had a multitude of children. Some of the descendants were fine people, but some inevitably turned out to be lazy parasites. "Like your father," Grandmother added.

Because Nhamo's totem was the lion, she wasn't permitted to eat one. "As if I would try," she said, smiling at Mother's jar. People who ate their totems lost their teeth or went blind or became sterile or occasionally turned into the forbidden animal. It was extremely easy to avoid eating lions, so Nhamo never worried about it.

Grandmother's totem was *moyo,* the heart, which meant she wasn't allowed to eat the heart of any creature. Aunt Chipo, Aunt Shuvai, and Mother's had been *shiri,* the bird, which would have been an enormous problem if it had meant any bird. Fortunately, the ban applied only to the fish eagle, who carried Mwari's messages. Uncle Kufa—and therefore his children—weren't allowed to eat the *gumbo,* or leg of the cow. They could eat any other part of the animal, though. Since cattle were almost never killed, the difficulty rarely came up.

Nhamo listed the totem, *mutupo,* and clan name, *chidao,* of everyone in the village. It was important to remember this information so she wouldn't marry a relative by accident. "Tazviona's *mutupo,* let me see, is—" Nhamo stopped in consternation. Tazviona's totem was the baboon. If Tazviona ate a piece of baboon meat, she would turn into the animal, and because she had a twisted foot—

Nhamo sat up and scanned the dark trees at the top of

the cliff. Don't be foolish. It's only a stupid animal, she thought. But she couldn't ever remember seeing a baboon that deformed. It wouldn't have survived.

"It's not my problem," Nhamo decided, firmly putting the idea out of her head. She lay back down and presently drifted off into the first of many fitful periods of sleep.

22

The lake water softened the clay Nhamo had so carefully applied. She had to paddle furiously after the crack opened again. She managed to grab an overhanging branch when she got close to shore, but the baskets got wet and even the mealie bag was dampened. It was nearly empty, anyhow.

Nhamo scrambled onto the large island and pulled out her stores before they were ruined. She guided the boat along the shore until she was able to drag it up a sandy beach. Then she rested under a *musasa* tree to consider the situation.

"At least I'm not in as much trouble as the baboon," Nhamo said to Mother. She could see him going over her campsite on the little island. He smelled the ground where she had prepared food, and devoured the pumpkin skins ravenously.

Nhamo's new home was able to support a baboon troop, monkeys, and many kinds of antelope. It could support her, too. The problem was what *else* lived on the large island. Something had frightened the baboon over the treacherous rocks.

"Maybe it was a snake," she said hopefully. Baboons went into screaming fits if they saw a snake. Nhamo was capable of going into screaming fits herself, for that matter, but she did have common sense. Snakes left you alone if you didn't upset them. Most of the time they ran from you just as fast as you ran from them.

"I might have to live here until someone visits the island," Nhamo decided. She couldn't possibly attempt a long trip with the boat in its current condition. The thought of the crack suddenly opening out of sight of land made her feel sick. She had seen no one fishing in all the time she was on the lake, but that didn't mean it didn't happen.

"Or I could *make* a boat," she said.

"*Now you're talking*," said Crocodile Guts from his seat by the *njuzu* hut at the bottom of the lake. "*You make a boat out of* mukwa *wood. It's so strong, even the termites won't touch it.*" He scratched his hair, and ghost lice crept over his fingers.

Nhamo shook her head. She was on friendly terms— so far—with the spirit world, but she found its presence frightening. For a moment she actually saw the fisherman as he lounged in his watery kingdom. An *njuzu* girl poured him a pot of beer.

"Thank you. It's good advice," Nhamo said politely as she made sure she was surrounded by real trees and real sunlight. She had a *panga* and Uncle Kufa's broken knife. Surely, with careful work, she could fell a *mukwa* tree and carve it into the shape of Crocodile Guts's boat.

She felt immensely cheered by the plan. All she had to do was survive until the craft was finished. It might take a long time, though. To be on the safe side, she ought to plant her uncooked pumpkin and mealie seeds.

She balanced the baskets in the branches of the *musasa* tree. It wasn't a good storage place, but it would have to do. She needed to find a campsite and shelter before dark.

Nhamo cautiously made her way away from shore. Now and then she stopped to memorize her surroundings. The lake quickly became hidden behind trees, only occasionally appearing when she climbed over a boulder. She picked a large fig tree near the water and an oddly shaped pillar of rock as landmarks.

The farther she got from the lake, the more nervous she

became. The place was *too* quiet. She flicked off a few ticks that had brushed onto her dress-cloth. They were large and hungry, probably left behind by antelope. She could see more of them clinging to the grass, waiting for dinner. She found a game trail that meandered until it met a wide grassland divided by a stream. Beyond rose a sizable cliff, topped by trees. She made out the prints of kudu, waterbuck, and duiker, the splayed mark of guinea fowl, the looping trail of a *burwa* lizard. Nothing dangerous.

The stream, lined with bushes and small trees, rushed along with a lively chuckle. The water was too shallow to hide crocodiles, so Nhamo sat down for a drink. It was clean and surprisingly cool. She washed her face and arms.

When she got closer to the cliff, she saw it was pitted with small caves. Many crevices and cracks, filled with plants, ran down its face. She found much evidence of baboons, although they were absent at the moment. In a clearing between the stream and cliff were two enormous *mutiti,* or lucky-bean, trees growing close together. Heavy branches stretched out almost at right angles to the thick trunks and gave Nhamo the idea of making a platform. Lucky-beans didn't attract animals, because their seeds, although beautiful, were poisonous. The trees would make a fine refuge.

The platform would take days to build, though, and Nhamo needed a place right now.

She set about exploring the cliff. Everywhere was the stink of dassies. They perched on boulders and squealed at her furiously before retreating. Their favorite places were painted with a thick coating of urine. She climbed farther up. She could camp inside one of the caves and watch the grassland for predators.

Predators.

What *had* frightened the baboon to the little island?

Nhamo couldn't hope for the luck she had had on the *njuzu* island, where she had found so much food. This place was too large. One excellent reason for living close to dassies was that they would give a swift warning of anything dangerous in the neighborhood. And provide an alternate meal for whatever was hunting.

Halfway up, Nhamo found a low cave partly filled with a drift of sand. She poked the *panga* around inside to drive out anything that might be lurking. The only thing she dislodged was a large scorpion, which she hurriedly flicked down the cliffside with the knife.

Well pleased, Nhamo returned to the *musasa* tree by the lake. Termites had already found and attacked the baskets. She knocked them off, getting several bites from the soldiers in the process, and hauled her belongings to the cliff. When she had everything stored at the back of the cave, she built a fire, boiled pumpkin, and toasted a few soldier termites she cornered in the baskets. It gave her a melancholy pleasure to eat the creatures that had so recently tried to bite *her*.

Nhamo spent the rest of the day scouting around the area she had chosen for her camp. She found several other small streams—they had been much larger, but the rainy season was already two months past. She noted a number of *mutowa* trees with rough, scaly bark. Their sticky sap could be used to trap birds. She found gourd vines to make more calabashes.

Food plants close to camp had been picked clean by the baboons, but she could forage in the woods as they did. And unlike them, she could fish and trap game.

That afternoon Nhamo cooked the last of her mealie meal. It was damp and would spoil anyhow. She would have to conserve as much of her other stores as possible for the dry season, which was coming. It made her sad to empty the sack. Aunt Shuvai and Aunt Chipo had grown this grain; she and Masvita had ground it. It had been made with the many, many hands of the village, and when it was gone she would have no more food that had been touched by her people.

But the bag had been woven by them. Nhamo stuffed it with dry grass and took it to the cave to use as a pillow. She could wrap her arms around it and bury her nose in its smell.

She gathered a heap of rocks by the cave mouth because she could hear the barks of the baboons in the distance. She backed into the opening and watched the forest on the other side of the grassland.

The baboons straggled out from under the trees in the slanting golden light of late afternoon. In little groups they came, talking and shouting. The young bounced around the adults, ambushing one another, rolling in mock battle, and shrieking for protection when an older animal lost patience and bared its teeth. Little black babies clung to their mothers' stomachs while older, brown ones rode on their mothers' backs. There were so many of them! Nhamo couldn't count that high!

They paused to drink at the stream. They jumped over the water and passed the lucky-bean trees. They found the cook-fire and stopped short. Nhamo held her breath. A large male shouted a challenge. His eyes flashed white and his big fangs yawned. The message was perfectly clear: *Come out, whoever you are, so I can rip you to shreds!*

"Oh, Mother," whispered Nhamo. She had expected the baboons to nest in the far trees. It was clear from the gathering below that they intended to climb the cliff. They would pass right by her cave. Nhamo had a sudden vision of the male baboon discovering her presence and deciding to remove the intruder.

Nhamo wriggled out and stood on the narrow ledge at the mouth of the cave. The troop down below reacted instantly. Several males gave the loud threat call: *Oo-AA-hoo!* Females gathered up babies with cries of alarm. The large male by the cook-fire puffed out his fur until he looked twice as big. *Oo-AA-hoo!*

"Go away!" shrilled Nhamo. She looked frantically for a quick way up the cliff. She hurled the stones she had piled at the mouth of the cave. One caught a male on the face. *Wah!* he barked, jumping back.

The baboons milled around, obviously upset by the strange creature in their sleeping place. They swayed back and forth, eyeing Nhamo. Then, as the sun went down, they suddenly made up their minds and headed for the trees at the edge of the grassland. Their outraged barks floated back on the evening air.

She had won! She had driven off a huge baboon troop. She slid back into the cave and let her pounding heart settle down to its natural rhythm. She felt like vomiting, so great had been her fear, but she had won! "I, Nhamo, have taken this cliff for my own," she said. "*And* the island. This is Nhamo's Island. I am the boss of all baboons."

Later, when she listened to the hoot of an eagle owl, the hiss of a genet, and the *hrrr-hrrr* grunt of a foraging honey badger, she didn't feel quite as confident. The night was full of activity—some harmless, some not. A dassie screamed as it was killed by some unknown predator in the dark.

"I'll get started on the tree house in the morning," she promised. The cave wasn't really comfortable: The ceiling was too low, and she hated the feeling of being trapped. Something kept crawling over her body, flickering its antennae as it puzzled over the addition to its home. Nhamo didn't fall asleep until the first streaks of dawn appeared in the sky.

23

So much work to do! Nhamo had to find food, build a shelter, dig a garden, cut down a tree, and carve it into the shape of Crocodile Guts's boat. The boat and garden would have to wait. Even the shelter was less important than an immediate food supply. She didn't dare use up her stores from the *njuzu* island until she was certain she could replace them.

The rainy season was past and so, therefore, was the largest supply of vegetables. Still, on the stony slopes of hills she found many small *tsenza* bushes. Their roots could be roasted like yams or even eaten raw if she was really hungry. In the marshy ground where the stream met the lake she found dense patches of sedge. The small brown tubers under the soil would be available throughout the dry season.

Wild spinach, *mowa,* was still present although sparse, and several varieties of wild beans had escaped foraging baboons. The beans were dry, but she could soak them. On termite mounds Nhamo discovered *jabvane* bushes with purplish black fruit, and in dense thickets near the water grew brambles with dark, sweet berries.

She found wild loquats and waterberries, monkey oranges, and *marula.* All had been plundered by baboons, but quite a lot of food was left. Nhamo noticed that some trees were hardly touched, and when she tasted the fruit she understood why. The animals had so much to eat they could afford to ignore food that tended to be sour. Later in the dry season they wouldn't be as fussy.

Nhamo collected a basket of the pale yellow *marula*s from the ground and returned to her cook-fire. In the middle of each fruit was a nut that, broken open, produced three edible seeds. Nhamo craved oil, so she ate the seeds right away. Some of the white, pulpy fruit she also devoured, and some she boiled to make a drink for later.

She found a number of large grasshoppers, pulled off the heads to remove the guts, and roasted them on a flat stone over the fire. She tossed them in a basket to knock off the wings and legs.

In the afternoon, Nhamo harvested gourds to turn into calabashes and storage pots. She cut slashes in *mutowa* trees and collected a ball of sticky sap. She hacked off the outer shell of a *mupfuti* tree and began peeling off long strips of the inner bark.

By sundown, Nhamo was exhausted. She lay in the mouth of the cave and wearily chewed and twisted the bark strips into twine. The bark tasted good—like raw beans—and gave her the illusion she was eating as well as working.

The cries of the baboons echoed in the trees across the grassland, but they didn't attempt to approach the cliff. In the middle of the night the unknown creature came out of its hiding place and whisked its long antennae over Nhamo's legs.

Day after day Nhamo toiled. She smeared bushes with the sticky *mutowa* sap and baited it with termites. In the evening she harvested small birds, which she gutted, wrapped in clay, and baked in coals. When the clay cracked, she pulled it off along with the feathers, and devoured the small morsels inside. She installed fish traps in the streams and set twine snares along small game trails. She caught cane rats, squirrels, and hares.

Every day she spent as much time as possible constructing a platform in the lucky-bean branches.

Nhamo cut down small, straight trees. She worked very carefully because she didn't dare damage the *panga*. She hauled the poles up into the lucky-beans with Crocodile

Guts's rope, and experimented with various configurations until she had a floor that was more or less level. She bound the poles together with twine. Next she covered the platform with a thick layer of thatching grass.

It was beautiful! Nhamo lay back on the springy grass with a sigh of satisfaction. No more cold, lumpy sand! No more feeling cramped like a worm in a nut! She began to plan all sorts of refinements: upper platforms to store food, a rope ladder, a barrier of thornbushes, a thatched roof to keep out rain.

Rain? Nhamo stopped in horror. The rainy season was *months* away. She would have to be away long before it began. When the violent storms arrived, the waves on the lake would become extremely dangerous. Nhamo looked up through the dark, fan-shaped leaves at patches of bright sky. As long as she kept busy, she could thrust away thoughts of her real predicament. Now they rushed back.

She was alone on this island. Now and forever. She would slowly grow old, without family or children, until she was too feeble to climb the tree. Her eyes would grow too dim to find water and her fingers too weak to dig for yams. She would starve like the baboon on the little island, unless a predator found her first.

"No! I will build a boat and sail away!" Nhamo cried stoutly. "I am Nhamo Jongwe, whose totem is the lion and whose people are descended from kings. I am a woman, not a little girl. I have Mother and Crocodile Guts for company, and—and—the *njuzu*." The *njuzu* still made her uneasy. For a moment she saw them gliding out of their huts with Aunt Shuvai's beads twined around their long bodies.

She climbed down the notches she had made in the lucky-bean trees, and went back to the boat. She had already ring-barked a thick *mukwa* tree to cut down later. She wandered to the tip of the large island and got a surprise. The water level had dropped during the night!*

Even she could jump from rock to rock to the little island

---

*When the floodgates at Cabora Bassa Dam are opened, the water level drops sharply.

now. The baboon must have escaped, she thought, but when Nhamo shaded her eyes, she could still see him crouched under a tree. He watched her dully. She threw a stone to get his attention, but he didn't react.

"It's not my problem," Nhamo declared, returning to her campsite.

She moved everything to the platform and began working on her ladder.

"Once upon a time there was a wealthy man and wife with only one daughter," Nhamo said as she alternately twisted and chewed the *mupfuti* bark into rope. She had calabashes of water and boiled *marula* juice, a pot of toasted grasshoppers, a basket of *tsenza* roots, and a small grass mat covered with ripe bramble berries. Higgledy-piggledy in the branches were wedged baskets of supplies, and on a corner of the platform, protected on two sides by branches, was Mother's picture, weighted down with stones.

Nhamo had to guard the picture carefully because the paper was tempting to termites. She normally kept it sealed in a jar with a tight-fitting lid, but the afternoon breeze was so pleasant she brought Mother out to enjoy it.

"This man and wife told their daughter not to speak to any young men," she went on. " 'You are too good for the donkeys who live in this village,' they said. 'You must wait until we find someone suitable.'

"The girl obeyed. Many young men tried to court her. They brought her presents and told amusing stories, but her parents wouldn't give her permission to speak. No matter how hard the young men tried, they couldn't make the girl react, and so one by one they gave up and found other wives.

"After a time the girl became discouraged. 'All my friends are married and have children. I think my parents don't want me to get married at all!' But she was a good daughter. Whenever a new suitor showed up, she obeyed her parents and kept her mouth shut."

Nhamo considered the rope she was making. Her first attempts at a really long strand had come apart, but she was getting the hang of it. She paused to wash the taste of bark from her mouth.

"One day, a poor boy from another village heard about the girl. 'Please make me a pot of rice and cowpeas,' he asked his grandmother. 'I'm going to court the girl who won't talk to anyone.'

"Grandmother laughed and said, 'What makes you think you'll succeed when everyone else fails?'

" 'I've got a secret plan,' he replied.

" 'If you want to waste your time, it's fine with me,' said Grandmother. She made him a big pot of rice and cowpeas, and he set off the next morning. He sat down next to a baobab tree near the girl's house and began stripping off the bark.

"After a while the girl came out and saw him making rope from the baobab bark. She walked past him several times, but he never looked up at her. When mealtime came, he ate with one hand while still making rope with the other.

"She went home and told her parents. 'There's a strange boy making rope out of baobab fiber. I walked past him several times, but he wouldn't look up.'

" 'Put on your best clothes and jewelry,' suggested her father. 'Then see what he does.'

"The girl put on her best clothes and jewelry. Her mother combed her hair and oiled her skin. The girl sat on a rock near the baobab tree for hours, but the boy never looked up. When dinnertime came, he ate rice and cowpeas with one hand while making rope with the other.

" 'I knew it!' cried the girl that night. 'You made me wait so long to get married, I've turned into an old woman!'

" 'Hush,' soothed her mother. 'Everyone knows you're the most beautiful girl in the village. Take him some food tomorrow and see what happens.'

"In the morning the girl again dressed in her best clothes. She cooked fine white *sadza* and spicy red relish. She presented it to the boy with a pot of water to wash his hands. To her surprise, he washed only one hand to eat with. He continued to roll fiber into rope with the other.

"When she reported this to her father, he went to the baobab tree and invited the boy to visit his house. 'Thank you, *baba*. I would like to do that, but I'm busy right now,' explained the boy. 'My grandmother's fields are next to a den of baboons, and she is worn out from guarding them. I am making a long rope to drag the fields closer to her hut.'

"The girl's father was amazed that anyone was powerful enough to do that. He hurried home and told his wife to make dinner. He sent his daughter to invite the young man to stay with them.

"'Please come,' she said shyly. It was the first time she had ever spoken to a young man. The boy quickly accepted. Now he spent every night at the rich man's house. During the day he made rope and talked to the girl. They fell in love with each other.

"'I want to marry you, but I'm too poor to pay *roora*,' the boy said.

"'That's all right,' replied the girl. 'Just promise to pull my father's fields closer to his house as soon as you have finished with your grandmother's.' The girl's father was delighted with the offer and married his daughter to the boy at once. They went off to his village and lived there very happily. They soon had many children.

"One day the girl's father came to visit. 'Why haven't you moved my fields yet?' he complained to his son-in-law.

"'Did you really think anyone could pull a field around with a rope?' His daughter laughed. 'That was just a trick we played so we could get married. I couldn't stand another year of not talking! Please come and see your new grandchildren.'

"The girl's father was annoyed at his clever daughter, but he liked his grandchildren, so he forgave her."

Nhamo flexed her hands. They were getting calluses from twisting so much *mupfuti* fiber. She munched a few grasshoppers and followed them with a handful of bramble berries. "I wish I could tie a rope around this island and pull it next to Zimbabwe," she told Mother.

Mother asked when she was going to work on the new boat.

"In a few days," Nhamo replied. "I have to make a garden where the baboons won't find it. I need food for the dry season."

Mother pointed out that the sooner she got started, the sooner she could leave.

"To be honest, I don't know if I can copy Crocodile Guts's boat."

Making a boat is easy, little Disaster, said Crocodile Guts from his bench at the bottom of the lake. *Use* mukwa *wood. It's so strong the termites won't touch it.*

"It's easy for *you*," grumbled Nhamo. "To me it's like carving one of Uncle Kufa's walking sticks." Uncle Kufa made them in the shapes of snakes, animals, and people, and sold them at the trading post. Nhamo had tried to copy him, but wound up splintering the wood instead.

Take little bites. That's what the termites do.

It made sense. Nhamo knew she wasn't going to hollow out the *mukwa* trunk with the *panga*. It was too long and anyhow too vital to her survival. She could chip away with Uncle Kufa's knife. Or even a sharp rock.

But first she had to plant a garden. Nhamo put Mother away in her jar and climbed down the lucky-bean tree. She had a plan, but she had been waiting until it became possible.

24

Nhamo shaded her eyes and looked across to the little island. At the foot of the bluff where she had built a fire lay a dark object. She squinted to be sure. It was the baboon. She sighed unhappily. She hadn't wanted him to die, but she couldn't carry out her plan until he was gone. The little island was an ideal place to plant a garden.

Nhamo hopped from stone to stone, all the while searching for signs of the crocodile. When she reached the final rock, she paused. The last channel was very deep. It was almost too wide for her to cross. A few months before, she would never have attempted it, but now she could swim if she miscalculated—and if the crocodile didn't get her first.

She took a deep breath and leaped. She fell on the sand, scraping both knees, and scrambled to put distance between herself and the treacherous lake. She cautiously approached the dead baboon. He lay on his back with his eyes closed. His twisted foot stuck up reproachfully.

"I'm sorry," whispered Nhamo. A few people ate baboons, she knew, but the practice wasn't common. As precarious as her food supply was, she wasn't even slightly tempted to cook this one. He had been alone like her, and his disability had set him apart from the other animals. She would cast his body into the water for the crocodile to find.

Nhamo poked the baboon with a stick. He sprang up with his fangs bared and his skeletal chest heaving. Nhamo jumped back with a shriek. She threw the stick at him and followed it with every rock she could lay her hands on. The baboon retreated, screaming. He tottered to the base of the bluff and fell over. He lay there churring with terror, his eyes wide open and unfocused.

"You horrible creature!" she yelled. "Why aren't you dead like you're supposed to be?" She squatted on the ground and hugged herself to stop shaking. They sat across from each other, the baboon whimpering and Nhamo trembling. After a while the baboon sighed deeply and relaxed again into the posture of impending death. He looked, Nhamo had to admit, like one of the many cholera victims she had cared for.

"You're only a beast," she said defiantly. The animal's eyes were haunted with fear. He feebly scratched his chest. "*Nyama,* that's all you are. Meat. If I wasn't so fussy, I'd cook you up at once." The baboon turned toward her voice. *Oo-err,* he said, like an infant calling for its mother.

"Oh, stop it!" Nhamo cried. She got up and returned to the beach. The leap back was easier—she had an idea of the range now. She could still see the baboon from the large island. "Don't think I care!" she yelled across the water.

Nhamo walked along the shore until she reached a shallow stream. She followed this to a meadow dotted with *marula* trees. She filled her dress-cloth with ripe fruit and tied it onto her back like a baby-carrying shawl. Then, naked, she returned to the rocks and proceeded to cross. This time she heaved a large stone into the water first. The crocodile was a fearsome, but cautious, beast. She had seen how it fled when it heard a strange noise.

Nhamo dumped some of the *marula*s near the baboon and laid a trail back to the beach. She put another small heap on the first rock, and then one on each of the easier jumps all the way back to the shore. "I'm only doing it so you'll leave my garden alone," she shouted. The baboon didn't react. She went off to harvest the birdlime traps.

That night she listened to the voices of the troop as they

nested in the trees across the savanna. They were more agitated than usual because the moon was full. Like people, baboons were restless at such times. She heard the low, soft, rhythmic grunts of the females and cooing of the infants, the rumble of the males, with now and then a challenging bark. They had trouble sleeping in the intense, white moonlight, as did she. In the village, everyone would spend the night around the cook-fires, exchanging stories. Nhamo shook her head to keep from thinking about the village.

In the morning the *marula*s were all gone and the little island was deserted.

Nhamo was unable to find large patches of soil, but she found many small ones. She cleared out weeds and broke up the ground with a sharpened stick. It was extremely hard work, and a hot wind made her throat ache. Fortunately, the drop in the lake had created a small bay on the far side of the little island. She dragged branches across the narrow inlet. The water could get in, but the crocodile couldn't hide in such a shallow place. She felt safe to draw water for her new garden.

Over the next few days she planted mealies, pumpkins, squash, tomatoes, peanuts, okra, and pieces of yam. The planting season was over, but if the weather didn't turn too cold before the vegetables ripened, she ought to get some results. She named the place Garden Island in honor of her work. Well pleased, Nhamo bathed in the small bay and washed out her dress-cloth. She would have to be careful with it. It would be terrible if it wore out and she had to arrive in Zimbabwe stark naked! She sang:

> "I have worked! I have sweated!
> And now I have a great farm.
> I will eat to my heart's content,
> For I am a soldier of the land,
> And a warrior whose weapon is the hoe.
> Even kings and ngangas respect me,
> Bringer of food and preserver of nations."

"I wish I did have a hoe," Nhamo added, wriggling her toes. Water striders skated away on their X-shaped reflections. Tiny fish darted here and there in the weeds. Old Takawira had been a fine blacksmith, Grandmother said. He had taken red soil and melted it into iron, but that was in the old days. Now people bought such things at the trading post.

"I'll have to make do with a sharp stick," she sighed.

That afternoon Nhamo feasted on a guinea fowl that had become entangled in one of her traps. She had never equaled the feat of eating one a day as she had on the Musengezi. They weren't as common here. Still, she regularly caught francolins and doves, and she was able to snare smaller birds in the lime traps. All in all, she was doing well, but she had yet to get through the dry season.

As the afternoon shadows slanted across the grass, Nhamo got a shock. The hoots and yells of the baboon troop didn't veer off into the trees. Instead, they came straight ahead. Soon she could see little groups of animals moving toward the cliff as they had on that first evening.

"This is *my* home," Nhamo shouted from her platform. She gathered rocks from her hoard and prepared to rain them down. The baboons gave her trees a wide berth, however. "I do *not* give you permission to visit!" she yelled. The animals glanced at her and continued their migration. The big male who had sniffed at her cook-fire that first afternoon approached and bared his frightening teeth.

Oo-AA-hoo! he shouted at the girl cursing him from the branches. *We're going to sleep here whether you like it or not!* Nhamo hurled a stone at him. His fur puffed out until he looked twice as large. His eyes flashed white with rage. Abruptly, he turned and trotted after the others. Last of all came a straggler, all skin and bones, hobbling on a twisted foot. The big baboon shouted at him, and the crippled animal cringed.

"He doesn't like me, either," Nhamo called with grudging sympathy. She wasn't in actual danger as long as the troop kept to the rocks, so she settled down to watch their antics.

The young ones scampered and wrestled. They turned flip-flops and chittered with excitement. The adults walked staidly among them, as elders should, and now and then pulled a tail to maintain order. The grassland between the stream and cliff was thick with them.

Nhamo watched with mixed feelings. They were a threat, but they were also company. The mothers nursing their tiny infants, the females who gathered around to admire, the youngsters leaping over one another all created the bustle of a peaceful village. Even the sullen males were not that different from Uncle Kufa and his friends at the *dare*.

"Uncle Kufa would be furious if I told him that," Nhamo said to Mother. "But it's true. That big one—I think I'll call him Fat Cheeks because his beard swells up when he gets angry. And the miserable creature I rescued from Garden Island will be Rumpy because something chopped his tail off."

Rumpy was pushed around by almost everyone. He cringed and groveled and chattered with terror, but no amount of bad treatment could drive him away. He seemed to have accepted his status as pariah. "The things people do to keep from being lonely," sighed Nhamo.

When she woke up in the night, she could hear the baboons murmuring among themselves on their rocky perches. "I'll put thornbushes around my trees in the morning," Nhamo muttered as she drifted back to sleep.

Nhamo was used to hard work, but she had always depended on others for help. Now she had to do *all* the gardening, *all* the water carrying, *all* the hunting, and still find time to cut down the *mukwa* tree and carve it into the shape of a boat. From the minute the red ball of the sun lifted above the lake to when it sank again in thickening layers of haze, Nhamo hurried from one chore to another.

She finished the rope ladder and barricaded the base of the lucky-bean trees. She built small platforms higher up in the trees. When she was out, she lifted the end of the ladder with a pole and draped it over a convenient branch. She didn't want to find baboons in her home!

Even with the correct raw materials available, Nhamo's basket-making skills were limited. She had to depend on the calabash vines to provide most of her containers. She chopped up old termite mounds and used the clay to make pots, firing them in heaps of coals. Even the ones that broke in the process were useful. She used the shards to roast termites. She spent every morning weeding and watering the garden, and every afternoon chipping away at the *mukwa* trunk. Between times she foraged for food. When she couldn't face chores any longer, she explored—cautiously.

The baboons ranged far and wide on the island. Sometimes they chose to stay in another area, and then the darkness rustled with unfriendly noises. Nhamo huddled on the platform, rocks at hand. Most nights, though, the animals preferred to stay on the cliff, and then she slept easily, soothed by their incessant murmuring.

The baboons filled the days with drama. The troop erupted with shrieks when someone encountered a snake. They churred excitedly when someone discovered a large scorpion—and muttered with disappointment as the lucky finder nipped off the stinger and ate the rest of the creature! Some things—vultures, for example—made them rub their faces and watch the sky uneasily. And some things they ignored, like Nhamo, most of the time.

Other animals, too, lived in the area around the cliff. Dassies snarled at anything that attempted to invade their rocky hideouts. Their fat bodies shivered with rage and their shrill cries pierced the air. Impalas grazed around the baboons as though they were bushes. Vervet monkeys cavorted as much as their larger cousins, and the babies of both species occasionally joined in play.

The main business of the male baboons, as far as Nhamo could tell, was to shove one another around. A stronger one would stare fixedly at some inferior, slap the ground, and fluff out his fur. Then he would stand up and slowly approach. The other baboon would quickly give up his seat. The first animal sat down in his rival's place with what appeared to be great satisfaction. Fat Cheeks was the most successful at this game and, predictably, Rumpy was the one who always got moved on.

Not all baboon activities had to do with threats, though. Babies, especially the tiny black infants, brought out the best in everyone. Even Fat Cheeks was reduced to lip-smacking foolishness when he attempted to entertain one. He lay on the grass and let the baby crawl over him, yank his beard, and put a foot in his eye without the slightest protest.

The least attractive, where infants were concerned, was Rumpy. When he felt threatened, he snatched up one of the tiny creatures and held it in front of him for protection. Sometimes it worked and sometimes, if the baby was old enough to protest, it only got him more soundly beaten.

Every morning and every afternoon, the animals busily groomed one another's fur. This was their greatest pleasure. The one being groomed lay down, eyes closed in ecstasy, as another searched for dirt and ticks. He or she would present an arm or leg if the other baboon's attention wavered. Everyone took part in this activity—except Rumpy. He had to sit on the edge of the gathering and morosely groom himself.

25

Nhamo tried to build an entire hut on the platform, but she soon found it was beyond her ability. Poles crashed down and calabashes shattered as she struggled to construct walls. She had watched the villagers make houses for years, but somehow, somewhere, she had missed a critical piece of information. There was a way to brace walls even in a tree, but Nhamo couldn't remember how it was done.

After her efforts clattered to the ground for the tenth time, she gave up. She wedged a pole across the branches over her head and leaned reeds against it to make a slanted windbreak. She lashed the reeds down and covered them with bundles of thatching grass, using many overlapping layers tied in place with *mupfuti* twine. It wasn't perfect, but she was too irritated to keep trying. "I'll be out of here before the rainy season starts, anyhow," she told herself.

Nhamo was lacking other important skills as well. How did you *finish* a reed mat, for example? Her attempts unraveled. She knew skins could be cured. It had something to do with soaking in mud and rubbing with ashes, but her rabbit skins smelled vile when she was finished.

The boat was the biggest problem, though. Slowly, painstakingly, Nhamo cut down the *mukwa*. When it finally crashed to the ground, her heart sank. How could she *ever* turn such a giant lump into anything useful? She couldn't even make a walking stick. She sat in Crocodile Guts's leaky craft all afternoon, too dispirited to try anything.

Nhamo crouched by the *mukwa* log scraping, scraping, scraping with a sharpened rock. It was slow work, but she was afraid of using Uncle Kufa's knife too often. *Mopane* flies circled her face, landing to drink moisture from her lips and eyes. She waved them away; they came straight back. The only way to discourage them was to sit directly in the sunlight, and it was too hot for that.

She stopped to watch flecks of light on the lake. Breezes ruffled its surface, and occasionally a tiger fish leaped after a low-flying dragonfly. Otherwise the lake was devoid of interest. Blue and endless, it lay between her and freedom. She never even saw a boat on it.

"If only I could strike it with my skirt like Biri," she sighed. Biri, a famous rain priestess, and her two brothers had founded the eland clan. They came from the north and were light-skinned like the Portuguese. "When they reached the Zambezi, Biri removed her skirt and struck the water. Immediately, it rose up on two sides like hills, leaving a dry path between," Nhamo said aloud to whatever spirits might be listening.

"'You will find your totem on the other side,' Biri instructed her brothers. As they crossed over, the ancestors played mbiras and drums from the depths of the water, and after they had passed, the river came together again.

"I suppose you'd find that frightening," Nhamo told the *njuzu*. "It would be like someone rolling up your house while you were living in it." She stripped away the green, resinous wood, pausing to remove a splinter from her thumb. "The older brother ran ahead. He came upon a dead eland and immediately cut it up into steaks. 'How could you be so foolish?' cried Biri when she saw what he had done. 'That was our totem. Now you will be forever unlucky.' From that time, the descendants of the younger brother were called the Tsunga, the Steadfast Ones, because he had honored the totem."

Nhamo tried to rock the log. It wouldn't budge. She poked her fingers into a gap beneath to get a better grip. A pain shot through her like a knife! She jerked away, and a large black scorpion scuttled out of the hole. It danced sideways, making a hissing noise.

Nhamo threw the scraping rock at it. It squirted venom at her in a fine spray. She grabbed a stick and pounded the creature even as it rose to attack again, banging it until its body was mush with the tail twitching feebly. She sank to the ground, dizzy with shock. "Oh," she moaned. The pain was so terrible, she couldn't think.

Nhamo stared up at the sun stabbing through the gray-green *musasa* leaves. The light dazzled her eyes, and her stomach rolled with nausea. "I can't stay here," she whispered. If she was going to be really sick, she didn't dare remain exposed. A jackal or honey badger could be just as lethal as a lion then. But she couldn't bring herself to move. Instead, she studied her hand until she found the puncture on the back. It was oozing slightly.

Nhamo sucked at the wound and spat out bitter liquid. Painfully, she forced herself to roll over and crawl to the lake. She scooped up water to wash the evil taste out her mouth. And then she collapsed with her face half in the mud. She wanted to lie there forever.

If only Masvita would cover her with a blanket. She could sleep until the pain went away. Someone will look for me if I don't return with the firewood, she thought dimly. But no, she wasn't in the deserted village. Nowhere near it.

At sundown, Nhamo remembered, the larger animals would venture down to the lake. And waiting for them under the surface would be the crocodile.

It didn't much matter whether something discovered her on its way into or out of the water.

She struggled to her feet. Slowly, with many stops to clear her swimming head, Nhamo crept back to the lucky-bean trees. The rope ladder was hooked over a branch. She sank down again and looked at it with despair. It seemed impossible to lift the long stick she kept at the foot of the trees.

Her hand and arm were on fire. And her heart was doing funny things. "Aunt Chipo is going to be furious if I don't start dinner," she murmured. At last, after several tries, she unhooked the ladder, and it flopped down within reach.

Nhamo had only a fleeting memory of how she got up. Once she leaned through the ropes and vomited on the ground. For a long time she seemed to be frozen in one place without moving at all. But eventually she dragged herself over the platform and pulled the ladder up for safety.

Her spirit had done as much as it could. Now it abandoned her and went to the place where the living walk with the dead.

Hhhuuu, she was cold! Her body was wet as though she had stood in the rain. Masvita came toward her with a blanket. "Hurry up," ordered Grandmother. "They won't wait all day!"

"I'll carry your pack," Masvita whispered, wrapping the blanket around Nhamo's shoulders. They walked swiftly through the forest, Grandmother in the lead, until they came to a great, shining expanse of water. There, gathered at the edge, was a troop of twenty young women and twenty young men, and standing on a rock above them was a beautiful woman. Her arms and legs were weighted down with gold bangles.

"That's Princess Senwa, Monomatapa's niece," whispered Masvita. Nhamo's eyes grew round. King Monomatapa lived at the beginning of time, long before even Grandmother was born. The young women and men played drums and mbiras, but they didn't seem joyful. And Princess Senwa's face was drawn with grief. Masvita untied her pack and laid it respectfully at the foot of the rock. It was full of honeycombs.

"Why is she so sad?" Nhamo whispered.

"You'd be sad, too, if your husband had abandoned you for another wife," Grandmother said harshly.

"But she's so beautiful . . . ," began Nhamo.

"As if that mattered. Men are like baboons. If one mango

tastes good, *two* must be better. Or three, or ten. They eat until they have to lie on the ground clutching their stomachs!"

"Didn't Princess Senwa object?"

"Of course she did," *Ambuya* snapped. "Prince Kakono, her husband, said that his men would laugh at him if he listened to her. Afraid of being laughed at! He hunts lions for sport, and he's nervous about a few snickers. What a fool!"

Grandmother fell silent as the princess raised her arms. Her servants began to wail. Nhamo watched with amazement as a herd of cattle was led to a cliff jutting over the water. Warriors urged them on with spears. The cattle rolled their eyes and bellowed, but they had no choice but to go forward until one after the other, they tumbled into the lake. They thrashed wildly and were drawn under by forces Nhamo couldn't see. She sank to her knees with horror.

Next, the warriors threw baskets of food away. One of them grabbed Masvita's basket and hurled it into the deep. Nhamo felt sick. All those delicious honeycombs! The soldiers cast away grass mats, pottery, and beads. Then they seized upon the young men and women.

"No," moaned Nhamo, hugging *Ambuya*'s legs.

The men struggled, the women screamed, but it did them no good. They were all sucked under the water even as they stretched out their arms for help. The warriors, their duty performed, followed the hapless servants to destruction. Princess Senwa looked on with grim satisfaction. She turned to gaze directly at Grandmother. "Tell my husband I await him," she said. Then she descended from the rock and threw herself over the cliff. Her body was so weighted down with gold, it disappeared instantly.

"Let's go back to the village," Nhamo pleaded, clinging to Grandmother's legs.

"Wait," commanded *Ambuya*.

Now another group of people arrived from the forest. A handsome man wearing a crown of feathers rushed to the water's edge and shouted, "Senwa! Senwa!" The others joined him with cries of alarm.

"That's Kakono," said Masvita. The prince climbed the rock and stood watching as his servants mournfully played their drums and mbiras. They were even younger than Princess Senwa's followers. "Kakono can only be waited on by people who have not yet married," Masvita explained. "His magic depends on it."

Nhamo thought he was indeed a magnificent being as he gazed at the lake where his wife had disappeared. "If he hadn't been such a donkey, it would never have happened," grumbled *Ambuya*. "Right now he's wetting his loincloth over what Monomatapa will do to him when he finds out."

Trust Grandmother to take the glamour out of the scene, thought Nhamo.

She heard the lowing of cattle and smelled their earthy breath on the wind. "Not *again*," she murmured.

Prince Kakono raised his arms. A new army of warriors drove a herd of cows over the cliff at spearpoint. They threw all the prince's wealth into the lake, and then they turned to the terrified servants. Masvita rose and began to walk toward them.

"No!" screamed Nhamo. Grandmother held her tightly. "Let me stop her! Please, *Ambuya*!"

Masvita turned and gave Nhamo a sad and tender smile. "It is the custom," she said.

"No! No!" shrieked Nhamo.

Grandmother held her with a grip of iron. Masvita walked to the warriors and they parted to let her pass. The others struggled as they were flung to their deaths, but Nhamo's beautiful cousin approached the water like a queen. She paused on the cliff to let the breeze ruffle her dress-cloth. Then she stepped off and fell like an arrow into the devouring water.

Nhamo wailed uncontrollably as the warriors and Prince Kakono sacrificed themselves, but her cries weren't for them. They *wanted* to die. They wanted to destroy everything to satisfy their stupid pride. The lake had turned blood-red, but it wasn't from the light of a setting sun. It was swollen with death, and it resounded with the boom of drums. The spirits were dancing under the water!

She could see them like the inhabitants of a great city in their finery and gold. The warriors were in their leopard skins and the servants in their bark dresses. Princess Senwa and Prince Kakono danced apart, apparently still not reconciled with each other. And in the center, unmoving, stood Masvita, gazing upward through the blood-red water.

Boom . . . boom . . . boom. The drums pounded. Nhamo flung her head from side to side to get rid of them. *Boom . . .* The movement only made it worse. Her head ached and her heart raced. Her body was soaked in sweat. She blinked at the lucky-bean leaves overhead. Ah! Even her eyelids hurt!

But she wasn't at the lake. Grandmother was still in the village, and Masvita was still alive. Whimpering with relief, Nhamo tried to sit up. She was overcome with muscle spasms. Her body jerked as though it belonged to someone else. Frightened, Nhamo lay as still as she could manage. Was she possessed? Her stomach felt like someone had punched it.

I'm dying, she thought. She had never heard of anyone dying of a scorpion sting, but she had never seen anyone stung by such a big one either. The way it sprayed venom at her!

"I'm not dead—yet," she whispered. She had come close, though. Grandmother had often told the tale of Princess Senwa and Prince Kakono, finishing up with, "And if the prince hadn't been such an ass, everyone could have been perfectly happy."

Remembering *Ambuya*'s acid remark made Nhamo feel slightly safer. It made the world seem solid, not a shifting mist of dreams. She listened to the baboon troop returning to their sleeping cliff. She could interpret all of the sounds by now. There was the squeal of babies who had tackled one another too vigorously. There was the soft grunt of a mother calling her child. There was Rumpy getting kicked off a rock by a bigger male.

The animals appeared almost civilized. They stole from one another, of course, and enjoyed terrorizing one another, but their crimes were minor compared to those of people. Even Fat Cheeks wouldn't march the troop into the lake to satisfy his pride.

26

Nhamo was afraid to climb down the ladder for two days. Her body wouldn't obey her: It jerked when she tried to remain still and went limp when she tried to move. The first day she was so drowsy, she didn't care. Then thirst drove her to pull herself up and hunt for the calabashes of water she had stored. She had laid in a good supply, fortunately, along with dried grasshoppers, fish, and fruit.

She fouled her bedding during the first day. That was unpleasant, but not as unpleasant as falling off the platform from sheer weakness would have been.

On the third morning, Nhamo threw the bedding out and ventured down the swaying rope ladder. She found the baboon troop still lingering by the stream. The water had subsided and would probably disappear by the end of the dry season. The animals no longer screamed when they saw her. They watched her with suspicion, but accepted her as part of the scenery much as they accepted the impalas and vervet monkeys.

She dabbled her feet in the stream. The baboons groomed one another in tranquil groups. Even Rumpy had maneuvered a half-grown female into combing his scruffy fur. It was nice having them around, Nhamo realized. She had come to depend on the cooing sounds, the lip-smacking, the sudden shrieking panics. They were—almost—people.

An older female whom she called Donkeyberry, because of the creature's fondness for the fruit, sat surrounded by a respectful gathering of younger females and babies. The animal most certainly dominated her group—or was it her family? Nhamo didn't know. Donkeyberry got first choice of food, and she was the one who decided when the others would move. She was—almost—like a grandmother.

Except that she had a young child. A mischievous baby, who had just changed from the black fur of the newborn to brown, climbed over the respectable old baboon's head. Nhamo called the baby Chisveru, or Tag, after a game she had played in the village. Tag scampered everywhere. He and the other youngsters held endless running, jumping, and wrestling matches with much shouting and even noises that sounded very much like laughter.

No matter how gloomy Nhamo felt, her spirit lifted when she watched Tag. His favorite game was to climb out to the thinnest branch on a tree, dangle by one skinny arm, and drop to the ground. Sometimes three or four youngsters went up the same tree, and then they followed one another off the branch, trying to land on the one who went before.

Tag fearlessly climbed over Fat Cheeks, ignoring the rumbles a foot in the eye caused. Fat Cheeks hardly ever lost his temper, although occasionally he did and sent Tag shrieking to Donkeyberry's arms. The large male wasn't as gentle with brown babies as he was with the tinier black ones.

"I wonder if you tell each other stories," said Nhamo to the elderly baboon, who was dozing with her paws tucked under her knees. Donkeyberry blinked at Nhamo and went back to her nap. "You certainly *seem* to talk. I wonder if you have relatives in other villages. Did a witch put a curse on Rumpy's foot? What do you do when someone gets sick? Do you have *nganga*s?" But Donkeyberry paid no more attention to Nhamo's questions than she would to a chattering bird.

Nhamo made her way to a stand of thatching grass to fetch more bedding. As usual, she scanned the dirt for prints. She knew that the island ("*My* island," she said to herself) had once been part of the mainland. Before the Zambezi rose, the animals had drifted here and there as they pleased. Now they were trapped. Whatever had scrambled to this higher ground when the lake formed was here forever. By merest chance the most dangerous creatures had been excluded.

Nhamo had found no evidence of lions or hyenas, buffalo or rhinoceroses. Hippos came ashore at night, but only in the marshes. They ignored the garden island and anyhow, to be on the safe side, Nhamo had planted everything out of reach. She had seen no wildebeests or zebras. She knew there were a few jackals, bushpigs, honey badgers, and porcupines. She had seen the gaping holes anteaters carved into the sides of termite mounds, although she hadn't seen the creatures themselves. She had seen many kinds of antelope: waterbuck, duikers, bushbuck, reedbuck, and a few large kudu, whose harsh bark sometimes rang through the forest.

As far as the small animals went, there was a wealth of squirrels, cane rats, and hares, as well as the irritable dassies, the tiny bush babies who squealed as they jumped from tree to tree after dark, and mongooses who slithered into holes as she approached. These were all, as far as Nhamo knew, that inhabited her island.

And of course whatever had chopped off half of Rumpy's tail.

Nhamo found nothing alarming in the dirt around the thatching grass. She quickly got out of breath slicing off new bedding with the *panga*. She rested under a *musasa* tree and idly snaked a long piece of grass into a termite hole. It came up with several angry soldiers attached, and Nhamo expertly twisted off the abdomens and ate them.

"I really ought to water the garden, but I'm too tired," she said. "I suppose it can wait another day. Ow!" One of the termite soldiers had transferred its mandibles from the grass to her finger. "I should check the traps. There's still food in the lucky-bean tree, though." The thought of walking anywhere was unappealing. She had a fit of dizziness whenever she stood up.

Nhamo wearily hoisted the bedding up to the platform. She burned the old grass, rekindling the dead fire with one of her precious matches. I mustn't let it go out again, she thought. She dragged a large green log over the flames. It smoldered and hissed—a thick smoke drifted over her platform—but it would burn slowly. As a bonus, the smoke would drive away mosquitoes.

Nhamo spent the rest of the day idling by the stream. In the afternoon the baboons returned, and she lay on a conveniently flat rock to watch Tag. He had discovered it was more comfortable to land on something softer than the ground. Nhamo held her breath as the baby dashed up a small tree and hurled himself onto the unsuspecting Fat Cheeks.

Wah! shouted Fat Cheeks as Tag bounced off his stomach. The baby ran for all he was worth to Donkeyberry, who gathered him into her arms and turned him over for a quick grooming session. When Tag was sure the large male had fallen asleep again, he repeated the performance. Nhamo was impressed with Fat Cheeks's patience. In spite of the creature's fearsome appearance, he was soft as potting clay where the baby was concerned. Tag was far less confident about jumping on other males, though. Once he blundered into Rumpy, who bared his fangs and sent him into hysterics.

Was Fat Cheeks patient because he was the chief and too dignified to react? Or was he, in fact, Tag's father? And if he was Tag's father, was he *married* to Donkeyberry? Nhamo found it all extremely interesting.

She felt better the next morning, but she got a nasty surprise when she made a tour of the animal traps. Every single one had been broken. She found fragments of bone and hair with the shredded twine. Of course a struggling animal would attract predators—she had been foolish to put off checking the snares. She studied the ground. Jackals had been present, and a honey badger—and a catlike creature as well.

It was too small for a leopard, too large for a wildcat. Nhamo had never been taught hunting, but her restless spirit had seized upon any information she overheard at the men's *dare*. She knew, therefore, that the only animals who could have made the prints were the serval or the caracal. The serval was a spotted animal about the size of a jackal. Uncle Kufa had given two serval skins to the *nganga* in return for headache medicine, and the *nganga* had made himself a ceremonial hat. Servals sometimes raided chicken pens, but generally they avoided people.

The caracal was half again as large—the height of a goat— and was a much bolder creature. Servals lived on mice, but a caracal could bring down an impala.

Nhamo had not heard of caracals attacking people, but their size and strength made it possible. She found droppings clotted with bone and hair. They could have belonged to either animal.

The fish traps were empty, which wasn't surprising. The streams were almost dry. The birdlime had entangled a few *quelea*s and a mouse that had been attracted by their fluttering. The garden on the little island was beginning to wither. The plants were stunted anyhow, with few flowers and less fruit. Nhamo didn't know whether the soil was bad or whether she had simply planted too late. She watered them morosely and returned to the *mukwa* log.

It was as big as ever, with hardly a dent to show for all her scraping.

Nhamo poked around the edge with a stick, but even after she had satisfied herself that no scorpions were lurking, she couldn't bring herself to carve. Instead, she cut down spotted aloe plants to make new traps. They were easier to prepare than *musasa* bark, although the twine they provided wasn't as strong.

As she pounded the long, tough leaves with a club and rolled the fiber into string, she thought about the dry season. The wind off the lake grew hotter every day. Food was going to get scarce soon. "I thought I'd be off this island by now," she grumbled.

Well, if she couldn't leave, she would have to learn to hunt. Nhamo went over the weapons she had observed in the village. The boys were trained to use bows and arrows, slings, clubs, throwing sticks, and spears. Girls, of course, didn't need such skills.

Nhamo examined the branches she had trimmed off the

mukwa tree. When she had found one long and straight enough, she whittled an end with the *panga*. "I wish I had metal for a spear point," she said. She remembered, though, that when Uncle Kufa made training spears for boys, he didn't waste precious iron. He hardened the tips with fire. He held the wood just so over the flame, turning it carefully so it wouldn't char. The results weren't as strong as a proper, man's weapon, but the boys could still bring in small game.

Nhamo gathered up her supplies and went back to the fire. She sharpened and fire-hardened and balanced the *mukwa* spear until it felt good to her hand.

She practiced throwing it at a rabbit skin. It bounced off and clattered to the ground. After many attempts, she decided her arm simply wasn't strong enough. She would have to thrust with the spear, using her weight to add force.

"Now what shall I hunt?" she mused. A kudu? Ah! That would be a prize! Nhamo's mouth watered at the thought, but she knew such a large antelope was beyond her strength. An impala? Nhamo considered her thin arms and lowered her expectations.

She had often observed the dassies as they foraged for grass. They hated sunlight but were too timid to venture out after dark, except during the full moon. This limited them to very short feeding periods at dusk. The rest of the time they crowded into crevices that were easily found by the streaks of dried urine staining the rocks.

Nhamo waited by a little cul-de-sac on the way out of one of these crevices. As the afternoon shadows lengthened, the dassies muttered among themselves and eventually clustered at the entrance to their den. A large male edged forward to check for enemies. Nhamo sat perfectly still.

I'm just another rock, she told the dassie as he suspiciously sniffed the air. He crept out farther; the huddled group inched behind him, *scuttle, scuttle, freeze; scuttle, scuttle, freeze*.

He came down the path by the cul-de-sac. Nhamo lunged. His instinct was to race back, but she stood between him and the others. He leaped into the cul-de-sac. She had already aimed the spear there, guessing that his panic would send him into the nearest gap. She impaled him against the rock. He screamed and gnashed his teeth.

The other dassies fled with shrieks, but Nhamo barely heard them. She was too terrified of being bitten. The dassie flopped wildly, snapping his sharp tusks. She didn't dare let go! With her free hand, she felt around for a stone and smashed him on the head. She struck him repeatedly until he stopped moving. Nhamo sat down and burst into tears.

"I don't like hunting," she sobbed.

You did it very well, said Mother.

"I didn't! It was even w-worse than dropping a r-rock on a guinea fowl."

But you did it. And on your very first try.

"That's true," Nhamo admitted. She wiped her eyes and looked at the dead animal. Its body was sleekly fat. Its meat would make a welcome change from mice and termites. Nhamo willed the trembling in her hands to go away. She got the *panga* and expertly prepared the carcass. Soon she had it roasting over the fire.

It was heavier than two guinea fowl! She could smoke-cure most of it for later, and still have a banquet tonight. Her salt was finished, but she had made a substitute some time ago.

Mutsangidza plants were common on the island. They were bushy herbs with purple, daisylike flowers, growing as high as her knee. Nhamo had soaked and then burned them. She mixed the ashes with water. She poked holes in a calabash and padded it with dry grass to make a sieve, because unfiltered *mutsangidza* ashes were slightly poisonous. The juice that dripped through was collected in a pot and boiled until only a white residue was left. The result didn't taste as good as salt, but it was better than nothing, and the same residue could be used to tenderize tough leaves or meat.

Nhamo felt elated as she feasted on the roasted dassie. She sang:

> *"I had mambas for breakfast*
> *To put me in a bad mood.*

Now I am ready for anything.
Run, dassies, hide in your holes!
I crunch up bones like a mother hyena
And hit flies on the wing with my spear."

She would make more weapons. She would make spears, throwing sticks, a bow and arrows, a sling. She would be chief of the island (*my* island, Nhamo thought happily as she licked the grease from her fingers).

And, she thought later as she snuggled up to the grass-stuffed grain sack, I've solved the mystery of Rumpy's tail. A caracal is exactly the kind of creature that would try to catch a skinny baboon.

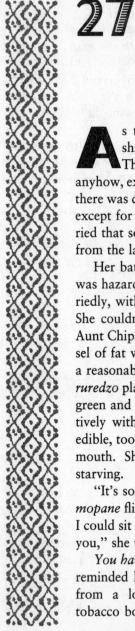

27

As the dry season progressed, the grass shriveled and many trees lost their leaves. The lake, which was receding gradually anyhow, experienced another sudden drop. Now there was dry land all the way to the little island, except for the final, deep channel. Nhamo worried that something might be tempted to invade from the large island.

Her bathing pool dried up. Collecting water was hazardous again, and she had to wash hurriedly, with one eye watching for the crocodile. She couldn't make soap with ashes and fat as Aunt Chipo had done in the village—every morsel of fat went down her throat—but she made a reasonable substitute from the boiled roots of *ruredzo* plants. The vines grew everywhere, their green and silver-white leaves contrasting attractively with rose-pink flowers. The leaves were edible, too, but they left a slimy feel in Nhamo's mouth. She didn't eat them unless she was starving.

"It's so *hot*," Nhamo sighed, brushing away *mopane* flies as she worked on the boat. "I wish I could sit at the bottom of a nice, cool lake like you," she told Crocodile Guts.

You have to be dead to do it, Crocodile Guts reminded her. He was puffing on a pipe made from a long-stemmed calabash with a clay tobacco bowl inserted in the round bulb of the plant. It was so much like Grandmother's pipe, Nhamo suddenly felt her throat constrict.

"How do you keep a fire lit underwater?" she asked to keep the lonely-sickness away.

Anything's possible in the country of the njuzu, the boatman said enigmatically.

"Don't you get homesick?"

I won't be here forever, little Disaster.

"What do you mean?" cried Nhamo.

You know the custom. My brothers have already divided up my things. If Anna was still alive, one of them would have been forced to marry her. I'd have liked to see that argument! Crocodile Guts laughed so hard he almost fell off his stool.

Nhamo nodded. She remembered the boatman's wife screaming insults at her husband.

She was a good person. Just a little noisy, Crocodile Guts said. *Everyone was annoyed when they found the boat missing, by the way.*

"How do you know all this?" asked Nhamo.

The njuzu *told me.*

Of course, thought Nhamo. Snakes went everywhere. She saw them rustling through the leaves, watching the affairs of the village from their dark lairs.

Anyhow, my family's going to have the coming-home ceremony at the end of the dry season. They've sent out all the invitations.

"And then?" said Nhamo.

And then I go home.

"But . . . what about me?"

You'll be on your way by then.

"What if I'm not?" Nhamo wailed. "You can't leave me!"

You'll have to work faster, little Disaster. You haven't been paying attention. The njuzu *can give you plenty of advice, but you have to pay attention.* Crocodile Guts knocked the ashes out of his pipe and packed it again with tobacco. An *njuzu* girl picked up a live coal from her cook-fire and carried it to him in her delicate fingers.

The underwater scene rippled and vanished. Nhamo was

alone next to the *mukwa* log. She hurled the scraping stone as hard as she could against a rock.

"How can he go off and leave me! Selfish man! He's living like a king at the bottom of the lake. He doesn't care what happens to *me*. All he has to do is let his pipe go out, and one of those creepy snake-girls lights it again!"

The image of the *njuzu* lifting the coal came to her mind. What a strange thing to do. What was it about that coal? Nhamo saw it glowing in her mind as she gazed at the *mukwa* log.

Of course!

Why was she spending so much time chipping away at the wretched boat when she could *burn* a hole into it?

"You're right. I haven't been paying attention," she apologized to Crocodile Guts. "I'm sorry I lost my temper. I'm an ungrateful child and I'm lucky you speak to me at all. I don't really think you're creepy, *Va-njuzu*," she added. "You just take a little getting used to."

That afternoon, Nhamo sacrificed her best calabash to the water spirits. She had decorated it with black-and-red designs from crushed berries. She filled it with lucky beans to make up for the lack of proper beads, and hurled it far into the lake. She poured *marula* juice into the water for Crocodile Guts because she didn't have any beer.

In spite of her new weapons, Nhamo's food supply grew smaller as the dry season struck with full force. Plants she could count on earlier were ravaged by baboons. Her traps were destroyed by jackals, honey badgers, and the caracal—she was certain of its identity now. Not only had she heard it meowing in the dark, but she also saw it make an absolutely stunning leap early one morning. It had spotted a dassie on the cliff. With breathtaking accuracy it sprang straight into the air—twice the height of a person—and plucked the hapless creature off its perch. After that, Nhamo reinforced the thorn-bush barrier around her trees and added a coat of birdlime to the bark.

She still managed to bring down the occasional hare or dassie, but she had to spend a long time hunting them. It took time away from her work on the boat. It was taking shape more rapidly now that she used burning coals to hollow it out.

One day, as Nhamo watched the baboon troop pass beneath her platform, she realized that they had many more sources of food than she. She had only explored a fraction of the island. Surrounded by an ever vigilant crowd of baboons, she could hardly be safer finding new hunting grounds.

Nhamo climbed down the ladder, hooked it out of harm's way, and, greeted by only one or two outraged *oo-AA-hoo*s, trailed after the creatures. At first the animals moved rapidly—they obviously had a goal in mind. She kept her distance. After a while, the baboons fanned out and began digging earnestly in the soil. They hauled up thick, juicy grass roots, knocked them against their arms to dislodge dirt, and proceeded to feed. The babies clustered around to snatch unguarded morsels. Nhamo dug, too, using a sharpened stick. She stored the roots in a carrying basket.

The animals turned over logs, ripped off bark, plunged their paws down holes (and sometimes withdrew them hurriedly), and picked over cassia trees for pods. Nhamo copied everything, with the exception of sticking her hand down holes. She wasn't *that* desperate yet. The baboons devoured beetles, grubs, maggots, grasshoppers, mice, and even scorpions. Nhamo shuddered when they nipped off the stingers. One of them uncovered a snake and sent the whole troop into a screaming panic. Nhamo went up the nearest tree, scratching herself badly.

"Stupid animals," she muttered, climbing down. Still, it was pleasant foraging with company. The baboons appeared to accept her presence. They allowed her to sit almost within arm's reach.

She collected grasshoppers and grubs, cassia pods, the black fruit of the buffalo thorn, donkeyberries, and sowthistle leaves. In the heat of the day, the troop rested in the shade of a *musasa* grove. The remains of a stream meandered through the rocks, and here and there were small pools of water at which the baboons—and Nhamo—could refresh themselves.

"This was an excellent idea," Nhamo told Mother. "I have enough food for several days, so I can stay by the boat for a while. The work is going quickly now that I'm using hot coals."

All at once she felt a tickling sensation on her back. She had tied rabbit skins around her hips to save the precious cloth for her eventual arrival in Zimbabwe, so everything from her waist up was bare. Nhamo felt horribly vulnerable. Something was inching its way across her skin.

Nhamo didn't scream. She didn't jump. Months in the wild had taught her the wisdom of sitting perfectly still until she found out what was happening. None of the animals were reacting, so the danger had to be small. *It's probably a scorpion*, she thought bitterly. *The baboons are probably* envious *of my good luck.*

Flicker, flicker. She felt a pinch, the scrape of a tiny nail. Very slowly, she turned her head. Her heart was pounding.

It was Tag. He looked up briefly and went back to his examination of her skin. He was *grooming* her!

Nhamo's emotions underwent a rapid change. She was relieved of course, and then pleased that the tiny creature had trusted her. And then—and then—she began to shiver. From some unknown depth, sobs rolled out of her. Tag jumped back, his mouth open in alarm. Nhamo wept until she thought she was wrung dry. All those nights she lay on the platform hugging the grain bag came back to her. What she wanted, what she desperately needed, was *touch*. Now she understood the hours the baboons spent combing one another's fur. Now she knew why they wore such blissful expressions and why Rumpy would put up with any mistreatment in order to lure someone into grooming his hide.

Donkeyberry and the other animals seemed to recognize her agony. They didn't move nearer, but neither did they flee. They watched her nervously. Tag was clinging to his mother's stomach. This wasn't the reaction he'd expected to get for being friendly.

"I'm sorry, Tag," Nhamo said, hugging herself tightly. "I like you. I really do." She made lip-smacking noises, aware of how ridiculous she must appear. I'm just like Fat Cheeks, she thought. Well, it didn't matter. No one was going to laugh at her here.

After a while, Tag untangled himself and began a wrestling game with another baby. The troop went back to dozing. Nhamo felt weak with emotion. It's probably my period coming. I seem to cry more easily then, she thought. In the afternoon she harvested wild cotton plants to use in her pads.

It made sense to work on the boat—but Tag's offer of friendship had made a deep impression on Nhamo. He was really like a naughty little boy. Perhaps Aunt Shuvai's baby was toddling by now, getting into mischief, making Masvita laugh. Nhamo didn't need to forage for a few days, but she found herself following the troop anyhow the next morning. At midday she rested with them, tensely waiting to see if the baby would approach her again.

He did. He picked through the rabbit skins, explored Nhamo's back, and then scrambled onto her head. She held herself tightly to keep from screaming. Tag found her head enormously entertaining. Her fur wasn't at all like anything he was used to. He pulled and prodded, chuckling to himself. Then he bounced off and scampered over to Donkeyberry, who was watching the scene anxiously.

"See, I didn't once try to eat him," said Nhamo. She felt her head ruefully. Tag was anything but gentle.

She grunted softly, the way the baboons did when they wanted to be friendly. Donkeyberry yawned. Nhamo had learned this meant the old creature was uneasy. "I don't blame you," Nhamo told her. "I can imagine Masvita's reaction if Aunt Shuvai's baby tried to pull out *your* hair."

Every day the troop traveled farther. Nhamo discovered hills and valleys she never knew existed. She passed an enormous fallen log that swarmed with bees, but she didn't dare try to get the honey. Only men did that, and sometimes they got more than they bargained for.

She found a shallow pool filled with water lilies: The bulbs would make acceptable food when other things ran out. She found a chocolate-berry tree loaded with juicy black fruit. The taste was pleasant enough, but the smell was disgusting. Masvita often said chocolate berries reminded her of bedbugs. Nhamo knew it was foolish to ignore any source of food, though, so she held her nose and ate.

The baboons, she discovered, were not above eating baby birds and mice. Fat Cheeks even killed a hare and snarled at anyone who tried to get a share. She wondered if he had been one of the culprits who had destroyed her traps.

One afternoon the troop didn't return to the sleeping cliff at all. Nhamo realized with horror that they intended to spend the night in the trees. It was too late for her to return alone. She climbed a tree with the rest and sat there miserably all night, with her legs aching and her body chilled. She jumped every time she heard a noise. In the morning she returned to her platform alone and spent the day in bed with her arms around the grain sack.

You really have to stop following baboons around and work on the boat, said Mother as Nhamo buried her nose in the comforting bag.

"I know," Nhamo sighed. "It's just . . . it's so *nice* to have company."

They're animals. You belong with people.

"I know."

You don't have much time, little Disaster, said Crocodile Guts. *When the rains start, you're going to have elephant-sized waves on that lake.*

Nhamo covered her head with the dress-cloth.

You can't play "let's pretend" now. This isn't the deserted village, Mother insisted.

Nhamo saw Crocodile Guts packing a string bag: He put in a pipe, fishing lines, and a reed flute she remembered him playing as he waited for fish to blunder into his net. The *njuzu* girls rose to the surface of the water and looked expectantly to the east, from where the storm clouds would come.

28

Nhamo grudgingly went back to work on the boat. Now and then she doused the coals and carved away the blackened bits with Uncle Kufa's knife. The *mukwa* tree was beginning to look like a real boat, or at least like a log with a very large hole in it. Nhamo labored for several days, but one morning the lonely-sickness struck her with such force, her spirit felt like it was being circled by hyenas. "It wouldn't hurt to gather supplies," she explained to Mother, to keep from being scolded. She armed herself with the *panga* and spear, and set off after the troop.

This time they went up a hill near the other end of the island. The territory was new, and Nhamo realized she would have to stay with the baboons because she wasn't sure of the way back. The animals located a rich stand of wild grapes in a dell partway up the hill. They fell on them ravenously. They didn't seem at ease, though, and she wondered why they had left such a good supply of food untouched before.

Fat Cheeks and the other large males kept looking around. Rumpy dropped his fruit when-ever anyone made a sudden movement. Nhamo found their nervousness contagious.

During the noontime rest, everyone sat much closer together than usual. Tag tried to pull off the bag Nhamo wore around her neck, and she had to push him away. He hurled himself to the ground. *Ik-ik-ik-ik,* he scolded, thrashing around in the dirt. He looked just like a toddler having a temper tantrum. Nhamo refused to look at him, and after a moment Tag scuttled off to play with someone else.

Rumpy went from female to female, trying to get himself groomed. He smacked his lips seductively, but it did him no good. One and all, the females turned their backs. "Some days are like that," remarked Nhamo.

She immediately regretted speaking aloud. Rumpy noticed her and halted in his tracks. He was trying to put a thought together in his mind, and she had an awful suspicion what it was: *This strange animal has been following us for days. Tag likes it. Tag grooms it, so it must be available to groom someone else.*

"Oh, no!" cried Nhamo as the scruffy baboon shuffled toward her, smacking his lips. She turned her back. Rumpy trotted in front of her again. *Oo-er,* he coaxed. "No!" shouted Nhamo. The other baboons flinched, but Rumpy wasn't discouraged. Everyone shouted at him. He was used to it. "Go away!" Nhamo yelled.

Rumpy fluffed out his fur. *I am a male and it is the duty of all females to obey me,* he seemed to say. Nhamo jumped up and grabbed a rock. The baboon instantly understood. *Oo-AA-hoo,* he barked angrily.

Fat Cheeks, who was lounging nearby, rose to his feet and roared a counter threat: *I am the chief here! No one else is allowed to push people around!* Suddenly, all the baboons were aroused. Their nervousness flared into rage. The males screamed at one another, tore off branches, and slapped the ground. The females gathered up their shrieking young. The whole dell erupted with wild cries.

Nhamo realized she was in danger. She dashed farther up the hill to put distance between her and the excited animals. Soon she couldn't see them, although she could hear their cries. "I'll stay away until they stop fighting," she decided.

The shouts were already dying down, but she didn't go back yet. She climbed higher. She had spotted an unusual tree* at the top of the hill. It had hand-shaped leaves and purple berries like the ones found on bramble vines. All around, the rocks were stained with purple splotches. The birds clearly fed on the tree, but that didn't mean the fruit was safe. Birds sometimes ate things that poisoned people. On the other hand, most of the things they ate were perfectly good. Nhamo cautiously tasted a berry: It was delicious.

She stored some in her carrying basket. She would try the new fruit on Rumpy before she ate any more. If he got a bellyache, it was no great loss.

She explored farther and found more of the unusual trees. All around was the silent forest, and she heard no birds. Vervet monkeys slipped through the branches like shadows sliding among the leaves. It was strange that they didn't make any noise.

At the very top of the hill, Nhamo found a crack in the rock. She followed it around a corner to where it widened to reveal a cave. Sand, which seemed too cool for the hot afternoon, surrounded the entrance. She dug her toes into it.

The mouth of the cave wasn't large. She knelt down to get a better look. And in the shadows where the sand disappeared into darkness, she saw a heap of skulls.

They were little skulls, belonging to monkeys. They stared out with empty eyes, and all around the ground was littered with tiny bones.

No wonder the monkeys were silent! This was the lair of the caracal!

Nhamo hurried down the hill and sat as close to Donkeyberry as the old creature permitted. She was relieved when the baboons made the long trek back to the sleeping cliff, rather than spending the night in the trees. They seemed as anxious to get away from the cave as she was.

Rumpy pounced on the new fruit. He relished every berry and showed no ill effects. But Nhamo was frightened to go

---

*A mulberry tree. Mulberries were introduced by the Portuguese.

back to the hill by herself. Nor did the baboons return to gather more grapes. One visit was enough for their nerves.

They soon learned to tear Nhamo's traps apart. First one, then another discovered the secret, until she couldn't get to the snares fast enough to salvage any food. The baboons learned about the birdlime, too, and all she found now were a few forlorn feathers. Her garden, never healthy, turned yellow in the heat. She was reduced to eating the pumpkin leaves when every one of the new vegetables was devoured by beetles. Here and there she managed to salvage a tomato, a handful of okra, a stunted yam. It wasn't enough.

She made a bow and arrows, but hardly ever hit her targets. She spent hours lurking by the dassie dens only to have them scale an almost vertical rock to escape. The dassies knew she was their enemy. They evaporated almost before she could see them.

As the food supplies disappeared, Nhamo felt a strange nervousness descend on the island. The baboons muttered more at night. The antelope were more wary, the birds readier to take flight. Nothing, she had to admit, had gone right since the day she looked into that bone-filled cave.

Most distressing, Rumpy had decided she was another member of the troop—a less important member. He began to play the kick-someone-off-a-rock game with her. He stared at her aggressively, slapped the ground, and swaggered over with his fur puffed out. Nhamo hurriedly moved away. With great satisfaction, Rumpy sat down in the place she had vacated. This was the first time he'd been able to bully anyone. He loved it!

He followed her around, demanding that she share her food. She retreated to the platform to eat. He sat below, watching intently. "I ought to throw this spear at you," she yelled at him. "I ought to chase you with a *panga*!" But actually, she was afraid. Rumpy might be a miserable speci-men compared to the other males, but he was still a large animal with lethal-looking fangs. She didn't know how far she could push him.

Nhamo foraged by herself these days, and she scurried

back to her trees before the troop returned. Rumpy made her too nervous to enjoy sitting with the baboons anymore. Hunting for food took most of her time now. She peeled the roots of wild geraniums and baked them in hot coals. They were so tough, it was like gnawing on a tree. She cooked their bitter leaves as a vegetable. She boiled cassia pods to make a thin, unsatisfying soup, and roasted spongy, tasteless water-lily bulbs.

All this filled her stomach, but it wasn't nourishing. Nhamo began to get dizzy when she stood up. She had to rest frequently on her foraging expeditions, and she realized that she was slowly starving. The sky remained a hot, dry blue with not a single cloud in it.

Nhamo sat by the *mukwa* log, too dispirited to work. It was hollowed out well enough, but the exterior still looked like a lumpy tree. Crocodile Guts's boat had been shaped to move smoothly in the water. The sides were braced to keep from warping. Altogether, his craft was a work of great skill, and Nhamo despaired of equaling it. She couldn't even roll the log over, much less drag it to the water—which receded farther from the work site every day.

Besides, she was bone-tired. The smoke from the fire she used to make coals made her head swim. She rested her cheek on the log and closed her eyes out of sheer exhaustion. Gradually, she became aware that things were awfully quiet. Not even the go-away birds* called in the heat. The air was breathless and still. The forest had that eerie quality she had noticed near the caracal's cave. Nhamo sat up quickly, in spite of her fatigue.

For two nights the baboons had chosen to nest in another part of the island. She listened for their distant shouts: There was nothing. Nhamo picked up the *panga*. I'll get some water quickly and go back to the platform, she thought. Watching the harsh shadows under the trees, she edged toward the lake.

---

*go-away bird: Looks like a cockatoo. It has a loud alarm cry that has spoiled many a hunter's chances.

If anything, the bright light stabbing through the leaves made things more confusing. She stopped several times when she couldn't immediately identify something. She knelt by the reeds and cautiously filled the calabash.

On a rock set back from the water was a large shape. The rock was flat, almost like a platform, and was overhung by a large fig with roots snaking down on either side. Her heart thudding heavily, Nhamo shaded her eyes. The shape began to look familiar. It was . . . a *kudu*.

A kudu didn't lie so quietly on its side unless it was dead.

She could tell it was a male by the huge, spiral horns. Its reddish brown back, marked by pale stripes, lay toward her, and one of the large, cuplike ears was silhouetted against the pale trunk of the fig. Nhamo clapped loudly. The kudu didn't move. If it was alive, it would have sprung to its feet.

It might have starved or died of old age. Or it might have eaten something poisonous. One thing was clear: It wouldn't stay on that rock long if the jackals and vultures discovered it.

Nhamo carefully made her way to the animal, looking around for possible rivals. She saw a trickle of blood glistening on the stone. It was still damp. She halted.

This antelope had just died—and not from starvation. Nhamo raised herself on tiptoe, craning her neck to see what was on the other side of the rock. Whatever had slain the kudu wasn't visible, but it—or they, since it must have been jackals—had to be nearby. No predators would abandon such a rich feast.

Nhamo lifted the *panga* and inched forward. The thought of all that meat made her reckless. She could snatch a morsel away from jackals. They were probably sleeping off their first meal nearby. She could see that the intestines and forelegs had been devoured. The hind legs were untouched.

The neck of the antelope was scored with teeth marks: It had been strangled. Jackals didn't do that. They weren't strong enough. They disemboweled their prey, devouring it while it was still alive.

Strangling was a technique used by caracals—but no caracal could have brought down such a large animal. A kudu stood taller than Nhamo and weighed ten times as much.

Only a lion or a leopard could have done it.

Nhamo was positive her island contained no lions. Their roars were too obvious. That left only leopards. *A leopard,* she thought. *How could I have overlooked it?* But she knew: When she had discovered the caracal's footprints, she had seized on that to explain Rumpy's injury. She had assumed it lived in the cave at the other end of the island. But why would an obviously starving baboon troop avoid a hill covered with wild grapes? Not because of a creature smaller than themselves.

How could I have been so stupid?

Nhamo's spirit threatened to abandon her. She felt like an antelope circled by hyenas. Sometimes an animal simply gave up and let itself be devoured. I am Nhamo Jongwe, a woman, not a little girl, she told herself. My totem is the lion. Lions are stronger than leopards. It wasn't much consolation, but it was enough to keep her spirit from entirely fleeing her. Keep thinking, she ordered her body.

Leopards carried their prey into trees, but the kudu was too large to lift. The big cat had eaten as much as it could manage and had withdrawn to rest. It wouldn't go far. For the moment, though, it was sated and perhaps even asleep.

Nhamo had gone beyond terror to a state that was almost a dream. She couldn't possibly run fast enough. She hadn't a hope of fighting off a leopard with a child's training spear. There was nothing she could do to protect herself, and so she did the only sensible thing left and began to cut off a big, meaty hind leg from the kudu.

It was too heavy for her to lift. She dragged it back to her trees and set about butchering it. She cut off long, thin strips of meat and laid them on her smoking-platform. Methodically, still in a dream, Nhamo built up a fire beneath. The trick was to bathe the meat in smoke without actually roasting it. Smoking preserved meat far longer than cooking did. She roasted some of the kudu, though, for immediate use. The rich food filled her with elation, but she was too shaken by the presence of the leopard to make up a victory poem.

In late afternoon, shouts in the forest told Nhamo the baboon troop was on its way to the cliff. Smoke-curing the meat would take at least two days, and she didn't dare leave it exposed. She would have to do the operation in stages. She hauled the meat into the trees and laid it out. The wind was so hot and dry, it would hasten the process of curing on its own.

The baboons drifted past below, and sniffed as closely as they dared to the fire. Rumpy bared his fangs at the smoking-platform and then looked up at Nhamo, who was watching from her shelter. She had the unpleasant suspicion that he knew exactly where the meat had gone.

29

"Once upon a time a farmer lived in the middle of a forest full of baboons," began Nhamo. It was late at night. Her nerves wouldn't let her sleep, so she decided to tell Mother a story. Nhamo hugged the grass-filled grain bag, and she had Mother's jar nestled next to her face. She knew the leopard wouldn't be a problem until he finished eating the kudu, but he was still out there.

"The farmer could never relax," she went on. "Day after day the baboons looked hungrily at his mealies. But every time they tried to get them, the farmer would pelt them with rocks from his sling.

"Finally, the chief baboon said, 'My brothers, we are never going to get those mealies. That man is much too watchful. He can make mistakes, though. He never guards the goat pen because he doesn't know we can eat meat.'

"'Hoo! Hoo!' cried all the other animals. 'Let's go raid the goat pen!'

"They killed a goat and roasted its meat. 'Do you know what would be really funny?' suggested the chief baboon. 'Let's sew our droppings into the skin and prop it up outside the farmer's hut.'

"'Hoo! Wow! What a great idea!' cried the other animals. They filled the skin with baboon droppings, sewed it up, and propped it against the farmer's door. Then they hid in the bushes to watch.

"Soon the farmer came out. 'Good morning, my fine nanny goat. What are you doing out of your pen?'

"The goat didn't answer.

"'Well, don't stand there blocking the door. Get out of the way,' said the farmer, but the goat didn't answer. The man shouted at the animal and then, when it *still* didn't answer, he lost his temper and kicked it.

"*Maiwee!* The stitches flew apart. The goatskin exploded and sent baboon droppings all over the hut. The farmer was furious. 'Wah! Wah!' cried the baboons, falling all over themselves with laughter.

"'I'll get them back for that,' the man said as he swept and washed out his hut. He dug a deep pit in front of his garden and covered it with branches. Then he lay down on the trail to the forest and pretended to be dead.

"The baboons discovered him. They pushed and prodded him. He didn't move. They sang:

> '*The farmer is dead*, hii!
> *What has killed him*, hii!
> *He died of grief for his goat*, hii!
> *With what can we repay him*, hii!'

"'We'll have to bury him,' said the chief baboon, so they carried the farmer into the forest and dug a grave. It was hard work, and soon the animals got bored.

"'Who cares if the hyenas scatter his bones,' said the chief baboon, wiping his face. 'The good thing is, he's no longer around to throw rocks at us. Let's go raid the mealies.'

"The baboons left the farmer and hurried back down the trail. They raced to the garden, fell into the pit, and were all killed. The farmer lived happily ever after and never had to worry about his plants again."

Nhamo hugged the grain bag and listened to sounds in the night. She heard the usual mutter of the baboons. They couldn't be too worried or they wouldn't talk.

It's going to be more difficult to finish the boat now, Mother said.

"I shouldn't have put it off," moaned Nhamo.

There's always something dangerous in the forest. You'll just have to be more careful.

"I can't work with that creature around!"

You don't have a choice, Mother pointed out.

The waves are as big as elephants during the rainy season, said Crocodile Guts from his soft bed in the *njuzu* village.

Nhamo got up and sat on the edge of her platform. She watched the starlit cliff with its murmuring baboons until dawn.

As she had hoped, the meat dried steadily during the night. It hadn't spoiled. As soon as the baboons were gone, Nhamo built up the curing-fire. Clouds of smoke billowed up through gaps in the platform, adding flavor as well as preserving the meat. Now and then she turned the strips to expose both sides.

"I can't possibly work on the boat until this is finished," she explained to Mother. Then, to keep from feeling guilty, Nhamo devised a method to protect her stores. She took two of the now-useless fish traps, plugged the small ends, and hung them by long ropes from the highest branch of the lucky-bean trees. The branch extended out over the grassland. She could pull the fish traps back by means of a string.

"I can store the meat inside, *Mai*. The birds can't reach it, and the baboons can't jump that high." To be on the safe side, Nhamo built a low fire on the ground below. If Rumpy tried anything, he was going to get a hot foot.

In the middle of the day, Nhamo made a quick trip for water. The stream was dry now, and she had to depend on the lake. She put the *panga* in the sling with the calabashes and kept the spear handy. She half intended to raid the kudu carcass again, but when she got to the shore, the antelope was gone.

All of it.

The leopard must have dragged it into a tree, she thought. The rock looked perfectly clean, though, without a trace of blood. Or perhaps there was blood. Nhamo was too unnerved to check closely.

In the afternoon she packed the fish traps with dried meat and suspended them from the overhanging branch. Well satisfied, she went to the stream to gather a few blackjack leaves for relish. The stream was dry, but a cool dampness still clung to the soil.

Oo-AA-hoo! The sound brought her instantly alert. The baboons were back early—and they had come almost silently. Suddenly, they were all around her in a milling crowd. It wasn't the chaotic, screeching mob she was used to. The animals slipped through the grassland like the vervet monkeys near the leopard cave. Even Tag was impressed with the seriousness of it. He rode on Donkeyberry's back without a single murmur.

Nhamo shivered. The males were unusually irritable. They snapped at one another and threatened the females. Now that the troop was close to the sleeping cliff, the animals spread out and applied themselves to digging in the soil. That in itself was unusual. At the end of the day the baboons preferred social activities: grooming, entertaining infants, lounging in friendly groups. They were clearly ravenous. Something had kept them from feeding.

Rumpy sniffed around the smoking-platform, barking as a coal singed his nose. He spotted Nhamo and trotted up, fur bristling, to demand the meager bunch of blackjack leaves. "Go away!" shouted Nhamo. Rumpy slapped the ground. She snatched up a stone and hurled it accurately at his head.

Rumpy danced back and forth with fury. He didn't cower as he usually did when she hit him. She suddenly realized he was dangerous. She grabbed the spear, which was lying against the thorn barrier, and quickly unhooked the ladder. As it flopped down, she thrust the spear at the angry creature to drive him back. Rumpy sprang forward instead.

He sent Nhamo crashing to the ground as he rushed to grab the ladder. His foot smashed her face into the dirt. By the time she recovered, he was already on the platform, raging through her possessions. His big teeth crunched into calabashes to get at the food inside. But what he really wanted—and could obviously smell—was the meat.

He hopped from branch to branch. He caved in the delicate smaller platforms. He found the fish traps hanging from the rope, but he couldn't reach them. The branch was too slender, and he didn't have the sense to pull them in with the string. Rumpy bounced up and down in the tree in a perfect fit of rage.

Meanwhile, Nhamo had grabbed a burning branch from the fire. She was terrified, but her survival depended on protecting her stores. She swung up the ladder and shoved the flames into Rumpy's face. He flinched back. She clambered around him, trying to drive him out of the tree.

Rumpy was beginning to lose his nerve. Nhamo approached him like a small and utterly reckless honey badger. She screamed insults. She cursed his ancestors. She felt like she wouldn't mind sinking her teeth into his throat.

Wah! shouted Rumpy. He dodged past her. His twisted foot stumbled against Mother's jar, and he fell with a shriek over the edge of the platform. Mother's jar rolled after him before Nhamo could reach it. It smashed open, and the picture, caught in the afternoon breeze from the lake, fluttered off and landed in the cook-fire.

Nhamo almost fell out of the tree in her haste. She ignored the fallen animal as she raced for the picture. The same puff of wind that had blown it away stirred the coals in the fire. They flared up briefly, caught the paper, and burned it to ashes before Nhamo even got close.

She knocked the coals aside with her bare hands, ignoring the searing pain in her fingers. But it was already too late. The picture blew away like the ashes that had been beaten in the mortar so long ago in the village, the day *Vatete* died.

Ambuya . . . , they whispered. *Sister Chipo . . . Masvita . . . beloved Nhamo. Please do not be frightened. I must go now. I know you will follow when you can.* The ashes floated off on the wind, carrying the message.

30

Nhamo lay on the platform. The ruins of her belongings lay around her, but she didn't bother to check them. The sun had passed over the trees once or perhaps twice since she had crawled to her present bed. She had drunk water—Rumpy hadn't been interested in those calabashes. She had eaten nothing. What was the point? She didn't even put her arms around the grain bag. She couldn't bring herself to touch it.

Below, the baboons ransacked the smoking-platform. Nhamo turned on her side and watched a line of ants move up the tree trunk. Perhaps they had found their way to the kudu meat. What difference did it make?

Once she stirred enough to climb out onto a branch to relieve herself. She saw that Rumpy no longer lay on the ground, so he must have survived.

More time passed. It was dark, then light again. She saw Fat Cheeks with Tag draped over his shoulders, and Donkeyberry searching the remains of the calabashes on the ground. Rumpy appeared. His limp was far worse. He moaned to himself as he struggled along, and the other baboons seized the opportunity to bully him.

The water ran out. Nhamo's tongue stuck to the roof of her mouth. Her body smelled strange—not dirty, exactly, but old, like a musty cave where animals had laired for a long time. Her head ached. It doesn't take long to die of thirst, she thought dully. She didn't think she had the strength to climb down the ladder.

Darkness came, and with it a cooling breeze. The sound in the leaves was like water rushing across the sky. The moon was growing again, and its milky light spilled through gaps in the tree's canopy.

I'm on my way, little Disaster, said Crocodile Guts. He had a string bag hefted over his shoulder. *My relatives have brewed beer and my oldest son has bought a goat to sacrifice at the coming-home ceremony. It'll be good to see them again.*

Nhamo didn't answer.

I suppose Anna will be there. I hope she's forgiven me for dying first. Crocodile Guts scratched his hair thoughtfully. *I would have liked a sacrificial bull, but times have been hard recently. My sons have promised me a bull as soon as they can afford it. I'll probably have to remind them.*

Nhamo watched him stride along the bottom of the lake as easily as a man on a forest trail. Just before he moved out of sight, the boatman turned and called, *The* njuzu *might be lonely for a while. Don't be surprised if they pay you a visit.* And then he was gone.

First Mother, now Crocodile Guts has deserted me, thought Nhamo. She watched the cool moonlight slide along the platform. The baboons stirred on their rocky perches. An eagle owl called as it floated along the upper airs.

Sh sh. Something was moving in the grass below. *Hhhhuh,* came a sigh. Nhamo tried to ignore it. So what if something wanted to kill her? She wanted to die.

The sounds went on, *sh sh.* Of course, she wanted to die on her own terms, not some horrible beast's. Her plan was to stay on the platform until her spirit was driven away by thirst. She had seen people die of cholera. Eventually, they fell into a fevered sleep that deepened until they simply let go. There were worse ways.

Nhamo put her eye to a gap in the platform. Two *njuzu* girls were weaving around the thorn barrier, looking for a way up. They lengthened their supple bodies until they were thin enough to slither between the thorns.

Nhamo felt a chill pass over her. She was too dehydrated to break out in a sweat.

Up they came until they reached the first foot hole Nhamo had carved into the tree trunk, before she made the ladder. Now the *njuzu* did a very strange thing. Instead of sliding around it, which they could easily have done, they searched until they found a fragment of wood. It might have been part of the storage platforms Rumpy had smashed.

One of the snakes carried the wood to the hole in her fangs and the other butted it into place with her head. In a moment the rift was healed. They went on to the next hole, and the next until the trunk was smooth again. Then they came to the ring of birdlime.

Nhamo had put it there to discourage the caracal. She watched to see how the *njuzu* would handle the problem. They slithered down the tree and gathered up dry grass. Back and forth they went, gluing the grass to the birdlime until it was covered up. When they were finished, they glided over it as smoothly as if they were rustling across a rock.

Nhamo had to admire their cleverness, but she realized she was about to have *njuzu* in her bed. She wanted to die, but she did *not* want snakes crawling all over her first! She crept to the other end of the platform. Her body trembled with the effort.

The *njuzu* coiled over the edge with their eyes glittering in the moonlight. One of them found a calabash Nhamo was certain was empty and dived her head inside. Water droplets twinkled as she rose again. Her mouth brimmed with water.

"No!" cried Nhamo, clinging to the trunk. "Go away!"

One snake twined around the girl's body, *ssuh*, and came up by her face. She lightly caught Nhamo's lower lip with her fangs and pulled the girl's mouth open with surprising strength.

"Aaugh!" Nhamo gasped. The other snake bent over her mouth and poured the shining water inside. It was cold, cold! It sank into her body like a frog diving into a lake. At once the *njuzu* shook themselves loose, rippled over the rim of the platform, and disappeared.

Nhamo was shocked to the very depths of her being. She clung to the tree, shivering violently. She had swallowed something offered by the *njuzu*. Did that mean she was condemned to live with them forever? Or did the rule only apply to food? One thing was certain: Her determination to die had completely vanished. Now she passionately wanted to live. She only hoped she wasn't too late to try.

Nhamo's first chore, as soon as darkness lifted, was to get water. She was badly dehydrated. Her skin was loose and her ears buzzed, but she was filled with a kind of strength that had been missing the day before. She dipped the calabash—the one the *njuzu* had used—into the lake and drank repeatedly. She lay under a tree to let the water take effect.

After a while she returned to the lucky-beans and ate some of the dried meat. The whole day was spent drinking and eating. She noticed that the tree trunk was still scarred by foot holes and the birdlime barrier was still intact. Was the *njuzu* visit only a dream?

But that night they were back, filling the holes in the bark again and gluing grass to the barrier. This time they didn't force Nhamo to drink. They murmured to each other as they rustled through the branches. Nhamo couldn't understand what they were saying, but the sound was oddly comforting. She fell into a deep sleep and when she awoke, they were gone.

Nhamo couldn't quite put her finger on it. She was sitting by the *mukwa* log, trying to shape the outside of the boat, when it came to her that something had subtly changed about the forest. The light was different. The sky remained as cloudless as ever, and the heat was even more oppressive than usual. Her body was covered with sweat that wouldn't dry.

Then she realized what had happened: Buds were swelling on the branches of all the dry trees. New leaves were forcing their way out. A subtle green hue hung over the forest. And that meant . . .

The rainy season was on its way.

During the dry season many of the forest trees lost their foliage. But unlike the vines and grass, they didn't wait until the first rains to start growing again. They *knew* somehow that the storms were about to arrive. Nhamo had seen it happen before. In two or three weeks towering clouds with swollen purple bottoms would rise out of the east. Branch-cracking winds and thunder that shook the bowl of the sky would descend on the island, along with torrents of life-giving rain.

She hadn't a hope of finishing the *mukwa* log by then.

Nhamo was appalled. She couldn't possibly cross the lake during the storms. She would have to stay on the island until the next dry season. Alone.

Nhamo stumbled back to the platform and lay in the shade of the lucky-bean canopy with her chest heaving. She wanted to cry—or scream—or throw something hard. So many emotions ran through her, she couldn't decide which one to feel. All she could do was lie there and pant. *Alone.*

The baboons returned full of complaints. Hunger and heat made them irritable. Nhamo watched Rumpy creep from one to another, trying to beg a grass root. They all shouted at him. He was again the scrawny bag of bones she remembered from the little island. Poor Rumpy, she thought. The high point of your life was when you knocked me down.

Nhamo lay back on the grain bag and tried to think. The grinding hunger that tormented the animals would go away when the rainy season arrived. Antelope would have young, and birds would build nests. Perhaps the leopard would return to its cave.

She wouldn't be able to build fires on wet days. She wouldn't be able to work on the boat. And all those months alone . . .

But look on the bright side, she told herself. The island will be full of food. The streams will run again, and the fish traps will become usable. This year she could plant her garden at the right time, although rising lake water might make it difficult to reach the little island.

By evening Nhamo was almost reconciled to the situation.

She munched a strip of dried kudu meat and choked down some of the horrid, tasteless water-lily bulbs as she made plans. She would rebuild her platforms and make a watertight shelter.

The full moon rose as the sun set. It was going to be one of those restless nights with the baboons awake and the dassies foraging.

Rumpy tried to climb the cliff and failed. His foot was swollen. Perhaps he had fallen on it when he tumbled out of the tree. He managed to reach a low shelf, where he ensconced himself in a crack.

The *njuzu* hadn't visited since the two nights after Crocodile Guts left. Nhamo was frankly relieved. She hugged the grain bag and considered telling a story to pass the time until she felt sleepy. Tell who a story? she thought sadly. Rumpy wasn't going to listen. He had cowered from her since she had thrust the burning branch in his face. She could hear him groan even now as he fidgeted under the bright moon. Anyhow, an animal wasn't the audience she wanted. She wanted *people*.

Oh, fine, she thought. If I can't get through one night on my own, what am I going to do in three months?

Cough-cough.

Her mind went blank.

Cough-cough.

That sound. She remembered it from the banana grove outside the village.

Cough-cough.

Silence.

What was it doing? Was it standing under the tree? She remembered the leap the caracal had made to pluck a dassie from a rock. How high could leopards jump?

Cough-cough.

Farther away now, it was moving toward the cliff. Nhamo let her breath out carefully. The baboons were absolutely still. Not a single infant whimpered. The troop might have vanished off the face of the earth. The dassies, who had been twittering to one another, had turned to stone. The whole grassland held its breath.

Then, a scream.

It was a terrible, wailing shriek, so much like a human that Nhamo stuffed her fist into her mouth to keep from crying out. It went on and on in ghastly agony. From her earliest childhood that scream came, with a memory of flowing, spotted skin and rending claws, and later of *Ambuya* tearing out her hair when they brought Mother's bones home from the forest.

And then it stopped.

The grassland waited.

The bright moonlight shone through the leaves, and water-laden air pressed on Nhamo's skin.

After a while a baboon infant whimpered. Its mother grunted softly in response. *Whow-whow* called a nightjar in a breathless voice. One by one the inhabitants of the grassland came alive. They were no longer in any danger. The leopard had selected its prey and they, with heartless ease, returned to their usual activities. The dassies twittered. A ground hornbill uttered its low, panting call.

But something had been subtracted from the chorus of night noises. Rumpy's characteristic moan as he moved his injured foot was no longer present.

31

I can't stay," said Nhamo, looking out over the endless lake beyond the *mukwa* log. She didn't know who she was talking to. The island, perhaps. "If I stay, I'll go mad. Or the leopard will get me." She felt it was only a matter of time. The great cat had marked Rumpy as his prey long ago. Grandmother said that if a lion or a leopard tasted someone's tears, it would never be satisfied until it got the whole person.

She considered dragging the log to the water in its present state. She could sit in the hollow and float along—but it would probably flip over with her inside. Anyhow, she couldn't even budge it. Nhamo contemplated Crocodile Guts's boat. "He said the *njuzu* taught him everything he knew about water. I wish they would do something for me."

Or had they?

Who taught her to swim? And who found her the island with the Portuguese grave? Who told her to hollow out the log with coals? *And who slithered up and down the tree fitting pieces of wood into the holes?*

"I have been such a fool," whispered Nhamo. *After many years even a good boat gets cracks,* Crocodile Guts had said the first time she met his spirit. *I used to plug them with sap from the* mutowa *tree.*

She turned Crocodile Guts's boat over and studied the bottom. The gap was as wide as her little finger on the inside, but it narrowed to a hairline outside. She could whittle a slice of wood to fit it—and pack it securely with *mutowa* sap and wild cotton fiber. It should last long enough to reach shore.

Nhamo worked feverishly all day. She mended every defect she could find, both inside and out. She poked sticky cotton into tiny gaps with a sliver of dassie bone. She held a glowing branch next to the wood to dry the seals. She harvested all her plants from the little island—leaves, seeds, and roots— leaving nothing to replant in the rainy season. Everything depended on this last attempt. She would succeed, or she would join the *njuzu* in their watery kingdom.

The next morning she said good-bye to the baboon troop. Tag scampered after a butterfly he hadn't a hope of catching, and Donkeyberry groomed Fat Cheeks by the dry stream before everyone set out on the daily search for food. There was no sign that any of them missed Rumpy.

Nhamo dragged the boat to the reeds and packed it with her stores. She had one fish trap still full of kudu meat, and a few yams and tomatoes. She was encouraged to see that the interior of the boat stayed dry as she paddled along, but to be absolutely sure, she rowed to the far end of the island and spent the night there.

As the sun rose, she set out again, keeping it at her back. The island fell behind her. It was still visible at sundown, and during the night the current drifted her partway back. The second day she forged on, and by nightfall she saw land again.

The forest went on and on, with here and there an inlet. After following the coast for several hours, Nhamo believed that she had reached the true shore and not another island. The dry-season current was so sluggish she was able to move much more swiftly than she had months before.

She saw plumes of smoke. People were living in the forest, but she never saw them. A natural caution kept her from looking for them. They might be cannibals. Nhamo had been away from humans so long, she felt like a wild animal who might be hunted instead of welcomed.

The days passed as she doggedly paddled along the shore. The air grew heavy with unshed rain, although the clouds still hid in Mwari's country. Sometimes she blundered into a side channel and wasted hours working her way back out. Sometimes she was so frustrated, she sat in the boat and cried. But always, eventually, her spirit rebounded.

Whenever she saw a *mutowa* tree, she went ashore to gather more sap and more wild cotton. She pulled the craft onto sandbanks and poked as much caulking as she could into the cracks. The inside of the boat became unpleasantly sticky. Dirt glued itself to her legs. Now and then thunder rolled from somewhere beyond the horizon. She saw lightning far off in the middle of the night, but no clouds.

At last Nhamo spotted a cluster of huts set back from the water. She studied them anxiously. The heat dried her eyes so much she could hardly make anything out. As she got closer, she observed women squatting on the shore, beating clothes on rocks. A girl with a switch sat guard over a cluster of babies. They were exactly like her own villagers! Nhamo's spirit leaped.

The women shouted and pointed at her. Nhamo struggled to control her fear. What was wrong with her? These were *people*. She had braved the lake to find them.

The women stared with frank amazement as she paddled toward the land. Nhamo realized she must present a strange sight. Her hair hadn't been combed since the day before she was to marry Zororo. She wore a girdle of smelly rabbit skins. She had a spear tied to her back and a *panga* stuck into a makeshift belt. The villagers moved away warily as she came ashore.

"*Masikati.* Greetings," said Nhamo, clapping her hands politely. "Have you spent the day well?"

"We have done so if you have done so," said one of the women. "What—who—are you?"

"I'm Nhamo Jongwe. I'm looking for my father."

"He isn't here," said the woman.

"Is this Zimbabwe?"

"It's that way." The woman gestured to the west. Her expression said, *I wish you were there rather than here.*

"Is it far?"

An old woman who had been sitting in the shade of a tree spoke up. "You weren't thinking of going in that boat, were you?"

"I was, *ambuya*," Nhamo said courteously.

"Let her go, Mother. It's none of our business," said the young woman.

"She's only a waif from the forest, Oppah," snapped the old woman. She turned to Nhamo. "You wouldn't get far, child. The border patrol watches that part of the river like vultures. Anyhow, the Zambezi speeds up where the Luangwa joins the main channel. If the soldiers didn't shoot you, the current would send you straight to the bottom."

Nhamo sat down in dismay. What soldiers? Why would anyone shoot her?

"You could take the road," the old woman continued, "but the border patrol would ask you for identity papers. Do you have any?"

"No."

The old woman nodded. "Then they'd send you straight back."

"Why?" cried Nhamo. "I only want to see my father. What difference does it make to them?"

"They just will. Ask anyone if you don't believe me."

"You're making her cry," said Oppah.

Nhamo couldn't help it. She had battled so long to get to Zimbabwe, one more obstacle was more than she could take. She began to sob. She curled up into a ball on the ground with grief.

"Don't do that!" exclaimed Oppah. "There's more than one path in the forest. Goodness, we sneak into Zimbabwe all the time. We'll tell you which way to go. Now tell me, how long has it been since you ate? You're all skin and bones!"

So the women helped Nhamo sit up, and the girl who had

been watching the babies ran off to fetch food. Soon Nhamo was sitting under the tree with a bowl of cold *sadza* and tomato relish. It reminded her of her own village, and she burst into fresh tears. Little by little, the women wormed her story out of her—or as much of it as Nhamo dared to tell. She left out the part about the *ngozi*. She didn't want people to think she was cursed.

"Imagine! Living with baboons for months! It's no wonder you look—ah, you look—" Oppah stopped in confusion.

"Oh, I wasn't alone," Nhamo said cheerfully. "I had Mother and Crocodile Guts and the *njuzu*, except I never got used to *them*—" She halted. Everyone was staring at her again.

"Please excuse me, but didn't you say your mother was dead?" inquired Oppah.

Nhamo realized she had made a serious mistake. "I *dreamed* of her," she explained. It was all right to dream of spirits. It was how the ancestors preferred to communicate.

"And the *njuzu*?" The friendliness in the gathering had suddenly evaporated.

"I, uh, dreamed of them, too." But Nhamo knew the answer was bad. Normal people didn't talk to water spirits, only *nganga*s did—or witches. The villagers were already suspicious of her weird appearance.

"Well, I think we should help this one on her way," Oppah said briskly. The others agreed, even Oppah's old mother. Nhamo's spirit sank. She had looked forward to a night surrounded by people, but now they wanted to get rid of her. The women gave her a small amount of mealie meal and took her to a road running along the far side of the village.

Nhamo was sorry to lose the boat, but it had begun to leak badly again. If the mouth of the Luangwa River was as bad as everyone said, it wouldn't have survived anyhow. Maybe it will sink out there in the lake and go to the country of the *njuzu*, she thought. They can tell Crocodile Guts where it is.

"Remember: Walk as far as the three baobab trees on the other side of the hill shaped like a waterbuck's ear. Turn right on the path and follow it until you see bright lights. Don't take any other path! The soldiers put land mines along the border during the war, and most of them are still there." With that, Oppah firmly sent Nhamo on her way.

What was a border? Nhamo wondered as she trudged along. She had the grain bag packed with mealie meal, yams, and dried kudu meat, plus a few tightly stoppered calabashes of water. She had the precious dress-cloth, Uncle Kufa's knife, six matches, two clay cooking pots, her weapons, and the bag of gold nuggets around her neck.

Big clouds were piling up in the east. She heard a distant grumble of thunder. Grandmother said if you heard thunder without seeing lightning, it was the voices of the *njuzu* celebrating the approach of rain.

What was the border patrol guarding that was so valuable? They had guns and land mines just to keep children from looking for their fathers. It didn't make sense. Nhamo passed the hill shaped like a waterbuck's ear and found the three baobabs. Beyond them was the path, clearly marked.

The sun was just past noon as she sat by the road to take a drink of water. A strange noise came from the west. It grew louder and louder. It wasn't like the tractor she had seen at the trading post or the airplanes she had occasionally glimpsed, although it came from the sky. Nhamo's nervousness increased as it approached: *Whap! Whap! Whap!*

It was louder than anything she had ever encountered. She dived into the bushes as a large object swooped down the road. She had a glimpse of a whirling tail and a bulbous body full of soldiers. They had guns! They were looking for her!

Nhamo plunged into the forest. She felt thorns tear at the grain bag. Her spear caught between two trees and brought her to a jolting halt before she wrenched it free and kept running. *Whap! Whap! Whap!* The thing curved around and came back. It flew in low over the trees where Nhamo lay spread-eagled in terror. It didn't see her. It went back the way it had come, and soon its noise faded into the normal sounds of the bush.

Hezvo! Nhamo never wanted to meet another one of those! She had to rest before she gained the courage to go on. When she sat up, she realized she wasn't on the path anymore. She was in the middle of the forest and she had no idea where the path was.

She couldn't see the hill shaped like a waterbuck's ear. The trees were too dense, and anyhow it might look like something completely different from this side. The only thing Nhamo was sure of was the direction of Zimbabwe. It lay toward the setting sun.

Sighing, she took stock of her belongings. The thorns had torn a large hole in the grain bag. She rearranged the articles inside to allow for it. The thorns had torn a sizable rip in her, too. A seam of blood ran from her shoulder to her elbow. She hoped it wouldn't become infected.

Nhamo hefted the grain bag to her shoulder and set off again. There was nothing else to do. She would tackle the problem of land mines when she actually reached the border.

The clouds were building rapidly. The thunder was closer, and now she actually saw streaks of lightning. The birds swooped and twittered. Leaves stirred on the trees. Termites boiled out of their nests, and Nhamo paused briefly to have a snack.

Soon she encountered a trail. She didn't know whether it was the correct one, or if it was made by people or animals, but it went in the right direction. She made much better time now.

The clouds gathered overhead. Their bottoms were dark and lumpy, and Nhamo knew a violent storm was imminent.

"I wish I could have stayed in that village," she mourned. Lightning crackled down. "Oh! That was close!" She smelled rain, a cool dusty odor that sent ripples of excitement through her body—but she wished she could find shelter!

Crash! Nhamo flinched. A rushing sound rapidly approached through the trees. The wind suddenly whipped the forest into a frenzy. Beyond the tossing branches she spied a hut, and farther on a wide, open space. It was a dried-up marsh pocked by the footprints of animals. In the eerie green light she saw the trails of buffalo, antelope, and elephant. *Crash!*

The hut was abandoned. Its door was gone and the grass roof looked unreliable, but Nhamo had no choice. The first drops of rain were pattering down. She quickly poked around the dark floor of the hut with a long stick. There didn't seem to be any snakes. She sat against the clay wall as far from the entrance as she could manage and watched the dense sheets of water sweep past.

Maiwee! The wind threatened to tear off the roof. Leaks appeared in several places, but Nhamo's spot stayed dry. She hugged herself against the sudden chill and watched the marsh thirstily drink up the first water of the season.

Crash! A tongue of lightning came down so close it blinded her. The bushes nearby exploded with startled buffalo, who had apparently been sheltering under the wrong tree. One of them bellowed loudly and charged across the marsh with its tail tucked between its legs. It got halfway and then, horrifyingly, the ground heaved up with a tremendous roar, louder than the thunder itself. Nhamo thought for an instant the creature had been struck by another bolt of lightning.

Clods of dirt flew in all directions, some of them raining on the hut. The buffalo was flung into the air. It fell back with its stomach torn in two and one leg completely severed. It flailed briefly and died with its tongue protruding from its mouth.

Grandmother had described land mines, but they were far, far worse than Nhamo had imagined. She had never dreamed such destruction was possible! Now she noticed a collapsed fence running along the edge of the marsh. The wire looped under and over termite-eaten posts on the ground.

"I g-g-guess I f-found the b-border," said Nhamo between clenched teeth.

She watched water pool around the ruined body of the buffalo. She realized she had made her own puddle on the floor of the hut when the land mine went off.

After the fierce front of the storm had passed, the rain lessened in intensity. Then it stopped entirely, and the sun came out. The ground steamed as the marsh dried. It would take several more storms for the ground to soften.

Nhamo broke open a rotted log with the *panga* and used the soft, dry wood inside to start a fire. She boiled the mealie meal. The food made her feel more courageous. "I can't go back. I don't know the way," she said as she shoveled the hot *sadza* into her mouth with her fingers. "I can't stay here, either." She rested against the side of the hut and studied the marsh.

Some animals had certainly crossed the border. She could see their tracks. "I could walk on the prints of an antelope," she said. Except that she didn't know how big land mines were. They might be as small as peanuts, in which case she could easily tread on one that an antelope hoof had missed.

But wait: Four or five elephants had been through when the soil was soft enough to take deep imprints. The brief rain hadn't eroded these. Her foot could easily fit inside one of them. "If an elephant isn't heavy enough to set off a land mine, I certainly won't do it," Nhamo declared.

It was one thing to figure out a solution, though, and another to enter a place where she had just seen a buffalo torn apart. Nhamo packed and repacked her goods. She experimented with different methods of carrying the grain bag. Finally, as the sun approached the line of trees in the west, she couldn't think of any more excuses.

Nhamo found the elephant trail in the forest and hopped from print to print until she reached the marsh. She took a deep breath and retied the bag to her back. "Well, here goes," she whispered. She began the trek across the wasteland. It was easy enough to jump, but impossible to rest. Once or twice she teetered on a print and almost fell over. She passed close to the buffalo. Vultures had found it, and a few silverback jackals nipped at the birds and wriggled through the massed feathers.

She was halfway across. The sun was very low now. Blue shadows streamed across the marsh. Soon the ground would be completely dark except for the glow from the sunset. Nhamo kept hopping. The spear came loose and clattered to the ground. She picked it up gingerly and went on. Closer and closer came the line of trees, and darker and darker grew the wasteland. The sun had set. The silvery light was confusing.

At last she came to the opposite side, and to be extra careful she followed the elephant footprints under the trees until she couldn't make them out anymore. Nhamo sat down to rest. She wasn't safe yet, not one bit, but she was surrounded by familiar dangers. After all her time in the bush, she found them far less unnerving than the land mines. She thought about climbing a tree to wait for dawn, but something caught her eye in the darkness.

It was a light, a brilliant light. It was brighter than a hundred cook-fires. It came from the first house beyond the border of Zimbabwe.

32

Filled with wonder, Nhamo made her way through the forest. There were several lights attached to the roof of a large, square house, and they illuminated a grassland surrounded by a fence. Nhamo tried to look directly at them, but they were too bright. They hurt her eyes.

The grassland was lush with plants, in spite of it being only the beginning of the rainy season. You could keep a whole herd of goats in there, she thought. They would be safe, too. The fence was higher than her head and topped with spiky wire. Not even a lion could jump it.

The inside of the house was lighted, too, and she could see a table. Nhamo's heart sped up. It wasn't just *any* table. It was like the one in Mother's picture, covered with cloth and dishes.

Oh! It was too marvelous to be real! It was *exactly* like the picture! Nhamo saw a woman in a print dress and white apron emerge from a room at the back of the house. She was carrying a tray covered with steaming food. Nhamo followed her progress from window to window until she reached the table.

Other people arrived, with light skins—much paler than Joao. There was a man, a woman, and two children. They sat down, and the first woman piled food on their plates. Even from where Nhamo squatted outside the fence, she could smell the rich aroma of meat. These must be the whitemen Grandmother had told her about. Nhamo thought they were fascinating.

She assumed the man had two wives, one light, one dark. He was certainly rich enough. The dark woman had no children, but perhaps she hadn't been married long. She was obviously the junior wife since she was doing most of the work.

Nhamo looked for a way into the grassland so she could peer more closely into the windows, which were open but covered by a fretwork of iron. She went round and round until she found a spot where the wire was loose at the bottom. With some work, she was able to pry it up. The gap was large enough to wriggle through.

But first she changed from the rabbit skins to the dresscloth. She hadn't forgotten how the women at the village reacted to her. She attempted to comb her hair with her fingers, but it was far too knotted. Then, inspired, she tied around her head one of the red scraps from the cloth in which she was to have married Zororo. It covered most of the knots.

She crawled under the fence and pulled her belongings through. She hung the grain bag from a stray wire halfway up and leaned the spear against it. But she couldn't bring herself to leave the *panga* behind. It had stood between her and destruction too often. She tied it to her waist.

Nhamo saw beds and tall chests with many handles in one of the rooms. In another was an easy chair wide enough to hold four people. She jumped when she saw something move on the wall. It was a person who seemed to be looking out of a shadowed room. When Nhamo raised her hand, so did the person. Nhamo had encountered mirrors in the Portuguese trader's house, but this was not a reflection. It was too tall and bony. Tufts of hair stuck out from under a head rag, and the eyes stared from a face gone skeletal. If Nhamo had met the creature on a forest path, she would have climbed the nearest tree.

There would be time enough later to figure out the picture, Nhamo decided. She crept along the grass on hands and knees, and rose silently to look into the room where the people were eating dinner. They used knives and forks. They spoke softly in an unfamiliar language. Once, when the children made a noise, the father became angry.

Nhamo eagerly tried to identify the food on the table. She recognized margarine and white bread. She saw a bowl of red paste that Grandmother had said was *jam*. One of the children—a boy—stuck his finger into it, and his older sister slapped his hand. The junior wife came in with a bowl of boiled potatoes covered with a gray sauce.

Nhamo's stomach complained at the sight of so much food. She was afraid the sound could be heard through the window. Then the junior wife took the plates away and brought—Nhamo had to think hard to remember the word—*cake*. It was covered with a yellow paste. The father poured himself a drink from a glass bottle.

By now, Nhamo was standing with her nose poked between the window bars. She didn't want to miss a thing. She incautiously took a deep breath to bring the heavenly odors closer—and the sound attracted the attention of the chief wife.

The woman screamed. She jumped up, dumping her cake to the floor. The children scrambled out of their chairs, and the father shouted, "*Voetsek!*" It was one of the few non-Shona words Nhamo understood. It meant "go away," but not the *go away* used for people. The word was meant for animals, and it was a terrible insult.

Nhamo dropped below the window and scuttled away. Her feelings were hurt. She *wasn't* an animal, in spite of living with baboons for so long. But of course the man was angry because she had been spying on them. She would have to approach the house again in the right way and try to apologize.

She hurried to the gap, but before she could reach it, the back door of the house slammed open, and several huge black dogs bounded out! They made straight for her. She scrambled under the fence, abandoning her grain bag and spear. She heard the precious dress-cloth tear and the *panga* rattle against the metal. Her head scarf snagged on a wire and was torn away. Panting, she came up the other side.

Two of the dogs fell upon the grain bag with snarls and flashing teeth. The man came out the back door with a gun. He yelled at the animals and they dropped the meat and proceeded to wriggle under the fence after Nhamo.

She didn't wait to see what happened. She ran for her life with the bullets whizzing over her head. The dogs set up a horrible cry as they galloped on. *Murder! Murder!* they howled.

Nhamo ran this way and that. She didn't know where to hide. She blundered into the forest and out again to a road. *Murder!* the dogs howled as they ran. Nhamo fled past more houses, where other dogs set up a clamor. She stumbled and fell, picked herself up, and dashed on. The lights of the houses stabbed through the trees, making it just possible to tell where she was going—except she didn't know where she was going.

Finally, gasping for air, she climbed a hill and abruptly reached the end of the road. The hillside had collapsed. The road broke off into a deep gorge. She couldn't go any farther. She was trapped.

Nhamo's chest heaved as she struggled to catch her breath. She saw the shadowy bodies of the dogs as they approached. She braced herself at the top of the hill and waited. Suddenly, she was possessed by an intoxicating—and frightening—sense of power.

"Whhhooo's going to be my next meal?" she screamed, brandishing the *panga*. "Whhhooo's going to sweeten my cooking pot?"

The dogs skidded to a halt and stared at her.

"I'm soooo hungry! I want a fat little dog for dinner! Will it be you?"—Nhamo thrust the *panga* at one of the animals—"Or you? Or *you*?" She advanced on the creatures, who backed away with nervous whines. "Too late! You can't make friends now!" snarled Nhamo. "I'll send my locusts to eat the hair off your backs! I'll brew your blood into beer. Whhhooo's going to sweeten my cooking pot?"

The dogs lost their nerve and ran—all except one. He was

the biggest. He launched himself at Nhamo and she met him with the *panga*. It was almost as though she wasn't there. Her arms and legs moved of their own accord. Her spirit sang as she fought, and when she dropped the dog's lifeless body to the ground, she howled with purest ecstasy.

All the dogs in the neighborhood went wild as Nhamo fled back down the road, skirted around the houses, and disappeared into the forest. She didn't know where she was going, only that she had to run, that she didn't belong with people who shouted *voetsek* and shot at her with guns. She plunged deeper and deeper into the bush until the sensation of power left her and she fell to the ground unconscious.

Who did you think gave you the panga, said Long Teats from her perch in the dead tree. Nhamo lay on the hard soil. Tsetse flies zoomed overhead. As the days passed, as she had wandered on, she'd encountered more and more of them.

"The Portuguese spirit," she said weakly.

Ha! He was no match for me with his Catholic spells. Forgive your enemies, indeed! I say kill them all as quickly as possible.

"My ancestors . . . the puff adder . . . ," murmured Nhamo. She was too exhausted to explain fully, but Long Teats understood.

Your ancestors have watched over you, little Disaster, but this time it was I who aided you.

"You're a witch. . . ."

Nonsense! I'm just someone who won't let herself be pushed around. What has goodness done for you? Tossed you from one nasty situation to the next.

"It's wrong to enjoy killing. . . ."

It's wrong to suffer, child.

Nhamo's spirit wandered. The hot, humid air of the forest buzzed with tsetse flies. Now and then chills seized her body. She was sick, no question about it, and lost. She had staggered on along trails for days. A few times she had seen houses, but the memory of the dogs came back to drive her away.

She hadn't seen people for a long time. She found the

remnants of a farm and gorged herself on bananas gone wild. They were unripe and made her stomach ache. A rainstorm briefly caused the streams to flow, but now she was dependent on the few pockets of water that hadn't dried up. She was hungry, thirsty, and weak—and her head thudded with pain.

Worst of all was the realization that she had been possessed by the spirit of a witch. Far from leaving Long Teats on the *njuzu* island, she had brought her along with the *panga*. Witches made you do evil things without your will or even memory. No village would allow you to stay. You became an outcast. Nhamo shuddered as she remembered the weird ecstasy of destruction the night she had killed the dog.

The dead tree was empty. Long Teats had flown off to plague someone else, but she would return. Nhamo was sure of it.

She forced herself to stand. She knew she ought to search for food, but she couldn't keep her mind on it. How her head ached! Nhamo paused as another chill wracked her body. The trail, which had seemed large at first, had dwindled until she couldn't find it anymore.

Thunder rolled in the distance. Rain would keep her alive awhile. It had already caused new grass to spring up. Soon the forest would be full of things to eat, but Nhamo doubted she would survive long enough to appreciate them.

She heard a strange humming in the distance. It was like a giant hive of bees. She wouldn't be able to smoke them out—her five remaining matches had perished at the same time as the kudu meat—but perhaps she could use a long stick to fish out the honey.

Nhamo staggered on. The humming came from an odd structure on a hill. As she drew near, she saw a door in the side of the hill, and from the opening came a rumbling sound and the lowing of cattle.

Nhamo stopped to clear her head. She had trouble focusing. The strange object was like a hut, but the sides were like finely woven cloth. She could see inside. *It was full of tsetse flies*. Nhamo shook her head again. She must be dreaming. Tsetses didn't live in hives. The flies were zipping into openings at the bottom, but they couldn't get out again. So many of them clustered on the screen that their buzzing made her ears ring.

She stood bemused until the pain in her head forced her on. She peered into the door in the side of the hill. A breeze laden with the rich odor of livestock blew against her face. It was dark inside.

The floor beyond the opening sloped down to a central chamber. Beyond lay another door filled with something that whirled round and round, and was the source of the breeze. In the central chamber was a pen containing many cattle and a few goats. Nhamo suddenly understood where she was. She had arrived at the underground country where the broken and thrown-away creatures lived.

She made her way down the slope. The cattle stirred uneasily as she approached. "Oh, beautiful cows," she whispered, running her hands over their warm hides. Among them were two nanny goats with swollen udders. Nhamo backed one against the fence and, ignoring its angry protests, helped herself to the milk. She drank until she began to feel sick again. Then she lay down at the feet of the milling herd and fell asleep.

Her spirit wandered in confused dreams. The voices of the underground people muttered as they lifted her. They carried her along a path with branches rushing past overhead. A silvery gray twilight soothed her burning skin. Presently, she was in a room with white walls where a woman sat reading a book by a window. Nhamo opened her eyes wide to make out the figure.

It was Mother.

33

I am *not* your mother," the woman said crossly. Nhamo sank into happy oblivion again. If Mother wanted to disagree, that was her business. *She* was not mistaken about the braided hair decorated with beads. She recognized the flowered dress. They were exactly like the photograph.

Nhamo dozed, woke to be fed, and dozed again. Never had she been so contented. After a while an old man dressed in a white robe sat by her bed and murmured charms. "Are you my grandfather?" she asked. The old man looked startled.

She snuggled into the bed, which was softer than anything she had ever known. A woman-spirit stuck a thorn into her arm. It hurt, but Nhamo accepted it as part of the strange rituals of the spirit world. Then the old man was back with a black book, which he read with his lips moving.

"Oh, Grandfather. I'm so glad to see you," Nhamo murmured. "*Ambuya* said I would meet you someday. Did you know Mother can read? She's so clever! Is Aunt Shuvai here? I miss her. . . ."

"Sh. You must rest," said the old man.

Nhamo obediently went back to sleep.

She talked to Mother, sharing with her things that had happened since the picture was destroyed. "Poor Rumpy. He never had any luck," she sighed. "I wonder whether he was really a human who had eaten his totem. Do you know?"

"He was only a baboon," said Mother firmly.

Gradually, Nhamo became more aware of her surroundings. The woman-spirit was called Sister Gladys.* She was kept busy mixing things up in bottles and writing in a book. She was very respectful to Mother. The old man was called *Baba* Joseph and he often came to talk. She didn't understand half of what he said, but it didn't matter. His voice was very soothing.

And gradually she became aware that she wasn't dead after all and that *Baba* Joseph wasn't her grandfather. But she stubbornly refused to give up on Mother. Other people might call her Dr. Everjoice Masuku. Nhamo knew differently.

She was so sleepy! It was all she could do to keep her eyes open more than a minute. She lay in the soft bed, and now and then drifted off into dreams.

"What's wrong with her?" said an unfamiliar man's voice.

"What *isn't* wrong with her? Malaria, bilharzia, malnutrition," said Mother. "When I picked her up, I could have sworn her bones were hollow."

"Her feet are scarred."

"That's an old burn. You should feel the soles. They're like hooves."

"How long was she out there?" the man asked.

"Months. She keeps raving about water spirits and a dead boatman and a baboon she thinks was human." The woman sat next to the bed. Nhamo could smell the soap she used.

"Is she insane?"

Insane! Nhamo was insulted.

"She was alone an awfully long time," said Mother.

Nhamo opened her eyes to protest when she saw the man. He was an enormous whiteman with a bristling beard. His arm was as big as her waist. "No!" she yelled, scrambling

---

*Nurses are called "sister" in Zimbabwe. Sister Gladys is not a Catholic nun.

out of bed. She fell to the floor with the sheet wrapped around her and tried to crawl away on her hands and knees.

"Stop that!" Mother cried. She hauled Nhamo back.

"No! No! No!"

"She doesn't seem to like you, Hendrik," Mother said as Nhamo tried to squirm out of her grasp.

The whiteman shrugged. "At least she doesn't think I'm her mommy." He lumbered out of the room, and Nhamo's breathing became regular again.

"Why are you so afraid of Dr. van Heerden?" Mother asked.

Nhamo told her about the man with the dogs and gun. She didn't mention Long Teats or killing the dog, however. She didn't want to be accused of being a witch.

"That's terrible! You probably don't know this, but not long ago we had a civil war here—white people against black. Some of the hatred is still around. I wish I knew the man's name. I'd set the police on him."

"How could he hate black people when his junior wife was black?" Nhamo asked logically. She described the house and the wonderful dinner.

Mother laughed. "Englishmen aren't allowed more than one wife, and anyhow they almost always marry Englishwomen. That was a servant."

"Is Dr. van Heerden English, *Mai*?"

"Don't call me *Mai*. I'm not your mother."

"Yes, Dr. Masuku."

"Dr. van Heerden is Afrikaans. It's a different kind of white person. He doesn't like to be bothered by children, so stay out of his way."

"Yes, *Mai*—Dr. Masuku."

After a few days Nhamo was allowed out of bed. She was given a new dress-cloth because the old one was torn and foul with dog blood. Sister Gladys had burned it. Nhamo's bag of gold nuggets had disappeared during the period when she believed herself dead. She was afraid to complain.

Dr. van Heerden must have taken it to pay for my supplies, she decided.

She was delighted with the new cloth, though. It was green and red with a pattern of *jongwe,* or roosters. "That's my name," she told Sister Gladys proudly.

Nhamo went to the long mirror at the end of the hospital corridor to admire herself. She stood there a long time. Then she folded up on the floor and burst into tears.

"Now what?" said Sister Gladys.

"I'm—I'm so *ugly,*" Nhamo hiccuped. The creature she had seen in the Englishman's house wasn't a moving picture after all. It was *her.* She looked like a wall spider with a burr stuck to its head.

"You're only thin," the nurse said kindly. "Anyhow, *Baba* Joseph says the important thing is the soul."

This did not make Nhamo feel any better.

As soon as she was strong enough, Nhamo volunteered to help. Sister Gladys was pleased to have someone to scrub floors. She taught Nhamo how to make beds and how to use the electric stove to prepare *sadza.* Nhamo was enchanted by the stove. No more collecting firewood. No more worrying about leopards creeping up on her in the forest. She loved electricity!

It was made by something Sister Gladys called a *generator.* Dr. van Heerden fed it a kind of smelly liquid, and it hummed away as it made the lights shine and the stove hot. Late at night the generator was turned off, and then they had to use lamps like the ones Joao had at the trading post.

Nhamo quickly saw that she had landed in a very strange village. It was called Efifi and was stuck in the middle of a wilderness. There were vegetable gardens, cattle and goat pens, and fields of lucerne* for the animals. There were the usual huts and granaries, but along with them were large buildings devoted to what Mother (Dr. Masuku, Nhamo reminded herself) called *science.*

Nhamo learned new words every day. *Science* was the

---

lucerne: Alfalfa.

kind of work people did in Efifi. It consisted of catching and destroying tsetse flies.

Tsetse flies carried a sickness that killed cattle, horses, pigs, goats, and donkeys. The livestock at Efifi had to be given medicine every few weeks or they would die. Normally, no one would have kept domestic animals in such a lethal place, but the creatures had a very special purpose.

They were bait. Every day they were driven into the underground chamber Nhamo had seen, and a huge fan blew their smell through the forest. Tsetse flies came from miles around. They landed on the trap, crawled inside to find something to bite, and couldn't get out again.

Dr. van Heerden brought live insects back to his science house (which Nhamo learned was called a *laboratory*). There he let them bite animals that had been painted with poison. The whiteman was also trying to put the smell of cattle into a bottle. He wanted to bait traps all over the forest.

Everyone at Efifi had something to do with science. Dr. Masuku was looking for a disease to make the tsetses sick. Nhamo was amazed to learn that flies could get sick, just like people.

Baba Joseph was in charge of the animal building. He cared for herds of *guinea pigs,* which resembled small dassies. The guinea pigs squealed shrilly when he brought them food. After a few days he let Nhamo feed them, too. She covered her ears when the little creatures streamed out of their smelly pens, but she was charmed by the confident way they nibbled lucerne from her hands.

Baba Joseph had several pets: a duiker antelope, a bush baby, a large tortoise, and an enormous warthog that waddled after him, begging for treats. Nhamo realized that the old man was a very great *nganga*. He could get wild animals to obey him. He was also in charge of a small crocodile Dr. van Heerden insisted on keeping. Neither Nhamo nor *Baba* Joseph liked the crocodile. It eyed them in a most calculating way and once, when Nhamo teased it with a stick, it rose up with its yellow mouth open wider than she had dreamed possible. She clawed herself halfway up the wall. *Baba* Joseph laughed so hard he had to sit down and wipe his face.

Other people at Efifi concerned themselves with farming, herding, and carpentry. Two men were detailed to drive away an elephant that liked to raid the fields. Every night they patrolled, calling out "*Iwe! Hamba!* Hey, you! Go away!" The elephant was well aware that no one was allowed to shoot him. He went where he pleased, and the only thing that could move him on were the large firecrackers the men threw at his feet.

They had to be extra careful, *Baba* Joseph said, because it was never certain whether the elephant was going to run away from or *toward* them.

Sister Gladys took care of the inevitable accidents.

The one thing Efifi did not contain was children, and there were almost no women. Everyone had another home where he kept his family, and which he visited regularly. Nhamo thought this was a strange arrangement, but Mother explained that Efifi wasn't a healthy place for children.

34

Nhamo worked steadily for whoever would allow her to help. She walked a fine line between staying invisible (no one would notice her and send her away) and being useful (they would think she was valuable enough to keep). She was determined to live at Efifi—if only to feast her eyes as often as possible on Mother.

Dr. Masuku, for her part, was often impatient with the little shadow she had acquired. "Go haunt someone else!" she would cry. "You hang around like a tsetse fly!" And Nhamo would fade away, only to reappear later when she thought Mother wasn't looking.

Nhamo observed Dr. van Heerden as he picked up dead flies with a pair of tweezers and put them into bottles. She was a little afraid of him. He was so big and hairy! His legs were like tree trunks, and nestled in the top of one of his long socks was a comb. Nhamo wondered if he used it to comb his legs. Dr. van Heerden warned her not to make any noise or touch anything or get in his way.

Once she had satisfied these conditions, though, he was willing to let her watch. In fact he became so absorbed he often forgot about her altogether. If he was feeling sociable, he called her his Wild Child and insisted she had been raised by jackals. "I saw your brothers near the goat pen, Wild Child. Tell them I'll make a rug out of them if they get any ideas."

Nhamo explained gently that she came from a proper village full of people.

"We'll see what happens when the full moon arrives. I bet you'll run through the forest with your tongue hanging out."

There was no shaking him. She knew he was trying to be funny, so she didn't take offense.

When Dr. van Heerden's work went badly, his beard fluffed out like Fat Cheeks's mane. "What are you smiling at?" he rumbled, peering at her over his bottles.

"I am happy," said Nhamo.

"Go be happy somewhere else, Wild Child."

The only person who never chased her away was *Baba* Joseph. He was stern, as an elder should be, but always welcoming. The fate of the old man's guinea pigs upset her, though. Dr. van Heerden painted them with poison and put them under little wire baskets. The baskets fitted so tightly the animals could hardly wiggle as cages of tsetse flies were placed over them. They yelped and cried as they were bitten. The tsetses swelled up with blood until they looked ready to burst. It made Nhamo sick.

"It's cruel," agreed *Baba* Joseph, "but one day the things we learn will keep our cattle from dying." He stuck his own arm into a tsetse cage. Nhamo covered her mouth to keep from crying out. The flies settled all over the old man's skin and began swelling up. "I do this to learn what the guinea pigs are suffering," he explained. "It's wicked to cause pain, but if I share it, God may forgive me."

Baba Joseph talked a lot about God. He and a number of the other villagers dressed all in white on Saturdays. The men shaved their heads and carried long wooden poles with a crook at the top. The women wore white head scarves. They met in the forest on Saturday afternoons to sing and pray. *Baba* Joseph was their leader.

"Excuse me, *Baba*. Are you Catholic?" Nhamo asked him.

"Catholic! Whatever gave you that idea?" The old man was affronted, and Nhamo was too overcome with embarrassment to say anything more.

"There's more than one kind of Christian," Sister Gladys explained. "*Baba* Joseph is a *Vapostori*. Those people don't believe in medicine—if they get sick, they'd rather die than take a pill. I think they're idiots."

Whatever their opinion of *Vapostori*s, everyone deferred to *Baba* Joseph, even Dr. van Heerden: "The old man looks at you with those luminous eyes," the Afrikaner told Mother, "and you find yourself saying, Yes, *Baba*. You want me to stand on my head with a flower up my schnozz? You got it, *Baba*."

In the evening, the doctor sat outside his hut and drank beer. It wasn't the stuff the villagers brewed. It came in brown bottles, like the beer Joao had given Grandmother long ago. Dr. van Heerden drank seven or eight, and the sweat poured off him like a river. At such times he let Nhamo lurk in the bushes while he talked to visitors.

It was a lot like the men's *dare,* although Mother and Sister Gladys sometimes attended, and Nhamo learned a great deal from the conversations. Unlike her own village, Efifi was a mixture of Shona, Tonga, and Matabele, with one Afrikaner thrown in. The language was generally Shona, but smatterings of other tongues cropped up when people became excited.

Dr. Masuku was Matabele. At first this bothered Nhamo. She had been taught that the Matabele, traditional enemies of her people, were as cruel as hyenas. But she couldn't imagine Mother doing anything bad. She knew it didn't make sense that she, a Shona child, had a Matabele mother.

Mother wasn't married, either, and never intended to be. "It's just another name for slavery," she declared. Nhamo thought this was astounding. How could you become an ancestor if you didn't have children? How could you become *anything* without a husband? But Mother insisted that marriage was the worst thing that could happen to an intelligent woman.

She and Dr. van Heerden argued about it frequently. "What you need is a nest of little babies, Everjoice," the Afrikaner would announce after his fourth beer. "I can see them cheeping, 'Mama! Mama!' You'll go all soft like a pat of butter. You've got motherhood written all over you."

"I'd rather swim through a pool of starving crocodiles," Mother said.

"Even the Wild Child knows." Dr. van Heerden held a bottle of beer against his face to cool off. "She follows you like a little shadow."

"The Wild Child has *imprinted* on me. I was the first thing she saw after her ordeal in the forest."

Nhamo didn't know what *imprinting* was and she didn't bother her head about it. Her spirit told her Mother's true identity. That was all that mattered.

Her life drifted on in an aimless fashion. She knew she ought to ask about nuns. She knew it was important to locate Father, but she couldn't bring herself to leave Mother. Sometimes, when she was washing sheets at the hospital or gathering vegetables for the guinea pigs, a great craving came over her. She carefully put down her work and trotted off to the laboratories.

Ah! There was Mother with her eye pressed to a metal tube called a *microscope*. Nhamo would watch for a while, suffused with happiness. Dr. Masuku would eventually look up and say, "Stop sneaking up on me! You made me break a slide!"

Little by little Nhamo took over *Baba* Joseph's chores. He was grateful to let her handle things that had become difficult for his old body. He watched her carefully and instructed her in new duties when he thought she was ready. She worked willingly, even feeding the warthog, which snorted alarmingly when she approached. The only animal she could not bring herself to care for was the crocodile. It was given an occasional fish and the bodies of the guinea pigs when they died.

She was particularly helpful on Saturdays. Saturdays were sacred to the *Vapostori*. They weren't allowed to work all day. *Baba* Joseph always worried that he had not left enough food and water for his animals, but now he could relax. Nhamo looked after everything—except the crocodile. It can dry up like an old cow patty for all I care, she thought privately.

When she was finished, she helped Sister Gladys, and then she hurried to the forest to spy on the *Vapostori*.

They spent the afternoon in a clearing. The men sat on one side and the women on the other with an aisle in between. One or another of the worshippers would stand and begin the singing:

> "Kwese, kwese,
> Tinovona vanhu hamuzivi Kristu. . . .
>
> *Everywhere, everywhere,*
> *We see people who do not know Christ. . . ."*

This was, Nhamo learned, a call for the *angels* to come down from Mwari's country and hover over the gathering. She had asked *Baba* Joseph if angels were the same as ancestral spirits, and he had been vague about it.

Next, the *Vapostori* knelt in the direction of the rising sun and extended their arms with the palms upward.

> "*Mwari* komberera *Africa, alleluia!*
> Chisua yemina matu yedu.
> *Mwari*, Baba, Jesu utukomborera. . . .
>
> *Mwari save Africa, alleluia!*
> *Hear our prayers.*
> *Mwari, Father, Jesus bless us. . . ."*

Nhamo understood why one would pray to Mwari and one's father, but Jesus was an *ngozi*. She didn't think it was at all wise to attract his attention.

Sometimes *Baba* Joseph would pace the aisle between the men and women and tell them stories or scold them if they hadn't been good. He warned them about drinking or taking other men's wives. "Doing these things is like making a telephone call to Satan," he cried. The others would echo his words or make their voices sound like drums or musical instruments backing up his sermon—although the *Vapostori* used no actual instruments in their ceremonies.

The whole thing was extremely pleasant to listen to.

After a while Nhamo left to check up on the animals. She lifted the tortoise from its pen and let it lumber across the animal house for exercise. "You mustn't drink alcohol or take one another's wives," she commanded the guinea pigs, who watched her hopefully for vegetables. "I won't warn *you* about making phone calls to Satan," she told the crocodile. "I'm sure you've done it many times."

Nhamo sat with her back against the duiker stall and surveyed her kingdom. She hadn't told a story for a long time—not since Mother's picture burned up. She had been too absorbed with watching Dr. van Heerden's beard fluff out like Fat Cheeks's mane or with the warthog trailing around after *Baba* Joseph. Besides, if Nhamo wanted to talk, Mother was easy to find—although often unwilling to listen.

Now Nhamo's spirit moved with the desire to speak. She paced between the cages as *Baba* Joseph did between the men and women of the *Vapostori*.

"Once upon a time there were three kings who went to Mwari and asked for the ceremonial stone that brings rain when needed," Nhamo said. "They lived in Mwari's country, so I think they were probably *angels*. Anyhow," she said, stroking the duiker, which confidently thrust its nose at her, "Mwari refused them, saying, 'I cannot give this stone to you because only your people would prosper. Rain is for everyone.'

"The kings became angry and said, 'We thought you were God, but it seems you were only fooling us. We don't believe you have any power. We won't obey you any longer.'

"Mwari said, 'I will give you each a sign so that you may know I am God.' He told the first king, 'You will die because your fingers will drop off. I give you the disease called leprosy.' To the second king he said, 'You will die because you will fall into the fire. I give you epilepsy.' And to the third king he said, 'You will die because your flesh will be consumed.

I give you tuberculosis.' Then Mwari cast them out of his country.

"The first king washed himself in a river and sacrificed a goat. His disease, leprosy, transferred itself to the goat, which was devoured by a crocodile. Since that time crocodiles have been able to give leprosy to humans.

"The second king put his spittle on the wings of a Namaqualand dove. Ever since then, the dove has been able to give epilepsy to humans.

"The third king breathed on a basket of wheat. His disease blew away with the chaff. This is why wheat chaff is able to give people tuberculosis."

Nhamo retrieved the tortoise, which had wedged itself between two guinea-pig pens. She pointed it in the opposite direction and gave it a trail of lettuce leaves to follow.

"I hope *Baba* Joseph has never touched that ugly crocodile," she said as she dangled a sprig of lucerne over the guinea pigs to see if she could make them stand on their hind legs. "I'm sure it's loaded with leprosy." In the far distance she heard the voices of the *Vapostori*. They were really getting into it. Sometimes they got so carried away they didn't even use words. They yodeled any strange thing as loud as they could, and the next day everyone came to work with sore throats.

35

'm off to Harare tomorrow," Dr. van Heerden told Mother as the sun settled behind the gray-green trees of the forest and a soft dusk stole out of the east. The doctors and about ten villagers, all men, were seated companionably outside Dr. van Heerden's hut. There was no room for such a crowd inside and besides, it was too hot. Nhamo was hidden by the leaves of a bougainvillea vine the Afrikaner had grown over a frame at the side. It cast a welcome shade against the hut in the afternoon and formed a convenient nook for someone who did not wish to be noticed.

Dr. van Heerden had given Nhamo a bottle of orange soda from the refrigerator earlier, but by now had forgotten about her existence. She spun out the pleasure of the cold drink as long as possible. She pressed it against her face and let the juice slide down her throat to make her cool from inside. Now all she had left was a few sugary drops. She applied them to her tongue, one by one.

"I'm taking Petrus"—the doctor named one of the villagers. "He needs to spend time with his family. I hear the wife has a new baby."

"And Petrus hasn't been home for a year," added one of the other men. Petrus casually knocked the man's stool over.

He wasn't angry, so Nhamo knew it wasn't a real argument. She sometimes had trouble understanding jokes at Efifi. No one in *her* village would have made such an accusation lightly.

"Bring us magazines," said Mother. The rainy season had kept the road too marshy to use for many weeks. All the old magazines had fallen apart.

Whenever Dr. van Heerden went to town, everyone made out a list of requests. His Land Rover returned as loaded as the tractor that visited the trading post.

"I'm making two quick trips if the weather stays good. I'm taking in bottles of cow smell to be analyzed."

Nhamo had watched the doctor try to collect the exact substance that attracted the tsetses. Nothing was overlooked: the breath, the sweat, the droppings. The last item was most interesting. It had to be collected absolutely fresh before it hit the ground. Dr. van Heerden crept up on a likely cow, bottle in hand. Sometimes he got what he wanted, and sometimes he got a surprise. Once a cow coughed as he was peering up its backside, with entertaining results.

"I think I'll bring Bliksem back for a few days. We can hunt jackals together."

Who is Bliksem? thought Nhamo. She hadn't heard of him.

"This place is bad for his health," Mother pointed out.

"*Ach,* a few days won't hurt. The old fellow needs a vacation."

Bliksem must be an elder relative, Nhamo decided. Perhaps he was Dr. van Heerden's uncle.

"Someday we have to send the Wild Child off, you know," Mother remarked. "It isn't fair to keep her without an education."

Nhamo's throat suddenly closed up. *Mother* said that? *Mother* wanted to get rid of her?

"She's learning plenty," said Dr. van Heerden. "Works harder than five of these buggers." He was into his fifth or sixth beer. The men rolled their eyes.

"You know what I mean. She can't read or add. She's totally unsuited for modern life—and she's bright enough to take advantage of good schooling. In fact, she's brilliant."

Nhamo's heart burned within her. Mother's praise meant nothing. *She wanted to get rid of her.*

"*Baba* Joseph can teach her." Dr. van Heerden tipped the bottle up over his red, sweaty face.

"*Baba* Joseph!" Mother sounded exasperated. "He'd teach her to speak in tongues. Besides, he doesn't have time— and neither does Sister Gladys, and neither do I, so don't ask."

"You'd make such a *wonderful* mother," Dr. van Heerden said sentimentally.

"Nhamo needs a proper school and a real family. She says she has a father at Mtoroshanga."

"The Old Man is very attached to her." Petrus offered an opinion for the first time. Everyone knew that the Old Man was *Baba* Joseph. "She called him Grandfather when she was sick. He lost a granddaughter years ago, and Nhamo reminds him of her."

"Oh, brother! Just what I need. Another one of *Baba* Joseph's pets!" groaned Dr. van Heerden.

Pets! So that's what they thought of her! Nhamo's skin was hot with shame. She was just another warthog trailing around after the Old Man!

"All right, I'll think about it." The doctor came to a decision. "I'll go through Mtoroshanga on my way to Harare. If I can scare up the Wild Child's daddy, I'll take her back with me and Bliksem. If not—well, there's always boarding school. The government makes grants for orphans."

The men and Dr. Masuku (*not* Mother, Nhamo thought angrily) went on to other topics.

That night she ground her teeth as she lay on the cot at the hospital. Sister Gladys had pronounced her the night watchman and given her the duty of calling for help if anyone became especially ill. But she was not a night watchman, only an ugly warthog allowed to sleep in a human bed as a joke.

In the morning, she hid when Dr. van Heerden and Petrus drove off. She didn't look for Mother—not once!—and she obeyed Sister Gladys in such stony silence that the nurse asked if she felt sick.

But Nhamo couldn't be angry at *Baba* Joseph. She reminded him of his dead granddaughter. That meant he thought she was human.

"I'll never smoke cigarettes or eat pork or birds with webbed feet," she murmured as she swabbed out the guinea-pig cages. She had paid close attention to the things *Baba* Joseph considered sinful. "And I'll *never* make phone calls to Satan." Satan, the old man had explained, was like an *ngozi* and witch rolled into one. He waited around for people to get careless. The minute they let their guard down—boom!—he possessed them.

"I'll be good, and *Baba* Joseph will tell everyone to leave me alone." Nhamo wiped the tears from her eyes as the guinea pigs gathered around her with earsplitting squeals.

She avoided Dr. Masuku so completely during the next few days that the Matabele woman (she was *that* now, not Mother) tracked her down in the hospital. "I never thought I'd miss your beady eyes on the back of my neck. What's the matter with you, Nhamo? Why don't you spy on me anymore?"

Because you want to send me away, thought Nhamo, but she replied, "I've been busy."

"Of course you have! Sister Gladys says she doesn't know what she'd do without you."

Borrow the warthog from *Baba* Joseph, I expect, thought Nhamo, but she said, "I'm glad Sister Gladys is pleased with my work."

"You're acting so—oh, I don't know! You seem angry. Has anyone upset you? I know it's difficult trying to fit in to a strange village without any children. If I can do anything . . ." Dr. Masuku trailed off uncertainly.

Nhamo stared straight ahead, not insultingly but not in a friendly way either. Dr. Masuku looked to Sister Gladys for help.

"It's probably her period coming on," Sister Gladys offered.

"That makes young girls nervous," Dr. Masuku said gratefully. "It took me *forever* to settle down. I think the whole process of menstruation is a joke played by God on women."

But nothing she said could coax a smile out of Nhamo. Dr. Masuku eventually went back to her duties, and Sister Gladys gave Nhamo an herbal drink that she said "would make the pains better."

The only one who could lift her bad spirits was *Baba* Joseph. He went about his chores in the same tranquil way, with a kind word for each of his pets and apologies to the guinea pigs when they had to be strapped under the wire cages.

He and she always had lunch by the livestock pens. As long as Dr. van Heerden was away, the cows didn't have to spend the day in the underground chamber. The windows of their building were securely screened, though. Even one tsetse-fly bite could prove fatal. As it was, the poor animals had to be given injections to treat animal sleeping sickness every few weeks.

"It always rests my eyes to see a fine herd of cattle," *Baba* Joseph said. Nhamo nodded. She loved their sleek brown hides and lucerne-sweet breath. The old man told her about how Jesus *ngozi* had slept in a cow's feeding trough when he was a baby. Nhamo, in her turn, related one of *Ambuya*'s stories.

"Once upon a time there was a couple with many cattle, but only one son. Their neighbors became jealous, so they hired a witch to put a curse on them."

Baba Joseph frowned, not entirely pleased with a tale about a witch.

"The parents became very sick," Nhamo went on hastily. "Just before they died, they told the boy to sell all the cows and move far away. But first he was to kill the black bull and travel inside its skin.

"The boy was mystified by the commandment. Still, he obeyed his parents. He killed the black bull, took out its intestines, and moved himself and his belongings into its belly. At once the bull began to walk! 'Eh! Eh! What a strange thing!' cried the boy."

Baba Joseph was definitely uneasy about pagan magic, but he was too interested in the story to object.

Nhamo continued. "The bull walked and walked. It went through forests and swam rivers with the boy inside. Finally, it reached the court of a king. 'O great king, may I stay with you?' the boy said from inside the bull's belly.

"The king was frightened. 'Get out of here, you demon!' he shouted. 'Whoever heard of a bull talking?'

"The boy went on to an old woman's hut. 'Respected grandmother, may I stay with you?' he asked.

"'What luck! A beautiful black bull!' she cried. 'You can stay with my cows as long as you like.'

"Every morning the bull led the cows to pasture. The boy came out of the bull's belly and played on a flute to pass the time. When he played, the rain fell over the old woman's fields, even though everyone else was having a drought. Mealies and pumpkins grew everywhere. Her cows all gave birth to calves, and their udders were so full of milk the old woman didn't know where to put it all.

"The people around began to notice how prosperous the old woman had become. Their children spied on the pasture and saw the boy come out of the black bull's belly every day. 'When he plays, the rain falls,' they told their astonished parents. The parents went at once to tell the king.

"The king sent his soldiers to take the bull away, but it tossed them on its horns. 'You turned me away when I asked,' it bellowed. 'Now your fields can turn to ashes for all I care!'

"When the people saw this, they threw out the old king and put the boy in his place. He became very powerful and eventually had many wives and children. He built a fine new house for the old woman. But the boy's father called the black bull away to the spirit world. Ever since, when a parent dies, a cow or bull is given the person's name and sacrificed when the spirit is brought home again."

Baba Joseph sighed. "You tell a fine story, Nhamo," he said. "But you haven't learned the truth yet. All those old beliefs are wrong. Only Jesus matters, and our future in heaven."

Nhamo said nothing. She had her own private opinions. Who had protected her on Lake Cabora Bassa? Who taught her to swim and to use boats? As much as she wanted *Baba* Joseph's approval, she couldn't ignore the evidence of her own eyes. Crocodile Guts, the *njuzu*, and Mother had been with her when she most needed them, and she couldn't turn her back on them now.

At the thought of Mother, Nhamo's spirit sank again. *Baba* Joseph, perhaps noticing, set her to work feeding a young calf that was learning to do without its mother's milk.

36

Nhamo was returning from the lucerne fields. She had been gathering food for the guinea pigs, but had been distracted by a black wasp that was running around a patch of cleared land. Dr. Masuku had widened her knowledge of insects. Now they were not merely something to be swatted. They had families and illnesses just like people.

The black wasp dashed up to a twig and flipped it over. It dislodged a pebble, scattered dry grass, and scurried along a fallen fence post. All at once it jumped back with its wings raised. A huge spider stepped out from under a leaf the wasp had disturbed. It was a baboon spider with long, shiny fangs! Nhamo dropped her bundle of lucerne.

But the wasp didn't flee. It plunged straight into battle, and the spider reared back with its fangs exposed. Faster than Nhamo could see, the insect was in and out of biting range. Its stinger dealt a blow to the spider's head. Very soon the spider began to stagger as though it were drunk. The wasp landed squarely on it now, almost embracing it with its black legs as it delivered another sting to the belly.

Nhamo was thrilled. This was every bit as exciting as a lion kill without posing any danger to *her*. What courage the wasp had to tackle something so much bigger! When the baboon spider was nearly dead—its legs quivered slightly—the wasp flew off. Nhamo wondered why it didn't stay to feast on its fallen enemy. She wanted to ask Dr. Masuku, but her spirit still burned with anger toward the treacherous Matabele woman.

Nhamo gathered up the lucerne and trotted off to the village. People had left their work and were moving toward the main road. She soon saw what had attracted them: Dr. van Heerden's Land Rover was being unloaded of its treasures. Dr. Masuku had a stack of magazines, Sister Gladys carried a box of disposable syringes, and the staff cook had his arms full of sugar bags. Dr. van Heerden was wiping his face with a red-checkered handkerchief.

"The *blerry** flies were after me, I can tell you," he exclaimed. "They thought I was lunch and dinner rolled into one." He opened the door of the Land Rover. "Come out, Bliksem! You've got some tasty jackals to find!"

Out of the door bounded a huge black dog exactly like the beasts that had attacked Nhamo on her first night in Zimbabwe! She dropped the lucerne again, but she didn't drop the knife she had used to cut it. The world seemed to disappear. She saw only the huge black animal leaping around its white master.

"Look, *meisie-kind,*** I brought you a playmate," said the whiteman. He pointed at her. The beast started for Nhamo with its red tongue lolling out of its mouth.

She stood perfectly still. She would not run any more than the wasp had fled from the spider. *Of course not,* whispered Long Teats. *Only cowards run from their enemies.*

"Nhamo! Don't!" shouted the Matabele woman.

The dog was almost upon her now, but something in her face checked its gait. It swerved to one side. Nhamo struck out, raising a red streak along its ribs. The dog howled fearfully. "It's too late to make friends now," she snarled as she turned to pursue it.

**blerry*: Bloody (a mild swear word).
***meisie-kind*: Girl child, kid.

"Stop it!" bellowed the whiteman. He threw himself between her and the dog. "*Voetsek!* Go away!" He gathered up the animal in one hairy arm and thrust the other before him to ward Nhamo off. He backed off hurriedly, with the whimpering animal clutched to his chest.

She paused just an instant. *Baba* Joseph said you should forgive your enemies. *Forgive your enemies, indeed! I say kill them all as quickly as possible,* cried Long Teats. Nhamo threw back her head and howled. Then she hurled herself at the whiteman and buried the knife up to the hilt in his arm.

She felt herself being dragged back from behind. Her wrist was wrenched so hard she could hear the bones snap. The Matabele woman grasped her from the front, holding her in a tight embrace, and the spirit of Long Teats suddenly fled into the blinding sunlight.

"Mother! Mother!" screamed Nhamo, and fainted.

She clung to Mother through the long afternoon, becoming hysterical if the woman had to leave for a few minutes. She told her everything she had kept hidden for fear of being sent away. She told about the *ngozi* and the escaped marriage. She told about the cholera epidemic and the *muvuki*. She told about the *panga*. "I thought it was a gift from the dead Portuguese. Really I did!" She told about being possessed by Long Teats and killing the black dog. "No one will want me now. I've turned into a witch," she sobbed. She talked until her voice gave out and still she clung to Mother and wept if the woman showed any sign of leaving.

Finally, when the sky grew dark, Sister Gladys gave her an injection to make her sleep and to lessen the pain of the broken wrist.

In the morning, Nhamo stared at the white walls of the hospital and refused to speak at all. Mother and Dr. van Heerden sat by her bed. His arm was bandaged and he was still angry about the injury to Bliksem. "He'll never trust a child again," he said. "Poor old fellow. He was only trying to play."

"Did you find her father?" asked Mother.

"I found his family. They weren't anxious to talk to me. They didn't trust white people."

"At least *they* didn't try to kill you," Mother said.

"I think she should go off to them at once."

"That's probably best."

Nhamo listened numbly. Her father's family wouldn't want her either when they learned she was a witch.

"Is she insane?" Dr. van Heerden asked for the second time since Nhamo had arrived at Efifi.

"How could she not be? All those experiences . . . ," Mother said in a sorrowful voice.

"I expect her relatives will know how to deal with it."

"And I expect better things of you!"

Mother and Dr. van Heerden turned to stare open-mouthed at *Baba* Joseph, who was dressed in his Sabbath white. He brandished his sacred staff with the crook on top.

"You think of throwing this child away as though she were a dead guinea pig! You plan to cast her immortal soul into eternal fire! *Woe be unto you, you whited sepulchers!* You speak with the voices of angels, and yet have not charity. You drive the little ones away when Jesus gathered them to his arms. *Shame on you, you hypocrites!* This child is possessed of a demon, and I will not rest until I have cast it out! I swear this before Mwari and his angels!" With that, *Baba* Joseph whirled around and strode from the room like a man of thirty.

For a moment Mother and Dr. van Heerden were too stunned to speak. "I think I've been sent to stand in the corner," the Afrikaner murmured at last.

"You and me both," said Mother in a subdued voice.

They listened thoughtfully to *Baba* Joseph's voice in the distance. He was exhorting someone to throw away a cigarette.

"Maybe we *have* been too hasty about getting rid of the Wild Child," said Dr. van Heerden after a while.

"Perhaps we have." Mother smoothed out the wrinkles in her skirt.

They looked at Nhamo, who gazed back at them full of remorse and sorrow, but also with the faintest beginning of hope.

37

She's going to look awful," said Mother as Sister Gladys shaved Nhamo's head. It was several weeks later and Nhamo's wrist had nearly healed, but she still had it bound tightly in a bandage.

"Demons get tangled in the hair," *Baba* Joseph explained. "That's why *Vapostori* men shave their heads."

"Why not the beards?"

"What an idea! The longer the beard, the holier the prophet."

Sister Gladys rolled her eyes.

Nhamo hadn't looked into a mirror since the day she thought she resembled a wall spider with a burr on top. Now the burr was gone. She didn't think it was going to improve her looks.

"Are you sure it's safe out there?" Mother said. "Karoyi Mountain is infested with hyenas."

"Nothing in this life is safe," replied *Baba* Joseph tranquilly.

"I can send a guard along with a gun."

"No outsider is permitted. Mwari will look after us."

Mother's expression showed she felt this was unlikely. "I think this is a mistake, but if Nhamo believes it . . ."

And Nhamo wanted to believe it with all her heart. *Baba* Joseph and the other *Vapostori* prophets were going to conduct an exorcism ceremony on Karoyi Mountain. Karoyi meant "little witch" and it had a reputation for being a gathering place of evil, although Dr. van Heerden said that was because of the hyenas that lived there.

Baba Joseph's eyes shone as he talked about how he was going to send Long Teats back to her smelly den in Mozambique. While he was at it, he might as well clean up the other witches who might be lurking on Karoyi Mountain.

"Don't overdo it, *Baba*," Mother said gently. "You aren't as young as you used to be."

Sister Gladys swept Nhamo's hair into a pile. It looked like a dead animal sprawled on the floor. Nhamo was given a white dress and a scarf for her naked scalp. She would be allowed to wear sandals until they neared the exorcism site. The *Vapostori* never wore shoes for their ceremonies because the ground where they prayed to Mwari was sacred. "Please don't make Nhamo carry anything heavy," the nurse instructed *Baba* Joseph.

The sky was black when they started out. Mother hung a flashlight on a leather thong around Nhamo's neck. "Don't use up the batteries," Mother warned as Nhamo delightedly clicked it on and off. The prophets, ghostly in their white robes, carried blazing torches. They had different symbols embroidered on their robes to indicate their rank within the church. Their bald heads shone in the flickering light. They walked off along a forest path with Nhamo in their midst.

She saw Mother and Sister Gladys standing in the doorway of the hospital as they moved away from the comforting lights of Efifi. Dr. van Heerden was in his house. He had not entirely forgiven Nhamo, but he had promised to keep the generator going until she returned.

On and on they went through the eerie sounds of night. An owl hooted softly as they passed its tree. Bush babies chattered. Water trickled in streams left over from the rains. Nhamo turned her flashlight on only when she couldn't see by the light of the torches. Once she aimed it into the forest and caught a pair of red eyes staring back. She didn't do that again.

The path gradually began to rise. It threaded between

boulders and past baobab trees with their roots firmly tapped into pockets of water in the soil. Soon they left the baobabs behind. They came to drier soil with strangler figs splitting the rocks. They passed close to a solitary *mukonde* tree, which raised many pale, leafless branches against the dark sky. They were careful not to touch it, for the sap was poison.

At last they arrived at the bare knoll of the mountain with only the stars for cover. *Baba* Joseph told Nhamo to remove her sandals. "Ow!" said Nhamo, stepping on a thorn. Once her feet had been like balls of baked clay, but Sister Gladys had made her work on them with a pumice stone. "Ow," Nhamo cried again, trying not to notice the pain.

"Be quiet," *Baba* Joseph said sternly.

The prophets must have gathered wood earlier because a great heap was already present at the center of the bare knoll. They thrust their torches into it. Soon it was blazing high into the sky. Nhamo wondered whether Mother could see it from Efifi.

At first the ceremony was exactly like the service on Saturday. The men sang *"Kwese, kwese"* to invite the angels to come down. "I imagine they'll need a *lot* of angels tonight," Nhamo said to herself. She took no part in the proceedings. The *Vapostori* sang and prayed until the flames died down to coals. Then they behaved very strangely indeed.

The men knocked the embers into a long, glowing line *and began to walk over them as though it were a path*. Nhamo stifled a scream. They not only walked, they *rolled* on them and placed hot coals in their mouths. No one seemed to get burned. Even the robes didn't catch fire.

After *Baba* Joseph had crossed over, he shook his staff and shouted. "I have heard! I have heard the word of God, *alleluia*! He said, 'You witches come out. You make your feet to go. You take your ugly toes somewhere else.' *Ehe!* I have heard it! The waters of the earth have witnessed it! *Fala-ula he!* God has said it! We don't want you anymore! *Zifokola hau!*"

Nhamo didn't know what all the words meant, but there was no mistaking the power that filled *Baba* Joseph. If she had been a witch, she would have leaped straight off the mountain.

The other prophets joined in, praying, cursing, prophesying together with a kind of weird music. After a while Nhamo realized they weren't the only ones making it. From all around on the dark hillside came the voices of hyenas. They had observed the intruders in their country. They didn't like it.

"I call on you, Long Teats!" bellowed *Baba* Joseph. "I say, Come here like the mangy dog you are! Come and see your power destroyed! *Mezu-kano-eh!*" The old man laid the *panga* on the hot coals. Nhamo hadn't seen it since she arrived at Efifi. A breeze caused the fire to leap again. The wooden handle burned to ashes.

On the edge of the hill, at the very rim of the light, was an enormous hyena with red-shining eyes.

"*Eh!* You have crawled out of your pile of dung! You have come to witness the superior power of Jesus!" *Baba* Joseph laid his hand on Nhamo's head. She wasn't expecting it and flinched.

"I will send you to hell along with damned Satan!" The *panga* burned in the fire with a sickening, metallic smell.

You miserable worm, came Long Teats's voice from the dark. *You're no match for me. I'll burst your lungs between my teeth like old rotten bladders.*

Nhamo hugged herself so tightly, her arms turned numb.

"You're stupid, like all witches," taunted *Baba* Joseph. He took out a bottle of holy water from a pack he had carried up the mountain. Nhamo had seen holy water blessed after the Sabbath ceremony. It was used to cure illnesses. "Watch this!" the old man commanded. He poured the liquid on the *panga*. It hissed up in a furious steam—and the metal snapped!

Aauu, wailed Long Teats. The hyena seemed to have shrunk. It was only a cane rat watching the fire with glittering black eyes.

"I command you to bring me the *ngozi*. I have words to say to him as well."

The form of the cane rat wavered. Its eyes became dull. *There is no ngozi,* sighed Long Teats.

"Don't give me your damned lies! I want Goré Mtoko!"

There is no ngozi. The cane rat came apart in shreds of air. It was only a blackjack weed at the side of a rock.

"*Alleluia! Alleluia!*" sang the *Vapostori* as they circled the broken *panga.* "Mwari save Africa!" they sang. They were beside themselves with joy. But *Baba* Joseph wasn't finished. He began striding up and down again, praying and prophesying, with his words sometimes shifting to an unknown, yet strangely powerful, tongue. Nhamo was sure it was the language of the angels. She was weeping with relief. She felt clean and free again. She was as happy as she had been when Masvita's face lost the deathly gray pallor of cholera.

"I call on you false gods of Africa!" shouted *Baba* Joseph, shaking his staff. "I call on the *njuzu* and on the *ngozis*! I call on the *vadzimu,* the ancestors of this girl."

Uh-oh, thought Nhamo.

The old man shouted challenges at the pagan spirit world. He ordered the spirits to line up like naughty children in front of an elder. Nhamo began to get seriously worried. She wanted to get rid of Long Teats, but no one had mentioned driving away the *njuzu.* And she *couldn't* part with the *vadzimu.* Although in one sense Mother had returned as a Matabele doctor, deep down Nhamo knew the truth. Her *real* parent was with the ancestors. And someday Grandmother would join her. . . .

"I don't want to lose *Ambuya,*" Nhamo cried out suddenly.

"Hush, hush," murmured the *Vapostori.* Nhamo shuddered. She didn't want to oppose them, but she didn't want to lose her family either. She stood up, desperately trying to think of a way to stop them. All at once she became aware that the other prophets didn't seem as confident as *Baba* Joseph. They stopped now and then to observe their leader's performance. When they began speaking the angel language again, they looked around as though they weren't sure what might be lurking in the darkness.

"I call on *mhondoro*, the lion spirit!" bellowed *Baba* Joseph.

"Respected elder, surely we have done enough . . . ," one of the prophets said.

"Nothing will be enough until we drive all false gods from this mountain! Don't lose courage, brother. Satan comes in many forms, but they are all worms compared to Jesus. Come forth, you maggot-infested hyena droppings!"

The coals had died down. By the cold, distant light of the stars, Nhamo could still make out the white robes of the prophets. Suddenly, they began to move erratically.

"*Eh!* I feel hands on my neck!" one of them cried.

"Don't touch me!" yelled another.

"Stand firm! It's only Satan!" *Baba* Joseph shouted, but the men stumbled around, fighting things they could not see. A scream and the sound of tumbling rocks told Nhamo someone had fallen over a cliff. The cries of the *Vapostori* filled the air. One by one they blundered into objects until all that could be heard were *Baba* Joseph's exhortations and the groans of men nursing injuries.

Finally, the fight went out of *Baba* Joseph as well. He sat down heavily, and his staff clattered to the ground. Nhamo flicked on the flashlight. "Are you all right, *Baba*?" she whispered. She crept up to him. He was slumped over with his head cradled in his arms.

"Broken reeds," he muttered.

"What did you say, *Baba*?"

"I fought with a rod of iron, but my brothers fought with broken reeds." He spoke no more. Nhamo huddled next to him. It wasn't cold exactly, but the early-morning air raised goose bumps on her arms. She heard moaning from half a dozen places. It occurred to her that the sounds might attract predators, and so she dragged unburned chunks of wood together and rekindled them with the still-hot coals.

She made *Baba* Joseph sit close to the fire for protection. Nhamo carefully hunted around the knoll for the injured *Vapostori*. She urged them to move next to the old man, but they stared at her blankly. She didn't know whether they were injured or possessed. "Please. I don't have enough fuel for more fires," she begged. They rocked back and forth, with their eyes staring.

"If I can't bring them to the fire, I'll take the fire to *them*," Nhamo decided. She set the longest branch she could find ablaze. But first she put on her sandals. "I don't think this is holy ground anymore," she said. "The *Vapostori* certainly don't act like it."

Methodically, she went from person to person, waving the burning branch with her good hand and shouting insults at any hyenas who might be lurking. At the bottom of a boulder she found the first victim. He seemed to be really hurt but, paradoxically, he was the only one willing to talk. "Water . . . ," he murmured. "Water. . . ."

The only water around was in the bottles *Baba* Joseph had brought. Nhamo knew that it was for healing purposes. The man by the boulder was certainly in need of healing, so she removed the containers from *Baba* Joseph's pack and gave the injured prophet as much as he could swallow.

By now the first faint streaks of dawn were appearing in the east. Early morning was a favorite time for animals to hunt, and she didn't dare let her guard down. What will I do if I really meet hyenas? she thought. Her wrist ached badly, and the torch had burned down almost to her fingers. The beasts weren't going to be frightened of a small female person with a flashlight.

"Wake up, *meisie-kind*," came a hearty voice. Dr. van Heerden came over the edge of the knoll with a rifle slung over his shoulder. He had a crowd of workmen with him. They fanned out at once to attend to the injured *Vapostori*. "Looks like you had a *blerry* square dance up here. You certainly live up to your name, Disaster. You've disabled half the farm crew."

Nhamo turned hot with shame.

"*Baba* Joseph put them up to it," Mother said sharply. She had walked more slowly than the others and was just coming up the mountain.

"Everjoice wouldn't leave me alone until I came looking

for you. Bang! Bang! On the door all night," said Dr. van Heerden.

"He had the binoculars trained on Karoyi Mountain from the minute you left."

"*Not* Karoyi Mountain," *Baba* Joseph murmured, raising his head.

"You rest, *oupa*,"* the Afrikaner said in a gentle voice.

"No witches here anymore. We threw them over a cliff."

"I'm sure you did, *oupa,* and a few *Vapostori,* too, by the look of it."

Daylight and the arrival of help brought most of the prophets back to their senses. Only the man who had fallen off the boulder needed to be carried back to Sister Gladys's hospital, and to be on the safe side a litter was used for *Baba* Joseph as well.

*oupa: Grandfather.

38

What happened up there, *Mai*?" asked Nhamo as she drank sweet milky tea at the hospital. Sister Gladys and Dr. van Heerden were splinting the injured *Vapostori*'s leg.

"I'll take this one to Harare. He needs an X ray," the Afrikaner told the nurse.

Dr. Masuku grimaced at the word *mai,* but didn't correct Nhamo. "What do you think happened?"

"*Baba* Joseph drove Long Teats away. I saw it. First she was a giant hyena and then, when he broke the *panga,* she turned into a cane rat, and then she became a blackjack weed. I threw it into the fire."

"Good for you," said Mother.

"But I don't understand how the spirits could throw the *Vapostori* off the mountain," Nhamo went on. "I thought Jesus was too strong for them."

"Jesus *is* too strong for them," *Baba* Joseph called from his bed.

"Go back to sleep," Sister Gladys said. "Do you know, not one of these fools will take an aspirin."

"Prayer is our medicine," insisted *Baba* Joseph.

"I think"—Mother lowered her voice—"that most of the *Vapostori* weren't born Christians. They were raised to believe in *vadzimu* and the *mhondoro*. It's very hard to turn your back on something you learned as a child."

Nhamo nodded. She wouldn't think of arguing with anything Grandmother had taught her.

"It's all right to exorcise witches. Everyone thinks they're bad. It's different when you try to get rid of your ancestors. I think the *Vapostori* threw themselves off the mountain without quite realizing it. They couldn't reconcile their childhood beliefs with Christianity."

Nhamo wasn't sure she understood this. "Do you believe in the spirit world, *Mai*?"

Mother sighed. "I'm a scientist. I've been taught not to believe anything that can't be proved, and yet . . ." She gazed at *Baba* Joseph, who had snuggled into the soft bed with a look of bliss. "He often infuriates me, but he's *old*. I've been taught to revere and obey such people. It's just . . . built in."

"Like motherhood," Dr. van Heerden said cheerfully. "I'm finished, you layabout." He put a final strip of tape on the injured man's splint. "If you don't take Sister Gladys's nice medicine, every bump of the Land Rover is going to make your eyes cross with pain."

"Prayer is our medicine," the *Vapostori* said mournfully.

"Speaking of ancestors, I think you should get in contact with your family, Nhamo," said Mother. "You have relatives in Mozambique and at Mtoroshanga."

Nhamo clutched Mother's hand. She had been forced to flee so often, the thought of going anywhere else was simply terrifying.

"I won't rush you," Mother said. "We ought to send a message to your Grandmother, though. I'm sure she wants to know you're safe."

"They might make me go back. To marry Zororo."

"There's no chance of that!" Mother's eyes flashed. "The very idea! Trying to force a child into marriage to save their own skins. *Ngozi* sacrifices are illegal in Zimbabwe."

"I'm . . . not a child."

"Oh, Nhamo! Having a few periods doesn't make you an adult. You have so much to learn—and you're so clever."

Nhamo looked down, smiling with pleasure.

"If she's so clever, tell me how she buggered up half the farm crew," said Dr. van Heerden as he helped the *Vapostori* hop out to the Land Rover.

Nhamo was happier than she could ever remember. She was accepted. She was safe. And everyone went out of his or her way to make her feel wanted. The cook made her special milk tarts from a recipe provided by Dr. van Heerden. Sister Gladys took time from her busy schedule to give her lessons in arithmetic. Mother let her look through the microscope at wiggling creatures that lived inside the tsetse flies and made them deadly.

Baba Joseph took a long time to recover from his night-long ordeal on Karoyi Mountain (which he renamed Angel Mountain). One of his sons performed his duties. Nhamo still helped, but she spent several hours a day with the old man, learning to read.

Once she realized the funny marks stood for sounds, she progressed rapidly. She took to reading with a fervor so extreme, *Baba* Joseph had to take the books from her hands by force. "Your eyes are not tractors. They are not meant to pull heavy loads," he said sternly. Still, Nhamo couldn't help sounding out every bit of writing she encountered. Some were in languages she didn't know, like English. It didn't matter.

Writing wasn't nearly as easy. Her fingers were callused from years of grueling work. The pencil wouldn't obey her, and she became so angry she wanted to snap it in two—except that it belonged to *Baba* Joseph. "Don't worry. I'll teach you to type," whispered Mother when she found Nhamo in tears over the writing.

But all in all, her life was blissfully free of care. She waited anxiously to hear from Grandmother. "It's hard to get a message to a place that doesn't even have a name," Mother explained. "I sent letters by several people—anyone who might be traveling in that area. They are to ask for *Mai* Chipo, Mother of Chipo, of the Moyo clan, whose childhood name was Nyamasatsi."

Weeks passed; months passed. Nhamo's hair grew back, softer than before, and Sister Gladys rubbed coconut oil into her scalp. The smell made Nhamo hungry. The nurse taught her to oil her skin as well, and to buff her fingernails with a piece of leather. She provided her with underpants, something Nhamo found annoying, but Sister Gladys insisted that civilized women wore them. She even came up with a strange strip of cloth with two bags at the front to contain Nhamo's growing breasts.

That was too much! The bags were uncomfortable. Besides, no one in the village had ever needed such a thing. Nhamo only wore it under the new dress Mother had given her for special occasions. The rest of the time she trotted around bra-less in her dress-cloth.

After work, she liked to sit in the watchtower that overlooked the lucerne fields. During the war, Mother said, it had been a guard post to protect Efifi from attack. Now it was slowly falling apart, but Nhamo could still lounge under the thatched roof and enjoy an afternoon breeze. On this particular day, she had a bottle of red soda from Dr. van Heerden's fridge. She had a peanut butter sandwich and a heap of guavas. She gazed contentedly at the distant shadow of Karoyi—now Angel—Mountain.

The sun dipped below the trees. A haze began to gather at the rim of the horizon. It spread out in a gray line, and a long, thin finger of it flowed toward the tower. Nhamo watched in amazement. It came from the east, from beyond the border of Mozambique, where her nameless village lay on the banks of an uncharted stream. It surrounded her with a swirl of gray ashes.

Cousin Tsodzo, Cousin Farai. Granddaughter Nhamo. Please do not be frightened. Your relative has died here. We know you would come if you could, the ashes whispered. And another voice sighed, *If I go to my ancestors before we meet again, my spirit will come to you in a dream. I promise it.*

Nhamo screamed and fell to her knees. The soda bottle smashed to the ground below. She stared into the east for a long, long time. The sky darkened. The first stars came out, and fireflies began to appear over the damp fields of lucerne.

She heard Sister Gladys calling her to dinner. The nurse came to the bottom of the tower and waited while Nhamo climbed down. "What's wrong?" said the woman, touching the girl's tear-streaked face.

"*Ambuya*" was all she was able to reply.

In the morning, Mother called her to her office. "I think it's time we visited your relatives at Mtoroshanga," she said.

39

Dr. van Heerden drove. Then he and Mother went off for a cool drink while Sister Gladys alone accompanied Nhamo. Since the Jongwe family was suspicious of white people, they probably wouldn't welcome a Matabele woman either. Nhamo wore her special dress with the bra underneath. It was hot and uncomfortable. She wore freshly cleaned sandals. Sister Gladys had styled her hair and given her clear polish for her fingernails.

She said Nhamo was beautiful, but Nhamo was afraid to look into the mirror.

Mtoroshanga was covered with dust from mining operations. Some of the houses were attractive; most were merely hovels. Sister Gladys said that many Jongwes lived in the part of town they were passing through. They all worked for the Big Chief Chrome Company, whose manager was Industry Jongwe, Nhamo's uncle.

Nhamo grew increasingly nervous as they walked. The Jongwes might not like her at all. They might think she was an ignorant Wild Child of dubious parentage. She realized that her mother and father might not have been married at all.

They came at last to a magnificent house with a large lawn and a drive that curved up to the front door. Sister Gladys opened the front gate and went in. Nhamo looked around in wonder. Flowering trees cast shade on emerald grass. They weren't even fruit trees. How could anyone afford to have trees that didn't produce food? And where did they get so much water when the rest of the town was dry?

The windows were covered with iron grilles and the roof was of red tile, like a Portuguese house. The front steps were the same color. They gleamed from a recent application of wax.

"Your father's younger brother Industry lives here," Sister Gladys said.

Nhamo was frozen with fear as the nurse rang the doorbell (a doorbell!). Soon a servant (a servant!) in a white apron answered it. She invited them to sit in the parlor while she called her mistress.

"They won't like me," whispered Nhamo as she gripped Sister Gladys's hand.

"They have to. You're family," the woman said placidly.

The servant brought them tea, which Nhamo was too distraught to drink. Then a tall, elegant lady in a flowered dress entered and introduced herself as Mrs. Edina Jongwe. Several children peeped out of a back room until the servant shooed them away.

"Dr. van Heerden phoned you about Nhamo," began Sister Gladys.

"Oh, yes. The whiteman," said Mrs. Jongwe distantly. "This is the alleged relative."

"Proud Jongwe's daughter," the nurse said.

"She's pretty," remarked Mrs. Jongwe. Her cold manner took the pleasure out of the compliment. "How old are you, child?"

"I—I don't know," stammered Nhamo.

"When she came to us, she didn't look over eleven, but actually I think she was around fourteen."

"Totally uneducated, I suppose."

"She grew up in a remote village," said Sister Gladys with a trace of irritation. "Since she's been at Efifi, she's learned rapidly. She can read like an adult, and Dr. Masuku is going to teach her typing. She's wonderful at arithmetic. I think she's a very intelligent child."

"How interesting. Well, my husband will be home around five. Perhaps you can come back then and discuss things." Mrs. Jongwe stood up. Sister Gladys pulled Nhamo to her feet.

They were shown to the door. Very soon Nhamo and the nurse found themselves at the foot of the gleaming red steps.

"I told you they wouldn't like me," said Nhamo.

"That witch," hissed Sister Gladys under her breath. "Did you see her fingernails?"

"They were very long," Nhamo said.

"That's to show everyone she doesn't have to work with her hands. I'd like to stick them into a nice hot tub of laundry."

Sister Gladys fumed until they found Mother and Dr. van Heerden at a grocery store. "Come back at five! I'm surprised she didn't tell us to use the servants' entrance!"

"It'll be too late to drive back to Efifi afterward, but we can stay at a hotel," Dr. van Heerden said, trying to calm the nurse down.

"If only we could find Proud. We could forget about the others," said Mother.

"Don't worry, Wild Child," boomed the doctor. "I'll corner your daddy. I'll tell Bliksem to track him."

Nhamo wished he wouldn't call her Wild Child.

The news of her arrival must have traveled, because at five a small crowd of Jongwes had gathered outside the gate to observe her. Nhamo, feeling extremely self-conscious, made her way past several dozen pairs of eyes. She didn't know how to react. Did you wave at strange relatives? Would they think she was rude if she didn't?

Mother and Dr. van Heerden had decided to accompany Sister Gladys on this visit. "I don't think it makes any difference *who* shows up," Mother said. "They're simply unfriendly."

"Or are hiding something," observed Dr. van Heerden.

They were ushered into the parlor and again served tea. This time Mrs. Jongwe was joined by her husband and his parents. Nhamo studied them covertly. Industry was dressed in a gray suit and shiny black shoes. His face was carefully bland. The grandparents were surprisingly youthful, or perhaps they had had easier lives than poor *Ambuya*.

What would *Ambuya* have made of these people? "Dressed-up donkeys," she would have judged them. "What good are claws on a woman?" she would have said about Mrs. Jongwe. "Is she going to hunt dassies for lunch?" Nhamo smiled with her head politely bowed.

"Let's have a look at the child," commanded Industry Jongwe, and so Nhamo was made to stand and turn before the assembly.

"She's pretty," remarked her grandmother.

"Yes, I noticed that," Mrs. Jongwe said.

"But she doesn't look like Proud."

No, the Jongwes agreed. She didn't look like Proud.

"She resembles my mother," said her grandfather. The others glared at him.

"Would it be possible to speak to Proud?" Dr. van Heerden asked.

No, that would not be possible, the others murmured.

"Why ever not?" exclaimed Mother.

The children clustering at the inner door scattered. From beyond, Nhamo heard the *tap-tap-tap* of a cane. The elder Jongwes turned, suddenly tense.

"*Why* can't we talk to this child's father?" Mother cried.

An old, old man came through the door. He was dressed in European clothes, but around his neck hung many charms and around his hips was tied a leopard skin. He was unquestionably an *nganga*, and, from the reaction of the others, a powerful and important one.

"Because Proud Jongwe is dead," the *nganga* said.

Nhamo stood perfectly still as the old man approached her. He lifted her face with a skeletal hand and turned her head from side to side. "She looks like my first wife," he announced.

A stir went through the room.

The old *nganga* sat in a chair hastily provided for him and motioned for Nhamo to sit beside him. "Tell me about yourself," he said.

She didn't think to hold anything back. She was convinced he would detect a lie. She told him about the village and her mother's death. She told him about the *ngozi* and how she had fled from an imposed marriage. She even talked about the leopard that had appeared to her by the water so long ago—if it *was* a leopard and not a trick of the light.

Now and then the *nganga* waved for a cup of tea or tray of snacks. He allowed Nhamo to rest between stories. Night fell outside. The smaller children were hauled off to bed, but no one else attempted to leave.

When Nhamo explained how the *njuzu* had led her to the garden island, the old man bent toward her with great attention. "I gave them Aunt Shuvai's beads," Nhamo said. "I didn't have anything else."

"You did the right thing," the *nganga* assured her.

Nervously, she told him about the dead Portuguese and the *panga* she thought he had given her, about the puff adder that had come from the ancestors, and about Long Teats. "But *Baba* Joseph sent Long Teats away," she said hastily. "He turned her from a hyena to a cane rat and then to a blackjack bush. I threw it into the fire."

"Good," said the old man.

By the time the story was done, the smells of good food had been coming from the kitchen for a long time. Nhamo realized it was very late. She gulped a mouthful of tea. It was only then that she looked up at the faces of the Jongwes. They were full of awe, and even fear.

"If this child hadn't resembled my first wife, I would still have accepted her," announced the old *nganga*. "She has obviously inherited my ability to communicate with the spirit world. She has been trained by the *njuzu*. I am pleased to welcome her into our family."

Dr. van Heerden, Mother, Sister Gladys, and Nhamo were sitting in the dining room of the Mtoroshanga Hotel. They had arrived just before the kitchen closed and were busily applying themselves to curry and rice. Nhamo sat between the two women. She needed them close to her, and she dreaded the morning, when they would leave her.

"You've landed with your bum in butter, and no mistake," said the Afrikaner, wiping his vast chops with a napkin.

"She's frightened, Hendrik," said Mother.

"*Ach,* that old man hasn't eaten anyone for *blerry* years, Wild Child. His teeth have gone soft."

Nhamo turned her eyes, which threatened to spill over with tears, toward him.

"Don't look at me like that! You must have learned how to make me feel guilty from *Baba* Joseph," rumbled Dr. van Heerden. "Listen, any kid in this dust bowl would give her right elbow to live in that mansion. The Jongwes are rich. They'll send you to the best school, buy you fancy clothes. You can't afford to pass up the chance."

"I know," Nhamo said tearfully.

"The witch almost bit off her long fingernails when the old *nganga* recognized Nhamo," remarked Sister Gladys.

"Please don't make her more nervous," Mother said. She put her arm around Nhamo, and Nhamo had to swallow hard to keep from crying. It was very clear that all was not harmony in the Jongwe household. Nhamo didn't know what was wrong, but she knew the addition of a Wild Child from Mozambique wasn't going to improve matters.

"Remember," Mother said softly, "if things don't go well, you can come back to us. We expect you during school vacations anyhow."

School! That was another thing Nhamo found worrying.

"I've got something of yours in my safe, remember," added Dr. van Heerden.

Nhamo looked up in surprise.

"Your *roora,* Wild Child. Your granny's gold nuggets."

"I thought—I mean, I expected—"

"—the old whiteman to pocket them," finished the Afrikaner.

Nhamo's face burned with shame. He had taken her in, saved her life, and asked for nothing in return. She had repaid him by slashing Bliksem and stabbing his arm.

"You more than earned your keep with work, Nhamo," the Afrikaner said, "even if you did disable half the farm crew."

She was too overcome to speak.

"This calls for ice cream all around," shouted Dr. van Heerden. The sleepy waiters moved toward the kitchen with resigned expressions on their faces.

The first thing Mrs. Edina Jongwe did was hand Nhamo over to the servants and instruct them to keep the girl out of her sight. Nhamo was glad to obey. She discovered this wasn't personal. Mrs. Jongwe didn't tolerate her own children either. They were shunted off to a nanny, who chased them around like naughty mice and fed them beer when she wanted peace. Nhamo was shocked.

Industry Jongwe had a second wife in another, smaller house. Her solitary child, a little boy named Clever, came over and tried to play with Edina's flock. The other children tormented him, but he was so desperate for company that he put up with it. "You can beat him if you like," Mrs. Jongwe said lazily, on one of the few occasions she deigned to notice Nhamo.

That means I'm not *quite* at the bottom, thought Nhamo. I can always thrash Clever if I feel out of sorts.

Instead, she went out of her way to be kind to the miserable child, with the result that he attached himself firmly to her. He was a whining, unattractive creature. In spite of his name he wasn't bright, and he had yet to master toilet training, although he was old enough to attend school.

Nhamo's grandparents slept all day and fought all night. Jongwe Senior had developed a taste for whiskey. The smell of his breath made Nhamo's head swim, and his loud, bullying voice filled her with alarm. He was her grandfather, so she owed him respect—but that didn't mean she had to stay near him. He was sometimes possessed of strange rages and would strike out with his walking stick and even smash the furniture.

Her grandmother treated him to what were referred to as "curtain lectures." She didn't dare humiliate the old man in front of the family, but she could—and did—scream at him behind closed doors.

Nhamo looked forward to school because it got her out of the house. Every morning she and five of Industry's children set out with book bags over their shoulders. The boys wore khaki uniforms, and the girls had blue-and-white plaid dresses. They all had heavy brown shoes.

Nhamo liked the uniforms. No one could tell she had never been in a school before, or had grown up in a *primitive* village. *Primitive* was one of the first new words she learned from Mrs. Jongwe. Nhamo was no different from any of the other girls until someone asked her a question. Then her extreme ignorance became obvious.

And yet, gradually, her ability to read and do math surpassed that of all but the oldest students. Only writing continued to defeat her. She held the pencil like a butter knife and her penmanship was as bad as Clever's. I hope Mother remembers to teach me typing, thought Nhamo. She looked forward to summer vacation.

She was sitting in the lush garden one Saturday morning with Clever clamped to her like a leech. "I wish there was school today," she sighed.

"I don't. I hate school," Clever informed her.

The nanny was trying to round up the other girls to dress them for a party. Nhamo wasn't invited. The girls ran around, taunting the poor woman. Suddenly, the nanny squatted and urinated on the lawn, just like a wild animal. At once she was up again, chasing the excited children. Nhamo closed her eyes. She had behaved in exactly the same way, before Sister Gladys introduced her to underpants.

"Tell me a story," demanded Clever.

He was the only person who cared to listen to her anymore, although he was a bad audience. His attention wandered. Nhamo remembered a Matabele tale she had heard from Mother. She decided to alter it slightly, to make it more interesting.

"Once upon a time the elephant had two wives," she began. "The senior wife was a hyena with many children, and the junior was a skinny jackal with only one little boy."

Clever listened with his thumb in his mouth.

"They hated each other, but they had to pretend to be friendly. One day the two wives were trotting down a path when they saw a band of hunters ahead with meat rolled up in grass mats. As the hunters walked along, blood dripped onto the ground. The smell almost drove the animals wild.

" 'I'm soooo hungry,' howled the hyena, baring her teeth.

" 'Meeee toooo,' wailed the jackal.

"They followed the hunters to a village and watched them store the meat in a granary. The granary was up on poles. In the wall was a single round window.

"As soon as the hunters were out of sight, the jackal leaped up to the window and wriggled her skinny body inside. 'Come on,' she called to the hyena. 'This place is loaded with food.'

" 'I'll never fit through such a tiny hole,' the hyena protested.

" 'I'll help you.' The jackal jumped out again. She let the hyena climb onto her back and she helped her struggle through the window. Then both of them began to eat for all they were worth.

" 'We'd better go now,' said the hyena after a while.

" 'You may never get a feast like this again,' the jackal pointed out. The hyena continued to stuff herself until her stomach was ready to burst. 'Just one more piece,' urged the jackal, holding up a chunk of meat. The hyena couldn't resist.

"The jackal leaped through the window again. The hyena tried to follow, but she became stuck. 'Help me, O junior wife! I'm trapped here!' she cried.

"But the jackal ran through the village barking at the top of her voice. This brought out all the hunting dogs. They spied the hyena stuck in the window and set up such a clamor that the hunters came to see what was happening. 'Look at that ugly beast!' they cried. 'She's eaten all our meat!' They ran into the granary and killed her at once. The jackal and her one son lived happily ever after with the elephant."

Clever had fallen asleep after—Nhamo wrinkled her nose—relieving himself on her skirt. She eased him to the grass. A chuckle drifted out of the grape arbor behind her.

"You have a wicked mind, little Nhamo," said the dry, old voice. "I wonder who the hyena and jackal are?"

Nhamo whirled around. It was the *nganga*, seated in the deep shade. She hadn't spoken to him since that first day.

"Go change your dress, great-granddaughter. We're going to visit your father," he commanded her.

41

She wore her best dress, the one Mother had bought her, and the bra. She was going to do things exactly right for this occasion. Nhamo thought the old man would take her to the local graveyard, but he led her to his house. It was a small place tucked away at the edge of the vast Jongwe estate. People were always waiting outside for advice. They came from all over the country, and they sometimes had to wait a long time for the *nganga*'s attention.

Nhamo spied a pot hidden in the thatch and halted. Horror nailed her to the spot. What did *nganga*s store inside such things? It couldn't be— she didn't want to know—

"I'm not the *muvuki*," he said in a whispery voice that made her jump. "I don't keep my oldest son's heart in a bottle."

Nhamo bit her lip. That was exactly what she had imagined. She looked cautiously at the dried animals hanging on the walls, the heaps of withered herbs.

"I've been too weak to undertake this journey until now," explained the old man. He waved to a young man at the back of the house. "Garikayi is my assistant. He will help us."

Garikayi loaded a car with bottles of water and food. He helped the *nganga* into the front seat and opened the back door for Nhamo. They set off on a steep road going up into the Umvukwe Mountains. It was here, Nhamo had learned, that the chrome mines lay. It was the only place on earth where that rare metal was found.

The car struggled up higher and higher. It curved around until the outside world had completely vanished. Nhamo's eyes opened wide. She had no idea this beautiful green country existed so close to the dusty streets of Mtoroshanga. Yellow weaver birds darted across the road. A stream overhung with palms wound beside them with a loud, heartening sound. She pressed her face eagerly to the window.

Eventually, they came to a meadow. The road deteriorated into a path scarred by deep ruts from the rainy season. They stopped. "Oh," sighed Nhamo, stepping out onto springy grass.

"We'll eat first," said her great-grandfather. Garikayi spread out a cloth and heaped it with food. He helped the old man sit down with his back against a tree. No one spoke, and Nhamo was just as happy to stay quiet. She was in awe of the *nganga* and hardly knew how to address him.

They had lemonade, peanut butter sandwiches, and a kind of pound cake with red jam. Nhamo was now knowledgeable about the food she had seen in magazines so long ago. She could never have imagined then that she would be eating them in a forest glade with her great-grandfather.

When they were finished, Garikayi packed up the food. They set off along the rutted path. The *nganga* had to be carried across the larger gaps. They came to a grassy hill dotted with gentians and pink ground orchids, and began to climb.

It was a long, slow process with many stops to allow the old man to rest. "Would you like to return, honored *Tateguru*?"* asked Nhamo.

"If I stop now, I may never have the strength to return. Your father appeared to me in a dream and asked me to bring you here," he replied.

So Nhamo went up behind him, to cushion his fall if he slipped, and Garikayi half carried him until they arrived at

Tateguru: Great-grandfather.

a jumble of rocks and timbers in the side of a cliff. The *nganga* sat down on a log to catch his breath.

All around were the green hills with the stream chattering below in the valley. Puffy white clouds floated overhead in a blue sky. Nhamo took a deep breath.

"I'm an embarrassment to the family. So are you," said the *nganga*. "We represent the past, which they are busy trying to forget." He patted the ground beside him, and Nhamo sat down. "They're Methodists when it suits them. That's a kind of Christian."

Nhamo sighed. *Another* kind of Christian. Why did they have to be so complicated?

"Industry went to church until he decided to take a second wife. Then he suddenly discovered his African roots. The Methodists don't approve of second wives. Even so, the others occasionally attend church and talk about bringing Zimbabwe into the twentieth century. They aren't pleased to have a traditional healer in the backyard, but I'm too powerful for them to ignore."

The old man signaled to Garikayi, who quickly produced cups and a thermos of sweet milky tea.

"My son—your grandfather—made his fortune in the mines."

Nhamo nodded. He was talking about Jongwe Senior.

"He dug his own tunnel into these hills and made a lucky strike. A lot of men work independently along the Umvukwe range. The place is like a giant anthill. As soon as he got money, he began to imitate the white people, and he changed his Shona name, Murenga, to Lloyd. He wanted to flatter the owner of the Big Chief Chrome Company, who was also called Lloyd. Unfortunately, the owner was killed by a land mine. Then the whites began to lose the war, and it became unfashionable to have a white name.

"As you know, the word *murenga* means 'revolution.' What wonderful luck! Lloyd-the-lackey turned into Murenga-the-revolutionary overnight. Oh, he was first in line for the victory parades, as soon as the guns were put away. At the same time I was promoted from being a senile old peasant to being a revered elder.

"Murenga was rewarded for his patriotism by being made manager of the mines. He had two sons, called Proud and Industry."

Nhamo straightened up. Here at last was information about Father.

"I think you've noticed Murenga's weakness where alcohol is concerned."

Nhamo was confused. She was unwilling to criticize her grandfather, but what was she to do when her *great*-grandfather wanted her opinion?

"Never mind. I shouldn't have asked. How could anyone in that house *not* hear the shouting and fighting? Murenga is an alcoholic. So, unfortunately, was Proud."

A breeze blew between the hills and bent the grass before it in long waves. An impala buck stepped onto the path far below, turned its head to observe the humans, and led a group of females across to the stream.

"Proud was a good boy," said the old man, his eyes soft. "He could have been such a fine man, but he started drinking when he was no older than you. I think he used to empty Murenga's bottles after he passed out. Your father always had such big plans! He was going to *own* the Big Chief Mine; he was going to run for Parliament. The sky was the limit. And then he met your mother."

Nhamo was jolted out of her reverie. "You knew about Mother?"

"I met her. She was just a little schoolgirl, but very, very beautiful. Proud should have been ashamed of himself. Did you know she was pregnant before they got married?"

"I—I—wasn't even sure they got married," Nhamo admitted.

"There was a terrible family row. Murenga refused to give his permission. I did, of course, but at that time I was only an ignorant old peasant. Murenga was in his I-love-whites phase. The Catholics at Nyanga married your parents."

Nhamo sighed with relief.

"I suppose Proud lied to the priest—neither of your parents was Catholic—or perhaps the priest felt sorry for your mother. He insisted that Proud get an official wedding license from the government, to make sure the marriage was legal. I still have it.

"Your parents traveled to your mother's village in Mozambique. The next thing we knew, Proud was back, and we got a letter asking for cattle to pay for a murder. It was like someone had tossed a beehive through the window. You wouldn't believe the fights!"

I might, thought Nhamo, remembering the noises that came from Jongwe Senior's room.

"Murenga disinherited his son. Proud announced he was going to earn his own fortune. He came here." The *nganga* gestured at the hill. "He was always full of great plans. He was going to dig the deepest, longest tunnels anyone had ever seen. And so he did. They collapsed one day with him at the very heart of the mountain."

Nhamo gasped. That jumble of rocks and timber—it was her father's grave! "Didn't . . . anyone dig him out?" she said.

"We tried, but the tunnels went in all directions. No one had any idea where he was when the accident happened. Finally, we conducted the funeral ceremonies here. Murenga wanted it that way, but I always wondered whether Proud's spirit was happy with the arrangement."

Nhamo was so overcome with a mixture of emotions, she began to cry. She was glad her parents had been married, but shamed that Mother hadn't been welcomed by the Jongwes. She was horrified to be sitting next to Father's grave—and yet relieved to know what had happened to him. She lay on the grass and gave herself up to weeping. The old man handed her a handkerchief when she was finished.

"I think we should go down now. I'm feeling tired," he said.

"Oh! Of course!" Nhamo was instantly concerned about her frail great-grandfather. She and Garikayi helped him back to the meadow. The sun had slipped low in the sky. The valley was filling up with green shadows.

"Let's have more tea, little Disaster," said the old man. "I have one last piece of information for you."

The ever resourceful Garikayi started a fire and boiled tea with water from the stream. He laced it with sweetened condensed milk. Nhamo thought she had never drunk anything so delicious. In a strange way it tasted exactly like the tea she used to prepare for Mother in the ruined village.

"I think there were *two* spirit leopards involved with your life, Nhamo," the *nganga* said suddenly. "Goré Mtoko's totem was the leopard. So is ours."

"I thought ours was the lion." Nhamo was appalled. If two people with the same totem married, it was *incest*.

"Ours is both the lion and the leopard. That happens sometimes when two powerful clans combine. Our praise name is Gurundoro, the people who wear the *ndoro,* the symbol of royalty. The Mtokos, by the way, are very remote relatives with different praise names, so you can relax. The marriage wouldn't have been incest, although it would certainly have been evil. My understanding is this: Goré Mtoko's spirit killed your mother and, I believe, caused your father's mine shaft to collapse. At that time Goré's revenge was complete.

"But your father's spirit was unsatisfied. He knew he had a child who must be brought to her true family. Proud told your mother his totem was the lion because it made him feel powerful, but he was really more like a leopard. A leopard hunts alone in the shadows. He doesn't face his enemies openly. I think your father's first appearance to you was by the stream."

"It might have been a trick of the light," Nhamo couldn't help saying.

"Yes, but why did you insist on telling everyone about it? He appeared again in the banana grove the night before *Vatete* got sick, and he left his print on her grave. He was driving you away from your mother's village."

"But the leopard on the island—"

"Tell me, did it ever harm you?"

"No," Nhamo admitted.

"From what you told me, it provided you with meat when you most needed it, and killed the baboon that was a danger to you. At the same time, it frightened you off the island. Otherwise, you might have spent the rest of your life there."

Nhamo clasped her hands. That was certainly true.

"Proud appeared to me in a dream recently, asking me to bring you here. I think he wanted you to understand what he had done."

All the way home, Nhamo was sunk in thought. She barely noticed the hills give way to the dusty plain, or the lights of Mtoroshanga as they approached. The *nganga* rapped on the door of Jongwe Senior's room as soon as they returned.

Jongwe Senior was slumped in an easy chair with a cut-glass decanter on a table beside him. His wife crocheted a blanket on the opposite side of the room. She must do that all day, thought Nhamo. The house is full of those crocheted blankets.

"I've come for the picture," said the *nganga*. Murenga stared at his father with red-rimmed eyes. He seemed not to have heard, but his wife put aside her crochet hook. The air in the room was full of the sweet, cloying smell of whiskey, and every corner was heaped with mementos of trips to England and South Africa.

Murenga's wife cleared away some porcelain statues of white girls in long frilly skirts. She folded up a lace tablecloth. From a tea chest underneath, she removed a portrait of a man in a suit and a woman in a long, white dress.

The *nganga* took the photograph without a word and led Nhamo from the room. "Phew! I need fresh air after that," said the old man, seating himself by the open dining-room window. The cool smell of lawn sprinklers drifted inside. "They rented the clothes." He tapped the portrait. "That's what Catholics wear when they get married."

Nhamo was afraid to look. She had imagined her parents' appearance for so long, she didn't want the image destroyed. But she finally had to open her eyes and acknowledge them. They were so young! Mother wore a gauzy white cloth over her hair and held a bunch of flowers trimmed with ribbons.

Father was cheerfully at ease in the whiteman clothes, while Mother seemed embarrassed. They were both extremely handsome people. "She looks like Masvita," murmured Nhamo.

"Masvita? Oh, your first cousin. That's not surprising," said the old man. "You're in the picture, too, little Disaster."

"I am?"

"Right here." The *nganga* pointed at Mother's stomach, and laughed at Nhamo's discomfort. "This picture belongs to you. I'll give you the wedding license tomorrow. It proves you really are a Jongwe, although sometimes I think that's not such a wonderful thing."

Both Nhamo and the old man winced as the first sounds of fighting erupted from Jongwe Senior's room.

42

Efifi looked exactly the same as Dr. van Heerden's Land Rover roared through the gate. Nhamo sighed with relief. She was so used to losing things, she was afraid Efifi had vanished. She ran to find *Baba* Joseph as the doctor unloaded supplies. Then she ran to the hospital to find Sister Gladys.

It was wonderful to be back! No matter how she tried, she couldn't really please the Jongwes, except for her great-grandfather. In subtle ways they made her feel like an intruder, and she suspected they always would. Efifi felt like home. She raced eagerly from place to place to assure herself everything was all right. The bottles were lined up on the same shelves in the hospital; the pumpkins were heaped in the corner of the cookhouse where they belonged. Even the same crows perched on the fence near the livestock pens.

Only she had changed. She had stylish new clothes, pink plastic sandals, and almost-emerald earrings in her newly pierced ears. One thing worried her, though: She no longer knew how to address Dr. Masuku.

Nhamo couldn't call her Mother anymore, now that she knew what Mother had looked like. And yet it seemed unfriendly to go back to "Dr. Masuku." She hesitated at the door of the lab.

"Nhamo!" cried Dr. Masuku in a delighted voice. "Oh, my! You really are a woman now.

Turn around. The Jongwes didn't pinch pennies on that cloth. And those earrings! You look beautiful!"

"Grandmother made me the dress," said Nhamo shyly. "She took time off from crocheting blankets."

"You told me about those wretched blankets."

Nhamo had written letters to Dr. Masuku in her clumsy, uneven scrawl. She started them "Dear Mother," although it made her uncomfortable to do so. This summer she would learn to type and would throw away pencils forever.

"I finally got a message from Mozambique," Dr. Masuku said. "I thought it was better for you to read it in person." She took out a piece of yellowed paper that had been folded and refolded. It had obviously been carried in someone's pocket for a long time. The writing was just as crabbed as Nhamo's.

"Dir Neese," it began. It took a moment for Nhamo to realize it meant "Dear Niece." The letter was from Uncle Kufa. It confirmed what she already knew, that *Ambuya* had died. Aunt Chipo was devastated ("veri veri sad"), but she was cheered up when Masvita had a baby boy. Masvita had married a man from *Vatete*'s village and was pregnant again.

Two children! Nhamo's eyes became distant as she calculated. They must have married her cousin off the minute her hair grew back. She remembered the fever dream she had after the scorpion sting. Masvita had sacrificed herself in the lake with Princess Senwa "because it was the custom," but Grandmother had held her, Nhamo, back. "*Ambuya* didn't want me to be like Masvita," she murmured.

"I'm sure she didn't," Dr. Masuku agreed.

"I ought to visit them."

"I'd wait awhile. They might still be worried about *ngozi*s."

Nhamo thought about living in the village again. She would have to spend her days pounding mealies and hauling water. She wouldn't have any books. Most of her fellow students hated studying, but Nhamo loved it—except for the writing. Well, as *Ambuya* said, even the best bowl of porridge has a few weevils in it.

"Dr. van Heerden and I need to talk to you," said Dr. Masuku. They went off to find the Afrikaner in the barn, supervising the birth of a calf. *Baba* Joseph was watching the procedure critically.

"I don't think you should have given her medicine to hurry it along," he said.

"She's weak from the *blerry* flies. I suppose you'll want to baptize the baby," Dr. van Heerden said, soaping his hands as he prepared to deliver the calf.

"*Vapostori* don't baptize animals. I can pray for *your* soul, however."

"Thanks, *oupa*," said the doctor. He wrestled the calf from its weakened mother. Nhamo's eyes grew wide as she watched the new life slide into the world. Animals had one spirit from Mother Earth, but people had an extra one from Mwari. She wasn't sure why you had to pray for it.

"I wondered where you'd got to," boomed the Afrikaner as he plunged his hands into a bucket to clean them.

Dr. van Heerden, Dr. Masuku, and Nhamo sat outside the cookhouse in the shade of a bougainvillea vine. The cook had provided a box of arrowroot cookies to go along with the tea.

"I've had this weighed," Dr. van Heerden said, tossing the bag with Grandmother's gold nuggets into Nhamo's lap. Her throat constricted as she looked at it. The red cloth was almost black with dirt, but it was the only surviving link to her life in the village.

"Your granny provided for you better than she realized. She had to sell her gold at a tiny fraction of the real price and probably didn't know what it was worth in the outside world. There's almost three ounces here. That's worth over four thousand dollars."*

Nhamo, who had recently been granted an allowance of fifty cents a week, could only stare at him.

"We think," said Dr. Masuku gently, "you should open

---

*Zimbabwe dollars.

a bank account in your name. We think it should be secret from the Jongwes."

Now Nhamo stared at her.

"Both your grandmother and mother were trapped by poverty. You can be free. That's why *Ambuya* gave you the gold."

"But why can't I tell the Jongwes—"

"Right now the old *nganga* rules the roost," said Dr. van Heerden. "When he dies, you can bet that Long Fingernails won't rest until you're out of the house."

"Tell me, does anyone there really care about your happiness? Aside from sewing you dresses to relieve the boredom of crocheting blankets," said Dr. Masuku.

"No," Nhamo admitted.

"Right now you're a doll for them to dress up. People get tired of dolls. You're far too intelligent to be turned into a family drudge or forced into a bad marriage. Women are never free until they can control their own money."

"And during the summers when you work here, your salary will go into the account," added Dr. van Heerden.

It was all happening too fast. Nhamo could only agree blindly and hope for the best. She felt uncomfortable about hiding the bank account from the Jongwes, but she had no illusions about Mrs. Edina Jongwe. Someday the woman might casually say, "You can beat her if you like" to a stranger, and then introduce him as her future husband.

"You know, you haven't once called me Mother since you returned," said Dr. Masuku. "Or used my name."

Nhamo hung her head.

"*Ach*, it just came to me: She hasn't called me Daddy in donkey's years," said Dr. van Heerden, stirring three spoonfuls of sugar into a fresh cup of tea.

Dr. Masuku pursed her lips in irritation. "I'll admit I was relieved about *Mother*, Nhamo, but you really ought to think of something. I won't accept 'Hey, you!' "

"I'm sorry." Nhamo's eyes filled with tears.

"Oh, dear. You look like I just hit you! Why don't you

call me Aunt Everjoice? I'll be your *vatete* and tell you all the secrets of womanhood."

"Like how to get the lipstick to stay inside the little lines," Dr. van Heerden said. Dr. Masuku swatted him with a magazine from a pile by the cookhouse.

Nhamo's eyes suddenly focused on the cover.

"Oh! Oh! It's the picture! It's Mother," she cried. She jumped to her feet. Startled, Dr. Masuku held out the magazine. Nhamo grabbed it and smoothed it out on the table. The back cover showed a woman wearing a white apron and a flowered dress. She was spreading white bread with margarine. Nearby stood a little girl with hair gathered in two fat puffs over her ears, and Nhamo *knew* the bread and margarine were for the little girl. She looked up.

The picture didn't look anything like Dr. Masuku.

"That's a *margarine advertisement*," exclaimed the woman. "Good grief! You were communicating with the spirit of Stork margarine all those years."

"Sh-she doesn't l-look like you," hiccuped Nhamo. "H-how could I have made such a stupid m-mistake?"

"Don't cry." Dr. Masuku hugged her tightly. "We always suspected you *imprinted* on me. It's not surprising after all you went through."

"What's *imprinting*?"

"When certain birds break out of the egg, they think the first thing they see is their mother. They follow it everywhere."

"Even if it's a jackal?"

"So they say. I don't think a bird with a jackal mother lasts very long," Dr. van Heerden remarked.

Dr. Masuku hesitated before she spoke again. "In one sense, you died after leaving the village, Nhamo. If the spirit world exists, you certainly went through it, and when I found you in the underground chamber, it was as though I brought you back to life. I was the first thing you saw after you broke out of the egg."

Nhamo looked from the magazine to the two doctors and back again. This was an idea she would have to think about for a long time. "The picture doesn't even look like my real mother," she said sadly.

"No, but wait. . . ." Dr. Masuku held up the picture. "This is fantastic." She marched Nhamo over to the hospital and made her look into the full-length mirror.

Nhamo had steadfastly refused to do this since the horrifying moment when she saw the wall spider with the burr stuck on top. She had to see bits of herself, of course, to attach earrings and so forth, but she had avoided putting the bits together.

Now she gazed in amazement at her image. She was taller and had a womanly figure. Her hair shone with good health, and her eyes no longer stared back from hollows. She wore a flowered dress and pink plastic shoes. The almost-emeralds glittered in her ears.

She was beautiful.

And she looked like the woman in the Stork margarine ad.

"I can't explain it," said Dr. Masuku in an awed voice.

"Auntie Everjoice. I like the sound of that," Dr. van Heerden said from the door of the hospital.

The last evening of summer vacation, Nhamo sat in the ruined guard tower watching the twilight fade. Out of the hazy east came three figures walking like people who have come a long way. They passed through the fence and moved across the fields without disturbing the leaves. They halted below the tower, one ahead, the other two hanging back among the tall fronds of a stand of mealies.

Little Pumpkin, whispered the foremost figure.

Tears began to roll down Nhamo's face.

You've done well, Little Pumpkin, said Grandmother. *A bank account at your age! If I'd had a bank account, things would have been different, I can tell you. Well, I said I would visit you when I returned to my ancestors, so here I am. What have you got to say for yourself?*

Nhamo explained about the Jongwes and her new life.

Bunch of donkeys, except for the old man, said Grandmother. *Still, what can you do? They're family.*

Nhamo talked until darkness fell and an evening wind made the mealies rustle. The other two figures came out into the starlight. Mother's face was young, so young! She looked like Masvita. Father was more difficult to see. Sometimes he seemed to be standing there and sometimes he was only a shadow padding silently along the fence.

We have a long way to go, said Grandmother at last. *Ruva is having her coming-of-age party. I don't want to miss it.*

But you will return? Nhamo wanted to ask.

The paths of the body are long, but the paths of the spirit are short, said Mother in a low, sweet voice. And then they were gone. And Nhamo was left with the wind blowing out of the forest and the fireflies hovering over the lucerne.

GLOSSARY

(Unless otherwise stated, words are in Shona.)

Ach (Afrikaans): Oh.
Ambuya: Grandmother.
Baba: Father; also a term of respect for any older man.
Binza: Otter.
Blerry (Afrikaans): A form of the mild English swear word *bloody*.
Bliksem (Afrikaans): Lightning. A mild swear word.
Bonsella (Tchalapa-lapa, pidgin Zulu): A gift.
Burwa: A giant lizard something like an iguana; also called a *leguuan*.
Chidao: Clan name or praise name.
Chikandiwa: A stroke (medical term).
Chisveru: Shona version of the game of tag.
Dare: Men's meeting place.
Dassie (Afrikaans): A hyrax. Also called an *mbira* (Shona) or rock rabbit (English). It looks like a giant guinea pig.
Donkeyberry: A small tree with rather dry, sweet berries containing large seeds, which are also edible. Also called a raisin bush or a *munjiri* (Shona).
Frelimo: Ruling party of Mozambique.
Gogodzero: Opening fee; it is paid to begin a divination.
Gumbo: Leg of a cow.
Gurundoro: People who wear the *ndoro,* a spiral disk worn by kings and spirit mediums. This is Nhamo's *chidao,* or clan name.
Hakata: Divining (fortune-telling) sticks, plain on one side with a pattern on the other.
Hezvo!: Good heavens!
Hozi: Communal storehouse raised on poles.
Iwe! Hamba!: Hey, you! Go away!
Jabvane: A many-branched small tree with juicy, purple berries.
Jongwe: Rooster.
Karoyi: Little witch.

Knobkerrie (Zulu): Club with a knob at one end.

Kugadzira: Ceremony to bring a spirit home to its grave.

Maheu: Drink made from leftover maize porridge and water; slightly alcoholic.

Mai: Mother.

Maiwee!: Oh, Mother! *Mama mia!*

Mamba (Zulu): The largest and most feared of African snakes. It is quick to bite if disturbed. Its poison can cause death within minutes.

Marula: A tree with yellowish green, plum-shaped fruit containing a nut with two or three oil-rich seeds inside. Very common and popular.

Masikati: Good day.

Mbira: A musical instrument with flat metal keys attached to a slab of wood or a hollowed-out gourd. It is played with the thumb or, if the musician is especially creative, the big toe.

Mealie (English): Corn.

Meisie-kind (Afrikaans): Girl child, kid.

Mhandara: Young woman.

Mhondoro: The lion spirit, spirit of the land.

Mhuvuyu: A weed with spearhead-shaped leaflets. The long, black seeds hook onto cloth and take time to remove. The cooked leaves taste like spinach. Also called blackjack.

Minha vida (Portuguese): My life, my love.

Mobola: A wild African plum tree.

Mopane flies: Stingless bees that like to drink moisture from one's eyes, nose, and mouth. Very irritating.

Mopane tree: A common tree with rough, gray bark and kidney-shaped pods. The wood burns very easily.

Mowa: Wild spinach.

Moyo: Heart.

Mukonde: A leafless tree with many soft, easily broken branches. Its sap is sticky and poisonous. Also called a candelabra tree or a *euphorbia* (scientific name).

Mukuyu: Wild fig tree.

Mukwa: Tree with attractive golden sprays of flowers. The wood is prized for making furniture and canoes. It is termite-resistant.

Mupfuti: A beautiful tree with rough, gray bark and reddish leaves at the beginning of the rainy season.

Muroyi: Witch. A very bad insult.

Musasa: A common and handsome tree with reddish leaves at the beginning of the rainy season.

Mutarara: Wild gardenia.

Muti: Medicine.

Mutimwi: Cord worn around the hips to protect one's fertility.

Mutiti: Lucky-bean tree. A heavily built tree with spectacular scarlet flowers and small red-and-black seeds that contain a poison like curare.

Mutowa: A small tree with corklike bark and very sticky sap. Also called a rubber tree.

Mutsangidza: A short, bushy plant with small purple flowers. It is inedible, but can be boiled to make a flavoring resembling salt.

Mutupo: Totem.

Muvuki: A medical specialist who deals with causes of death.

Muzeze: A handsome tree with spectacular masses of yellow flowers. The bark, roots, and leaves are used to cure stomach pain, sore throat, and pinkeye.

Muzhanje: Wild loquat trees. They have round, rusty-yellow fruits about the size of plums, with hard skins. The leaves drop off to form a crackling carpet that gives away the presence of any animal beneath.

Mwari: God.

Ndoro: Round disks worn by kings.

Nganga: Traditional healer.

Ngozi: An avenging spirit.

Ngwena: The crocodile; name of an unlucky pattern in the divining sticks.

Nyama: Meat.

Oupa (Afrikaans): Grandpa. To call someone grandfather is always meant kindly in both Afrikaans and Shona.

Pakila: Panpipes.

Panga (Zulu): A large knife or machete.

Picanin (Tchalapa-lapa, pidgin Zulu): Child.

Quelea: Small birds that travel in huge flocks; they are a major pest of grain crops.

Roora: Bride price.

Ruredzo: A common trailing plant with pink flowers somewhat like snapdragons. The boiled roots produce a soap substitute.

Sadza: Stiff cornmeal porridge.

Shiri: Bird.

Shoko: A vervet monkey.

Shumba: Lion.

Takutuka chiremba: Traditional greeting on entering a *muvuki*'s territory. Literally: "We have scolded you, doctor."

Tateguru: Great-grandfather.

Tsenza: A small shrub with yellow flowers growing from tubers under the soil. The tubers taste somewhat like turnips. Also called wild potato.

Tsotsi: Common hoodlum.

Tsunga: The steadfast ones; a praise name.

Va-: Honored; added to the beginning of a name.

Va-Ambuya: Honored Grandmother.

Vahukwu: Welcome.

Vapostori: A sect of Christianity founded by Johane Maranke in 1932.

Vatete: Respectful title for paternal aunt.

Voetsek (Afrikaans): Go away! The word can be extremely insulting.

Vukiro: Sacred grove.

Womba!: Amazing!

Zango: A charm against witches.

Zaru: Disagreement; name of a particular fall of the divining sticks.

THE HISTORY AND PEOPLES OF ZIMBABWE AND MOZAMBIQUE

RECENT HISTORY OF ZIMBABWE AND MOZAMBIQUE

From 1964 to 1974 Mozambique was embroiled in a war of liberation from Portugal. Independence was declared in 1975, with the political party Frelimo taking over the government.

In 1963 the British attempted to grant independence to their colony Zimbabwe (then called Rhodesia). A small English tribe living in the country took over the government. They ruled until 1979, when independence was finally achieved after several years of fighting.

Nhamo's journey takes place around 1981. Land mines were still in place along the border, and relations among white people, the Shona, and the Matabele were sometimes hostile.

THE SHONA

The ancestors of the Shona arrived from the north between A.D. 1000 and 1200 as a collection of tribes with a common language and a distinct culture. The whole group was not referred to as Shona until the nineteenth century.

Histories of several royal lines were preserved in oral poetry, but the most famous king was Monomatapa. Monomatapa lived in the fifteenth century, and tales of his splendor reached the first Portuguese traders on the coast of Mozambique. He was supposed to rule a vast kingdom from the Kalahari Desert in the west to the Indian Ocean in the east.

Throughout southern Africa are the traces of an ancient civilization. The most important site is the city of Great Zimbabwe. This is located inland from the southeastern coast of Africa in present-day Zimbabwe. The city center was on a hilltop that was naturally protected from attack by a large outcrop of granite. Because it was situated on a high plateau, it was safe from the disease-infested tsetse flies that were common in the lowlands. This made it possible for an economy based on cattle to exist. Large amounts of rain made the land good for farming, and, rich in minerals, the earth could be mined for granite, iron, copper, and gold. The ancient Zimbabweans traded gold for glass beads, porcelain, and silk from as far away as China.

The city was only one of many such structures. More than 150 stone enclosures were built over several centuries from Mozambique to South Africa, but it is unknown whether they were part of a large kingdom or the remains of several small ones. The word *zimbabwe* means "stone enclosure" in Shona.

THE MATABELE OR NDEBELE

Mzilikazi, one of Shaka Zulu's generals, was allowed to leave the Zulu tribe with three hundred warriors. He built up his own tribe (the Matabele), but was driven out of South Africa by encroaching white settlers. He moved into southern Zimbabwe around 1836. Mzilikazi brought with him the powerful military organization of the Zulus and was able to establish a kingdom at the expense of the resident Shona. At the time of independence, the Matabele made up about 19 percent of the population. The two tribes, Shona and Matabele, have had a long history of mutual hostility.

THE BRITISH

The British tribe is composed of several subgroups: the Scots, Irish, Welsh, and English. One of these, the English, has been dominant for several centuries. The British gained control of Zimbabwe around 1890, but not without violent dissent from the Shona and Matabele. Several uprisings occurred before 1965, when the British lost control of the country. From 1965 to 1979 Zimbabwe was ruled by a small minority of English tribesmen.

THE PORTUGUESE

The Portuguese first settled in East Africa in the fifteenth century. They pursued a policy of conquest and trade with the interior for five centuries, and developed the slave trade from around 1600 until the late nineteenth century. In the twentieth century, a great number of Portuguese immigrated to colonies in Africa. After Mozambique and Angola became independent in 1975, many of these people moved to South Africa, Zimbabwe, or back to Portugal.

THE AFRIKANERS

While the Afrikaners' language is based on Dutch, only about a third of their ancestors actually came from Holland. They are a mixture of Dutch, French Huguenots, and Germans. They also clearly have a few English, Malay, Hottentot, and black African ancestors as well. In spite of this mixture, they form a distinct culture with strict Protestant ethics. Beginning in the late seventeenth century, they established farms throughout South Africa. In 1906 only about 6 percent of them lived in cities, towns, or villages.

Some of the early Afrikaners became wandering farmers, or Trekboers, and performed amazing feats of courage and endurance. Each group was highly individualistic, with a patriarch and a holy mission to find the Promised Land under the guidance of God. Some, hazy on geography, thought they had reached the Nile River when they were about halfway up South Africa. Trekboers went as far as Kenya in their wanderings, and many settled in Zimbabwe.

THE TRIBES OF MOZAMBIQUE

Many Shona-speaking people live in Mozambique. Other cultural groups include the Maravi, the Yao, and the Maconde. The most important influence on the tribal system of northern Mozambique was the slave trade. This was carried on by Arab traders, the Portuguese, and the Yao from the sixteenth century on, but became epidemic from about 1790 to 1840. Serious depopulation and great displacement of people occurred. This permanently disrupted the traditional culture. One group, the Tonga, appears to be the remnant of several groups of fleeing people rather than a genuine tribe.

The Portuguese in Mozambique gave up slavery in 1890, although it had become technically illegal years earlier. At this time the majority of the Yao converted to Islam in order to keep trading slaves with the Muslim sheikhs on the coast and with the sultan of Zanzibar.

THE BELIEF SYSTEM OF
THE SHONA

Shona culture is extremely complicated. The following is intended only as a brief overview.

MWARI

The supreme being of the Shona is usually called Mwari, although he—or she, for Mwari is both—is known by many praise names. Mwari could best be described as Natural Order. Anything thought contrary to Natural Order, such as the birth of twins, must be put right or disaster will follow. Mwari may not be referred to as "it" because he/she is a sexual being involved with the mysteries of fertility. He/she is a bringer of rain, and one of his/her praise names is Dzivaguru, the Great Pool.

Great Zimbabwe, the ancient city, was a religious shrine that operated as a spiritual and governmental center in the same way as Westminster Abbey in England. In the nineteenth century a ceremony was held in the ruins of Great Zimbabwe every second year. A black cow was sacrificed as a request for rain. Two other cattle were killed, one for the priests and one to feed the wild animals of the forest. The latter carcass was left near a building known as the temple. If it was devoured, it was a sign that Mwari had accepted the prayers. The high priests who transmitted the messages of the spirit world to ordinary people were—and are—called the Ear, the Eye, and the Mouth. I changed the latter to Arm in an earlier book to indicate the physical way in which things are communicated through possession in Africa.

Now the center of the religion has shifted to the Matopos Hills near the city of Bulawayo in southern Zimbabwe. This is the one place on earth where the voice of Mwari can still be heard. Below the priests is a lower circle of devotees called the *mbonga* and the *hossanah*s. *Mbonga* are virgins dedicated to the service of the god. They care for the shrines until they reach puberty, when they are expected to marry.

The *hossanah*s are young men who dance during ceremonies and carry messages for the priests.

The *mbonga*, when they marry, move to another status as mediums for tribal spirits, and when they pass child-bearing age they become very important as *muchembera*, priestesses who brew the sacred beer used in ceremonies.

THE MHONDORO

A *mhondoro*, or lion spirit, is concerned with the land and its people as a whole. Because the Shona are actually made up of several tribes, each tribe has a *mhondoro* and a lion-spirit medium. The *mhondoro* is concerned with general problems, such as rainfall and famine.

THE MUDZIMU

The *mudzimu* (plural, *vadzimu*) is a more personal spirit belonging to a family. Each person has at least four, his or her parents and patrilineal grandparents, who may make contact to warn of impending danger or to demand that some wrong be righted. Other ancestors may or may not take an interest in their offspring. One consults a specific male or female ancestor through a spirit medium to receive advice on personal problems. Certain family spirits may become interested in their descendants and teach them skills. This is why particular abilities run in families.

Old people are considered to be close to the spirit world and therefore are cloaked in power. The elderly are treated with great respect in Shona society.

SHAVE

A *shave* (plural, *mashave*) is someone who died far from home and therefore couldn't receive proper burial rites. A *shave* can possess anyone he or she likes, to impart knowledge. This is what happens when an unusual skill shows up in a family, for example a computer expert in a family noted for hunting. Race or tribe is unimportant in this possession. The original names of the spirits are not known, so they are referred to by the attributes or skills they impart. Some of the more popular *mashave* are Mazinda, who teaches one how to dance; Rotunhu, who imparts the art of healing; Nkupa, who teaches generosity; and Rokuba, who turns people into kleptomaniacs.

Rokuroya makes people act like witches. This is a particularly bad *shave,* and people who sleepwalk are suspected of being possessed by Rokuroya. In the bad old days they used to pound wooden pegs into the heads of sleepwalkers and leave them to die in the bush.

Chirungu is my personal favorite. He or she is the spirit of a white person, who makes people dress in pure white clothes, sit in chairs, drink boiling tea, and crave hard-boiled eggs.

NGOZI

An *ngozi* is an angry spirit who can cause madness, illness, and death. A murder victim, a parent mistreated by his children, or anyone else who has a grievance left over from life may turn into an *ngozi.* The wrong must be corrected before the spirit will agree to depart.

VARI KUDENGA

The *vari kudenga,* or people of the sky, live in Mwari's country and are very powerful. At the same time, not much is known about them. They are said to be the source of newborn souls.

VARI PANYIKA

The *vari panyika,* or people of Middle Earth, include living humans, visiting ancestral spirits, and animals. The boundary between humans and animals can be weak, and some people have the ability to change from one to the other. Most people don't want to be overwhelmed by the animal world; it's considered extremely dangerous. One way to fall into the clutches of an alien form is to eat your own totem. A totem is the symbol of your family or clan.

Certain people have a special ability to contact the spirit world. These mediums are highly respected, unless they devote themselves to evil and become witches. Witchcraft is thought to be hereditary, but it sometimes shows up in a normal family. It is a serious crime to accuse someone of witchcraft in Zimbabwe because accused people may commit suicide. This is partly because of the social isolation that overtakes such individuals.

VARI PASI

The *vari pasi* are the people who live under the earth. A lot is known about them. The ancestors live with them, and sometimes living people fall into their realm.

Some of the most important inhabitants of the underworld are the *njuzu,* the water spirits. They protect lakes and rivers. If they are angry, they travel through the air like whirlwinds, bringing drought to the land beneath them. *Njuzu* take the shape of attractive men or women, but they can metamorphose into snakes, fish, or even crocodiles. They sometimes carry off people in their whirlwinds or pull them into their sacred pools.

Traditional healers, or *nganga*s, are often kidnapped and trained by *njuzu,* but they have to be very careful. They must never accept food while they are in the spiritual realm or they will be condemned to live in it forever.

CHRISTIANITY

Catholic missionaries arrived in southern Africa along with the Portuguese. Most of the other Christian groups have established churches in the past hundred years, but there are a few genuinely African sects. One of the most widespread is the *Vapostori,* or Apostles.

In 1932 Johane Maranke, the grandson of a chief and a member of the Methodist church, fell into a trance and began "speaking in tongues" after experiencing a vision. He and his family believed he had received the inspiration to establish a new church from the Holy Spirit.

The new system spread rapidly. It was against traditional religious practices and considered ancestral spirits to be evil demons. It also had a full set of rules, communicated to Maranke in his visions.

Vapostori may not drink alcohol, smoke tobacco, or eat pork. They may not use medicines, although they are allowed holy water and the laying on of hands at healing ceremonies. The men shave their heads and let their beards grow. On the Sabbath, Saturday, *Vapostori* meet outdoors for confession and prayer. All wear white, and the men carry shepherd's crooks.

While they reject the traditional Shona religion, they do believe in witchcraft and have ceremonies to deal with it.

TOTEMS

When a child is born, he or she is given the father's totem name. This identifies the infant as belonging to a particular clan. This name, or *mutupo,* refers to an animal or part of an animal that must not be eaten. The child also receives a principal praise name, or *chidao*. This refers to a much smaller and more closely related group of relatives. A person can marry someone with the same *mutupo* but not the same *chidao*.

Examples of names are:

mutupo	*chidao*
Gumbo (leg)	Sambiri (The possessor of fame)
Soko (baboon)	Murehwa (One who is spoken about)
Soko (baboon)	Vhudzijena (White-haired, venerable)
Moyo (heart)	Chirandu (Great Beast, probably elephant)

A man with the totem Soko-Murehwa could marry a woman with the totem Soko-Vhudzijena, but not someone in his own *chidao* group.

BIBLIOGRAPHY

Major sources are indicated with an asterisk. Sources of Nhamo's
stories are indicated with a dagger.

Altmann, Jeanne. *Baboon Mothers and Infants*. Cambridge, Mass.:
Harvard University Press, 1980.

*†Aschwanden, Herbert. *Karanga Mythology*. Translated by Ursula
Cooper. Gweru, Zimbabwe: Mambo Press, 1989.

*†———. *Symbols of Death*. Translated by Ursula Cooper. Gweru,
Zimbabwe: Mambo Press, 1987.

*†———. *Symbols of Life*. Translated by Ursula Cooper. Gweru, Zimbabwe: Mambo Press, 1982.

*Bourdillon, M. F. C. *The Shona Peoples*. Gweru, Zimbabwe: Mambo
Press, 1982.

Bozongwana, Reverend W. *Ndebele Religion and Customs*. Gweru,
Zimbabwe: Mambo Press, 1983.

Broadley, D. G., and E. V. Cook. *Snakes of Zimbabwe*. Harare, Zimbabwe: Longman Zimbabwe, 1993.

Chigwedere, A. S. *The Forgotten Heroes of Chimurenga*. Harare, Zimbabwe: Mercury Press, 1991.

Corfield, Timothy. *The Wilderness Guardian*. Nairobi, Kenya: The
David Sheldrick Wildlife Appeal, 1984.

Dale, D. *Shona Mini-Companion*. Gweru, Zimbabwe: Mambo Press,
1981.

*Daneel, M. L. *The God of the Matopos Hills*. The Hague and Paris:
Mouton & Co., 1970.

*Drummond, R. B., and Coates Palgrave. *Common Trees of the High-
veld*. Salisbury, Rhodesia: Longman Rhodesia, 1973.

*Ellert, H. *The Material Culture of Zimbabwe*. Harare, Zimbabwe:
Longman Zimbabwe, 1984.

*Estes, Richard Despard. *The Behavior Guide to African Mammals*.
Berkeley, Calif.: University of California Press, 1992.

*Fortune, George. *Elements of Shona*. Salisbury, Rhodesia: Longman Rhodesia, 1957.

Gelfand, Michael. *An African's Religion*. Cape Town, South Africa: Juta & Company Ltd., 1966.

*————. *Diet and Tradition in an African Culture*. Edinburgh and London: E & S Livingstone, 1971.

*————. *The Genuine Shona*. Gweru, Zimbabwe: Mambo Press, 1973.

*†————. *Growing Up in Shona Society*. Gweru, Zimbabwe: Mambo Press, 1979.

*————. *The Spiritual Beliefs of the Shona*. Gweru, Zimbabwe: Mambo Press, 1977.

*————. *Witch Doctor*. New York and Washington, D.C.: Frederick A. Praeger, 1964.

*Gelfand, Michael, S. Mavi, R. B. Drummond, and B. Ndemera.*The Traditional Medical Practitioner in Zimbabwe*. Gweru, Zimbabwe: Mambo Press, 1985.

*Ginn, Peter. *Birds of the Highveld*. Harare, Zimbabwe: Longman Zimbabwe, 1972.

*Grainger, Colonel D. H. *Don't Die in the Bundu*. Cape Town, South Africa: Howard Timmins, 1967.

Guy, Graham, Alan MacIsaac, P. Papadopoulo, and Dr. D. G. Broadley. *The Bundu Book of Mammals, Reptiles and Bees*. Harare, Zimbabwe: Longman Zimbabwe, 1972.

Hannon, M. *Standard Shona Dictionary*. Harare, Zimbabwe: College Press, 1987.

*†Hodza, A. C., comp. *Shona Folk Tales*. Translated by O. C. Chiromo. Gweru, Zimbabwe: Mambo Press, 1987.

*†————. *Shona Praise Poetry*. Edited by George Fortune. Oxford, England: Oxford University Press, 1979.

Hove, Masotsha M. *Confessions of a Wizard*. Gweru, Zimbabwe: Mambo Press, 1985.

Jenkins, David, R. B. Drummond, S. Mavi, J. F. Ngoni, and R. Williams. *The Bundu Book of Trees, Flowers and Grasses*. Harare, Zimbabwe: Longman Zimbabwe, 1972.

*Jules-Rosette, Benetta. *African Apostles*. Ithaca, N.Y.: Cornell University Press, 1975.

*Kenmuir, Dale, and Russell Williams. *Wild Mammals*. Harare, Zimbabwe: Longman Zimbabwe, 1985.

*Kileff, Cliff, and Peggy Kileff, eds. *Shona Customs: Essays by African Writers*. Gweru, Zimbabwe: Mambo Press, 1992.

Lightfoot, Christopher. *Common Veld Grasses of Rhodesia.* Salisbury, Rhodesia: Government Printer, 1975.

Minshull, Jacqueline, and Janet Duff. *Arachnids: A Classification.* Bulawayo, Zimbabwe: The Natural History Museum of Zimbabwe, 1993.

Munjanja, Amos M. *Everyday Shona and English.* Harare, Zimbabwe: Write and Read Publications, Literature Bureau, 1994.

Nelson, Harold D., ed. *Mozambique: A Country Study.* United States government publication, Department of the Army, 1985.

———, ed. *South Africa: A Country Study.* United States government publication, Department of the Army, 1981.

———, ed. *Zimbabwe: A Country Study.* United States government publication, Department of the Army, 1983.

*Plowes, D. C. H., and R. B. Drummond. *Wild Flowers of Rhodesia.* Salisbury, Rhodesia: Longman Rhodesia, 1976.

*Reid-Daly, Ron. *Staying Alive.* Cape Town, South Africa: Ashanti Publishing Ltd., 1990.

Skaife, S. H. *African Insect Life.* Cape Town, South Africa: Struik Publishers Ltd., 1994.

Smuts, Barbara B. *Sex and Friendship in Baboons.* New York: Aldine Publishing Company, 1985.

Stein, David Martin. *The Sociobiology of Infant and Adult Male Baboons.* Norwood, N.J.: Ablex Publishing Corporation, 1984.

*Steyn, Peter. *Wankie Birds.* Salisbury, Rhodesia: Longman Rhodesia, 1974.

†Stockil, C., and M. Dalton. *Shangani Folk Tales.* Volumes I and II. Harare, Zimbabwe: The Literature Bureau, 1987.

*Stuart, Chris, and Tilde Stuart. *A Field Guide to the Tracks and Signs of Southern and East African Wildlife.* Harare, Zimbabwe: Tutorial Press, 1994.

Swaney, Deanna, and Myra Shackley. *Zimbabwe, Botswana & Namibia.* Hawthorn, Australia: Lonely Planet Publications, 1992.

*Tredgold, Margaret H., in collaboration with H. M. Biegel, S. Mavi, and Dr. Hugh Ashton. *Food Plants of Zimbabwe.* Gweru, Zimbabwe: Mambo Press, 1986.

Viewing, Dr. K. A., J. W. Sweeney, and P. S. Garlake. *The Bundu Book of Geology, Gemology and Archaeology.* Salisbury, Rhodesia: Longman Rhodesia, 1968.

Nancy Farmer is the author of the 1995 Newbery Honor Book and best-seller *The Ear, the Eye and the Arm*, as well as the novels *Do You Know Me* and *The Warm Place*.

For many years a resident of Zimbabwe and Mozambique, she now lives with her family in Menlo Park, California.